The Ragged End

By the same author

Plays

MacRune's Guevara
In the Heart of the British Museum
Shades of Heathcliff
The British Empire

Criticism

Beckett the Playwright (with John Fletcher)
Graham Greene

As editor

J. G. Farrell, *The Hill Station*

The Ragged End

JOHN SPURLING

WEIDENFELD AND NICOLSON
London

First published in 1989 by
George Weidenfeld and Nicolson Ltd
91 Clapham High Street, London SW4 7TA

All rights reserved. No part of this publication may be reproduced, stored in a retrieval system, or transmitted in any form or by any means, electronic, mechanical, photocopying, recording or otherwise, without the prior permission of the copyright owner.

Copyright © John Spurling 1989

British Library Cataloguing in Publication Data

Spurling, John 1936–
The ragged end.
I. Title
823'.914 [F]

ISBN 0-297-79505-8

Filmset by Deltatype, Ellesmere Port
Printed in Great Britain by
Butler & Tanner Ltd
Frome and London

DEDICATED

(Millamant: Would you have me give myself to you over again?
Mirabell: Ay, and over and over again.)

TO HILARY

who has never dwindled into a wife

Prologue

I

'Two bébés,' said Patrick, the man from the garage, whispering hoarsely against the noise of the band.

James Biggar looked dubious.

'You are human being,' said Patrick, encouragingly, 'You can dance with them or go away or you can dance and they will go with you, it not matter.'

James glanced sideways at the 'bébés' and didn't fancy them.

'You are stranger here,' said Patrick, 'you are loneliness.'

James shook his head. He was offended. True, he'd only been in Balunda a few weeks, but he was already proud of feeling at home. Here beside him at his table in the Unity Bar, smiling complicitly, was his newest friend Rachid. Somewhere in the crowd by the bar, under the notice 'No Bone-to-Bone Dancing', was his driver Jacob who had introduced him to Patrick in the first place. Back at his house outside the town were his steward, Bartholomew, and the night-watchman, both of whom were certainly his friends. Then there was his interpreter, Mr Epia – much too respectable and godly a man to be seen in the Unity Bar, but full of warmth and kindness – plus any number of well-disposed acquaintances – village headmen, schoolmasters, government servants, policemen – whom he had met in the course of his duties as a plebiscite officer. One of them, a registration clerk called Edward Banga, smartly dressed in white shorts and shirt and almost incoherent with drink, had just taken the unsuccessful Patrick's place beside the table. Edward wanted James to dance with his sister. The sister, wearing a blue dress with white dots, wasn't very pretty, but slim and appealingly shy. James stood up and escorted her into the mob of dancers.

For a while they danced high life with the rest, pounding rhythmically with their feet, swaying at the hips, making juggling movements with their hands, but seldom touching each other. James enjoyed dancing and soon got bored with this undemanding form of it, so, seizing his partner's hand, he began to jive, twirling her under his arm, twirling himself under hers, passing front to front and back to back, every so often catching her round the waist and going into a controlled spin. The other dancers left a space round them and after a time everyone in the place was watching them, calling out encouragement and clapping. James was exhilarated and though his clothes clung to him as if he'd been bathing in them and he could hardly see for the sweat running down over his eyes, he kept on leaping and turning, slipping in some complicated footwork to make up for his partner's obedient but lacklustre performance. The band – castanets, drums, pieces of stick, trumpet and saxophone – kept on and on playing. At last James felt a hand on his shoulder.

'Sorry, sah,' said Edward Banga, 'My sister is too tired.'

James stopped and bowed awkwardly to the girl. She didn't look at him, but was led away by the staggering Edward. James sat down at his table and lit a cigarette. He felt dazed but pleased with himself. The other dancers returned to their gentle shuffling and swaying. Rachid was looking at him with amused admiration.

'I'm afraid I got carried away,' said James.

'You're a good dancer.'

James shrugged modestly.

'But I tell you what,' said Rachid, 'these people dance and then go away for sex. You dance instead of sex.'

James saw Jacob, his driver, and asked him to take Edward's sister a bottle of beer, giving him the money. When Jacob returned to say she was grateful, James asked him to drive them home. But as they were leaving the table, a woman came up and began talking urgently and angrily to Jacob.

'What does she want?' asked James.

'She says you almost killed her sister. She wants you to send her five bottles of beer.'

'Nonsense,' said James. 'She could have stopped any time she wanted to.'

But he thought afterwards, as he got into a cold bath at his house, that she probably couldn't. She had been a present to him, just as the headmen gave him live chickens when he visited their villages. In return he gave them packets of cigarettes and shared his whisky with them. He had behaved insensitively. Five bottles of beer was the least her relations might have expected for the use he'd made of her.

James had come to Balunda straight from university. The Empire was being dismantled, so Balunda's people were to be offered the choice of uniting with one or other of its larger, already independent neighbours. Some thirty young men, just down from Oxford and

Cambridge, were selected to organize this plebiscite, under the supervision of experienced colonial administrators, and the United Nations sent a team of observers – among them James's Lebanese friend Rachid – to see fair play.

The British had occupied Balunda for about fifty years, introducing a modern superstructure, but scarcely altering the ordinary living conditions of most of the population. Although each plebiscite officer was provided with a smart grey landrover and a driver, James found that much of his area had to be travelled on foot. The adjoining areas were worse. David Rutland, who had unwisely impressed the board of selectors with his climbing experience, was in charge of a semi-mountainous area without any roads at all. Tony Cass had the river area and had to go everywhere by canoe. The only comparatively cushy area was Simon Carter's, around Lugard, the small port serving as capital, where there were not only metalled roads, but a general store with a British manager and a well-appointed modern hotel.

James's base was a small wooden house standing on a cleared knoll and surrounded by forest. The forest was like nothing in Europe. It covered the whole land as far as the escarpment three hundred miles from the sea, where the grasslands began. Every break in the forest was either a river or a man-made clearing hacked out for a road, a village or a town. The trees were enormous and shut out the sun, not only because their tops formed a canopy, but because the hot vapour that rose from them created a dense pall of cloud. Beneath and between the trees was a tangled subsidiary growth of smaller plants, climbing creepers and ground-cover and a thick, warm stench of rot. Birds, reptiles, insects and animals inhabited the forest, but one seldom saw any of them except the insects and a few hornbills. James had never imagined that a jungle could seem so empty of life. The intense humidity meant that he was constantly bathed in sweat and his energy and patience poured away with the sweat.

Nevertheless, fresh from England, James had energy to spare. The plebiscite officers had clearly been chosen as much for their impressive physique as for more abstruse qualities of leadership and enthusiasm. Assembled for their initial briefing in the Provincial Assistant's office, it occurred to James that Tony Cass, David Rutland, Simon Carter and he might be the elite of a warrior tribe, the bodyguard of a chieftain or a British Imperial version of Dumas' musketeers. All of them were in their early twenties and stood six feet or more, all were long-legged, broad-shouldered and straight-backed, with intelligent faces, well-defined jaws and a commanding set to their heads. Simon Carter and he were more willowy, less rugged than the other two and no doubt for that reason had been given the less remote areas, but every one of them, if he had not been brought here to begin the process of withdrawal from Balunda, might have stayed to govern it.

Standing under the large mango tree at one end of the village of Mbola, flanked by his interpreter, James began his careful, sentence-by-sentence explanation of the choices facing the villagers assembled in front of him.

'Do you wish,' he asked, using the portentously impartial phraseology of the printed leaflets, 'Balunda to achieve independence by joining the independent republic of —— or the independent republic of —— ?'

And Mr Epia, sounding less even-handed, translated into pidgin:

'You go see if you want to be free wi' British or wi' French.'

The birds were twittering excitedly among the mangoes above their heads and they had to strain their voices to be heard, but as he completed the bureaucratic part of his task, James felt inspired by its essential nobility – hadn't he come with the gift of freedom? – to a passionate peroration in which he urged them to think long and carefully, since they were choosing not just for themselves but for their children and their children's children – 'you pikins and you pikins' pikins,' in Mr Epia's rendering.

But the villagers had already begun to make more noise than the birds. They did not, it seemed, consider that it was any sort of freedom to be handed over to either of the neighbouring countries. Why couldn't they have their own independence? James, whose eyes were still watering from the emotion he had aroused in himself, descended from his rhetorical heights and replied shortly, as he'd been instructed, that he couldn't answer that question. They had two choices, not three.

After the meeting James sat in the back doorway of the hut set aside for him – it was a rectangular affair made of wattle and mud, with a grass roof, an uneven earth floor and large, open doorways opposite one another, so that chickens and the odd small black pig wandered through freely – and drank whisky. He didn't usually care for the stuff, but here it seemed more necessary and less potent than in a northern climate, replacing his lost energy without making him particularly drunk. Bartholomew was cooking his supper and heating water for his bath. Someone nearby was drumming incessantly. Bartholomew told him it was for a dance in the village that evening. After a while James began to read the book he'd brought with him – a battered copy of the autobiography of Sir William Butler.

Butler was a member of the so-called Wolseley Gang, the group of army officers led by Sir Garnet Wolseley who tidied up most of the Empire's small outbreaks of violence in the later nineteenth century. Butler was in Burma and India soon after the Mutiny, in Canada for the Red River Expedition, in the Gold Coast for the first Ashanti War; he followed Wolseley to Cyprus and Natal, Egypt and the Sudan and finally, risen to the rank of general, held his own command in South Africa until the outbreak of the Boer War. He was also well-known as a travel writer and he married the artist Elizabeth Thompson, whose Crimean battle painting *The Roll-Call* had astonished London and been bought by Queen Victoria when it was shown at the Royal Academy in 1874.

Butler had never visited Balunda, but his experiences not far round the coast leading the Akim against their traditional enemies, the Ashanti, made salutary reading for someone who had just encountered the rainforest for the first time. Coming straight from the invigorating climate of Canada, where he had been exploring the northern Rockies, Butler had used his health and strength up to their limits and far beyond. By the time he crossed the Prah River and led a small force of his reluctant allies into Ashanti territory, his body had shrunk almost to its skeleton. He could make a circle with his finger and thumb and run it all the way up his arm from wrist to shoulder. But although he had nearly died of persistent fever and had been frustrated at every turn by the superstition, procrastination and debility of the people he was trying to help, so that his efforts had mainly ended in failure, he bore no grudge. On the contrary, he asked himself in retrospect why he should have expected any trust from people who had been robbed, tricked, demoralised and enslaved by Arabs and Europeans for four hundred years. Why should tribes which had been overrun and slaughtered by the Ashanti only six months before, without getting any effective help from the British, have been so foolhardy as to invade Ashanti-land just because an unknown and inexperienced white officer asked them to?

Thinking about the meeting at which he had brusquely refused to discuss the impossible third choice – genuine independence – James felt ashamed.

'It is a peculiarity with many of our people,' wrote Butler, 'that they do not know how much they do not know. There is nothing in a land before they came there. History began when the first English traders arrived.'

Bartholomew came to tell him the bath was ready. James undressed and got into the rickety canvas structure with caution. He was aware that astonished village children were peering round the doorway and through gaps in the walls and was sorry when Bartholomew chased them away. He felt like a child himself – so much of what he was experiencing was brand new, but at the same time part of a pattern well understood and taken for granted by others. This absurd bath, for instance: he had not asked for it, it was part of the equipment laid on by the government, packed as a matter of course by Bartholomew and carried through the forest on a man's head so that he, James, could sit soaping himself in a few inches of tepid water, with his bottom encountering all sorts of odd bumps in the floor through the canvas, and be surrounded with the furniture of civilization even where no roads ran.

The dance was unlike anything James had ever seen. It took place at the far end of the village, in a large and completely empty hut. The band was in the middle – a man with a long, deep-throated drum, another beating a flat, many-faceted piece of wood with sticks, two or three others rattling gourds, chanting, clapping and handing out tots of local gin, which were drunk at a gulp from a single communal glass. The dancers – men, women and children, some of the women with nodding babies strapped to their backs – circulated slowly round the room in a continuous ring, shuffling their feet and jerking their shoulderblades in time to the beat, their bodies slightly crouched. Every so often the big drum gave an extra bang and stopped, but then resumed after half a minute. There was no other interval. The scene was lit by two small hurricane lamps, one hanging on the wall, the other standing on the ground beside the band. James stood for some time in the doorway, among a crowd of onlookers which included Bartholomew, some of the carriers and Mr Epia, changed from the khaki outfit he wore for walking and the coloured shirt and long trousers he kept for interpreting into a voluminous white toga. Round and round went the dance, without variation, neither gloomy nor ecstatic, neither companionable nor solitary, neither exactly a rite nor quite a pleasure. After a while the monotony of the spectacle made James feel tired and he made his way back to his own hut. Writing his diary at the folding table, he could still hear the drum – rubrubrub rub rubadubadubadub. In one corner of his room a row of chickens perched quietly on the poles provided for them, their heads cocked to the sound and their eyes blinking, but making no other movement. His own cockerel, tethered to the fireplace, had tried to flutter up to join them, but was now also lying still.

Indeed, James thought, he was a stranger, but not loneliness. The dance was a mystery to him, but though he might not fully understand the Balundans' community, he admired and even envied it and felt no sense of exclusion. On the contrary, they made him constantly welcome and gave him a sense of belonging in spite of his strangeness, as if this life were more natural to him than his own, as if he were beginning to remember something long forgotten.

Early next morning, when it was still cool, he stood in the street looking at the lines of huts with smoke oozing out of their thatch, the chickens, pigs and goats wandering through the open doorways, the small cultivated area of cocoa and plantain bushes intervening between the huts and the surrounding forest. He could almost see it as a village in Northern Europe before the Romans and imagine himself his own Iron-Age ancestor.

At breakfast his increasing satisfaction with the world and himself was curbed by another passage from Butler's autobiography.

'When a white man speaks to a black one,' Butler asked a local friend in the Gold Coast, 'what does the black man think of what he is told? Does he believe it?'

'No,' replied the African, 'he thinks every word the white man says is a lie.'

James read the passage to Bartholomew as he brought a boiled egg and coffee to the folding table and asked if he agreed.

'Na true!' said Bartholomew with feeling and then smiled. 'Except you, sah. I never hear you lie.'

Several months later, when the vote had been counted and the Balundans had decided in favour of joining their ex-British rather than their ex-French neighbour, the plebiscite officers were given a week's break. They still had to swap areas and hear the appeals, mostly lodged by politicians of the losing party, but meanwhile the four musketeers – David Rutland, Tony Cass, Simon Carter and James – took a trip up-country in two of the landrovers. David's vehicle was off the road for repairs and James had just sacked his driver and was waiting for a replacement.

The trip began with a visit to an acquaintance of David Rutland's, a man called Arthur Rimington, who was in charge of road maintenance. Rimington had a house provided by the government, but he had lived there for a long time and transformed it into something entirely his own. From the neat green lawns and well-stocked flowerbeds to the colourful rugs on the floor and the personally designed, locally made furniture, it all expressed the owner's meticulous energy. Rimington himself was a small man in his thirties – almost absurdly dwarfed by his four tall guests – with a long face, thick stand-up hair cut short round the sides in military fashion and pale grey eyes. David had told the others a little about him: that he had been in Balunda longer than any other European, except perhaps one or two of the missionaries, that no one knew the local people better than he did, that in fact his official job in the Public Works Department was less important than his unofficial position as a link between the government and the people. What he had not told them, because Rimington always liked to keep his surprise fresh for newcomers, was that Rimington had a particular hobby.

After he had given them a drink on the verandah, Rimington ushered his guests into the main room of his house. It was a large space, divided into smaller areas by built-in glass cases, jutting out into the room in the manner of a museum. The exhibits were alive. Every case contained a different variety of snake and when one sat down on the benches either side of the dining table, the glass was only a few inches away. Behind James's head were two small, thin, bright green creatures, one of which struck viciously at the glass as he turned to examine it.

'Yours is a green mamba, James,' said David with relish, from the other side of the table. 'Don't annoy it, it's deadly.'

'At least it's prettier than yours,' said James, indicating the fat brown creature marked with a white streak which was behind David's head.

'Rhinoceros viper,' David said, delighted with his role as temporary expert while Rimington was out of the room attending to something in the kitchen. 'Also deadly, but slower.'

'What does he keep them for?' asked Tony Cass, irritated by David's superior knowledge.

'He's fond of them.'

'He makes a bit of a thing of them, doesn't he? They must be intended to frighten people and give him a feeling of power.'

'Not at all. He likes to have them round him. He likes to watch them and talk to them.'

'They're very beautiful,' said Simon Carter, 'but I'm not sure they increase my appetite for lunch.'

The meal was of a standard James hadn't come across before in Balunda. Rimington told them his cook came from the French side, but that he'd trained him himself. His steward's expertly unobtrusive waiting at the table would have done credit to a good restaurant. Rimington kept a sharp eye on him and once reproved him for putting his thumb over the edge of a clean plate.

'What are you going to do when Balunda becomes independent?' asked Tony Cass.

'I shall stay, of course,' said Rimington.

'Will they want expatriates?'

'To begin with.'

'I'm sure they'll need you,' said David, who clearly admired Rimington without reserve.

'They will,' said Rimington. 'In any case, I've no wish to go anywhere else. This is where I live. What are you chaps going to do when this job's over?'

'I might try for the Foreign Office,' said Tony.

Rimington looked as if he didn't approve, but said nothing. 'And you?' he said to James.

'I want to be a writer.'

'Want to be? I should have thought you either were or you weren't.'

'I mean I want to write for a living. If I can make a living.'

Rimington stared at James for some moments as if he were appraising his prospects and finding them poor, then turned to Simon.

'I haven't the faintest idea,' said Simon, refusing to be cowed as James had been.

'None of you feels like staying in Africa?' said Rimington.

There was silence, then Tony said:

'Even if we did, I doubt if Africa would welcome us.'

'Would you expect it to?' asked Rimington, with scorn. 'Must you have everything on a plate? Can you only give what people beg you for?'

Tony looked at him angrily. It was the sort of remark Tony might have made himself, James thought, and he obviously hated receiving it.

After lunch, at David's insistence, Rimington put on a glove and lifted the green mamba out of its case. It writhed around in his grasp and slithered through his fingers, until it could have bitten his bare arm if it had struck backwards. He talked to it a little and then put it back in the case. Outside on the lawn, where Rimington let some of the snakes move about, controlling them with a forked stick, they discussed the plebiscite. In spite of their professional impartiality, none of the plebiscite officers could disguise their relief at the result. How could a country organized on the British systems of law, government, education, measurement, speaking English as its only common language, with mainly Protestant rather than Catholic missions, have amalgamated successfully with another that was equally French in all respects? James suggested that if Balunda was too small to be independent on its own, then it might do better to remain under British rule for a few more years.

'What would be the good of that?' asked Rimington.

'At least we could build them a few more roads.'

'They need more than roads.'

'But will they get what they need if they're just a province of someone else's country?'

'What they need most is to get shot of the British.'

'Aren't you British?' asked Tony.

'I am British, yes, but not proud of it.'

He picked up his snakes and put them in a basket to carry inside.

When they were driving away, half an hour later, Tony said to James, sitting in the back of his landrover with their two stewards and the luggage, 'What a self-satisfied little creep! Just the sort of phoney old colonial you'd expect Ruggles to admire.'

The nickname he had invented for David sounded almost affectionate, but James was sure it was really intended to diminish him, with its suggestion of boys' romances and public-school camaraderie. James didn't want an argument with Tony, so he murmured agreement, but he felt the visit to Rimington had put them all in a bad light. For him personally it was another twist in a steady process of disillusionment.

During the registration period he'd been informed of a fraud in one of the villages. Immediately he'd begun an intensive investigation, himself checking every flesh-and-blood villager against the names on the register. The task hadn't been as straightforward as he'd envisaged. The names themselves were confusing, several of the villagers seeming not at all clear whether a name belonged to them or not, who its owner was, whether he or she was dead. After several days of appalling discomfort from heat, argument and mental effort, he eventually arrived at a list of some thirty names which couldn't be accounted for and took his list triumphantly and indignantly to the Provincial Assistant, so as to get permission to strike the names off the register. His superior seemed, if anything, embarrassed. He made it obvious that he regarded James less as a white knight of justice than an ignorant meddler and James retired to his lonely house in the forest with a sense of grievance and suspicion.

Of course he should have realized that to the Colonial Office Balunda was of no importance at all, simply a tiresome piece of territory which, now that they were no longer interested in collecting territory, had to be got rid of as quickly as possible. The people they chose to administer this rapid disposal would hardly have been of first-rate quality. As for the under-officers – himself, Cass, Rutland, Carter and the rest – they were little more than boys, immature, inexperienced and cheap.

But James's disillusionment went beyond politics. He had lost his first naive admiration and affection for the people themselves. His energy had evaporated and left behind irritation and impatience with the fecklessness, unreliability, drunkenness and venality of nearly everyone he had to deal with. He excepted Bartholomew and Mr Epia. But Jacob, his driver – more than that, he had thought, his friend – was the worst offender of all. He had cheated with the petrol, flogged the spare tyre and tools and been more and more often drunk in charge, so that James had several times barely escaped with his life. He'd had every excuse to sack him long since, but had repeatedly forgiven him. Now that he'd finally done the terrible thing, dismissed Jacob without a reference and probably reduced him and his family to starvation and despair, he felt that the failure was as much his as Jacob's and that sense of failure spread out to engulf the whole of his brief career as an imperial functionary, a leader of men, a respected stranger. He was not so magnanimous as William Butler: he couldn't make allowances either for his own inexperience or for the wretched history of the Balundans. He simply wanted to get out and go home as soon as he could.

II

David Rutland returned to Balunda a couple of years later. By then he had set up as a sculptor and it was his friend Arthur Rimington who offered him his first serious commission. He was to make a bronze head of Balunda's first President, Marius Nakimbi. Having changed planes at Abidjan and landed at Tumba airport — it was little more than a flat piece of ground covered with a rusty metal grid and set about with a few sheds — David found Rimington waiting for him inside the reception area. They passed straight through Customs and Passport Control on Rimington's nod and, emerging into the open on the far side, were greeted by a detachment of soldiers, smartly dressed and drilled, who came to attention while their officer saluted. Rimington — not himself in uniform, but wearing much the same outfit of long khaki shorts and bush shirt he had worn in the days before independence — gave the soldiers a friendly wave and led David to a dark green landrover. His luggage was loaded into the back. The driver got out and gave his seat to Rimington.

'I thought we'd prefer to be on our own,' said Rimington.

The soldiers and the landrover's driver got into an army truck and the two vehicles set off in convoy for Rimington's house, fifty miles away.

'I haven't moved,' he said. 'Saw no point in it, since the place suited me. Marius wanted me to live in Molo so as to be close to him, but I thought a little independence of my own wouldn't be a bad thing. You're looking well. Very decent of you to come out like this — I must admit I persuaded Marius he wanted his mug done by a pukka European artist mainly because I reckoned a visit from you would do me good.'

'I hope I won't let you down,' said David. 'I've not had a tremendous lot of experience yet with portrait busts.'

'I thought you told me you were going to be the new Michelangelo.'

'Certainly I am,' said David, fully convinced of his future genius, even though he was diffident about his present abilities.

'Well, then, what does experience matter?' said Rimington. 'Early Michelangelos are just as good as late ones, aren't they?'

He laughed and David's qualm of self-doubt was dispelled. Rimington's company always made him feel as if he were part of one of those close-knit bands of purposeful adventurers from the pages of Buchan or 'Sapper' which he had read as an adolescent. Even in the days when David had first known him, when he was a comparatively humble member of the colonial establishment, Rimington had exuded the confidence and command of a minor potentate. By now, as David knew from his letters, he was in fact, though not officially, the most powerful person in Balunda after the president.

As he drove slowly and carefully over the pot-holed road, Rimington talked about his adopted country. Shortly after Independence Balunda and the ex-British neighbour it had voted to join had become involved in a civil war. The outcome was that Balunda itself, together with the western section of its neighbour, had emerged as a brand new nation. President Nakimbi himself did not come from Balunda. He belonged to the Koruba tribe which had dominated Balunda's neighbour and whose skills as entrepreneurs and administrators had also made them an important element in the comparatively backward Balunda. The new country was called Balunda in deference to the larger territory whose people had fought side by side with the Korubas, but in almost every respect it was now a greatly expanded Koruba-land, with Korubas holding almost all the leading posts in the government. Even the capital had been moved from the Balundan port, Lugard, to the inland city of Molo, which in the old days had been just over the border from David's plebiscite area and Rimington's house.

The Korubas, however, had never been noted as fighters and although with their customary intelligence and application they had turned themselves into efficient soldiers for the duration of the civil war, they were content afterwards to leave the professional army mainly under the command of Balundan officers, including that redoubtable white Balundan, Colonel Rimington. It was generally acknowledged, Rimington assured David with satisfaction, that the elite force of veterans trained and led by himself had clinched the final victory in the war. The Leopards, as they were called, remained in being after the war – it was a detachment of them that had greeted David at the airport and was now escorting them in the truck behind. Indeed, Rimington said, he went nowhere without them. He himself was a close friend and adviser of the president, but held no government office. Even his position in the army was anomalous. The army's chief of staff was a Balundan called Brigadier Ozo – an ex-sergeant-major in the British Army – who was nominally Rimington's superior. But Ozo exercised no control over the Leopards, who formed a kind of privileged Guards regiment round the president.

'Nakimbi's not very popular at home,' said David.

'I don't imagine I am either,' said Rimington. 'After all, we broke up a country which had been created by Britain and we were enabled to do so by supplies of arms from the French. In fact they're still giving us financial aid.'

'It's not that so much,' said David, 'as that Nakimbi's left-wing.'

'Is he?'

'He's getting aid from China and the Soviet Union.'

'That's what you've read in the newspapers?'

'Isn't it true?'

'We've certainly had Chinese and Soviet delegations here, but I don't think they've chipped in with anything substantial. Marius isn't keen to belong to anybody's camp.'

'He's got a one-party state, hasn't he? And he's nationalized everything in sight.'

'True,' said Rimington. 'It's not a British democracy, but then it's not a very British sort of country, David. You must take us as you find us. We're doing the best we can in fairly adverse circumstances.'

The roads had certainly deteriorated since David was last here. Rimington was not, of course, any longer responsible for them. But the villages they went through looked mostly unchanged. There were some abandoned huts and others whose grass roofs were being replaced, but most of the damage done by the war had already been put right. There was not, after all, a great deal of damage that could be done to places that were principally made of mud and grass in the first place. They passed one more substantial building – a wooden store of the kind that used to be run by Syrians or Lebanese – which was still a blackened wreck, and David asked if it was true that Nakimbi had expelled the foreign traders.

'Many of them were ruined by the war, David. Starving people looted their stores. Yes, it's true that the richer ones were persuaded to leave.'

'Persuaded to leave?'

'Expropriated, then.'

'You mean, kicked out?'

'It's really no good criticizing us, David. We've been through hell and back. People – especially British people – have done their best to stop us existing at all. We're starting from scratch.'

Rimington's own house appeared to be almost unchanged. The snakes were still in their glass cases in the living room, even the steward was the same. There were no signs of Rimington's increase in status, except that a soldier guarded the gate and a new stone building to house the Leopards had gone up next to the servants' quarters.

'The rest of the Leopards are in Molo, behind the president's palace,' said Rimington. 'We switch the personnel round from time to time and of course I'm often staying in the barracks in Molo myself. I like to keep in close touch with my men, for obvious reasons. Their loyalty is important to me – and of course to the president.'

The next day they drove into Molo, again with the truckload of soldiers behind them, and drew up on a large sweep of gravel in front of the palace. Molo was built round a nucleus of large public buildings: a hospital and mission school, a church, a prison and law courts. The palace had been the British Commissioner's residence – a handsome white building longer than it was high, with a modest portico – but it had been enlarged since with wings on either side, each crowned with an oriental-looking dome.

'Some money's been splashed about here,' David said, but Rimington made no reply. Later he admitted that the building had been done by a rich Lebanese, hoping to ingratiate himself with the new regime, but that he and Nakimbi had quarrelled over the terms at some point and one wing was unfinished. David, aware by now how sensitive Rimington was about deficiencies in his adopted country, forbore to ask what had become of the Lebanese.

President Nakimbi received them in his large, impressively furnished office. There was a huge desk, a small library of books, a new Persian carpet, a long table with high-backed chairs (presumably for Cabinet meetings) and several fine African carvings. Whatever difficulty there was in repairing the roads, there was no lack of civilization here. Nakimbi himself was very black, tall and well-built, with a strong, intelligent face and watchful eyes. He didn't look much more than thirty. He wore a native robe and cap but spoke with an Oxford accent. According to Rimington he had been born a paramount chief's son, educated at an English public school before Oxford, been called to the Bar in London and then practised as a barrister in his native country until independence. After that he had become a leading Koruba politician whose opposition to the majority tribes had led directly to the civil war. He welcomed David warmly and arranged the first sitting for the late afternoon; then he gave David an airmail copy of *The Times* and suggested he explore the palace grounds or relax on the verandah while he, Nakimbi, conferred with Rimington.

The conference went on for the rest of the morning. David decided to walk into the city. It was very hot but he had not had any exercise, except getting in and out of aeroplanes and cars, since he'd been in England two days ago. He left a message with one of the president's staff that he'd find his way to the Leopards' barracks where he was to have lunch with Rimington, and set off down the drive and past the sentry at the gates. There were not many people in the better streets and indeed not much cause for them to be there, since the shops were closed and seemed to have nothing in their windows. The people he did see stopped to watch him with literally open mouths. He supposed that, apart from Rimington, they had hardly seen a European since the British had left. There was more life in the market area, a broad dusty circle with a big, shady tree in the middle and set about with more or less permanent covered stalls, but it came to a complete halt with David's appearance. He felt like someone from another planet, not just another country. It seemed almost incredible that a mere two years earlier he had walked about towns and villages not so very far from here without any sense of being alien. He had always been smiling at people in those days, because they had constantly greeted him. Now if he smiled they looked away. Very soon he'd had enough of it and stopped at a stall sparsely stocked with yams and plantains to ask the way to the Leopards' barracks. The man either couldn't understand him or didn't wish to and shook his head nervously, but a bystander pointed vaguely to the streets behind. It seemed to be almost the opposite direction to the way he'd come and he remembered Rimington mentioning that the barracks were close to the palace, but he didn't like to appear churlish and thought he could circle round once he was out of sight.

It wasn't so easy. This part of Molo was an unplanned sprawl of gimcrack shanties – made out of odd pieces of wood, corrugated iron and any old scraps – set along narrow dirt tracks which wound about arbitrarily and were spaces between the shanties rather than anything so continuous as streets. The place was teeming with people, some of whom stopped to stare at David marching doggedly past their doors in what he began to suspect were small circles leading nowhere. Others, busy with their own lives and tasks – women with babies on their backs queuing for water at a standpipe, men sitting morosely in doorways, children playing in the dirt or chasing each other amongst squawking chickens and cringing pi-dogs – hardly noticed him. David had no sense of fear – the squalor and poverty of these people made them seem, like the dogs, more pathetic than threatening – but he began to wonder what on earth he could do to break out of this endless maze. If there had been any kind of bar or café he would have stopped for a rest and a drink – he was desperately thirsty – but there wasn't even a tree he could sit under. He just had to keep walking.

At last he saw a battered black Humber nosing towards him between the shanties. In the better part of the city there were a few vehicles and he'd seen mammy-wagons near the market, but here a car seemed almost as out of place as he was himself. Perhaps this was a taxi or at least someone who might speak English and be able to direct him or even offer him a lift. The car was not too careful how it went, knocking over a can of water left by one of the women, dislodging a piece of somebody's fence, narrowly missing a child which had not noticed it coming. But nobody protested, all made haste to get out of the car's way and disappear into their homes and when it finally braked in front of David he realized that hardly a single person was still in sight. The sun was shining on the windscreen and he couldn't make out who was inside, but he smiled in a general way and went round to the driver's open window. There were three young men in the car, all dressed in white shirts and dark trousers and looking as if they belonged to a different city altogether, one with thriving banks and businesses.

'I'm looking for the barracks,' said David politely but firmly. 'Somewhere near the president's palace, is it?'

'Get in!' said the man behind the wheel.

'You can take me there?'

'Get in!' said the man, more aggressively.

David disliked people who gave him orders. He scratched his head and looked at the man as if he was amused.

'Are you offering me a lift or taking me for a ride?' he asked.

The man stared at him insolently. David now saw that he was wearing a revolver in a holster on his belt. So was the man next to him. Aware that this was some kind of contest and resisting the temptation to lose his temper, David stared back with what he hoped would pass as relaxed confidence. After a while the driver turned slightly and opened the door behind him, then lit a cigarette and dangled his elbow out of his window as if he had no further interest in David. Deciding that anything was better than continuing to wander round this dismal slum, David got in. Almost before his door was closed, the driver put the car into gear and moved off with a screech of tyres, accelerating between the shacks as if they had been put there only to serve as an obstacle course and knocking down anything that got in his way, whether frightened chickens or projecting corners of the shacks themselves. They soon reached a district where there were stone two-storey houses with neglected gardens and then, coming in sight of the back of the palace, surrounded by a high wall topped with barbed wire, they stopped at the barred and guarded entrance to a barrack-square. No one in the car had said a word and now the driver turned and opened the back door again.

'You get out!' he said.

'Thanks,' said David, smiling round at all three.

'Okay,' said the man in the front passenger seat.

'No charge?' asked David. 'Well, thanks again.'

There was no response and as soon as he was clear of the car it squealed round in a tight turn and sped away, covering him with dust.

When he told his story cheerfully to Rimington over a drink in the Leopards' regimental mess, Rimington showed no amusement at all.

'Unfortunate,' he said. 'Not your fault. I should have warned you. But you really must not stir a foot in this country without consulting me first. You don't know the rules. Nor does anyone, as a matter of fact. But maintaining a strong position is the basic rule, so that you're capable of playing to rules of your own.'

'Who were the people in the car?'

'Police. Not exactly that. Not quite what you and I mean by police.'

'They were perfectly helpful, as it turned out, if not very chatty. Perhaps they were busy.'

'They were instructed to find you and bring you here, but probably disappointed to find you so easily. They'd have liked you to have been abducted, or at least molested in some way. Then they could have pulled down a few houses, shot a few of the occupants, taken away others for questioning. They can usually find excuses for that in any case, but a missing protégé of the president would have given them extra scope.'

'Did you send them?'

'I'd have them all exterminated if I could. They belong to the PSD – Public Safety Department – and come under the Minister for Home Affairs. In my opinion he and his department constitute Public Danger Number One, but Marius thinks they're essential and if they decide a matter is within their sphere, it's not worth arguing. I suggested I might go out and find you myself, but Marius thought that would upset the Minister, so this has been a little positional improvement for the PSD.'

'I'm sorry. I had no idea I was a piece on your chessboard.'

'You were wise not to try to resist them.'

'If they'd just explained who they were and what they'd come for . . . '

'Of course they wouldn't do that. Explanation doesn't appeal to them and in any case they'd have given themselves a lot more pleasure if they'd been able to provoke you into resistance. They could have knocked you about a bit and then beaten up the neighbourhood and taken in a few residents to answer for your injuries.'

'Why do you go on living here, Arthur?'

'It's my home. Besides the PSD doesn't frighten me. I'm almost the only person it doesn't. So if I weren't here, they'd have things all their own way.'

David enjoyed his first session with Nakimbi. He'd decided to dispense with a preliminary drawing. Nakimbi's powerful head and lively face, in which one was constantly aware of the muscles round the mouth and of the eyes set deep in their arches, made him keen to start building it directly out of the clay. The session was not in Nakimbi's office, but in a delightfully cool, arcaded courtyard at the back of one of the new wings. A small fountain played into a rectangular pool, and there was the beginning of a lawn and many young plants beginning to climb the pillars of the arcade. Except for the brilliant light they might have been in a Moorish version of an Oxford college. David remarked on the likeness and Nakimbi agreed that he had asked his architect for something in the Oxford spirit, but the architect, being Middle-Eastern, had given the place ogival instead of rounded arches. They talked about Oxford – Nakimbi had been there a few years before David – and found that since they had both read law, they had been taught by many of the same lecturers.

'McGinty on tort,' said David.

'Dire,' said Nakimbi.

'I gave up on McGinty,' said David.

'Not I,' said Nakimbi. 'I was a disgustingly conscientious student.'

'I expect you got a First.'

'You mean you didn't?'

'I got a Third.'

'Shame on you!'

'I never had any intention of being a lawyer,' said David. 'I always wanted to be an artist. Besides, I spent most of my time rowing.'

'Ah, I should have guessed you were a rowing man. For me it was tennis and debates in the Union.'

By the time they parted that evening they were on first-name terms and the head was beginning to reach an interesting stage. David spent much of the next day idling by the president's swimming pool or sketching the palace and its grounds, looking forward keenly to the next encounter with his sitter. Nakimbi was late for the session and his mood had changed completely from the day before. He looked angry and preoccupied and made no attempt to keep up a conversation. David tried to concentrate on his modelling, but found himself, or at least his fingers, affected by the atmosphere, so that nothing came right.

'Shall we stop?' he said at last. 'I'm doing more harm than good.'

'How many more of these sittings will you need?' asked Nakimbi irritably.

'That depends. If it goes like yesterday, only three or four, but if it goes like today . . . you can see, it's gone backwards, if anything.'

'It's not very good,' said Nakimbi, turning away after a brief inspection.

'No. But I don't take all the blame to myself.'

'Why not? You're the artist.'

'The artist is sensitive to his sitter.'

'Oh, the sitter's fault, is it? I never heard that before. Only that bad workmen blame their tools.'

Nakimbi sounded so contemptuous that David wondered if he would come the next day. However, the next three sittings were better. Nakimbi was not very forthcoming conversationally, but he showed flashes of humour and friendliness and it was these, David realized, that gave him the face he had started on. Nakimbi's face in anger or withdrawal became like a mask, partly alarming but mainly, from the sculptor's point of view, flat and dead. When he talked with animation, though, when he wanted to charm his audience, above all when he laughed, the face, strangely enough, became more powerful, more regal; and it was as a king, a condescending, amused but also majestic ruler that David wanted to portray him. When they parted after the fifth sitting, Nakimbi too was pleased.

'You have got the forehead and the eyes and the nose,' he said. 'But I think the chin should be sharper.'

'Not when you smile or laugh.'

'But you have not shown me smiling or laughing.'

'It's a composite image. I didn't want to give you a particular expression, so I've put the laugh in your chin instead of your mouth.'

Nakimbi looked as if he wasn't sure whether David was making fun of him. 'Well, I'm glad you're on top of it again, David. I was so afraid you were going to get a Third for sculpture.'

Rimington had been away from Molo with most of the Leopards for the past few days. David had been staying alone in Rimington's quarters in the barracks and eating with the three officers who remained behind. He got on well with them, as he did with most straightforward, energetic and optimistic people, and they played cards or ping-pong together after supper. Rimington had forbidden him to accompany them on their night excursions after women, but David didn't think he had to behave entirely as if he were back at school and Rimington his headmaster, so on the third night he did go with them and was glad he did, because the part of the city they found themselves in, though it was hardly metropolitan, was at least more cheerful and animated than those dreary places he had visited on the first day. This was more like the Balunda he remembered. On the way home in the officers' landrover, lying half asleep and three-quarters drunk in the back, he was suddenly aware that they'd stopped and that the two officers in front were having an argument with somebody in the road.

'Where you been, soldier?'

'No business of yours, my friend.'

'My business what I say is my business. Who you got in the back?'

'You lef 'em, my friend, or be wuss for you.'

'I give you bad trouble you don' show me who you got in back.'

'You give me bad trouble already wastin' my sleepin' time.'

'What is this?' David asked in what he thought was a low voice. His companion in the back quickly put a hand over his mouth.

'You got someone there. I hear 'em,' said the voice outside.

'You move that ol' wreck in front of my jeep or I go ram 'em,' said the officer in the driving seat.

'I am tellin' you, get out!' shouted the man in the road, now very angry. David recognized the voice of the PSD driver who had picked him up on the first day. 'I goin' to search this jeep, 'cos I don' like anything I see or hear about you.'

The landrover suddenly shot forward, spilling David and his companion into a tangle on the floor. There was a clang and a heavy jolt, the vehicle veered steeply sideways and then they were speeding up the road and into the barracks. The wing of the landrover, when they got out unsteadily and inspected it, was badly crushed, but they were all in high good humour, laughing and clapping one another on the shoulders as they staggered into the building.

'Was it a Humber?' asked David. 'The PSD car you pranged?'

'That Humber!' said the officer who'd been driving the landrover, laughing so much he could hardly get the words out, 'I been hoping to smash that Humber ever since I first seen it.'

'I too,' said David happily. 'What a highly successful evening!'

Rimington returned the next morning. He already knew about the events of the night before, but didn't reproach David. Indeed he seemed remarkably cheerful. When David asked if it wouldn't make his bad relations with the PSD worse, Rimington replied that that couldn't be helped. The PSD had initiated the incident by stopping the landrover, an action obviously intended to provoke the Leopards. They probably knew that David was in the back, but the important thing was that no one had got out of the landrover. If they had, there might well have been fatal results, since both parties were armed and drunk.

'But won't you have trouble with the Minister for Home Affairs?' asked David.

'I doubt it. He's had a bad week.'

'How's that?'

'He's lost two of his supporters in the Cabinet.'

'Sacked or resigned?'

'Discontinued.'

'What does that mean?'

'They won't be seen again.'

Rimington's triumphantly vindictive tone shocked David.

'Was this Nakimbi's doing?'

'Not precisely. He prefers to play sides to middle, but in this case – you're a rowing man, David, what's that term for dipping your oars and missing the water?'

'Catching a crab.'

'Exactly. Those two on that side caught a crab and Nakimbi had no option but to chuck them to the crocodiles.'

'Not literally?'

Rimington laughed, but it sounded forced.

'What a terrible idea you have of us, David! We're not quite that barbaric.'

'What sort of crab did they catch?'

'They were doing deals, dear boy. Deals with Brits across the border. Not the sort of thing we can tolerate. Bad crabs. And now you've demolished the back end of a PSD limousine. Not a good week for Home Affairs.'

'And what happened to the missing ministers, Arthur? If it wasn't the crocodiles?'

'They bit the dust, David, one way or another. Don't ask me exactly how. I wasn't there.'

David's last session with President Nakimbi that evening was coloured by this conversation. He had never found any fault in Rimington before, never doubted that he was a wise and good man. Now just as the delightfully primitive Balunda he had known seemed to have turned into a baleful black Ruritania, so his old friend was transformed into a crafty and even lethal politician. As for Nakimbi, it was impossible now to imagine him as a charming and civilized, far less a majestic ruler. Nakimbi himself, nevertheless, no doubt because the factional struggle that had been worrying him was now settled, was again gracious and forthcoming. It was David's turn to be gruff and uncommunicative.

'You had a late night, David,' said Nakimbi. 'Like all artists, you are lacking in self-discipline.'

David grunted and scraped clay off the right cheek.

'But why should I blame you? When it comes to women, I lack self-discipline myself.'

The more David worked on the head, the more he lost the likeness. He stopped putting clay on and taking it off again and stood back to calm his nerves and try to understand what had gone wrong.

'What about your friend, though? I have known Arthur for some years now, but I have never discovered if he has women or not. What do you think, David?'

'I don't know. I've never thought about it.'

'If he did have women, surely you would know?'

'You're suggesting he's queer?'

'Not necessarily. But he's like a scoutmaster, don't you think? The way he runs his Leopards. Aren't you reminded of a scoutmaster?'

'You're probably right.'

'Don't misunderstand me. Every country, like every boy, needs a scoutmaster in the formative years.'

A scoutmaster who took out rivals, thought David and suddenly decided, depressed by the way he'd spoilt the head and couldn't see how to retrieve it, that he'd had enough.

'I've lost it,' he said.

Nakimbi walked carefully round the clay head and shook his real one.

'Too bad,' he said. 'Go to bed early tonight and try again tomorrow.'

But the sittings were not resumed. Rimington took David on a trip down to the coast at Lugard and told him that Nakimbi had decided he couldn't spare David any more time.

'But he liked you a lot,' said Rimington. 'He even wanted you to stay and work here. He thought you'd make a first-class officer in the Leopards. I'd have liked you as my second-in-command, dear boy, but it won't do. It's hard enough to get away with even one white officer in a black state. A pity.'

David left the unfinished sculpture with Rimington. He didn't see Nakimbi again before he took the plane from Tumba to Abidjan. The president was up-country by then, visiting a huge hydro-electric project which Rimington said was stalled for lack of funds. The money to complete it had gone into the Swiss bank accounts of the two missing ministers. So he and Nakimbi believed. At any rate that was the public excuse for their disappearance and in Rimington's view it was well worth the price.

Part One

1

I

They sat under an apple tree in David Rutland's garden. It was a reunion some twenty years after the three of them had first met in Africa and only James Biggar had been sure it was a good idea. He had been stirred to phone and arrange this visit by a sentence added to David's regular Christmas card – 'We really must meet again.' David had responded warmly at first and then, when James rang again a month or two later to suggest including Tony Cass in the visit, distinctly less so. As for Tony, his first enthusiastic curiosity to see 'how Ruggles has weathered' had become, by the time James called for him at his house near Shepherd's Bush, a kind of ribald gloom.

'This is a terrible idea,' he said, as they joined a queue of traffic crawling on to Barnes Common. 'What on earth are we going to talk about? Old times? Last days of empire?'

The traffic remained heavy most of the way and they arrived jaded and slightly sickened by exhaust fumes. David lived in a village near East Grinstead, just into Sussex. His house, quite large and comfortable, had been built in the thirties in a vaguely Georgian style, with a semi-circular gravel drive in front and a good-sized garden behind.

James and Tony sat in old basket-chairs and drank white wine. It was June, not a very hot day, but the sun shone intermittently, the birds sang, the roses were out, and their appetites began to return. Susie Rutland, whom they had not yet seen, was presumably putting lunch together in the kitchen. Meanwhile, James took stock of their host.

He had grown larger. Powerfully built, as you would expect of a former rowing Blue, he still carried the extra weight quite naturally, suggesting generous size rather than mere fatness, and he remained distinctly handsome, though his face was inclining to be flabby round the jawline and had acquired quite deep wrinkles in odd places. He was sitting higher than the others, on an upright metal chair, and was drinking whisky. James soon realized that he was already drunk and his first relief, when David opened the door to them, to find a strange house in a strange village inhabited by a still recognizable old friend with whom he had always been able to relax, gave way to a sense of disorientation. He didn't properly know this man. Strangeness, after all, prevailed over familiarity. James's arms were hurting – he had been pressing them with unnecessary force against the sides of his chair. The basketwork creaked as he shifted position. Tony poured himself a second glass of wine.

'Children nearly grown up?' he said, indicating the decayed swing and overgrown sandpit at the far end of the garden. 'How many have you got?'

'Just the standard two,' said David, perhaps defensively. 'What about you?'

'Four or five,' said Tony, with the pride of a man who relished his role as a father.

'Haven't you counted them recently?'

'Four on the ground and a fifth in prospect.'

The ostentatious energy in his voice seemed to sap David's. He groaned and put a hand to his head.

'Little screamers,' he said. 'No nights and a plague of nappies. Collapsing pushchairs and knotted baby-straps. Lost socks and shoes. Mending broken toys. Sticky chairs and jelly on the carpet.'

'I like all that,' said Tony, in his booming voice. 'Noise, emergencies, demands to be met. Hate to have to put my feet up when I come home.'

'You're afraid somebody might think you middle-aged?'

'No, I just need activity.'

This was becoming a bullfight. David showed signs of temper, of putting his head down and making inaccurate charges. Tony was clearly going to dance round him inserting barbs wherever he liked. James intervened to distract him.

'It seems to me a case of more is less. You can't give the same attention to five as you can to two.'

'Nonsense!' said Tony, brushing him aside and waiting eagerly for David's next charge.

The intervention had distracted David instead of Tony. He twitched his shoulder and slowly swayed his head.

'I don't think I've given enough attention to two,' he said sadly. 'One minute they're with you and you're just getting back into the swing of family life – childhood, all that – next minute they're gone and it's all over for another generation.'

His sadness overwhelmed James like a sudden fog. The summer

day, the roses, the sun just emerging from a cloud were immediately neutralized, drained of their warmth and colour. He stared at the garden table and was aware of half-obscured rings where glasses had stood on jollier occasions. He had meant to hold off smoking until after lunch, but now he reached for his pipe and began to fill it, at the same time reaching for words to fill the uncomfortable vacancy around him with the same professional reflex as when something went wrong in the continuity studio at Broadcasting House.

'Yours are at boarding school?'

'Not a very good one. They weren't bright enough to get into a good one.'

James felt embarrassed for David and wished he had come alone. He cast about to change the subject, but Tony forestalled him. His hunting instinct had been switched off by David's pathos.

'Didn't you go back to Balunda?'

'Yes, I did.'

David was hardly drinking his whisky, but he touched the glass with his hand as if that was a comfort in itself.

'I went back to do a bust of Nakimbi. Arthur Rimington invited me. It wasn't a great success. Nakimbi got bored with the sittings and I didn't get much of a likeness. So I came home. Matter of fact, even if I had got it right, it wouldn't have lasted long. Nakimbi got thrown out a year or two later and they broke up all his statues.'

'Do you still make sculpture?' asked James.

'Sometimes.'

There was no sign of any in the garden, nor in the hall or sitting room they had passed through to reach it. David had been serious about his sculpture after his return from Africa, renting a proper studio, studying books about Donatello and Michelangelo, though he had never been to an art school. Then, about the time James had stopped seeing him, he had taken the Law Society exams, moved out of London and settled for a steady job with a firm of solicitors. James was nostalgic for those days in the studio, when they sat about talking for hours, drinking coffee and imagining themselves innovative, profound and famous. Perhaps David's abortive trip to Balunda had destroyed his confidence. James thought it more likely that Susie Rutland had made him face reality. She had been with him latterly in the studio, but was probably only waiting for the right moment to bend him to a safe profession.

'What was it like?' Tony was asking.

'It wasn't like. That was the problem.'

The easy warmth, the sense of physical enjoyment that James had always liked in David suddenly flashed back. James wanted to cheer him on, to get the whole day back into that mode, a good day out with old friends who could make jokes about themselves and each other without offence. Tony Cass wasn't having it.

'The place. Balunda? How much had it changed?'
'Totally.'
'What do you mean, totally?'

The side of Tony that James didn't like was his rudeness. Tony no doubt considered it forthrightness – a straightforward desire for truth and clarity – but it came across as a bid for superiority.

'What I say. Totally.'

'You mean the roads weren't where they used to be, the towns had shifted, nobody spoke English, there were no law courts or hospitals? Or do you just mean it wasn't run in a British manner any more?'

'The roads and towns were probably more or less in the same places. The rest as you say.'

'You're exaggerating. The war only affected pockets of the country.'

'The war completely devastated the whole country. Nakimbi kicked the ruins into a sandcastle for his own benefit and now the latest civil war will have scattered that again. When we were there originally – you and I and James – it was a possible place. Not for long, but for a six-month holiday. When I went back it was one of the nastiest places on earth and by now it must be top of that league. Law courts? Hospitals? You must be joking. Nobody in Balunda would even know what the words mean.'

Tony was temporarily silenced by such vehemence. Then he took a more judicious tone.

'You haven't been there for at least fifteen years.'
'You haven't been there for twenty.'
'I read the papers.'
'Newspapers or Foreign Office papers?'
'Both.'

'The newspapers hardly ever bother to cover it and if the foreign Office thinks that Balunda is anything more than a stretch of bush inhabited by survivors of a holocaust in various stages of mental and physical collapse, it's being misinformed. Why doesn't it send you to see for yourself?'

'I'm not in that section.'

'Well, avoid it, is my advice. Africa in general is a write-off. Balunda in particular is the nadir of human history.'

Now he was spoiling his case and sounding more like a drunken blimp than an expert. Tony took the offensive again.

'I'm not surprised you couldn't get a likeness of Nakimbi, if that was how you saw his country. The British have never been able to see Africa in its own terms. Even sensitive people like Sir Richard Burton who appreciated and admired Indian and Arab culture were crassly contemptuous of the Africans.'

'Culture!' said David. 'Good God! Culture is not what it's about.'

But what it was about he was in no state to elaborate. The patch of excitement he had passed through must have disturbed the delicate coalition of alcohol and blood in his veins. He settled lower in his chair, almost as if some invisible surface had risen above his head.

'But still, fifteen years is a long time,' said James, anxious to keep the conversation more than the topic alive. 'Isn't Nakimbi back in power?'

'God help those bloody wogs!' said David and grasped the edge of the table with both his large hands as if he were going to push it over.

The word was presumably meant to enrage Tony, but he had already lost interest in arguing with an incompetent adversary. He got to his feet and walked off to inspect the garden. David took his hands off the table and put them on his knees. James sipped his wine and thought of the long, dreary drive back, first into London to deposit his passenger and then all the way out again to his own home in the suburbs. He looked up and saw David smiling at him.

'Nice of you to come all this way, James,' he said. 'I hear you on the steam from time to time, when I'm shaving, so you haven't gone out of my life quite as much as I've gone out of yours.'

'I often think of those days in your studio,' said James, not very truthfully.

'Happiest days of our lives?' said David ironically.

'No, but happy enough to remember . . . with pleasure.' James's sentence trailed away. He still couldn't be sure who he was speaking to, his old friend or the alcoholic interloper.

David put his glass back on the table and stared at it for some time in silence. Clearly his brain had ceased attempting consecutive conversation as his body had ceased attempting strenuous exercise. James wondered how he pursued his profession as a lawyer. Perhaps he kept all his energy for that.

'The trouble is,' said David at last, 'I could never finish anything. Except races or games, which finished when you passed the tape or the whistle blew. I never finished a single piece of sculpture. Did you ever finish that poem you were writing?'

James was disconcerted. The poem, his contribution to the literary section of that artistic powerhouse of the future represented by David's studio, had neither been finished nor discontinued. It still existed in a drawer of his desk at home and was still, in theory, awaiting completion. It was an ambitious piece, an epic modelled on Virgil, intended to run to twelve books like the *Aeneid*, but in Shakespearean pentameters. The subject was the Victorian soldier William Butler. James had got as far as the third book – Butler's exploits in the First Ashanti War – and then, like someone attempting a long swim underwater, had come up for air and realized that he could not sustain such a mighty artistic venture in a vacuum. His life and the life around him had no connection with the poem. He had thought they had when he began, but the connection had been lost somewhere in the midst of those exhausting struggles with metre and vocabulary. He had meant to try again when the problem became clearer, but it never did and its urgency receded. Yet, although he no longer thought of himself seriously as a poet or as any kind of writer, he had not relinquished that poem. Its existence, unfinished, impossible, somehow nourished him, his idea of himself. It was still his subject, even if he had failed to exploit it and saw no prospect of doing so.

'Not yet,' he said and then, apparently evading the question, 'but do you still have any contact with Simon Carter?'

'Nope,' said David, implying that he didn't wish to.

'I met him the other day in the lift at Broadcasting House. He's grown a Zapata moustache and was wearing a tropical suit. He looked like the hero of a Hollywood version of Conrad. Apparently he's doing the catalogue for an exhibition of the work of Lady Butler. You know, the lady who painted *The Roll-Call* and *Scotland for Ever* – romantic military subjects.'

'I thought Simon Carter liked modern art – abstraction and all that crap.'

Perhaps David did continue to make sculpture. His feelings still seemed to be engaged, as they always had been, on the side of tradition.

'The point is that Lady Butler was married to Sir William Butler – my man, the man my poem is about.' James's normally pale face was flushed, he sounded indignant.

'Well?'

Of course, it was ridiculous. James had no monopoly on Butler, let alone his wife. No one except a few close associates of nearly twenty years ago even knew he had meant to write the modern *Aeneid* around Butler's life. But still, Simon Carter was one of the few and James couldn't help feeling it was a kind of theft.

'If you finished your poem you could publish it to coincide with the exhibition,' said David.

He was pleased with the idea. Obviously he wished James and his poem well. But James felt a challenge had been issued – now the whole affair of Simon Carter and the exhibition had been made infinitely worse. He felt vulnerable in David's eyes. Agitated, he reached for his wine glass, saw that it was empty and, not liking to help himself to another, began knocking his pipe out against the heel of his hand.

Tony Cass returned from his inspection of the garden.

'Now then, Ruggles!' he said in his most schoolmasterly manner.

'Another drink?' asked David, picking up the bottle near its base and holding it out towards Tony.

James always enjoyed watching David touch and hold things,

making one aware of their shape and weight, as if every object he handled were a sculpture. Tony waved the bottle away.

'What about lunch?' he said.

II

There was no lunch, since Susie Rutland had gone to London. She had fixed the day some weeks before for a shopping expedition and lunch with her mother and had understood from her husband that his friends were coming the following week. The muddle only emerged at breakfast that morning when Susie asked him why he wasn't going to the office. She flatly refused to spoil her day in order to save his.

Susie took the train to London soon after breakfast and, arriving at Victoria, made her way down into the tube. She had arranged to meet her mother for coffee at Harrods. Standing on the platform and glancing up at the board to see if a train was announced she noticed a man admiring her. She had a strong, lively face and a good figure, and dressed in bold colours to set off her dark hair and eyes. She was pleased with her own appearance and enjoyed being seen as one of the fortunate ones.

There was nothing on the board and several minutes had passed. She had time in hand, but she was tired of standing and of avoiding the man's eyes. She walked down the platform, which was becoming crowded, and looked for a bench. The station tannoy began to cough and splutter and after a moment or two issued recognizable words:

'May we have your attention, please! We regret that all trains on this line are unavoidably delayed. This is due to a person on the line at Euston. London Transport apologize for the inconvenience. Thank you.'

The message was repeated as the crowd on the platform began to eddy to and fro, some making for the exits, some dithering between going and staying, some looking for a map of the Underground to replan their journeys. Susie decided it would be easiest to walk. She was already, almost instinctively, going quickly up the stairs away from the platform. It was as if the 'person on the line' were just inside the mouth of that very tunnel – not so much the person as the person's unhappiness. Susie hated and feared unhappiness. She avoided films or plays or books or TV programmes with unhappy subjects. She excluded unhappiness from her own life as far as possible by actively seeking happiness on all fronts: arranging parties, picnics, outings for the children; buying and wearing bright clothes; cooking delicious meals; cleaning the house and renewing the curtains, the covers, the wallpaper; taking holidays in cheerful, popular hotels; above all, through art – making her own or attending exhibitions. She had been an art student when she first met David. Her paintings were mostly watercolours of flowers, fruit, gardens or sunny views through windows, done in a bold, bright style derived from Vanessa Bell and Matthew Smith.

She left the station and struck through the gracious spaces of Belgravia, feeling her spirits lift at once among these grand buildings, wide streets and squares and new, expensive cars. She didn't dislike the rich. It seemed to her only natural and sensible to be rich and she had always vaguely hoped she would be herself. Besides, she and David were not badly off, could do most of the things they wanted to, even if at a more modest level than would have suited the owners of these houses and cars, so that in a sense she already belonged to the order of the privileged and shared their outlook. Heavy banks of clouds moved in a slow, stately fashion behind the tall, stately buildings. The sun emerged briefly and flashed off clean windows and large areas of fresh white stucco. Susie strode along briskly, noting that she wasn't going to be very late for her mother and thinking that she was grateful to London Transport for making her walk. No, not of course to London Transport, but to that unknown person who had certainly not foreseen that anyone would be grateful to him or her. Rather the reverse, she supposed. The person had no doubt been well aware that his or her action would disrupt the journeys of hundreds or thousands of other people, but had not cared, had considered the disruption trivial compared to his or her own needs. A selfish person, certainly, unhappy because selfish. But what depth of selfish unhappiness would it take to do that – to go down from this upper air into that rat-hole and publicly reduce oneself to a pulp?

Susie wanted to stop thinking about that person. She tried to distract her thoughts by looking at a bright orange, green and red flag jutting out over the porch of one of the houses across the square – some unknown country's embassy. She found herself thinking of David's doomed lunch party, the friends even now making their way through the suburbs towards those pallid sandwiches and too often reheated pies and sausages at The Brown Bull. She felt embarrassed for David and then for herself. They would not blame him, their disappointment and repressed anger would be directed at her. She had never met Tony Cass, but she had once known James Biggar quite well – he had been invited to their wedding, though she couldn't remember if he had come. He wasn't a bad fellow, a bit dull and serious, but polite and kind. He would be hurt by what she had done – not done. Worse still, David would be hurt. She had behaved badly, she recognized that now. She wished she could have undone the day, thrown it away like an unsuccessful painting and started it again with all its elements recomposed. She had turned into Sloane

Street and was passing an art gallery with a mixed exhibition of Cornish abstract paintings. Distressed and confused, forgetting the time, she went into the gallery, nodded to the woman behind the desk and gradually relieved the biting self-recrimination inside her with the airy optimism on the walls.

When she left the gallery she felt much better. Perhaps she was partly to blame for David's and his friends discomfiture, but wasn't David more so? He had taken her for granted as his cook and hostess, had not even consulted her timetable, had not bothered to discuss what they might eat for lunch, had treated her, in short, exactly as he used to treat her when they first knew each other, before they were married, when he was playing at being the artistic genius in that studio in Chelsea. She had put up with it then, out of some idea that he might be a genius, but chiefly out of selfless, uncalculating love for him. His love for her had been much less exclusive than hers for him – there were two or three other girlfriends, quite apart from his sculpture and his circle of male friends – but their marriage and changed circumstances had slowly altered the balance of their relationship, so that she and their two children had become the centre of his life. It occurred to her that this sudden attempt to revive the past with his friends had been a sort of unconscious desire on his part to escape from her or at least to reduce her importance to him. In that case, her behaviour had not only been justified but necessary.

She was in sight of Harrods now, late but not by more than ten minutes or so, and feeling quite herself again. As she was about to turn in at one of the doors in Hans Crescent, a woman came out and made for a taxi which was waiting in the street. The woman got into the taxi and it drove away. Who was she? Susie was sure she'd met her somewhere. On the other hand, if she had, she'd surely remember her name. She was at least ten years younger than Susie and not just pretty, but instantly attractive – a quality of warmth, openness and relaxed self-confidence emerged even in those few seconds between the shop's and the taxi's doors. Her quietly expensive clothes and hair-do and the waiting taxi suggested that she was used to luxury; and the way she looked neither to right nor left, but didn't seem to evade the admiring glances of the passers-by, argued that she might even expect to be recognized. Perhaps she was a film star – but there was a modesty, an absence of the artificial which made that seem unlikely. Her glamour was that of the beautiful girl next door, not of the unapproachable diva.

Susie stood for some moments in the street, visualizing the face, trying to place it and failing. She was reluctant to go inside and find her mother. She wished she could be turning out into the Knightsbridge traffic inside the taxi with that woman, sharing her day, experiencing the happiness she radiated. But as the taxi disappeared westwards, she felt chilled, diminished, reduced to the level of all the ordinary people hurrying past her. Her own life, she saw, was just as drab, scrappy and meaningless as theirs. She was not, after all, one of the fortunate ones.

She pushed wearily through the glass doors and went resentfully towards the coffee shop to meet her mother.

2

I

Simon Carter, walking towards Holland Park tube station, recognized Maria Dobson immediately when he caught sight of her on the other side of the street. She was unlocking the gate of the garden at the centre of the square and talking to a brown Burmese cat which, although it could have slipped under the gate, seemed to be waiting to leave the garden with her. Simon didn't often watch television, but he'd singled her out as his favourite newscaster. She was not only more attractive than any of the others, she was also, he was sure, more intelligent. He could imagine having a conversation with her.

He slowed his pace and observed her covertly as she pulled open the gate and stopped to pick up the cat. At that moment, on the other side of the garden, a large dog began barking and a moment or two later appeared, rollicking and bounding, in the middle of the lawn. The cat tensed. Simon could see the fur on its thin tail fluffing up into a dark brown plume. Suddenly, after a moment's indecision, it put its ears back, flattened itself to the ground and bolted across the road, straight into the path of a passing car. The car struck it a glancing blow and drove on as if nothing had happened. The cat was flung into the gutter almost at Simon's feet. Maria Dobson had been shouting 'No!' as the cat bolted and now she ran across the road herself without looking either way – fortunately there was no second car – desperately repeating 'No, no!' as she reached the gutter where Simon was bending over the cat's limp body.

'Still breathing,' he said. 'No damage to be seen.'

He looked up and saw that she was too shocked to reply. Her face was red and she was crying.

'Your cat?' he asked.

She nodded.

'Have you got a vet?'
She nodded again.
'Go and ring him,' he said. 'Where do you live?'
She pointed to a house a few doors up the street.
'Go and ring him now. Leave the door open, and I'll bring the cat.'
She didn't move. He stood up and faced her. She seemed absurdly small for someone whose face usually filled the screen, but of course he was standing on the kerb and she in the road and besides he was a tall man.
'Please!' he said urgently, waving his hand as if to break her trance. She seemed to be staring at his moustache. Feeling it itch, he brushed it down energetically with one finger. 'It's important to do something quickly. Cats give up.'
Pulling herself together, she ran away up the steps, opened her front door and disappeared. Simon removed his light cotton jacket, laid it on the road and eased the cat on to it. Then he picked up the bundle and carried it slowly up to the first floor. Maria Dobson was putting the phone down as he entered.
'The vet says I'm to bring him round straight away,' she said, still looking dazed.
Simon laid the cat on the long-haired rug in front of the fireplace. It wa a big, airy room with tall windows, pale green walls and a white carpet. The armchairs and sofa, also pale green, looked brand new. There were one or two prints on the walls – the sort of characterless things advertised in Sunday magazines or sold in up-market furniture shops – but there were also three long shelves of books which looked as though they were read, not just chosen to decorate the room.
'Taxi?' he said.
She dialled for one, while he opened the jacket a little to make sure the cat was still alive.
'The blood's from his mouth,' he said, pointing to the stains on his jacket.
When she had secured the taxi she seemed to regain her initiative, went and fetched a blanket and laid it over the bundle on the rug.
'The vet said he had to be kept warm.'
'There's no sign of injury outside,' said Simon. 'Maybe he'll be lucky. Nine lives. How many has he used already?'
'He's never had anything like this happen to him.'
She was kneeling on the floor, wiping her cheeks with the back of her hand, sniffing to keep her nose from dripping. Simon would have liked to lend her his handkerchief, but felt inhibited. They were total strangers. She must have had the same feeling.
'It's terribly kind of you,' she said, 'but don't let me keep you any longer. The taxi's coming and I can manage now.'
'I'm in no particular rush,' he said. 'I'll come with you. Better with two.'

'It's terribly kind of you,' she repeated and smiled for the first time. He smiled back, shrugged and went over to the window to look out for the taxi. He felt guilty, afraid she would notice he was enjoying her company more than worrying about the cat. But when he glanced back into the room he saw that she wasn't thinking about him at all. She was wholly taken up with the cat, staring at it, perhaps willing it to live, and then beginning to cry again.

'What's his name?' he asked.

She broke down completely and this time he felt able to offer her his handkerchief. She wiped her eyes and blew her nose.

'Vronsky,' she said at last.

He felt extraordinarily happy, as if they had ceased to be strangers, even though they still hadn't exchanged their own names.

When the taxi arrived, Simon carried Vronsky down to it and held him on his knee as they whisked over Campden Hill. The effort of counteracting the corners and abrupt slowings-down made his shoulders and legs ache and he was too concentrated on keeping the bundle steady to pay much attention to Maria.

'Have you got a cat yourself?' she asked, no longer sounding close to tears.

He glanced up and saw that she had been at work on her face and looked almost like the person he was used to on the screen: light brown hair, straight, sharp-ended nose, prominent high-set cheeks pleasantly softened by their roundness, gently arched eyebrows over warm brown eyes, her hairline and jaw in profile making an almost perfect semicircle.

'No,' he said. 'I'm ridiculously sentimental about animals. If I had one and something like this happened to it, I'd go to pieces.'

He was aware that he was exaggerating, trying to make himself more interesting, and spoke lightly to make that clear, but she took him quite seriously.

'This must be dreadful for you, then.'

'Yes,' he said, still keeping his tone light, 'It's what I've always hoped wouldn't happen. Being the person that had to cope with an injured animal.'

'But you needn't have done. I could have coped.' She began to sound as if it was his fault that she hadn't.

'Of course you could. But that was no excuse for me to walk on as if nothing had happened. Life has a way of searching out people's weaknesses.'

'You mean it was some kind of test?' she said. 'But if so, it was a test for me, not for you. Since Vronsky is my cat.'

'Of course. But since I happened to be passing, it became my test too.'

'No, I don't think so. You don't even know the cat, so it can hardly be quite the same for you as for me.'

She turned away and looked out of the taxi window. Was she offended with him? He had assumed too much.

'I'm sorry,' he said. 'It was tiresome of me to impose myself in this way.'

The taxi turned into a mews off Gloucester Road and stopped when she banged on the glass.

'I'm sorry,' she said. 'I didn't mean to make you feel . . . I couldn't be more grateful . . . It was sweet of you . . . and brave of you, considering your own feelings about animals.'

Embarrassed now by her fervour as well as her reassumed glamour, thinking that he had oversold himself as an animal-lover, he abruptly opened the taxi door and got out awkwardly, cradling Vronsky in his arms, saying hastily:

'Will you pay the cabbie? I'll go straight in.'

II

A pair of tattered gumboots abandoned on a beach; a German helmet upside down and filled with fir cones under a receding avenue of pines; a ruined clapboard lighthouse and a huge rusty anchor lying in windswept grass, in front of a pale, misted sea: Andrew Wyeth's paintings at the Royal Academy bothered Simon. He had asked his editor for more space than usual, but what was he going to write? There was so much detail, such sharpness of focus, such subtle colours and textures, such a powerful New World puritan flavour – yet he felt strangely antipathetic to the work. Should he plunge into the whole question of realism? But that was the most impossible of all the questions about art – better not to get involved with it.

Behind his uneasiness with Wyeth lay a much greater uneasiness about the long introduction he'd agreed to write for the proposed exhibition of Elizabeth Thompson's work. He'd definitely decided to call her by her maiden name rather than by her married name, Lady Butler, but that was all he had decided. He was becoming increasingly dubious about the whole project and the more he looked at these extraordinarily skilled, super-realistic, yet invincibly enigmatic paintings of Wyeth's, the more inadequate he felt as the expositor, let alone critic, of either Thompson or Wyeth. It was not just their skill that he couldn't begin to emulate, but also the labour that had gone into their paintings. Thompson had bought a field of rye from a farmer near Henley. Then she and her mother and some local children had trampled down the crop and she had sketched the result to use in her painting of the battle of Quatre Bras. She had gone to Chatham and had three hundred men of the Royal Engineers in specially made uniforms of the Napoleonic period demonstrate the old British battle-square for her. She had stood with her sketchbook in the Royal Horse Guards' riding school at Knightsbridge while two troopers on chargers rode straight at her and pulled up two yards short, showering her with sawdust. Wyeth's subjects were less ambitious, but every blade of scrubby grass, every small shell on the beach, every pine needle had been studied and recreated in paint with the same laborious care.

Filled with loathing for his own slothful, patronizing, facile profession, he shook himself, grimaced, shifted his burden of press handouts, photographs and the exhibition's catalogue to the other hand and moved on to the next painting. It was called *The Virgin* and depicted a young, well-built girl with reddish hair straggling down and curling up over her shoulders, her arms folded under her breasts. A shaft of light from the door of the barn in which she was standing lit her right breast and shoulder and her strong, homely face, turned sideways. She was completely naked. Simon supposed that, although the girl was uncompromisingly modern, the title alluded to the Virgin Mary. He found the painting shocking, not because of that, but because the girl was so obviously modest. Looking sideways out of the picture as she did, towards the shaft of light or the coming of adulthood or the angel of the annunciation, whatever it was, she wasn't aware of the viewer. The viewer, therefore, was forced into the role of voyeur.

As Simon went on staring at the naked girl, he thought of the incident with the cat a few days ago. The vet had diagnosed an internal haemorrhage and put Vronsky in an oxygen tent. Simon and Maria Dobson had left together and he had hailed her a taxi. He had not gone with her though he lived just round the corner from her, feeling that she wanted to be rid of him. He'd written down her phone number so that he could inquire about the cat's fate and then walked home in an odd state of mind. Trying to analyse his feelings in front of this painting of the naked girl, he wondered if there wasn't some connection. Maria Dobson had been equally disturbing. Not that she was unapproachable but that, just as with the girl in the painting, he felt she should have been. He had no right to be looking at this girl's naked body, he had no right to catch Maria when her defences were down. On the other hand, he couldn't pretend that he wasn't delighted, in both cases, to have been granted the privilege. The most disturbing element was that it went so far and no further. There was little satisfaction in being the voyeur of a painted image on a canvas and not much more in having briefly shared a taxi with a distraught Maria Dobson. But whereas the one offered no possibility of going further, the other did, so that there was really no comparison between the two experiences. Moreover, the Maria Dobson experience had involved at least four sets of different and possibly conflicting disturbances: his and her feelings about the cat, his about her and hers about him.

In that light, his reaction to the painting began to seem simple. So much for realism. It was just as much an abstraction from life as any other kind of art. On the other hand, was he being fair to the painting? He, not the painter, had imposed a meaning on it and was now accusing it of being limited to that meaning. Typical of a critic! Yet the painter was certainly imposing a subject on him. An arrangement too. He was confronting the viewer with the girl's nakedness in a most blatant way. You could look or you could look away, but if you looked you saw. There was nothing else to see. The wooden walls and door of the barn were mostly in the shadow, the hay piled up behind the girl disappeared into darkness. Simon had missed the hay until now. That also had two meanings, hadn't it? It alluded to the stable in Bethlehem and to the traditional bed for a peasant girl losing her virginity.

But was his encounter with Maria Dobson, after all, so much more complicated. His horror at seeing the cat's accident had been mixed with intense pleasure at the sight of the cat's owner running across the road in despair. She was immensely attractive. He wanted to see her again.

Moving away from the painting at last and allowing several other critics who had been hovering impatiently round him to compete for the full frontal position, he went in search of a drink. Refreshments were provided for the press in a dark, panelled room along a corridor, but the people taking these refreshments were none of them from the better-known papers. Simon helped himself to a glass of wine and a sandwich and overheard an oldish woman asking another if she couldn't somehow help her to place the occasional freelance piece with her magazine. The second woman rejected her pleas quite coldly, but the first woman wouldn't give up. A peculiarly ugly man, short with a very large head, was greedily shoving in towards the table for another glass of wine. Two others, both bald, one with thick glasses and the other with an unkempt beard, were running over the week's crop of private views, peering over each other's shoulders to see who else was in the room, rapidly clearing a plate of sandwiches at their elbows.

'What an unattractive lot we are!' thought Simon, looking round to see if there was anyone he could bear to talk to. 'What a half world we live in!'

'How are you?' said a voice beside him.

It was his cousin Freda, whom he never met except at these press views.

'I hope you don't mind my saying so,' she said, 'but you're getting to look awfully like Uncle Percy. Of course I hardly remember him at your age and he had a quite different moustache, but from the back it was strange. You're not offended?'

'Not at all. I liked Uncle Percy. I should think he was good-looking in his prime.'

His great-uncle had died in his eighties, a few years before. Simon had been proud of him for his shy, Edwardian manners, his hand-made clothes and general air of distinction, but above all for his knighthood, earned in the Indian Civil Service. It was no great distinction, judged objectively, but it made him stand out from the ruck of clergymen, doctors and lawyers whose line ended with Simon. The family tree which had put out so many branches in the last century must have come to feel the lack of its own necessity, for one by one the branches had dried up without issue. Freda was married, but childless. She had a younger brother who might still marry, but Simon himself – a generation behind Freda – was so far the only grandchild of Uncle Percy's many brothers and sisters and he, it seemed, was no more the marrying kind than Uncle Percy. The Carters were as doomed as the D'Urbervilles and they hadn't even had their days of glory.

'Did you ever go through that diary of his?' Freda was asking.

'Not yet. But I mean to.'

After Uncle Percy's death, Simon and Freda had helped one of his sisters go through his effects and Simon had taken away the diary.

'I don't suppose you'll find much in it,' said Freda. 'He was a dull man.'

'Was he? No, he could be quite amusing, surely, in that ironic way?'

'I thought he was conceited.'

Freda still had the manner of a little girl, though she was well into her sixties, and Simon suddenly felt incensed. This was what had kept the Carters down all these centuries, this disapproval of anyone who raised his head above the parapet.

'He probably thought we were all such bores that he found it difficult to talk to us.'

'That's what I mean by conceit,' said Freda.

'Did you like the show?' asked Simon, with an irritated smile.

'I loved it. Wyeth's such an honest painter, so true and simple. I specially liked the nude. That's what I call a good picture.'

'You mean, well painted?'

'Yes, it is well painted, but I mean morally good. Wholesome.'

Wholesome? It had made Simon feel the opposite and he thought the artist had meant him to feel like that. More for the sake of provoking Freda than starting a serious discussion, he said:

'You didn't find it pornographic?'

'Not the slightest. It's just about the cleanest, healthiest picture I've ever seen.'

'Not even erotic?'

'You men have such dirty minds.'

'It was painted by a man.'
'But not with that in mind. Not *at* all.'

One of the Carters' family tricks was to emphasize the wrong word in a phrase when they felt hunted or confused. It was a way of saying that words weren't important, that conversations meant nothing, that they were only polite exchanges like handshakes and that to pursue a topic which was uncomfortable or required effort was ill-mannered and even foolhardy. Simon decided to go home at once and write an article probing the 'wholesomeness' of Wyeth's paintings. After that he would make a point of reading Uncle Percy's diary. Thirdly, he resolved, as he said goodbye abruptly to his cousin, that he would ring the number he'd been given and ask after the cat.

III

The opening sentences of his piece on Wyeth's 'wholesomeness' had cost Simon much time and thought, but once he got them, the rest flowed easily. He took the three pages of typescript into his editor's office with an air of self-satisfaction, forgetting that Andrew Mowle never praised anything, only doggedly marked up the copy, complained about semicolons (which he believed to be effete) and usually finished by pushing the thing to one side with a noncommittal grunt if he had no particular holes to pick in it.

On this occasion, though, sitting hunched forward in his chair, his thin white arms lying on the desk, his fingers nervously playing with the corners of the paper, his large head tilted a little sideways, he seemed almost to be enjoying himself. There was the ghost of a smile on his severe mouth.

'Worth a visit?' he said when he'd finished reading.

This was high praise.

'I hope I made that clear,' said Simon.

'Your point about the sexuality of innocence is well taken.'

Simon didn't recall making any such point.

'This nude in the stable . . . ' said Andrew.

'It's simply the difference between a scene you might have stumbled on in real life and the same scene set up by an artist. It can only be pretended innocence, especially when the artist is as technically skilled as Wyeth. I'm not sure it would be any different as done by a naive artist – Douanier Rousseau for example.'

'The point, though, is that it's sexy.'

'Well, perhaps. But I don't think it's quite as simple as that. The artist's purpose wasn't primarily to create an erotic image. Rather the opposite. I think he was after an image of innocence. The difficulty is in the nature of innocence and the act of showing it when you're aware that it is innocence.'

'But you obviously find the image erotic,' said Andrew.

'True. But that's part of the difficulty – for the artist. If he wants to portray innocence, I mean. The naked body inevitably sets up the wrong expectations in the viewer.'

Andrew was silent, not pondering what Simon had said, which he'd hardly listened to, but following some line of thought of his own.

'Take TV!' he said at last. 'I happen to be involved at the moment in a series on the Third World – as writer and presenter. The working title is *Latitudes South* and the idea is to open people's minds to the positive side of post-colonial independence. Anyway, the producer of the series is a man called Michael Arley. Do you know him?'

'I'm afraid not.'

'It doesn't matter. He's quite young, very bright, very ambitious.'

Andrew stopped talking, lit a cigarette and then, picking up the loose pages of Simon's review, shuffled them together, paper-clipped them and tossed them into a tray on his desk.

'Michael Arley's current girlfriend,' said Andrew, 'is one of the newscasters. I've never met her, but whenever I see her on the box I get odd feelings about her.'

Simon smiled, but Andrew's expression remained stern.

'She turns me on, of course. But that isn't what I mean. That's a perfectly straightforward feeling in itself. The odd feeling is to do with her role. She's there to read the news, okay. She turns me on – and others too, no doubt. Okay. But which role is she hired for? The roles are in conflict. They distract from one another. A sexually attractive newscaster takes your mind off the news. So is this deliberate on the part of her bosses?'

'I suppose they reckoned she might improve the viewing figures.'

'Right. So she's hired as a kind of courtesan. But isn't this more than a matter of attracting the punters? Isn't it also, most likely, a way of blurring and manipulating the news?'

Simon smiled again. He could never take people with political convictions seriously. They seemed to delight in loading every aspect of life with more weight than it deserved. They were always looking for occasions of moral indignation. Their world, confined basically to two armed camps, the goodies and the baddies, was a perpetual conspiracy by the baddies to get the advantage.

'I met one of the courtesans the other day,' he said casually.

'What was her name?'

'We didn't introduce ourselves,' said Simon, still pretending to be only distantly interested in the subject.

'What did she look like?'

Simon wasn't prepared to describe her.

'Maria Dobson?' he said, as if he wasn't sure there was a newscaster with that name. 'I think that's who she was.'

'Maria Dobson is Michael Arley's girlfriend,' said Andrew.

Simon described the accident to Maria's cat and how he'd helped her to take it to the vet. Andrew, who seldom troubled even to appear to listen to what other people said, unless it was extremely short and part of an argument that interested him, sat staring at Simon as if every word of his story was important.

'And you haven't seen her since?' he asked finally.

'No, I meant to ring her to find out what happened to the cat, but I haven't got round to it.'

'Why was her cat called Vronsky?'

'I suppose she's keen on Tolstoy. A lot of people are. I daresay a lot of people call their cats Vronsky.'

'Where does she live?'

'Quite near me. That's how I happened to be passing when the accident occurred.'

'And you've got her phone number?'

'I suppose I've still got it.'

'On you?'

Simon felt in his pocket, brought out his diary and looked at the flyleaf, where he'd written it down.

'Why? Do you want it?'

'I told you, I don't know her, never met her. Why don't you give her a ring now and find out about the cat?' Andrew pushed the phone across his desk.

'All right.'

Simon was reluctant to do so. His feelings about Maria were still confused. The news that she had a steady lover – even though he couldn't have expected otherwise – made him the less anxious to clarify them. Nor did he want her to have to tell him that the cat had died. Nevertheless, he felt it necessary to keep up his pretence of being well distanced from the whole episode. He dialled the number and listened to the ringing tone, while Andrew leaned even further across his desk as if he meant to take part in the conversation. Simon now hoped there would be no reply, but Maria's voice interrupted the tone and Simon told her who he was and nervously asked for news of Vronsky.

'As good as new.'

'Really? I'm delighted.'

'The haemorrhage seems to have healed up completely.'

'That's marvellous.'

'I'm terribly grateful for what you did.'

'Nothing at all.'

'I'm sure you saved his life.'

'No, that was the vet.'

'Well, him too. I've been very lucky.'

'You bring out the best in people, I expect.'

'I should have rung you myself to thank you.'
'I'm glad I happened to be there.'
'I can't thank you enough.'
There was nothing more to say unless Simon cared to broach another topic. Andrew's eager face, hardly a foot away, added to his embarrassment.
'Anyway,' he said, 'it's very good news. I'm extremely relieved. See you about sometime, I dare say.'
'I dare say.'
She didn't sound as if she thought it likely or wished otherwise.
'Goodbye.'
'Goodbye and thank you again.'
He put the phone down.
'It's okay. It survived,' he said as he got up to leave the office. Andrew had pushed his chair back and was sitting with his chin on his chest, his arms hanging down and loosely clasped between his thighs. He seemed to have no further interest in the cat, Maria Dobson or Simon.

3

I

The fiasco of their visit to David Rutland drew James Biggar and Tony Cass together again. Tony was to bring his family to lunch with the Biggars on the next convenient Sunday. James, with his wife Judy and their two sons, lived in Riverley, a commuter suburb on one of the main lines from Waterloo. The line, on which James travelled to and from work, passed through a cutting right beside their garden. The house was small, but it stood in nearly an acre of ground. Judy was the gardener, but James helped with the heavy work and he relied on the garden almost as much as on his wife for his sense of contentment. Domesticity, he had decided, was the best thing that life had to offer. Calm, order and goodwill were the qualities he valued most and it seemed to him that the garden expressed all three, adding besides aesthetic pleasure, which he could not quite justify as a moral quality, but without which moral qualities were never very attractive. He had once tried to write a sequence of poems, in the style of Horace, to celebrate the perfection of his wife, his cottage and his garden, but the thing had petered out, chiefly because Judy had disliked it.

James's periods of domestic contentment were slashed through with a background of chronic anxiety. He worried about money, about his own and his family's health, about his children's education, about the house and the car, about the state of the country and the world, but most of all about time. His job as a continuity announcer demanded a perpetual awareness of the clock, an exactitude measured in seconds, and although in the controlled environment of the studio his sense of timing had become second nature, so that he was hardly ever worried by the performance of his duties there, the outside world tortured him with its looseness and shapelessness. It was like a parcel he could never be quite sure he had wrapped and tied securely. Potential disaster lurked just ahead of him. He might miss his train, the train might be delayed or cancelled. His watch might be wrong. He might have misremembered the time at which he was expected in the studio. He was aware of how much this excessive fear of being late damaged his enjoyment of life and fed on itself – he had written a poem comparing the pendulum of the grandfather clock in the hall to the Sword of Damocles – but he couldn't shake it off.

The Cass family was late, but this didn't trouble James. His anxiety about time referred only to himself. What did trouble him was that William and Stephen, his two sons, just back for the summer holiday from their boarding school, resented the lunch party. They didn't know any of the Cass children and had looked forward to relaxing and slopping about on this first Sunday of freedom. James remembered very well what it was like as a child having to keep your end up with other children, expecially strange children with whom you had nothing in common except that your parents were friends, but he pretended not to understand their complaints.

'Surely it's more interesting to have people your own age to lunch? You know how boring you find the grown-ups.'

'But we don't know these people,' said William, the elder.

'You'll soon get to know them.'

'Why should we?' asked Stephen, the more rebellious of the two.

'You may find you have interests in common.'

James was wrong. His own children, expecially William, were inhibited with strangers, preferred indoor to outdoor pursuits, spoke only if spoken to and then as briefly as possible. The four Cass children, the moment they emerged aggressively from their car like an army unit spreading out to occupy a piece of invaded territory, were clearly going to be intolerable guests. There were two boys and two girls, the boys roughly the same ages as William and Stephen, who were fourteen and twelve respectively, the girls younger, but all bursting with energy, fiercely competitive and as uninhibited as their father. They had been round the garden, climbed the trees and broken a branch, put the swing out of action and caught one of the goldfish in the pond before James had offered Tony and his wife Diana – heavily pregnant with their fifth – a drink. William and Stephen, meanwhile, stuck close to the grown-ups and James saw that to suggest they showed the Cass children their rooms and possessions was out of the question. It would have been like handing them over to a violent and unscrupulous enemy. He prayed that Judy would have lunch ready quickly.

'Have you got anything for us to do?' said Christian, the oldest Cass child, to William.

'What sort of thing?' asked William stiffly.

'You haven't got a tennis court,' said the elder girl, Martha.
'No,' said Stephen. 'Have you?'
'We play badminton,' said Tricia, the younger girl. 'It's faster than tennis and anyway we live in London and our lawn's not big enough for tennis.'

She implied that it was infinitely better to live in London, but that if you had to live outside it, you might partly redeem yourself by having a tennis court.

'What about a trampoline?' asked Martha.
'No,' said Stephen, almost with satisfaction.
'You need a new swing,' said Tricia.
'No we don't,' said William. 'Neither of us uses it any more.'
'This place is very boring,' said Jack, the younger Cass boy, partly to his father and partly to James.
'We don't find it so,' said James, with tight lips, the blood mounting to his head.
'Perhaps they've got a football you could kick around the lawn,' said Tony Cass, obviously considering his child simply truthful rather than rude.
'Can you find a football, William?' said James.
'I don't think so,' said William. He could have done, but he hated football and saw no reason to put himself out for these ruffians.

Lunch was fortunately not long delayed, but it was dominated by the Cass children. Judy talked to Diana about babies and education, James and Tony toyed with a few current topics, political and social, William and Stephen sat disapprovingly silent, while the Cass children criticized and rejected the food, compared the house and its arrangements unfavourably with their own and tried to draw William and Stephen out on the subjects of their car, their school and their holidays. James was relieved that his children were astute enought not to respond, but he felt more and more angry and uncomfortable. It was the anger that made him uncomfortable. It diminished him in his own eyes to be so provoked by these uncouth children.

Tony had got on to the subject of America, which he had visited several times, both North and South. James, who had never crossed the Atlantic, seized on the topic as an oblique way of criticizing the Cass children, berating the North Americans for their absence of long-established traditions and therefore of stability and civilization. He tended always to be pro-European and anti-American, but on this occasion he was deliberately exaggerating his attitude. Tony reacted contemptuously.

'But you've never been there. You know nothing about America.'
'I've read their books and seen their films. I've met plenty of Americans. The world is run by Americans. How can we help knowing about them?'

'This is just ignorant prejudice. Of course the world's run by Americans. They're the best people to run it since they're more advanced than the rest of us.'

'More advanced? Most of them are backwoods barbarians. They know nothing about the rest of the world and care less. They're not more advanced, just richer.'

'What America does today, the rest of us do tomorrow. I call that being more advanced.'

'It depends what you mean by "advanced". The drug culture, the psychiatric culture, lack of a welfare state, complete subservience to Capitalism with a big C, everybody carrying guns, consumerism run mad, children badly educated and undisciplined.'

He had reached the real point of his tirade. Tony seemed to understand, for he didn't reply at once, but glanced across the table at one of his own children, just then pushing aside a plate of Apple Charlotte:

'Ugh! it's got bread in it!'

'I don't mind the bread,' said another, 'but it's too sweet.'

'I'm hungry,' said a third, who had rejected most of her first course.

'The way you think of Americans,' said Tony, 'is the way everybody used to think of us. People with power throw their weight about, people without it naturally dislike them. But it's especially hard for us to accept being a second- or even a third-class power. It makes us behave like grannies, disapproving old grannies.'

That was it exactly, James thought. The Cass children made him feel like a granny, they deliberately put him in the position of a granny, and Tony had very neatly shot him down. He fell silent, discouraged, dissatisfied with himself, recognizing Tony as more intelligent, more forceful, better informed, more admirable in every way than himself. The Cass children, he saw, were trained to prosper in the new world, but he had put the leg-irons of the old on his own.

After lunch, they drove in both cars to the nearest bit of open country. Part of it was now a golf course, but there was a pleasant area of woodland and a footpath across fields which led back eventually to the road and so to where they had parked the cars. James made up for hardly having spoken to Diana during lunch by walking beside her through the woodland section; Judy walked with the reluctant William and Stephen, discussing plans for the holidays and restoring their good humour; Tony set himself to exercise his four storm-troopers by running races with them, testing their knowledge of wild flowers and trees, which they were only too glad to display, and competing with them at estimating distances. Diana spoke to James, but her eyes and most of her thoughts were on her husband and children. James asked her about the baby to come.

'Do you want a girl or a boy?'
'I don't mind. Why should I?'
'Girls are supposed to be less trouble to begin with, but worse later on.'
'I don't think it makes much difference. Ours have all been very easy.'
'What will you call it?'
'We always wait till we see it to decide what to call it.'

Diana had been working as a secretary in the Foreign Office when Tony met her. Did this perpetual assertion of superiority come with the job, James wondered, or did the Foreign Office only employ people who were already like that?

'I suppose you won't be having much of a summer holiday this year?'
'We'll be taking our holiday in September. Tony's booked a hotel in the Dordogne for the two of us and the baby.'
'What about the others?'
'My mother will come and hold the fort.'
'You're lucky. My mother wouldn't be up to that any longer and Judy's is dead.'
'My mother's a tough number. The children adore her.'

Natural selection, thought James. Perhaps if England bred enough families like the Cass clan, she'd rise to being a first-class power again. On the other hand, it was more likely that all the Cass-type people would eventually emigrate to America, leaving England to sink under the weight of its timid and flaccid Biggars.

The party had emerged from the woods and stopped to admire the view from a low ridge. The path crossed the golf course at this point and beyond was an avenue of poplars leading to a farm.

'I like that,' said Tony.

James immediately felt better, as if it was his landscape that had met with Tony's approval.

'It always reminds me of that painting by Hobbema,' he said.
'Which one do you mean?' asked Tony.

James couldn't remember its title or even where he'd seen it. The sun was quite hot, but there was a fresh breeze as they descended towards the poplar avenue. The Cass children were roughing up one of the bunkers on the golf course. Tony and James were walking together ahead of the rest.

'Will you keep in touch with poor old Ruggles?' asked Tony.
'I shouldn't think so,' said James. 'Too depressing.'
'I wish you would.'
'Why don't you, then?'
'I hardly know him. But he likes you.'
'Well, I like him, of course. But we don't have much in common any more.'

'The thing is,' said Tony, 'that he does still correspond with Rimington.'

'Is Rimington still in Balunda?'

'Oh yes, at the moment. So far he's managed to survive all the changes of regime.'

'The Vicar of Bray.'

'Not really,' said Tony. 'Rimington doesn't keep his head down. He survives the opposite way, by being the toughest character in the place.'

'I thought Balunda wasn't part of your section?'

'It's not, but naturally I still have an interest in it.'

'You want me to keep tabs on Colonel Rimington through David Rutland?'

'That would be helpful.'

'Why?'

'He could prove an embarrassment to us.'

'I don't see why. He hasn't kept his British nationality, has he?'

'The important thing in foreign policy is not to be taken by surprise. Nearly all the major cock-ups are caused simply by not being ahead of the game.'

'What am I supposed to do? Get hold of Colonel Rimington's letters to David and leave microfilm of them in rabbit-holes?'

'Don't be silly!'

'Do I get paid for spying on my old friend?'

'Rimington's not your friend and no one's asking you to do any spying.'

'And if I get any information about Rimington, what shall I do with it? Ring you at the Foreign Office?'

'No, I'll ring you.'

'Ah. There is some element of secrecy, then?'

'You really are making a mountain out of a molehill.'

'But since I'm supposed to be the mole . . .'

'Forget it, James, forget it! It's not really worth the bother.'

They had passed the poplars and the farm at the end of them and turned on to a footpath between hedges. Tony strode on ahead and James, looking back, saw that they had left the others some way behind and that Diana was sitting down against a bank. He called to Tony:

'Diana seems to be tired.'

Tony stopped and came back.

'I thought you said it was a short walk.'

'I was forgetting she had to carry all that extra weight.'

They hurried back to rejoin the others. When they reached them, Diana was just being helped to her feet, with two of her children pulling on each arm. She smiled at Tony.

'I was a bit out of breath and hot,' she said.

They all walked back the way they had come, Tony arm in arm with Diana, their children, more subdued now, following them and talking among themselves. James walked beside Judy, William the other side of her and Stephen the other side of him. The sun flashing off and on their faces as they entered and left the shadow of each poplar was tiring and eventually almost soporific, but James was in a better humour than he had been all day. He loved to have his family round him as they were now and no immediate reason for argument or even talk. If ever one was happy, he told himself, it was at moments like this, out of doors on a summer afternoon, without thought of the past or the future. No regrets, no anxieties, no present disturbance. But, of course, without the knowledge and experience of those miseries, one wouldn't enjoy their absence with the same force. He smiled at the banality of his reflections. But wasn't his contentment itself banal? Wasn't all contentment banal? Then roll on the banal! Surely this was the secret of all human endeavour, to be walking with your wife and children down an avenue of poplars and nothing to disturb your contemplation of your own happiness? Weren't all actions, all politics, all revolutions, all wars, all careers directed to achieving this simple outcome or something like it? Weren't all stories, plays, poems, paintings, symphonies only deliberate arrangements of disturbance, so that you could emerge finally in your avenue of poplars and appreciate what you'd achieved against the odds? No doubt it was because he had just escaped becoming a spy that he felt so particularly pleased with the ordinariness of his life.

'I think you might have made a bit more effort with your guests,' said Judy to William and Stephen.

'They weren't our guests,' said William.

'With our guests, then,' said Judy. 'Dad and I make an effort with your friends, don't we?'

'I wish they'd decide not to stay for tea,' said Stephen.

They were crossing the golf course again. Several parties of golfers were dotted about on the fairways.

'I wish somebody's golf ball would hit one of them on the head,' said William.

'Four golf balls,' said Stephen, 'bong, bong, bong, bong!'

'That's rather unkind,' said Judy.

But William and Stephen were off on one of their long-running comic-strip fantasies. The golf balls became cannonballs, hand grenades, rockets. The Cass children were blown up, vaporized, carried off to distant planets where further unpleasant experiences awaited them. The saga took William and Stephen in excellent spirits all the way back to the cars. They found Diana very much overtired and to everyone's relief it was decided that the Cass family would go straight back to London without stopping for tea.

'I'll give you a ring in a few weeks,' said Tony to James, as they shook hands by the cars, 'in case you have any news of poor old Ruggles.'

II

'I've rung you several times. You're always out.'
'I often work in the evening.'
'Couldn't Judy answer the phone once in a while?'
'She's often out in the evenings too.'
'Who with?'
'Local committees. School events.'
'Sounds fishy.'

The caller hadn't said who he was and James would have liked to pretend he didn't know. Tony Cass naturally assumed that he couldn't be mistaken for anybody else and it was a pity he was right. Self-esteem seemed to be one of the vices the gods approved of and rewarded with further cause for it.

'Have you been in touch with Ruggles?'
'Sorry, no, I haven't.'

Several months had passed since the Cass family's summer visit to the Biggars and it had been at the back of James's mind to make contact again with David Rutland. It was probably because Tony had particularly asked him to that he hadn't.

'It looks as if Ruggles's friend may be in trouble.'
'Do you mean Rimington?'
'I can't go into it on the phone. When are you next in town?'
'The day after tomorrow. But not till four.'
'Can we meet for lunch?'
'I was hoping to do some gardening.'
'Oh, come on, James!'
'I've told you I don't want to be involved with this business anyway.'
'You're being childish.'
'I can't think of anything much more childish than amateur espionage.'
'Don't be such a drip!'

James paused, found no suitable reply and put the phone down. He was shaking with anger. He had finished with Tony Cass – he didn't know how he'd put up with him so long.

Rain was spattering intermittently on the windows. It was a depressing afternoon of heavy cloud and gusts of wind. James went out into the garden and walked about moodily. Most of the flowers were over and the leaves were beginning to fall. The drizzle obscured his glasses and drips from the trees ran down his neck. Perhaps he had been unnecessarily mulish with Tony. Those coarse and inappropriate inferences about Judy had set the direction of the whole conversation. From then on, James realized, he had been determined not to be helpful. No doubt his tone of voice even more than his words had conveyed that and Tony had responded accordingly. Even so, it was Tony who wanted his help, not the other way round, and it was surely up to him to find a better way to get it. If obtaining this sort of information was part of what he was paid for, then he wasn't doing his job very well. James, in his capacity as a taxpayer, ought to write to the Foreign Office and suggest that Tony was incompetent and should be replaced. The thought made him smile. He imagined Tony being posted to Paraguay or St Helena or some other dreary outpost for fallen Napoleons. Or perhaps Balunda. 'Good morning, Cass!' he heard the under-under-secretary saying as Tony stood humbly in front of his desk, 'You seem to have made a balls-up of this Rimington file, so we're sending you to Balunda to find out for yourself.' And then the humiliating scene as Tony had to go home and admit to snobby Diana and the five children that he'd been demoted and would probably never get his K after all.

James groaned aloud. He was going on like a schoolboy. Did one never escape those patterns laid down in early youth? Was one like a boat with a keel and ribs laid down in the boatyard and only thinly disguised by the boards and barnacles and other accretions of age? As a child James had wanted people's admiration and approval. He had generally received them at home, but seldom at school. So he had grown up with a mixture of self-confidence and diffidence and his reaction to Tony was perhaps typical of his relationship to the outside world. Rather than take it on and shape it to his own purposes, he preferred to retreat into his own private world where his value was not in dispute. It wasn't that he wasn't competitive, but that he didn't care to compete where he didn't have an odds-on chance of winning.

In the tiny world of radio announcers there was virtually no competition, because no hierarchy. When he first became an announcer, one of the older ones congratulated him on joining 'the last profession left for a gentleman'. That was it, of course. A gentleman was someone who didn't compete, didn't have to, because his status was assured. He himself had been taught to behave like a gentleman and rewarded for doing so with approval and had learned the lesson so thoroughly that he couldn't now behave in any other way. Therefore he was content to remain an announcer because it asked nothing more of him. Therefore he had been angry with Tony Cass, because Tony wanted him to do something ungentlemanly and was contemptuous of him for jibbing at it. But the true cause of his anger and present disturbance was his sense of being in the wrong. He could argue as much as he liked that he was morally in the right, but he couldn't convince himself because he no longer fully accepted that moral code. It was out of date and he was partly out of date with it. He was programmed to be a gentleman and conscious of being an anachronism. So to some extent he had changed, in consciousness if not in behaviour, but the change was a weakness, since it left him dangling helplessly between the two worlds. He should contrive either to behave less like a gentleman or have the courage to be out of date. No, it was not a question of courage, but of conviction, of belonging. He belonged neither to the past nor the present.

Wasn't that the story of William Butler's life? In 1884–85 he took part in the attempt to rescue General Gordon from Khartoum. The commander of the expedition was, as always, Garnet Wolseley and he gave Butler, then forty-six, the task of designing, building and organizing special boats for the transport of troops and supplies up the Nile and over its cataracts. Butler succeeded heroically in getting the boats built in sufficient numbers and record time and in overcoming the natural obstacles; but his worst struggles were not with the Nile, but with the factions in the army who thought other routes and other methods of transport more likely to succeed. As it became clear that they were losing the race with time, Butler's rage and frustration burst out even against his hero Wolseley. The Gordon expedition was the end of Wolseley's unbroken run of success and from then on his reputation gradually faded.

Butler, perhaps the most adventurous, optimistic, attractive and certainly the most idealistic of all Wolseley's Arthurian knights, was soured by the expedition and its aftermath. Left in the desert to guard the frontiers of Egypt, he wrote to his wife Elizabeth: 'Is it not strange that the very first war during the Victorian era in which the object was entirely noble and worthy should have proved an utter and complete failure, beaten at the finish by forty-eight hours? These things are not chance, they are meant, and the men and nations who realise that fact are fortunate, for they can learn.'

James wondered what the British were supposed to learn from the failure of a noble and worthy cause, when so many ignoble and unworthy ones had succeeded. Presumably that virtue doesn't pay. Certainly the last two wars of the Victorian era were as piratical as anything in their history. Kitchener's triumphant revenge for Gordon's death, exacted thirteen years later at the battle of Omdurman, was closely followed, in 1899, by the Second Boer War. A year before its outbreak, Major-General Butler was sent by Wolseley – now Commander-in-Chief at the War Office – to Capetown to command the British troops in South Africa. There could hardly have been a less suitable officer for the job in the whole of the British army, especially since from the moment of his arrival he was also required to act as Governor and High Commissioner in the temporary absence of Sir Alfred Milner. Nobody had told Butler – how could they? – that the faction that wanted war with the Boers was being secretly encouraged by Milner himself. Gradually, however, Butler's eyes were opened to the true absurdity of the position he had been occupying: a man who wanted peace and brotherhood with the Boers standing in the shoes of a man who wanted to destroy their independence and make them part of a new British viceroyalty to rival India and Egypt. But Butler's new position, once Milner had returned and relieved him of his civil duties, was hardly less absurd. He was still commander of the forces which were supposed to be ready for a war that was being engineered against his wishes and without anything being admitted openly by his own political superior. Less than three months before the start of the war, Butler resigned his command and returned to England, where he found himself 'the best abused man in England', violently attacked in the press as responsible, by his failure to warn the government of their military unreadiness, for the repeated British disasters of that last autumn of the nineteenth century.

James stood staring through the dripping hedge at the trains passing in the cutting below. It was the rush hour and he could almost see the returning commuters inside spluttering over their evening papers at the news of the surrender of the Gloucester Regiment at Ladysmith, the Boer encirclement of Mafeking and Kimberley and the double defeat of Lord Methuen at the Modder river and General Gatacre at Stormberg. Nothing had changed. There had always been honourable men and they had always been the dupes of those such as Rhodes and Milner who knew how to manipulate events. The commuters, believing everything they read because they read it, did not associate honour with General Sir William Butler at all. He was either a traitor or an incompetent, but probably both, and some of them, as soon as they got home, would write to tell him so. After the Butlers' return to England, Elizabeth tried to spare her husband by intercepting the worst of these anonymous letters.

Suddenly remembering that he was not alone either, James went into the house to see if Judy was back from her school. She was drinking tea in the kitchen.

'Have you been for a walk?' she asked.

'Just round the garden.'

'Why didn't you wear a mac?'

'I didn't realize it was so wet.'

'You're soaked. You'd better change before you give yourself a cold.'

'I'll be all right.'

'No, you won't. Go and change!'

As if reluctantly, but secretly delighted that she had noticed and cared what state he was in, he went upstairs and did as he was told. When he returned to the kitchen he told Judy about the phone call from Tony Cass and his decision to break off relations with him for good.

'But I like Tony,' she said.

'Pompous ass!'

'Why don't you get in touch with David Rutland anyway and find out what's going on?'

'What's the point of that?'

'You'll know more than Tony. You'll feel in a stronger position.'

'But I'm not interested in what's going on. It's not my business.'

While Judy cooked the supper, James went and rang David. Susie Rutland answered the phone.

'David's not very well, I'm afraid.'

'I'm sorry. Shall I ring again in a day or two?'

'Was it anything special?'

'Not really.'

'I was very sorry to miss you and your friend when you came down. Did David explain? I had a long-standing engagement with my mother. But I felt bad about not making you any lunch. That pub is terrible.'

'It really didn't matter,' said James. 'We were there to see David, after all.'

There was a slight pause. James's polite smoothing-over of that memorably awful day must have persuaded Susie that he really did care about David. Or else she was clutching at straws.

'I'm worried about him,' she said.

'His illness?'

'Partly. No, not exactly. I can't explain on the phone. I suppose it wouldn't be possible to meet? I need somebody's advice.'

'Of course. Do you want me to come down there? I'm working the day after tomorrow. I could probably manage next week.'

'It's rather urgent. Couldn't I meet you in town?'

They arranged lunch on the day James was returning to work. It was the time he had already denied to Tony Cass and the arrangement gave him particular pleasure on that account. Judy wasn't so pleased.

'But you hardly know her.'

'I used to know them both pretty well.'

'That was twenty years ago.'

'Not quite as long as that.'

'I still think it's odd. Whatever can she want to consult you about?'

'It can only be David's drinking, can't it?'

'What do you know about that? You hardly drink at all. Do you fancy Susie?'

'I haven't seen her for at least ten years.'
'Did you fancy her then?'
'No. I didn't even like her much.'
'Where are you having lunch?'
'I don't know. We're meeting in the BH foyer.'
'I don't know what to think about it. You're so uncharacteristically cheerful.'
'It does us all good to be needed.'

That, James thought, was the truth of it. He did feel cheerful, he did look forward to the lunch with Susie but he was sure it was because she was asking something of him, not for any darker reason. It occurred to him then that he'd not felt the same about almost the same proposal from Tony. But that was because it came from Tony, who only meant to bully him.

III

It was nearly one o'clock. The foyer of Broadcasting House was busy. People were crossing between the lifts and the triple doors, and all the seats were occupied by visitors waiting for members of staff. Susie Rutland was not among them. James nodded to the commissionaires as he came in from Portland Place and then, since there wasn't a seat, stood inconspicuously in a corner. For the umpteenth time he read the grand Latin inscription dedicating 'this temple of the arts and muses' to Almighty God, carved on the marble lintel over the commissionaires' heads, and thought of Lord Reith and the beginnings of the BBC. Britain had already nearly collapsed into bankruptcy then and Hitler was on the way up in Germany, but the BBC was armoured in dreams of enlightenment and civilization. This building with its small windows and sheer, curving walls partly resembled a fortress, but although Reith certainly intended to fight for the values of civilization, it was not a defensive thing. It also resembled a ship – liner more than warship – and it was made to carry missionaries rather than weapons. The Thirties – at least the early Thirties – still had the energy of enthusiasm, even if the old Victorian certainties were being kicked to pieces and the world was finding its way back into hell. As long as this building remained the headquarters of the BBC, the seat of its Director-General and governors, some element of that stern Reithian enthusiasm would survive.

Whenever James thought about the BBC in the abstract, he felt warmly towards it, although he spent half his time when he was inside the building grumbling about its failings with his colleagues. He had never particularly liked any of his immediate superiors and he had hardly ever met the big bosses who came and went with the various power shifts inside the small ruling politburo, but he still felt loyalty to the organization. Perhaps that was how one felt towards the Church if one was a Roman Catholic. Perhaps in a curious way Lord Reith, the St Peter of the BBC, still held the keys to Broadcasting House and, from the presence of the Almighty God he had invoked, rattled them menacingly at the insecure, materialistic time-servers who occupied his chair.

Susie Rutland came through the doors and immediately attracted the attention of most of the men waiting in the foyer. She paused and looked around, half shy because she felt she had stepped into a world more glamorous than her own, half confident of the personal impression she knew she was making. She missed James, tucked away in his corner, and moved towards the receptionists' desk. James, at ease in his own world and proud to be seen as this attractive woman's cavalier, stepped forward and intercepted her.

'Susie!'

'Hello, James!'

Were they to kiss? He hesitated, rapidly estimated the distance to her cheek and missed the moment. They shook hands.

'Where shall we eat?' he asked.

'You choose,' she said.

'Well, if you've never seen it, the canteen has a splendid view over the rooftops.'

'I'd like that,' she said.

The canteen was crowded and they could only find places at a table already occupied by two actors from the repertory company. The rest of their cast were crammed round another two tables and exchanging theatrical gossip, but these two, both weary-looking men in their late fifties or early sixties, were earnestly discussing house prices in the Home Counties. James and Susie made polite inquiries about each other's children until the whole crowd of actors suddenly rose like a flock of birds and made for the door. The two elderly ones at their own table, now comparing their vegetable gardens, remained where they were and then, becoming conscious of the silence behind them, looked round, consulted their watches and scurried away.

James apologized, as he had already, for the food and the unceremoniousness of the place, but Susie was clearly delighted with everything. She was a regular listener to radio programmes, including plays, and knew several of the actors' names. James, describing and naming as many as he could for her, basked in their reflected glory and then started to entertain her with his repertoire of BBC stories, chiefly frightful gaffes by announcers who were drunk or who thought their microphones were switched off. By the time he got up to fetch two black coffees, they were both flushed with the unexpected success of their meeting and, as James returned to the table and was greeted with her smile, he felt younger and more optimistic than he had for years. At the same time he felt a pang of disloyalty to Judy. It wasn't she who had battened down hatches on him, forced him to live such a dull and unadventurous life. He had chosen it for himself – or rather for both of them – and she had acquiesced. Perhaps he should have married someone quite different, who would have driven him out of his shell. On the other hand, Susie was clearly not that someone, since she had if anything imposed the shell of suburban respectability on the once ambitious and promiscuous David. So it was just that he and Susie, two cautious and controlled people, were enjoying a little break from their routine selves. He smiled at the thought. What an adventure, after all! A *tête-à-tête* in the BBC canteen, a lunch-time rendezvous for which he had virtually obtained permission from Judy. No doubt Susie had also cleared it with David.

'What's so funny?' asked Susie, stirring her coffee.

James told her; and, by revealing that he thought it an adventure at all, made it more adventurous.

'No, I didn't clear it with David,' said Susie. 'For the simple reason that David wasn't there to clear it with. Otherwise, you're quite right, I would have.'

'But I thought he was ill,' said James. 'Do you mean he's in hospital?'

'He's not ill,' said Susie. 'Or at least I hope he isn't.'

'Where is he, then?'

'In France.'

James was taken aback. This was much worse than he'd expected, not a gentle adventure, but some sort of crisis. Susie read the consternation in his face.

'He's in France to see a friend.'

James said nothing. He still felt they were on dangerous ground.

'Not a woman friend, but a man. You probably know him. Colonel Rimington.'

'I met him, all those years ago in Balunda, but he was David's friend, not mine. What's he doing in France?'

'I don't think anybody's supposed to know he's there. David had a letter, saying that he'd had to leave Balunda and needed help. It all sounded very dubious, melodramatic. David had to book into a particular hotel and wait to be contacted.'

'I see.'

'He rang me up as soon as he got there, but since then I haven't heard a thing.'

'How long is that?'

'Several days. When you rang I was already worried, that's why I asked if we could meet and I thought I could always cancel our lunch if he rang or came back before today. But still nothing.'

'I see.'

'What do you think I should do?'

Susie was almost in tears. As long as she had kept the thing to herself she had bottled up her feelings with it, but now they threatened to overwhelm her. She wanted reassurance. But the story worried him quite as much as her, perhaps more so. The question was whether he should mention Tony Cass and the Foreign Office to Susie. It would increase rather than allay her worry and he wasn't at all sure whether he had the right to tell her. He had refused to help Tony, but he had not reckoned on being sucked into the affair from the other side. If there were sides. Susie was still looking at him, clearly on the edge of breaking down. He decided not to tell her for the moment.

'Have you tried ringing the hotel?' His announcer's voice was as steady and casual as eighteen years' practice could make it. He sounded as if it was only a matter of David's having gone out for a half-hour stroll.

'I haven't got the number.'

'But you know the name of the hotel and the town?'

'Yes.'

'So no problem.'

'But do you think I should?'

'If he rang you from the hotel, I can't see what harm it would do the other way round.'

'No.'

'There's nothing secret about David's whereabouts, after all. He went quite openly to this hotel. Rimington may want to contact him secretly but David is a respectable solicitor with a British passport visiting a friendly country.'

'But why haven't I heard from him?'

'He must be with Rimington. Rimington may not have a phone.'

'Why didn't he ring me before he left to say he'd be out of touch?'

'The business may be taking longer than he expected. But there's no point in asking all these theoretical questions until you've at least established whether he's left the hotel and if so, whether he hasn't left a message.'

James's manner more than his arguments had its effect and Susie calmed down. He would like to have known more about why Rimington had left Balunda, but was afraid to ask her in case the details should prove too alarming. Besides, he was sure she didn't know the details. He conducted her through the corridors and down in the lift to the foyer, reiterating his advice that she should ring the hotel and giving her the number of the continuity suite where she could contact him if she needed to.

This time they did kiss and it was only after Susie had disappeared through the doors and James turned towards the lifts that he realized how much he'd deceived himself as well as her with his reassuring manner. He felt very worried indeed, for David, for Susie, but chiefly for himself. If Susie went home, tried the French hotel and got no satisfactory answer, she would certainly come back to him. And then what? Must he then get hold of Tony Cass? He seemed to have gone through a looking-glass into a world he only recognized from fiction and films. He made his way to the announcers' room to check his schedule and look up the pronunciations of the names in the day's news.

His first job was to record the credits for a radio play and when he arrived at the drama studio in the basement he found the cast that had been lunching in the canteen. They had evidently been through a hard day and were mostly slumped about on chairs round the studio, while three or four of them, standing at the microphones in the centre, re-did a passage that had gone wrong. They had to do it several times before the director was satisfied and there was a general atmosphere of near-mutiny. The director was a small, stiff man with a neat little beard and moustache that looked as if they had been stuck on. He glanced up irascibly as James entered the control cubicle and gestured to his secretary to give him the sheet of credits.

The passage finished, the actors were released for their tea break and James took their place at the microphones. He had once wanted to be an actor and thanked his stars that he was not. To push yourself across that threshold between reality and make-believe was not so hard when you were young and scarcely knew the difference anyway, but to do it as you got older must be an almost intolerable strain. Those house prices and vegetable patches, let alone the shopping, the cooking, the children and their education, the annual holidays and travel arrangements! All heavier and heavier weights holding you down in the world's reality, while in the next room the masks and tinsel of make-believe looked more and more dried up and faded. The play they were recording was a new translation of *Peer Gynt*. What a misery, to be compelled for your living to try to animate this poetic whimsy, pretending that the world and its materiality were of no account, when the truth was exactly the opposite! At least he, James, was on the right side of the threshold, standing firmly outside the make-believe, putting the frame round it, declaring its true nature, shutting the door on it.

In his firm, neutral voice, priding himself on his ability to read almost anything without stumbling or mispronunciation, he topped and tailed Ibsen's fantasy, listed the actors with rhythmic precision, left the right pauses, faultlessly completed his task in a single take. The studio manager behind the glass of the control cubicle raised his thumb, the director smiled, perhaps for the first time that day, and spoke through the intercom:

'Thank you, James. Perfect! If only you could do the whole damn play for us!'

IV

Still no word from David. Susie, alone in the five-bedroom house which she loved both for its space and the status it conferred, wished for once that it was smaller. She had made it comfortable and cosy with warm colours, velvet or flowered curtains and cushions, pretty lamps and lampshades and her own bright paintings of fruit, flowers and gardens, but it was meant for family life. Her children were away at boarding school, her husband had disappeared. The house, intended to symbolize and support their sense of unity and mutual happiness, was forlorn, like a hutch made for a pet which has died or escaped. In the darkness outside, it was raining steadily.

She had got nothing out of the French hotel. David had stayed there one night and then moved out. What to do next? Surely one didn't ring the police about a husband absent in France? They would be certain he had a mistress there. Was she certain that he hadn't? She couldn't tell them he'd gone to meet a mysterious refugee from an African revolution. They would want details and she had no details. The only thing she could do was to phone James. Of course, there were friends she knew better than him, but they were mostly neighbours and she dreaded letting them in behind her guard. David's two partners in the firm of solicitors already made allowances for his drinking – they would assume this was a further downward stage in his rake's progress, would pity her and mark it up against him. And even if she sank her pride and confided in them or in some other local friend, would any advantage come of it? Would they have any better idea of how to proceed than she did? Having chosen James as her confidant, she had better stick to him.

She switched on Radio Three. He'd told her the phone wouldn't disturb his announcements, but she wanted to make sure of choosing the best moment for him. Besides, she was still reluctant to admit that further action was necessary. David might still ring. The programme was a symphony, a slow, sad piece which she was half inclined to switch off at once, but inertia overcame her, and a desire to put off the moment of going to the phone. The limping melody on muted violins and cellos gave way to a more cheerful passage. Flutes and oboes suggested birdsong. She could almost imagine spring blossom. She thought of David when she'd first met him. It was probably more summer than spring, a warm day in Hyde Park. She was sitting on a bench sketching the sailing boats on the Serpentine and he sat down at the other end of the bench. She could sense him looking at her and lost her concentration. Annoyed, she gave him a direct stare, saying nothing, but meaning 'bugger off!' He didn't look away but caught her eye and said pleasantly, 'I'm an artist too.' To anyone else who had tried that obvious ploy, she would no doubt have replied 'So what?' and pretended to go back to her drawing, but David was so handsome, his manner so relaxed, his large smile so disarming, that she immediately smiled back and, without a second thought, accepted his offer, whatever it might be: conversation, friendship or, as it turned out, a relationship which had lasted from that day to this.

The orchestra's strings were suggesting sharp gusts of wind and soon worked themselves up to a brief storm. The cymbals marked the climax and then the storm blew away, leaving the same limping theme as before, but this time more distant and dreamlike, as if the whole passage had been recollection instead of direct experience. There was a pause. The audience shifted, cleared its throat, blew its nose and settled again and the music resumed in a quite different, throbbing, extrovert mood. But Susie was hardly aware of it. She was still thinking of David, the David who had picked her up beside the Serpentine, escorted her to the cafe for a cup of tea and a piece of cake, taken her from there to a pub somewhere in Knightsbridge and, hours later, seeing her on to a bus back to the flat she shared with three other girls, promised that tomorrow he would be at his studio all day and only waiting to show it to her. She didn't keep him waiting. He was still in his bath when she arrived at 9.30 am and he received her wearing his towel like a South Sea islander and displaying his impressive torso. They spent the day together and after a couple of weeks she packed her belongings, said goodbye to her three flatmates and moved into David's studio.

It all seemed incredibly easy. No decisions were required of her, she couldn't recall having any doubts. It was as if she had drawn a winning ticket in a lottery, as if by sitting on that particular bench on that particular day between the hours of three and four in the afternoon, she had unwittingly qualified for the handsome stranger. More than handsome. At that time he appeared overwhelmingly fortunate, socially privileged, athletic, Oxford-educated, and on top of everything a talented and ambitious artist. She admired his sculpture as easily and wholeheartedly as she loved him and took it for granted that he would soon be famous and successful. For a while she continued her own studies at the art school, but they hardly seemed to matter beside his work and she left the school before her final year. Her naturally optimistic view of life, fostered by the easy circumstances of her own upbringing as the only child of affluent parents, was confirmed by this rapid and effortless translation to a new stage of maturity and independence. David, some years older than her and with more experience of the world, offered her the advantages of a father as well as a lover. Her mother, suspicious at first, had quickly accepted him, deferring to his advice, treating him almost as if she, rather than Susie, had acquired a new partner.

But good fortune, she thought, like silver, needed regular burnishing. Theirs had steadily tarnished. How could she have imagined that a man who so effortlessly picked her up would not do the same with others? The first phase of their relationship was for her a long and exhausting struggle with rivals: women he had known before she ever met him, others he met afterwards. Patiently and ruthlessly, believing in the validity of her lottery ticket and rejecting theirs, she saw them off one by one and persuaded him finally to marry her. Wouldn't she have done better just to let him go, to have recognized that their happiness was temporary, her ticket dated? His sculpture came to nothing, his extrovert good fellowship turned to excessive drinking, his love and care for her into a kind of domestic subservience, broken from time to time by rages, sulks or passing affairs with women who didn't know him and for whom he could still briefly resuscitate his old charm. Certainly he was fond of the children, certainly he depended on her, even if he didn't love her, but what did she have left of the original David and all the good fortune that seemed to come with him? She continued to live as if she had him and it, she kept up the pretence. But really, if she faced up to it, if she looked in her cupboard, the silver was irredeemably black.

The music was ending in a long, surging climax. A noble, triumphant tune surmounted obstacles and drove steadily onward. Towards what? A great river flowing into the sea, a wave of horsemen riding into the sunset? The finish was two quick little flourishes, a hand waved twice, dots in the distance, the composer turning his back on all that effort of creation with a deliberately dismissive gesture – take it or leave it! To Susie the whole piece suddenly seemed alien and false. It was a masculine solution to a masculine problem. It was a dream of doubts and difficulties overcome by the will and transformed into a flourish of self-assertion. Yet the flourish was implicit from the beginning. The doubts and difficulties were placed there only to justify and enhance the self-assertion, which was the real object of the exercise. The audience was applauding enthusiastically, but she felt crushed and rebellious. The rules of this symphony were the rules of the male world. They did not apply to her half of the human race. Nevertheless, she had been brought up to accept them and live by them and so had most of her sex. No doubt that enthusiastic audience contained at least as many women as men.

The voice announcing the credits and the end of the first part of the concert was not James's, but as the applause faded it was he who gave the length of the interval and prefaced a talk on nineteenth-century nationalism in music by some American professor. Her moment of alienation and anger passed as quickly as it had come. This was the time to ring James. She switched off the radio, went to the phone and then hesitated. Undoubtedly a kind of telepathy existed between people who knew each other well: at this very moment David too might be beside a phone, picking up the receiver, dialling the number of his home. She willed it to be happening, trying to see his face, his smile, his large hand grasping the receiver. And suddenly, making her jump, the phone did ring. She picked it up and could hardly speak.

'Yes?'
'Mrs Rutland?'
'Yes.'
'I didn't recognize your voice. This is James Biggar.'
'James.'
'Have you heard from David?'
'Nothing.'
'What about the hotel?'
'Nothing. They don't know where he is.'
'I'm sorry. Look, I've talked it over with Judy. My wife. I hoped you wouldn't mind.'
'No, of course not.'
'I couldn't think what to do for the best.'
'I wish I could.'
'Judy says that, short of alerting the police, the only thing she can suggest is for you to go over there yourself. I've got to work here for the next four days, but Judy will be free at the weekend and next week is half-term, so she could come and squat in your house, be at the end of the phone, while you were away. Would that be any use?'
'It's too much to ask.'
'Not at all. Judy would be only too happy to do it if the idea appeals to you.'
'You are the kindest, most wonderful people.'
'You can do the same for her one day, when I disappear.'

Susie was irritated by the buoyancy of his tone. Of course he would never disappear, of course he and Judy could feel all the more secure and pleased with themselves by comparison with David and herself. But as soon as James had rung off, she was overcome by a sense of her ingratitude and envy. She phoned his wife, whom she'd never met, and talked to her for nearly an hour. Then before going to bed, she wrote to her sons to tell them that she'd be away in France for a few days, but that a friend would be staying in their house and would be in touch with her. She would ring David's partners in the morning with the same message and perhaps, to give a plausible reason for her joining David, hint that they were thinking of buying a holiday home in Normandy.

In the bathroom she found Radio Three on the dial of the transistor radio and switched it on. James was still there in his studio, announcing a piano sonata by Schubert. The sturdy, faintly melancholy tune was interspersed with cascades of clear, clean notes. She washed her teeth and did her exercises and began almost to look forward to the trip to France; then, as the pianist started the second movement, her mood changed again. She sat on the edge of the bath, while tears ran down her face.

'I miss you,' she thought and a moment later said it aloud, as if the thought needed to be expressed to be complete.

'It's too sad without you,' she thought and said that aloud too.

'Don't you miss me?' she thought, but for some reason kept that to herself.

Gradually Schubert's exquisite compound of pain and courage – unhappiness exorcised by energy – calmed and comforted her. She waited for James to back-announce the sonata, then switched off the radio and went to bed.

4

I

Andrew Mowle and his wife no longer slept together, but they continued to share a flat. There was only one bedroom, so Andrew slept on the sofa in the sitting room, but he went on storing his clothes in the bedroom. In the days when they had still been in love, during the first three years of their marriage, they had quarrelled quite violently, but now that they expected nothing of each other except civility they only bickered in an almost mechanical way, as if they were characters in a soap opera which neither of them took very seriously. They were both busy people. Liz ran a small art gallery. Andrew took occasional extra-mural classes in history for mature students as well as being the literary editor of the *Equalizer*. Their revised form of marriage suited them better than the original version. They could eat, rest, sleep, without having to keep up the defences they needed during the day's work and whenever they discussed separating completely they ended up agreeing that there was no point in it, since neither of them really wanted any permanent relationship but the one they had.

After the interview with Simon Carter at the *Equalizer* when Simon had described his meeting with Maria Dobson and then spoken to her on the phone, Andrew realized that his life had to change. He must finally part with Liz because he was infatuated with Maria. The fact that he had still not met her and, that so far as he knew, she wasn't even aware of his existence hardly seemed to matter. He had recovered all his youth and hope. He was back in the days of adolescence, when to attend the Sunday morning service in his father's church had been the high point of the week because it was also attended by a pretty girl from a neighbouring village. He would sit through the prayers and readings and stand up for the psalms and hymns in a daze of pleasure from her mere presence.

Sometimes she would be sitting in front of him and he would be able to look at her as often as he liked; sometimes she would be across the aisle and he would continually glance that way and very occasionally catch glances from her. He never spoke to her, never even got to know who she was, and after a few months she disappeared, leaving him gradually to accept that that particular pleasure, like a box of chocolates that had been eaten, was over.

His secret love for the girl in his father's church had been anticipated and perhaps prepared for by earlier romances in the chapel of his public school. In those days he had been in love with younger boys, two or three at a time, and the arrangement of the chapel seats, facing each other like choir stalls across the central aisle, had been wonderfully suited to this purely visual kind of mating. Unlike the girl in the church, he had got to know one or two of the boys in the chapel, but he had never had any physical contact with them and would hardly have known what form it could have taken. Love, he believed then, was one thing and sex another, though he understood that they could be linked at some later stage. Of course, now that he was in his forties, he had gained a more pressing sense of time and direction – or perhaps better say had lost the timeless, directionless condition of youth – and knew that if you loved someone it was not just a state but an action. His present happiness, therefore, could only be maintained by steadily improving his position *vis-à-vis* Maria, by devoting his energy to her pursuit and capture.

Since, as a committed socialist, he believed that all human problems were fundamentally economic, he began by reviewing his finances. He was a fervent egalitarian and believed passionately in a future world without capitalism, where no one would have more or less than he needed and where it would be as criminal to profit at your neighbour's expense as it was now to steal his possessions. Unfortunately, he had always had difficulty in staying within the limits of his own income. He might have defined his own needs as greater than those of people lower down the social scale, who had never acquired the expensive habits of his class, but he was not a hypocrite and knew very well that he was preaching what he failed to practise. He might perhaps have justified himself by claiming that as long as capitalism persisted it was impossible to live as if the world were not capitalist. In fact, he felt ashamed of himself and, if anyone accused him of inconsistency, would quietly admit it and drop out of the argument. Short of a revolution, he could not see himself changing his ways and no doubt, like a smoker who half hopes to find the pub closed when his cigarettes have run out, Andrew's desire for a revolution in the state was strengthened by his desire for changes in his own behaviour.

As soon as he woke on the day after his indirect encounter with

Maria, his radiant happiness flooded back over him. Whistling and singing, he dressed and shaved in the bathroom, made coffee and toast, glanced indifferently at the front page of the paper, ate his breakfast standing up and carried his second cup of coffee to the desk in the sitting room. Nearly an hour later when Liz put her head round the door to say goodbye before she left for her gallery, she was surprised to see him seated at the desk with pieces of paper arranged all round him. Usually on a weekday morning he sat reading the newspaper until it was time to go into the office.

'What are you doing?'

'Accounts.'

'At this time of year?'

'Crisis.'

'What sort of crisis?'

Normally he only did his accounts in May, when he was preparing them for his accountant to submit to the Inland Revenue. Doing his accounts always put him in a foul temper and he was about to lash out at Liz for interrupting his calculations, when he suddenly remembered that he was a man reborn and a smile spread over his face. Liz, who had expected an outburst when he turned round furiously in his chair, was nonplussed.

'Hopelessly in debt,' he said, beaming with pleasure.

'That's nothing new,' she said, still trying to grasp what it was that was new.

'But hopelessly,' he said, almost chuckling.

'It doesn't seem to bother you.'

'It bothers me a lot,' he said, suddenly beginning to look angry again.

'I still can't see why it particularly bothers you this morning,' she said, relieved that he was seeming more like himself again.

Another wave of happiness came over Andrew. He looked at his wife standing uncertainly in the doorway and saw her almost as a stranger. Moreover, she was a stranger he liked. Slight and trim, with her fair hair cut short and her small nose slightly wrinkled because she was puzzled, she seemed younger and more boyish again, as she was when he first met her. He could see why she had appealed to him then, but also what a mistake he'd made. He'd married her for her lively innocence, but the innocence had swiftly turned to self-confidence and then self-assertion and the liveliness to sharpness and aggression. He had loved her chiefly because he liked her company. Later he had disliked her company and later still found he could tolerate it. He could see now that she was a perfectly nice person whom he would be happy to meet and talk to from time to time almost as if they'd never lived together.

'Aren't you going in to the *Equalizer* today?' she asked.

'Yes. But I'm doing this first.'

'You're very odd,' she said, then finding an explanation, 'Are they going to do your Third World thing?'

'I don't know,' he said lightly, 'but I hope so. It's crucial.'

'Crucial, is it?' The slight sneer that usually infused their dialogues was coming back into her voice.

'Absolutely crucial.'

'Well, I'm off.'

'Okay. Enjoy yourself!'

He couldn't keep the bounce out of his voice and her curiosity about him almost made her stay longer. But she was hanging a new exhibition today and needed all the time she could get.

'I'll probably be late back,' she said.

'Okay.'

He had turned round again and was staring out of the window. She spent a few more minutes finding her handbag and left the flat. The sound of the front door closing roused Andrew from his rapturous contemplation of the houses opposite. He took a fresh piece of paper and wrote at the top on the left, 'INCOME'. Underneath that he wrote, 'Equalizer – 12,000', and below that, 'Classes – 1500', and below that, after some thought, 'Odds and Ends – 1000 (if I'm lucky)'. He thought again, wrote 'TV Series' and then crossed it out, drew a line and put 'Total – 14,000'. He sat back for a moment, pursed his lips, found and lit a cigarette. At the top on the right he wrote 'OUTGOINGS' and underneath, 'Half Mortgage –1300' followed by 'Half Rates – 205'.

'I suppose I'll have to keep contributing to this flat,' he said aloud. 'But would she have to, if she moved out on me?'

Below these entries he wrote 'Mortgage on new flat – 230?' and 'Rates on new flat – 410?'.

'And will I have to pay electricity and gas and water and telephone on both flats?' he asked himself. 'Surely not telephone?'

He sat back and stared out of the window, aware that it was hopeless to try to draw up a proper balance sheet without more knowledge. He would have to speak to his accountant. He started another column at the bottom of his sheet of paper headed 'DEBTS' and wrote under it 'Barclaycard – 450' and 'Overdraft – 300' and, after another pause, 'Mother – 2500'. He stubbed out his cigarette and was overcome first by lethargy and then irritation. He picked up the piece of paper, crumpled it violently with both hands and threw it into the wastepaper-basket. However he juggled them, the figures were never going to allow him to move into another flat. He must either stay where he was or defy the figures and hope for the best. If the TV series came off he would be laughing. If it didn't, it would be that much more difficult even to meet Maria anyway. So he must proceed on the assumption that the series would come off, otherwise his life was ruined. Having reached that simple conclusion, he felt better again and, shuffled all the papers on his desk back into the file where they belonged.

He was packing his cycle-bag and wondering if perhaps the TV people would pay him so handsomely that he needn't worry about money for at least another year, when the phone rang.

'Hello?' he said pleasantly, his mind running on 15000.

'Liz?' said the voice at the other end of the line.

'Out,' Andrew said with satisfaction. He knew who he was speaking to. The slight regional accent, the gruffness, the tone of grievance: all belonged to a down-at-heel, drunken, comprehensively bearded poet called Ben Brooks. He was an old friend of Liz – she'd known him before she met Andrew – but Andrew loathed him. The loathing was mutual, especially since Andrew had turned down one of Brooks' poems for the magazine and published somebody's three-line hostile review of one of Brooks' slim volumes.

'How can I get her?' asked Brooks.

'Ring the gallery.'

'What's the number?'

'Haven't you got it?'

'I've probably got it somewhere, but I don't see why you can't give it me.'

'I'll have to look it up.'

'All right, then, look it up!'

Andrew took his time, maliciously conscious of adding at least 50p to Brooks's phone bill.

'Still there?' he said innocently, when he had finally picked up the receiver again.

'Been round the block for it, have you?' said Brooks angrily.

'Ready?' said Andrew, in his kindly teacher's voice, and began dictating the number over the answering splutter.

'I didn't hear the first part.'

Andrew dictated it again, more slowly.

'That's better,' said Brooks.

'Right. Anything more I can do for you?'

'Why don't you do something about that magazine you work for? Nobody reads it. It's shit.'

'I'll pass your comments to the editor.'

'You do that. With my compliments.'

There was a pause. Andrew abruptly put the phone down and, in case it should ring again, quickly collected his things and left the flat. Downstairs in the hall he unlocked his bike, attached the pannier bag to the rack, put on his trouser clips and wheeled the machine down the steps and out to the pavement.

The fine weather had gone. It was still dry and very warm, but the sky was overclouded. Ben Brooks's phone call had disturbed Andrew's happiness. As he pedalled through the heavy traffic, his disturbance increased. The roads seemed to be even fuller than usual of badly parked cars, careless pedestrians, noisy and overbearing motorcyclists, murderous lorry drivers and competitive commuters.

'A whole world of shits,' he thought.

'Shits to the right of him, shits to the left of him volleyed and thundered,' he recited as he negotiated a tricky crossing. One stream of traffic turned left, but he had to go straight on, clinging to the precarious safety of the thin white line between two rushing columns of steel. One of the cars brushed his pedal and nearly had him down in the path of another immediately behind it.

'You were wobbling,' said the driver of the second car, slowing beside him for long enough to make his accusation and then speeding away before Andrew could reply.

'Fuck you!' Andrew shouted after him, wishing he could shoot the man's tyres flat like the pursuers in a car chase on the movies.

By the time he arrived at the *Equalizer*, large drops of rain had begun to fall.

'Life,' he told himself, as he heaved his cycle in at the door and chained it up in the entrance hall, 'is mainly insupportable. At least the life of urban, Western, twentieth-century man. It is pointless, ugly and humiliating. The only things that make life supportable are appetite and passion. Temporary appetite for a meal or a fuck or a new car, more lasting passion for a cause, a course of action, another person. Life is then transformed from a negative into a positive and the world from a hive of shits into a mysterious and exciting buzz of anticipation and stimulation. Therefore,' he continued as he walked slowly up the stairs, 'seek out the buzz where ye may find it and let the rest go to hell! What it may cost to move to a new flat and whether I can conceivably pay for it are completely irrelevant. The alternative is a life reduced to correcting other people's reviews, measuring up columns, swearing at shits in cars and talking on the phone to Ben Brooks.'

He stopped at the door of his office on the top floor. It had gone very dark and through the skylight over the stairs he saw a flash of lightning.

'But I'm in love,' he reminded himself, 'I don't need any arguments.'

II

The Third World series cleared its first hurdle. Andrew was commissioned to do a treatment. The problem was that until he'd completed the treatment there was no occasion to see any more of the producer, Michael Arley, and if he didn't see Michael, how was he going to meet Maria? The only solution seemed to be to move into a new flat of his own, so that he would have a private base from which to conduct the long campaign that might be needed to separate her from Michael.

Meanwhile, of course, he did see Maria, regularly and obsessively, on the screen. It was worse than not seeing her at all, but he couldn't help himself. The image fed his passion in the way that alcohol feeds a thirst. It inflamed him without ever satisfying him. A person sat in the studio and read the teleprompter, but there was no person on the screen. Her voice and expression varied ever so slightly according to whether the item of news was grave, disastrous, happy or amusing, but her character was completely excluded. And the more of this characterless, but still irresistibly attractive simulacrum he saw, the less he could imagine the three-dimensional, flesh and blood Maria who had briefly stepped out of the screen into Simon Carter's life.

He couldn't hide his condition from his wife, who at first thought, when she noticed his moods fluctuating wildly between exhilaration and moroseness, that he must be meeting some real lover. The truth made her laugh, but his angry reaction convinced her that at least his need to move out into a flat of his own was genuine, even if he was unable, in his state of feverish impotence, to make any practical arrangements himself.

'You could surely borrow the money?'
'Where from?'
'The bank. A building society. Your mother.'
'I already owe her.'
'I've got a thousand or two saved up. I could lend you that.'
'A thousand or two!'

Nevertheless, the generosity of her offer broke a small hole in the icy wall of inaction that surrounded him. A few days later he told her he was going to visit his brother.

Luke Mowle had a farm on the border between Surrey and Hampshire. He was older than Andrew and unmarried. As small children they had been good friends, but their temperaments and talents were entirely different and their school careers forced them steadily apart. Luke was a slow, dreamy boy who got through his preparatory and public schools without disgrace or distinction. For a while he worked in an insurance company, but when his father died he used the money he inherited to buy a farm. He and Andrew had been at the same preparatory school, but Andrew won a scholarship to a more prestigious public school than Luke's, went on with another scholarship to Oxford and took a First. At that point, just as his brother was beginning to settle into farming, Andrew deliberately kicked away the academic ladder he had climbed so successfully, turned down the Fellowship he was offered and became a kind of professional radical. He would try anything that looked new and subversive, but nothing that was too well rooted in the past. He and his brother had been divided for a long time by their relative intellectual attainments, but their political differences split them apart completely. Luke was a convinced Tory and became literally red in the face if Andrew even attempted to argue the case for socialism. Since some aspect of socialism was the only common factor in Andrew's various interests and activities, this left them nothing to talk about except their childhood or their mother. They had not met at all for several years and Andrew had never visited Luke's present farm.

The drive down, in his small dented Renault, did Andrew good. The sun was lighting the autumn colours and the combination of attending to the road and avoiding a collision with other road users – Andrew was a clumsy and uncertain driver – as well as finding the way through unfamiliar territory temporarily eliminated Maria from his mind. The farm, when he found it, down a side road and up a rough track of its own, was not what he expected. He had spent little time in the country since leaving home and knew no farmers except his brother, so that his idea of a farm was still largely based on the toys they had played with as children: neat little metal fences; an assortment of animals; a golden yellow beehive haystack; a brightly painted tractor and trailer; a farmer in a brown suit with a stick; and a milkmaid on a three-legged stool. Of course he had seen real farms and knew that they also contained mud, manure and more sophisticated machinery, but he was quite unprepared for the shapelessness and squalor of Luke's farm. Everything looked half or wholly abandoned: quantities of old tyres and discarded plastic sacks, rusting tractors, outbuildings patched with corrugated iron and standing amongst thistles and nettles, Heath Robinson fences, gates held in place by pieces of wire and string. There was no sign of any animal, though the sea of churned-up mud and dung in an enclosed yard suggested that there must be cows somewhere. The track led round the corner of this yard to a short stretch of gravelled drive, flanked by lawns, chestnut trees and one or two flowerbeds. The farmhouse was quite small, built of bricks, and had no particular character, but it looked solid and cared-for compared to the rest of the place.

Andrew was so depressed at first that if he had been cleverer at backing his car he might have turned tail before ever setting eyes on the house. He had come, after all, not for pleasure or old times' sake, but simply in order to borrow money from his brother. The appearance of the farm made him think that his brother probably needed to borrow money even more than he did. The house and the ordered space in front of it restored his spirits a little. He parked his car and got out. The air at least was what one expected of the country, fresh and pleasantly tinged with the smell of earth. The sun was being gradually blotted out by large cloud-masses, but it was still quite warm. A dog was barking. Andrew walked towards the house and recognized his brother peering out of a small downstairs window. A moment later, the dog – a young golden labrador – shot out and stopped a few yards short of Andrew, barking furiously until Luke emerged, shook hands and led Andrew into the kitchen. The dog, called Fergus, now squirming and rolling his eyes and allowing himself to be patted, followed them in.

Luke was taller and thinner than Andrew and carried himself with a stoop. His face was remarkably soft and pale for a farmer and with his receding hair he was beginning to resemble their father, the vicar. His large, rough hands, however, had certainly been used out of doors over many years and he didn't wear glasses as their father had. The kitchen was bare and basic, reasonably clean, but cheaply and impersonally furnished. It seemed to be the room his brother lived in, for it contained a battered armchair – the dog went and flopped down beside it – and in the corner, a TV set. The sight of that immediately recalled Maria and Andrew set himself at least to re-open diplomatic relations with Luke.

'Have you seen anything of Mother?' he asked.

'Not really. Too far for her to drive and I can't leave the farm.'

'Haven't you got help?'

'One man. He needs constant supervision.'

Their lunch consisted of a ready-made steak and kidney pie heated in the oven and served straight out of its foil container, accompanied by tinned peas and followed by bread and cheese, also still in their wrappings, and fruit from the supermarket. Andrew had brought a bottle of wine. Under its influence their tight and sporadic conversation gradually loosened up.

'You've never thought of getting married?' asked Andrew, manoeuvring towards the purpose of his visit.

'I've thought of it often. I'd like to be married.'

Andrew was surprised. He'd never thought of his brother as anything but a confirmed bachelor.

'You mean married in the abstract?'

'Not at all. There's usually someone around I'd like to be married to.'

'There is now?'

'Oh yes.'

'Have you asked her?'

'Certainly not. She'd be fearfully embarrassed. So should I.'

'But if you don't ask . . .'

'Oh, I know. Asking is the stumbling block. If we had arranged marriages like people in other countries . . .'

Andrew had never seen Luke as a shy person. He hadn't been shy at home, of course, and being the elder had always seemed enviably assured and established in his courses, more like a grown-up than a fellow child.

'If you were really in love with someone – someone you knew – I don't see how you could avoid asking. It becomes a necessity.'

'Not to me. I imagine I was born with low blood pressure. You, of course, quite the opposite.'

'What an interesting idea! The race perpetuated by people with high blood pressure. And so by natural selection the blood pressure would get higher and higher as time went on. I wonder if there's any evidence of that. Does it account for the constant acceleration of technological and social change in the developed world? It's in the under-developed countries, after all, that they still have arranged marriages, allowing people with low blood pressure to go on reproducing themselves.'

Luke was smiling. 'What rubbish! You haven't got any children. I should have thought people with high blood pressure probably did more talking than reproducing.'

'As a matter of fact,' said Andrew, 'Liz and I are probably going to separate. That's why I came to see you.'

'I'm sorry. I liked Liz. I've hardly ever met her, but I liked her.'

'So did I. Still do, off and on, but it doesn't work.'

'Not having children?'

'I don't think that has much to do with it.'

There was a silence. Andrew had decided not to mention Maria, since he was almost sure Luke would disapprove of his discarding one wife in order to try to acquire another.

'If I were to get married,' said Luke, 'it would not be to have children. Nor would it be because I was bored and lonely. Never been bored in my life. If you're not bored, you're not lonely. It would be, I think, for religious reasons.'

Andrew looked at him in amazement. His brother had never, so far as he knew, shown the least inclination towards religion.

'I don't mean anything to do with the church. When I said I'd never been bored in my life, I was exaggerating. I was always bored in church, except when I was embarrassed because Father was doing one of his pulpit spiels, trying to provoke people.'

'That's unfair. He didn't do it to provoke people.'

'He did provoke people.'

'That was a side-effect. He said what he believed.'

'Sometimes.'

'Maybe you're right.' Andrew was wary of being drawn into any sort of ideological conflict with his brother.

'In any case,' said Luke, 'he should never have been a clergyman because he didn't care for the church. No more do I. To me it's detestable not because it's worldly, but because it isn't worldly enough. Its teaching, its message is a complete lie. There is no God, there is no other world.'

'Well, I agree with you, but that makes us both atheists. Where does religion come into it?'

'Religion doesn't have to be a belief in God. Religion is the recognition of what this life is, a temporary condition shared with every other living thing, ending with the annihilation of the individual. Of course, everything goes round again physically, is recycled over and over again, as long as the planet lasts, but for the individual consciousness, so far as we know, there is only the one go. Like a fair. "No readmission once you have left the grounds." My ticket is more than half used up. I've begun to see life as very precious, therefore. If I married it would be to someone who was able to share that feeling with me and make it all the stronger.'

Andrew made no reply. He didn't agree with his brother. For one thing he was younger and still felt he had plenty of time ahead of him; for another, he believed in the collective progress of mankind towards better and more equal conditions and, although he was nothing if not an individualist himself, could not find anything very stirring in the idea of simply making the most of one's personal ticket. But he wanted particularly to avoid this sort of divisive argument, so he sat staring at his empty glass until he could gracefully change the subject.

'Can I see the farm?'

'Of course, if you want to. There's not much to see.'

He sounded pleased, all the same. They left the lunch things where they were and, with the dog bounding wildly around them, strolled out across the lawn. The clouds had now entirely obscured the sun and the light was grey and depressing.

'You do some gardening.'

'Not really. I plant the odd thing from time to time and keep it tidy, but you don't need a garden when you've got the country all around you.'

Not much of the country could be seen from the farm. It lay in a slight hollow and was partly enclosed by woods.

'How much of this land belongs to you?' asked Andrew, waving his arm to indicate the surroundings.

'Not an enormous amount.'

'Do you grow anything? Crops, I mean.'

'Oh no. It's just pasture. This is an awfully dull farm, I'm afraid, from the visitor's point of view. Nothing but a lot of cows, the grass they eat and the milk they turn it into. An extremely primitive and simple business, if it weren't for the Min of Ag and the EEC with their paperwork.'

They walked through the milking shed, with its rows of stalls and suction hoses. In a separate compartment at one end was a great shiny metal tank to which all the hoses led. Luke lifted the hinged lid to show Andrew the milk inside.

'That's it. That's the end product. My liquid assets, so to speak.'

The phrase jarred on Andrew. It was as if his brother had guessed the purpose of his visit and was demonstrating its absurdity. A tank of milk bought nobody a flat in London.

'Help yourself!'

Luke was holding out an aluminium measuring jug. Andrew shook his head, which felt heavy and thick from the wine at lunch. He was not so much refusing the milk as acknowledging that this route towards his goal was proving a cul-de-sac.

They came out of the shed and stood beside a small paddock.

'I had a horse at one time,' said Luke, 'but it seemed an unnecessary expense. I really prefer walking to riding. Shall we take a walk now?'

Andrew would rather have driven straight back to London. The austerity of his brother's life made him restless. It seemed pointless even to ask him for a loan. He liked romantic and exotic landscapes, but this gently undulating countryside bored him.

'It needn't be a long one. Do come for a walk, Andrew!'

'Okay. Why not?'

Fergus the dog seemed to understand immediately that the walk was on and rushed off ahead down a rutted track. Andrew was touched by his brother's warmth. As children they had taken each other for granted. The distance between them as they grew older had made Luke seem an alien, self-enclosed figure and in any case Andrew tended to take others as they came, or appeared to come. He was not curious about people as he was about ideas or social phenomena. People could be interesting or useful or even stimulating, of course, but it seldom occurred to him to look at the person instead of what the person was looking at. Luke, however, constantly surprised him, no doubt because he thought he knew him, but had never really got to know him.

They went down the track after Fergus, through a gate and into a beech wood. As they walked, Luke came alive in a way that Andrew had never suspected he could. He seemed to know every bird, insect, tree and plant personally and as he pointed them out and talked about them, the whole place sprang to life around him. He and his dog – peering, pricking its ears, sniffing, stopping, starting, zigzagging, backtracking – were equally absorbed by the multiplicity of sights, sounds and smells. Andrew was spellbound. His headache vanished and was replaced with a tingling in his scalp, as if he were being stroked there.

They came out of the wood into a field that rose to a hump in the middle, then struck down through a second field to a small stream running through a strip of copse. There was a narrow wooden bridge and they leaned on its rail and looked down at the water, while Fergus investigated rabbit holes among the tree roots. Luke was silent and Andrew, partly released from his spell, wondered whether this might be the moment to mention that he needed money. For an instant he wondered why he needed money, then remembered Maria. The whole thing, he saw now, was ridiculous. As long as Maria was attached to Michael, she was out of his reach. If he succeeded in cutting out Michael, he could hardly hope to go ahead with the TV series, on which his finances depended. He had somehow associated having a new flat with having Maria, but on the contrary the one precluded the other. He had got everything in the wrong order. The TV series was the key, both to making contact with Maria and to being able to set up house independently of Liz. Furthermore, the TV series must be finished or at least well on the way to being finished before he could cut out Michael.

They walked on. Luke and his dog were still fully occupied with the innumerable delights of their world, but Andrew's new clarity of mind had partly returned him to his own world and he no longer paid more than casual attention to his brother. They emerged on a narrow metalled road with high hedges and approached another farm, whose sheds were new and shiny and which seemed altogether more modern and prosperous than Luke's. A confused, high-pitched noise coming from one of the sheds grew louder as they got nearer and, as they passed the shed, blotted out every other sound.

'What is it?' Andrew asked.

'Pigs.'

'What's the matter with them?'

'The sows have just been separated from their litters.'

'Does it have to be done so brutally?'

'I detest this kind of farming,' said Luke, 'but it's the only kind that really pays.'

They quickened their pace to leave the noise behind. Luke, after his moment of bitterness, seemed to have to put the pigs out of his mind. Farming, after all, was his profession and even if he didn't approve of his neighbour's business methods he was too used to them to be shocked. His philosophy – his religion of a brief and precious individual life – was not romantic, but a realistic assessment based on his own close observation of nature. These pigs – and probably most pigs, not to speak of calves, lambs, chickens, turkeys, cattle, all the creatures exploited by man – had drawn a short straw. Man himself, the master, looking to his own interests, apparently freer, but according to his own timescale just as doomed and pathetic as the pigs, walked quickly past and thought of something else. But Andrew found it difficult to think of anything else. The pigs' squealing stayed in his ears even after they had left the road and were crossing a large field back towards Luke's farm. He didn't usually trouble himself about the miseries of animals – he was seldom made aware of them – but this first-hand evidence of the callousness which supported somebody's prosperity revived and sharpened his instincts for reform and revolution. It was no good walking past. It was nearly as bad to walk past as it was to do the thing in the first place. It was a lie to pretend that you were helpless. If men could set up these cruelties, men could also put an end to them.

Andrew stopped in the middle of the field. He had almost decided to go back. What he would do when he got there he wasn't yet sure. Open the barn door and release all the pigs? Hammer on the door of the farmhouse and tell the farmer what he thought of him? Luke and Fergus were some way ahead before they noticed Andrew's absence and both stopped to wait for him. The field was full of Luke's black and white Friesians. They had interrupted their grazing to stare at the walkers and then had begun to move towards them. While Andrew had been debating with himself, they had closed in on him and now, as he started to signal to Luke that he was turning back, they took alarm and jostled and stumbled into a struggling barrier between him and the way he had come. He had little experience of cows and was nervous of them, so he stood where he was, hoping like a person on whom a bee has settled that if he didn't excite them, they would go about their business. The inquisitive cows moved nearer. Andrew changed his tactics and began to try to shoo them away with small excited gestures. But although the cows in front shied away from him and tried to retreat, those behind were still pressing forward and the whole herd became even more densely packed and restless. Andrew began walking slowly backwards in the direction of Luke, but the cows closed up on him and he found himself on the edge of panic. He was rescued by Luke, who returned and drove the cows back. The brothers crossed the remainder of the field in silence, followed at a short distance by the herd.

'It's nearly milking time,' said Luke, as they passed through a gate and found themselves back on the track to his farm. 'That's why they're restless. What were you trying to show me when you stopped?'

'I've forgotten,' said Andrew. 'Nothing of importance.' He was ashamed of the incident and even more ashamed of having been so easily diverted from his protest on behalf of the pigs.

They reached the farm's outbuildings and walked up the gravel drive towards the house.

'Cup of tea?' asked Luke.

'I think I'll get back,' said Andrew.

'Really? But we haven't talked about your divorce, whatever it was you wanted to ask me.'

'I don't know,' said Andrew. 'Maybe we won't get divorced. Can't afford it.'

'Are you short of money?'

'Of course I'm always short of money, but I suppose the real problem is that I'm in love with someone else.'

His mind seemed to be out of control, issuing signals he had told it not to.

'Why is it a problem? If you're no longer in love with Liz.'

'Because Liz and I and this other person obviously can't all share the same flat.'

'So it is a problem of money.'

'In a sense.'

'Do you want me to lend you a bit?'

'Good Lord, no! I'm sure you've got none to spare.'

'Not to spare. I can't give it to you, because in this business you need a safety net for bad years. But I could easily lend you ten or fifteen.'

'Ten or fifteen?'

'Thousand. You could pay me back gradually. Without interest, of course.'

'It's extraordinarily kind of you.'

'I made a profit when I moved here. I suppose I ought to spend a bit on the look of the place, but it's all perfectly functional at present. So the money's just sitting there for an emergency. Your emergency is my emergency.'

'I'd rather not take away your safety net.'

'I've left everything to you in my will anyway, so think of it as half yours already.'

Even though Andrew had decided he didn't want a new flat yet, his brother's generosity was so insistent that he couldn't reject it. It was as if Luke had invited him down in order to press money on him and, driving away from the farm half an hour later, Andrew suspected his brother must have guessed the purpose of his visit and determined it should be successful and creditable to both of them. Usually if you borrowed money, it soured a relationship. Luke had contrived to turn what had hardly been a relationship at all into a friendship. The concept of brotherhood was not often associated with real brothers, but he felt Luke had deliberately set out to restore that meaning to it.

So he was now virtually committed to a move. But was he any nearer to Maria? His mind turned to the TV treatment. He found himself freshly excited by it. The feelings aroused by the incident of the pigs and his failure to do anything for them were channelled into what he was sure he could do something about: the exposure of British neocolonialism. He would pull no punches, smooth nothing over, demonstrate . . .

A large Ford, hooting furiously, brushed past him with inches to spare and surged away ahead with contemptuous speed. He would demonstrate that that quarter of the world's population which

Birtain had once treated as little better than pigs were brother humans, worthy of respect, admiration and love.

III

'My head aches –
Too many nights spent screwing
Corks out of bottles
And afterwards spewing.
My loins ache –
Too many nights spent screwing
My cork into your bottle
And afterwards doing
The same again.'

Andrew crumpled the piece of paper into a ball and threw it furiously into the wastepaper-basket. His secretary looked up in surprise and said mildly:

'No good?'

'Bloody awful!'

'I think he may have wanted it back if we weren't going to print it. Wasn't there an s.a.e.?'

'Let him rot!'

The poem came from Ben Brooks and was entitled 'Same Again, Liz'.

'It's all lies, anyway. He drinks beer, not wine. As for screwing, he couldn't screw a frozen chicken.'

'I shouldn't think many people could,' said the secretary demurely.

'Nothing else would come within a mile of him,' said Andrew, taking the rest of the post into his own office.

But, as a matter of fact, it was only a couple of days since Ben Brooks had spent the evening at Andrew's flat and he was more annoyed with Liz than with Brooks. She seemed to be deliberately encouraging his visits because she knew that nothing drove Andrew out of the flat more quickly.

When Liz got home late that night, Andrew was working on this TV treatment. She had been to a private view at somebody else's gallery and then out to supper and she was a little drunk. Andrew told her about the poem, not quoting it, but giving the gist. She laughed.

'Sounds quite a good joke,' she said.

'At your expense.'

'At yours, I should have thought.'

'Did you put him up to it?'

'Of course I didn't. If I really wanted to draw blood, I'd get him to write you poems about your *princesse lointaine*, wouldn't I? As it is,

I've been extremely loyal to you and haven't said a word about her to Ben. Don't push me too far!'

'What does that mean? I'm not conscious of pushing you at all.'

'You seem to think you can have me as a wife without any of the bother of being a husband.'

'Do you mean you're jealous?'

'I'm bloody fed up. The age of troubadours is past. I think all this flat-hunting is just a diversion and I'm not giving up any more of my time to it or to anything connected with your obsession with that newscaster.'

Ever since he had returned from the day at his brother's farm, Andrew had occupied most of his spare time visiting estate agents, combing lists and newspaper columns and seeing over likely properties. He had relied throughout on Liz's help, as if the new flat was to be as much for her as for him, and up to now she had allowed him to take her help for granted, in the hope that he would finally move out and leave her to remake her life without him. It had not occurred to Andrew that she was not as involved in the details of his problem and its solution as he was.

'I'm sorry Liz. You were taking an interest for my sake and I thought it was because you found it amusing. Women are so kind and long-suffering and men are selfish bastards.'

He wasn't being ironic, but abasing himself in his own characteristic fashion, by discovering the general in the particular.

'I don't think men are any more selfish than women, but they're probably less observant, better at making themselves believe they're not being selfish.'

'I'm sorry. I've been insensitive.'

'That isn't the point. There's no way you can hurt me, therefore insensitivity isn't the problem. The problem is boredom. Your long-distance love life bores me. Your other life bores me too, but not quite so much, because it doesn't impinge quite so much.'

Without waiting for a reply she left the room and went into the bathroom, locking the door.

Andrew sat without moving, considering what she'd said. His first reaction was that she had hurt him deeply. As she'd clearly meant to. Then he wondered if she had meant to, but hadn't simply said the first thing that came into her head after a long, tiring day. Next he decided that she had meant to hurt him, but only instinctively because she was actually hurt herself, in spite of her denial. And he concluded that since he was able to weigh up all these possibilities, he couldn't have been all that much hurt. And, not for the first time, he was aware of the essential unreality of these marital bouts. They had both read too many books, seen too many plays, films, TV serials in which every conceivable variation of this sort of exchange had been played, to take it for real. It was a dead form and the content was dead also. Their arguments and insults were additionally unreal because they belonged to the past. It was as if they were unable to communicate except according to this ancient ritual, because their having come to an end of each other was all they had in common.

Suddenly, with great excitement, Andrew turned back to his desk. That was the way to begin the series: with a corny scene of marital sparring. Wasn't the Third World in the same position as the wife in a broken marriage, raped, exploited, disillusioned, but still economically dependent on her aggressive and much stronger despoiler? Wasn't he – the parliamentary, militaristic, capitalist West – openly contemptuous of her clumsy attempts to get by on her own, to live according to her philosophy, not his? This was the theme and he would find his variations in the different post-colonial histories of the divorcees. Of course, he mustn't allow the theme to overwhelm the material, it was only a washing line to hang it on; but it was necessary in a popular medium to adopt a popular approach and here was a way of presenting an intrinsically forbidding subject so that every man and woman in the living room would get the point.

Delighted with himself and his idea, feeling that the world owed him a living again and that he'd done a fine day's work, he decided he deserved some sleep, rose from his desk and went towards the bathroom. As he reached the door and turned the handle, having forgotten that the room was already occupied, it opened and Liz, in her nightdress, confronted him.

'Sorry,' he said, standing aside.

'I'm sorry,' she said. 'I didn't mean to speak like that. I didn't mean what I said.'

'I didn't think you did,' he said, unable to recall exactly what she had said.

'We don't have to part as enemies,' she said. 'I wanted to say that I'm glad you've fallen in love, even if it's such an absurdly conceptual affair. I wish you well. I'm not jealous, because I know we stopped loving one another some time ago. I suppose I'd like to be in love again myself – so perhaps it was envy not jealousy that made me lash out at you. Anyway, I'm sorry.'

He looked at her blankly for a moment or two. He was touched by her sudden sweetness, but her words confused him. He was not applying them to himself, but trying to fit them into his new theme for the series. India? Was this the Indian variation? Hardly. That would require some other country to be displacing India as the jewel in Britain's crown. Of course there was no such country. He was cast down. Would his precious theme prove a will-o'-the-wisp? No doubt he was frowning at the thought. Certainly he must have looked stern and withdrawn. He saw she was on the point of crying and at the same time heard her words with their original simple meaning, as if his brain had stored and replayed them like a telephone answering machine. Yes, indeed, he had loved her, loved this very person standing in front of him for just the way she looked at him now, unsure of herself and of him, fearing his cruelty and indifference, offering only kindness and generosity. She looked especially small and vulnerable with her bare feet and arms and smelled of the expensive soap he had given her for her birthday. She was still his wife, still closer to him than anyone else in the world. He kissed her gently but enthusiastically. She held on to him and he kissed her again, this time with sexual desire. He removed her nightdress and ran his hands all over her body, then led her slowly into the bedroom and drew back the covers of the double bed, made up with only one pillow. She lay and waited for him while he rapidly pulled off his own clothes and joined her in the bed he hadn't occupied for at least a year. They made love and slept afterwards with their heads close together on the single pillow. Andrew got up once in the night and at the door of the bathroom remembered the new theme for his series. He was no longer quite convinced of its usefulness. On the other hand, he felt as if some great burden had been lifted. Going into the sitting room to collect the pillow from his bed on the sofa, he thought of Maria. The thought neither excited him nor gave him pain. He returned to the bedroom congratulating himself on being at last free of his obsession.

5

I

Having honoured two of his resolutions, Simon Carter forgot the third until the autumn. He had been to see an exhibition of Indian paintings. They were from Rajasthan, the north-western area of small states ruled by Rajput princes in semi-independence until India became a republic in 1947. The court painters of seventeenth-and eighteenth-century Rajasthan were less sophisticated, less naturalistic and more stylized than the Persian painters imported by the Mughal emperors, but they had a vigour of line and a brilliance of colour which were more quintessentially Indian. On the whole, Simon had always preferred Mughal painting, perhaps because it was more international. You could to some extent enter it, become part of the scene depicted and share its worldly pleasures. The Rajasthan painters, especially those influenced by Mughal art, offered you that too in a less convincing way, but the element of Hindu myth predominated.

As he studied the catalogue, Simon began to change his mind. Normally he liked to understand things thoroughly enough to be able to explain them to others. But in this case he had no desire to understand more about the Hindu myths. He welcomed their obscurity, or at least the obscurity of their brief exegesis by some European scholar at the back of the catalogue. Why should that be, he wondered. It was certainly not laziness on his part or indifference to the nuances of a foreign culture. On the contrary, he wanted more of that culture, not less. But it was as if he wanted to approach it in a manner alien to him, without the intervention of rational thought, as if he wanted to grow into it in the way a child grows into its own culture and only begins to make sense of it much later. So was it simply the sense of being a child again that he wanted? Was it a sort of return to medievalism, a reaction against the freedom and burdens of a more sophisticated world?

It was already quite late at night, between 2 and 3 am, but Simon sat on at his desk. His elbow on the catalogue, his hand supporting his chin, he stared vacantly at the bookcase along one wall of the room while his mind painstakingly interrogated this rebellion against the mind's dominance. He was tired, though. His train of thought broke off and his eyes started to see the books on the shelf and to run along their titles. *The Siege of Krishnapur, A Passage to India, The Raj Quartet*: a lot of his novels seemed to be about India, though he wasn't conscious of its being a special interest of his. At the end of the shelf was a row of black hardbacked notebooks without titles – Uncle Percy's diaries. Simon got up from his chair, fetched them and stacked them on his desk. He pushed the catalogue aside, opened the first notebook and began to read. The firm, plain handwriting was as clear as print.

The hours went by, the sun came up, the birds in the gardens and squares around were singing and still Simon read on. It was not a particularly intimate diary, nor were the events particularly striking in themselves, but the gradual accumulation of detail drew you inexorably into Uncle Percy's world and the acidity of his comments gave it a certain individuality and immediacy.

Percy Carter had joined the Indian Civil Service in 1910, at the age of twenty-four. At the end of 1913 he was posted to the small town of Firkola. It was a remote, primitive place with an enervating climate and very little choice of European company. After three years in India the young Percy was already growing peppery and contemptuous, changing his servants every six months, sneering at the government edict forbidding the use of the word 'native' for 'Indian', complaining about the stupidity of his European superiors and the unreliability of his Indian subordinates and finding relief only in reading, riding and playing polo, tennis or cards. 'I can imagine no place more detestable than this,' he wrote in his diary and made a list of the eight or nine other Europeans who shared it with him: 'those in square brackets are negligible, those in round utterly impossible.' Two names appeared without brackets. The only Indians Percy encountered were servants or, in his capacity as a magistrate, criminals and he found fault with them all, especially the Muslims.

However, in the autumn of 1914 he was seconded from the ICS to the Political Department and given the job of tutor and guardian to the fifteen-year-old Maharajah of Dehrapur, one of the princes of Rajasthan. 'This is the ideal job,' he told himself with uncharacteristic and misplaced optimism. The Maharajah Badan Singh had succeeded to his throne at the age of six, after the early death of his father, but he would not receive the power that went with it until he was eighteen. Meanwhile his princedom was ruled by its State Council under the guidance of Dehrapur's British Political Agent and he himself was in the care of his mother, the Maji Sahiba, and his official British tutor. Badan Singh had been sent briefly to a public school in England, but withdrawn when the First World War broke out. Now he was to be educated at the special school for the Rajput nobility in the city of Ajmer and the twenty-eight-year-old Percy Carter was to be his surrogate father, succeeding an elderly married major who had retired.

The first meeting between Percy and Badan Singh – his mother and friends called him 'Badi' – took place not in Dehrapur itself, but in the Rajasthan hill-station of Abu. It was July, the hot season in the plains, and all those that could had migrated to the cooler slopes of Mount Abu. The young Maharajah, his mother and their entourage were in residence at Dehrapur House. Percy was invited to stay at the British Residency and introduced to his new charge at a formal dinner a couple of days later. He was immediately impressed with the Englishness of the boy, his good manners and his good looks. The Maji Sahiba could not immediately let her son entirely out of her sight, but it was arranged that Percy and Badan Singh should have a bungalow not too far from Dehrapur House and then, after a fortnight or so, provided that the Maji Sahiba was still happy with the new tutor, she would allow them to go off on their own to stay in Kashmir for the remainder of the hot weather.

Abu was extraordinarily beautiful. Heavily forested, full of flowering trees and exotic birds, it was a maze of hills and gullies and small winding tracks. Most of the houses, grand and small, official and private, nestled in their gardens and shrubberies within half a mile or so of a large artificial lake, behind which rose the upper crags of the mountain. There were cricket and polo grounds, tennis courts and a golf course, and excursions could be made to spectacular views of the plains below or to the famous Jain temples of Dilwara, set among hills and mango trees to the north-east of the lake.

Sometimes on foot, sometimes on ponies, once or twice by car, Percy and Badan Singh explored this paradise together during the next fortnight. Their expeditions were occasionally more planned and formal, such as that with the Maji Sahiba and entourage to Sunset Point for the view, but often they were on their own or accompanied only by the Maharajah's older cousin, a stout and indolent young man of about twenty. It was clear from the diary that the irritable and cynical Percy who had sweated and cursed his luck in Firkola had temporarily vanished, to be replaced by someone who, if not precisely in love with his companion, was so charmed and flattered by his high spirits and schoolboyish deference that he spent his days almost in a state of ecstasy. Not that Percy ever quite dropped his ironical and critical guard, even in his diary. He was still quicker to remark on the physical unfitness of the Maharajah's cousin or the fussiness of his mother than on the beauties of the scenery. But his references to Badi – as he now called him – were consistently admiring. Behind the brief prosaic entries, noting a walk by the lake, a boating trip, a game of tennis or golf or the fact that Badi found English food insipid, so that they compromised by eating partly English and partly Indian food, Simon sensed that his great-uncle was enjoying more than a holiday. Simon had never been to India himself, but he had read enough books and seen enough films and television serials to be able to picture the pair of them – the tall, grave tutor and the lively, glamorous boy – moving through that exotic setting in their impeccably laundered clothes like the principal figures in a romance.

Then, after two weeks, with the blessing of Badi's mother, they took the train to Srinagar, capital of Kashmir, where they were again entertained by the British Resident and again settled into a rented house with their servants and their ponies around them and this time, in the absence of the Maji Sahiba and her entourage, only Badi's apathetic cousin and the constant background of the British official world to intrude on their idyll. Srinagar, with its lakes and canals, was an even more enchanting place than Abu and Badi, who already knew it, immediately set about introducing Percy to these fresh delights. But at this point Percy's background and training reasserted themselves. As long as the boy's mother had been in the offing, he had not felt any need to assume the responsibilities of his job. He had been required only to make Badi's acquaintance and reassure his mother that he and Badi liked and trusted one another. Now, in Srinagar, he was indeed tutor and guardian and although he was content for a few days to go on behaving as Badi's privileged guest, he was determined after that to recall them both to their duties.

On the third morning in their house in Srinagar, as they ate breakfast on the verandah and Badi as usual said, 'Now, Sahib, what about today? Shall we take a boat on the lake?' Percy did not respond with his usual easy acquiescence. Instead, he put his hand in his pocket, drew out a folded sheet of paper and said:

'Today, Badi, we begin work. I have drawn up a timetable. Have a look at it!' And he unfolded the paper and passed it across to Badi.

Badi said nothing for a while. He looked at Percy as though he was seeing an altogether new person at his breakfast-table and then, sitting back in his cane chair, began to study the piece of paper. Percy had divided each of the six working days of the week into four sessions, devoted to such subjects as Indian history, general knowledge, Dehrapur history, religion and the reading of books and the daily newspaper. Badi looked up.

'Today is Thursday,' he said.

'Yes. So it will be Newspaper, followed by English Essay, followed by Dehrapur History and, after lunch, the Indian Penal Code.'

'Wouldn't it be better to start on Monday, since that is the beginning of the week and the timetable is arranged that way? Then we can still go on the lake today and perhaps riding tomorrow.'

'I think it would be better to start today.'

The boy was silent. In the diary, Percy described the episode as a battle of wills, but it was surely himself he was battling with? Need he have confronted Badi quite so abruptly with this change of programme, if he was not trying to deliver a shock to his own system? Their relationship, he wrote, became different from that moment on. Badi himself seemed to alter in character, becoming distant and devious. But wasn't it that for the past fortnight Percy had found a new character in himself which his old character was now desperately rejecting? No doubt his official position required him to do so in some measure, but did he really believe that in order to teach and guide the prince he had to appear as his master instead of his friend, to substitute overt discipline for shared experience? Between the pages of the diary Simon found the very piece of paper that had crossed the breakfast-table on that morning in Srinagar some sixty-five years ago. The columns were ruled in red pencil, the days, times and subjects were laid out in Percy's plain, confident handwriting and underneath he had added his signature, over a rubber stamp reading 'Tutor and Guardian to HH the Maharajah of Dehrapur'.

Simon pushed his chair back, opened the curtains and stood for some time staring out at the autumn morning. The Percy Carter who had been selected for the ICS and then picked out for the sensitive job of training this prince – a local hereditary authority skilfully welded into the greater authority of the British Raj – had called himself to order. The daily newspaper, the English essay, the history of Dehrapur and the Indian Penal code were martialled like bodyguards around him. The freedom and luxury of Rajasthan and Kashmir were now strictly confined to evenings and Sundays, the careless happiness of Abu was banished for ever. What else, after all, could he have done? He was an alien Englishman, a government employee, not there for his happiness but for his living and his service. He was allowed to enjoy India provided that he also ruled it. He was to alter India, not be altered by it. His fear of losing control of himself was reinforced on every side by the necessities of empire.

Simon went to bed and dreamed of a painting by one of the Rajasthan masters. At the centre of a paradise garden sat a young prince with pearl earrings and necklace and a jewelled cap with a feather. Women served him with wine and sweets and he held a pink rose between the thumb and forefinger of his left hand. Around him the garden, in several shades of green, was filled with flowers and birds, but strictly ordered by a grid of pink paths and formal fountains. Sometimes Simon seemed to be looking at the garden from above, sometimes walking in it, along the paths, but he felt he was trespassing and that the prince was only ignoring him because he despised him.

II

One of the lords of television was giving a party in his house in South London. Simon and his host had known each other as undergraduates but had hardly met since and he wondered why he'd been invited. Jack Dillon kept an eye on the theatre, books and films, but not, Simon thought, on the visual arts. Certainly there was nothing of interest on his walls. Perhaps he wanted to repair that omission; more likely, he was feeling his age and wanted to remind himself of the past. When Simon arrived, Jack welcomed him warmly, praised a radio interview Simon had done recently with a well-known artist and then, after introducing him to one or two other recent arrivals, disappeared into the throng of courtiers and fellow potentates. Simon was left on the fringe of a desultory argument between a Tory politician and a belligerent left-wing playwright.

'You talk about Victorian values. What you mean is a licence for greed, corruption and selfishness.'

'Not at all. I haven't mentioned Victorian values.'

'The Prime Minister has.'

'Perhaps. But Victorian values is a red herring.'

'You disagree with the PM?'

'I don't think the values alter. Individual responsibility, honesty, straight dealing, realism, courage . . .'

'Haves and have-nots are what you mean by values. The haves have value and the rest don't.'

'That isn't what I said and it isn't what I mean.'

Simon moved away and caught sight of a writer he knew slightly. She was with a group near the window, most of whom seemed to be fellow writers. They were talking eagerly about sales and authors' contracts, capping one another's stories about the meanness and inefficiency of publishers. Simon joined them, was introduced and contributed the story of his own first book – an introduction to American Abstract Expressionism which had been his only real success with a small public, but which he had foolishly sold outright.

'Don't you have an agent?' asked one of the writers.

'I do now.'

The discussion shifted to agents. It was noticeable, one of them pointed out, that most agents, like publishers, lived in luxury, whereas most authors, even apparently successful ones, were down-at-heel, if not actually on the poverty line.

'We are just the cows that supply the milk,' said the writer Simon knew, 'and of course if our milk dries up or doesn't sell, there are always plenty of other cows to take our place.'

'But still most people would rather be writers than publishers or agents,' said a tall, balding man with a plummy voice. 'The rewards aren't purely financial.'

'Writers are exploited by the employers and middlemen,' said a small, thin woman with a pallid face, short, bleached hair and an angry mouth. 'Just because the workers enjoy their work, they don't have to accept exploitation.'

Simon, feeling that he didn't mind if he never heard another opinion in his life, withdrew from the group and went in search of more to drink. People were descending the stairs to the kitchen. The whole basement had been converted into one room and fitted with cupboards, shelves and work-surfaces in a pleasant light-coloured wood. There was a crowd round the food laid out on the central table and people who had already filled their plates occupied most of the chairs round the walls. Simon placed himself near the corner of the table where there was a pile of clean plates and waited his turn. The Dillons' visual sense seemed to be all concentrated in their kitchen. Somebody – presumably Mrs Dillon – had taken trouble with the general look and feel of the room and its fittings, but that was only a setting or frame. The cold banquet on the table, even though it had been partly picked to pieces by so many hungry guests, was the work of art. The prevailing colour was green – salads, sauces, avocado paté, apples, grapes, melons – sharpened with pink – salmon, underdone beef, taramasalata, bowls of raspberry mousse – but this light and fresh effect was set off with dark, rich interludes or punctuation marks – caviar, black olive paté, chocolate cakes, purple grapes. As he finally reached the edge of the table, Simon paused a moment to take a complete view of its contents, which he had so far only been able to see between the bodies of those in front of him. Then, still with his eyes on Mrs Dillon's masterpiece, he put his hand out for a plate and found that someone else was grasping it at the same moment.

'Sorry!' he said, taking his hand away.

The other person had also taken her hand away.

'You were first,' she said.

He looked up. It was Maria Dobson.

'I thought it must be you,' she said, 'I remembered the back of your head.'

'How's the cat?' he said.

'Vronsky's terrific. You wouldn't know anything had ever happened to him.'

'Can I help you to something?'

'Doesn't it look wonderful?'

'Would you like to sit down?' he asked when he had filled two plates.

They found two chairs just inside the door.
'Are you Beeb or independent?' she asked.
'Neither. I'm an art critic.'
'That makes a change. What are you doing here?'
'I used to know Jack when we were both at Cambridge.'
'Are you a freelance critic?'
'Yes, but I have a regular job with a weekly magazine.'
A tubby man with frog-like eyes and a Roman hairstyle came and stood over them.
'Where's Michael?'
'Somewhere about,' said Maria.
'Always hopeful, I am.'
'Hopeful of what?'
'That he'll be on a slow boat to China.'
She turned away from him.
'What's your favourite kind of art?' she said to Simon.
'Hard to say. I'm very eclectic. If you press me, I'd have to say contemporary British.'
'Really?'
'Just because it is contemporary. About us. That gives it an edge that even Renaissance painting doesn't have. Renaissance painting may be greater, more skilled, richer in content, more absorbing in most ways, but it's about another world. It touches us at one remove. Our own painting is the immediate raw response to our world. I'm fond of history, but mainly because it's part of what we are now. We're the sharp end of history – or better say, the ragged end.'
Simon stopped abruptly, afraid that he was talking too much, but the pop-eyed, overweight man hovering over them had moved away and Maria was still looking at Simon as if she was listening carefully through the racket of conversation all round them.
'I can't say I've ever looked at contemporary art in that way. It's always seemed to me a bit of a con.'
'A lot of it is. But then in a sense all art is. I mean, to produce it at all, the artist has to con himself into thinking that he's got something to express and is able to express it.'
'Are you an artist as well as a critic?'
'No. Never been able to con myself sufficiently for that.'
'Who are the artists you admire?'
'Is this an interview?'
He had made her blush. If she had been anyone else, he would have hurried to cover up her embarrassment, partly from good manners, partly because other people's embarrassment embarrassed him, but he couldn't take his eyes off her excitingly pink face and besides he felt that she was the more self-possessed of the two of them and could bear a little embarrassment, so he let his challenge stand.

'I'm just very ignorant,' she said. 'I thought you might give me a few names to look out for.'

He frowned and began to collect names in his head, looking down at the floor so as not to be distracted by her face. But he had hardly begun to mention them aloud when he was interrupted by the appearance on Maria's other side of a slight young man with wiry, dark hair and thick black eyebrows that met over his nose. Jigging about restlessly with a bad-tempered look on his pale face, he suggested a conceited schoolboy. Simon thought he might have been Welsh, but couldn't place his faintly rural accent.

'You're doing all right, then,' he said, indicating Maria's plate of food.

Maria introduced him as Michael Arley and it depressed Simon to recall that this was Andrew Mowle's producer on the Third World series, the man Andrew had said was Maria's lover. Michael nodded irritably in Simon's direction, but took no further notice of him.

'I haven't eaten anything,' he said, implying that he'd expected her to fill a plate for him.

'There's plenty left,' she said, in a mild but offhand tone, dismissing the subject, but continuing to look at him.

Michael finished the wine in his glass and shifted about beside her defiantly, willing her to accompany him to the table and take an interest in his needs. She sat tight and then, as he still said nothing, turned to Simon.

'You were just telling me who I ought to admire.'

'Certainly not. No "ought" about it.'

Simon felt uncomfortable with the way Michael was standing next to them, making their conversation public and self-conscious. There was a burst of loud laughter from a group nearby and Maria looked instinctively in that direction, as if she wanted to be rid of both the men beside her. When she turned back towards Simon, Michael abruptly moved away. He seemed undecided for a moment, then made for the door instead of the table.

'You're in demand,' said Simon. 'I'm afraid I'm monopolizing you.'

'Most of the people I come across aim to monopolize people,' she said.

'No doubt I do too. Politeness is only a way of covering one's tracks.'

He tried to smile but his face felt stiff and inflexible. He had become more self-conscious than ever. She too, perhaps, since she reached for her glass. It was empty.

'Shall I get you some more?' he asked.

'Yes, please.'

'And maybe you'd like a piece of chocolate cake?'

'No thanks. Perhaps a few grapes.'

As he queued to fill the glasses on the other side of the kitchen, unable to see Maria through the people coming and going from the table, Simon was tempted to leave at once. By vacating his chair beside her, he had surrendered his chance of getting to know Maria. Someone else – probably Michael – would have occupied it and she would be relieved not to have to persist with their sticky conversation. He only felt a mild regret. She flattered him with her attention – it was like being singled out by minor royalty for a brief display of his expertise – and he couldn't deny that sitting next to her and watching her face gave him pleasure, but there was no future in it. It wasn't that he thought she was too good for him or even that he was too good for her – rather that the worlds they lived in were too different and that neither of them was really interested in more than a tourist excursion over the frontier.

He cut himself a slice of chocolate cake, broke off a stem of black grapes for her and, holding the plate in one hand and the two glasses of wine precariously in the other, edged his way back to her through the crowd. When he saw her again and saw that there was, of course, somebody sitting beside her, he no longer felt like writing off their relationship so easily. The man beside her was a well-known journalist who had recently become an executive of one of the independent TV companies. He was a large, handsome, clever man, whose face gave the same impression as Maria's of being unusually visible, a screen constantly lit for the projection of his personality. He and Maria were talking in a relaxed way, as if they knew each other well.

'Isn't Michael involved in some Third World project?' the journalist was saying.

'I believe so,' she said.

'I wonder if he'd be interested in interviewing Nakimbi. The ex-president of Balunda.'

'Yes, I know who you mean.'

'He's taken refuge in France. I could put Michael in touch with him.'

'I should think he'd be very grateful.'

Simon moved closer, holding out the two glasses of wine almost under her nose. The journalist got up at once.

'Your chair?'

'I can easily stand.'

'I'm on my way anyway.'

They sized each other up briefly, both tall, but the journalist bulkier. Maria did not introduce them and they saw nothing in each other to warrant further investigation. The journalist laid his hand on Maria's arm by way of farewell and took himself off. Simon hastily sat beside her. His own uncharacteristic sense of urgency surprised him and he immediately began to speak, as if this was a variation on musical chairs in which, to keep your seat, you were required to say the first thing that came into your head.

'This isn't my world at all,' he said. 'I feel like somebody up from the sticks among all these well-known faces.'

'Are those for me?' she asked, taking the grapes he'd forgotten to give her from the plate on his knee.

'Of course. I'm so sorry.'

'It's a very narrow world,' she said. 'It sometimes reminds me of those closed circles of aristocrats and high-up bureaucrats in Tolstoy's novels, a lot of self-important frogs hopping about in a stagnant pond.' The mention of Tolstoy gave him the same stab of pleasure as he'd felt when she told him her cat's name. It suggested they might have interests in common after all.

'I'm sure your world isn't half as narrow as mine,' he said. 'The contemporary art world is tiny. It revolves round its own navel in a way television never could, because television has an audience. It almost makes me envy the Victorians.'

He smiled and she smiled back, encouraging him to go on. But for a moment he suffered a mental blackout. His current of thought was short-circuited by his consciousness of her and of himself sitting next to her. In a panic, trying to think what he'd been going to say next, he took a huge mouthful of chocolate cake and got whipped cream all over his moustache. Wiping it vigorously with his handkerchief, he caught her eye. Her smile was broader still.

'People with moustaches shouldn't eat chocolate cake,' he said.

'Everyone seems to be nostalgic for the nineteenth century these days.'

'Not me,' he said. 'I think the British were at their absolute worst then.' What he had been going to say came back to him. 'But at least people weren't locked into their own narrow enclaves of specialization. It was a good time for artists.'

'Wasn't Victorian art mostly second-rate?'

'Maybe, but it had a public. When Frith showed *Derby Day* at the Royal Academy they had to rail off the space in front of it so that the people pushing and shoving to see it wouldn't damage it. And as for Elizabeth Thompson's *Roll-Call*, that was every artist's dream come true.'

'I don't think I've even heard of that.'

He looked at her suspiciously. Was this another interview question? No doubt it was part of her training to set nervous people at their ease and to draw out what the programme-maker wanted. In this case she was doing it perhaps only to keep the conversation going until somebody more interesting turned up to interrupt them and allow her to escape. Not that he was usually a nervous person – he was an experienced radio broadcaster, used to taking off from a crude question into a detailed and properly illustrated expression of his views – but here the rules were different. He felt it was himself rather than his views that mattered. Was he measuring up to the privilege – the time and attention – being granted him? She had stopped smiling. She even looked a little nervous herself. He remembered her looking like that when Vronsky had been lying on the rug in her flat, her nose a little pinched, the muscles tight around her mouth. He found he was still holding his handkerchief and put it away in his pocket. She was not going to cry this time. Suddenly he felt intensely happy. She did want to hear what he had to say and he wanted to tell it to her. He wanted to tell her all he possibly could, as if he were answering that ultimate Chinese exam question: 'Write down everything you know.'

'She was twenty-seven,' he said. 'A year earlier she'd had her first painting accepted by the RA. A military subject. She was always obsessed with soldiers. It was skyed – hung high up on the wall – but it got good reviews and was bought. Then that winter she began painting *The Roll-Call*. It was a commission for a Mr Galloway of Manchester. Her old headmaster found her suitable models, nearly all ex-soldiers and one of them actually a Crimea veteran. The family doctor took her round the pawnshops and helped her find old uniforms, helmets, haversacks, etc. When the thing was finished it went off to the Academy and was accepted. At the end of April she went in for Varnishing Day. *The Roll-Call* wasn't skyed this time, it was hanging on the line in the second room and there was a crowd of artists in front of it, including the big cheeses – Calderon, Prinsep, du Maurier, Millais – all wanting to meet her. By Monday, when the show opened to the public, Elizabeth Thompson and *The Roll-Call* were famous. Brass rails had been discontinued by this time because they made other artists envious, so they had a policeman instead to keep the viewers from damaging the picture. Then it was taken across to the Palace one night for Queen Victoria to see it and she virtually compelled Mr Galloway to allow her to buy it.'

'What does *The Roll-Call* look like?'

'It's just a row of exhausted, shattered soldiers formed up in the snow after a battle, with the sergeant calling their names to see who's still alive.'

'Any good?'

'Unforgettable. The subject's sentimental, but it's treated very simply, very matter-of-factly.'

'What happened to her afterwards?'

'She had some more successes, then gradually went out of fashion. She married an Irish major called William Butler. He was in hospital recovering from fever after a campaign against the Ashantis. His sister used to read him the papers as he lay in bed and when she read him the news of *The Roll-Call's* success, he said as a joke, "I wonder if Miss Thompson would marry me." But he didn't meet her until two years later and it was another year before they married.'

'He married her for her success?'

'He was successful himself. I think they fell in love. It's hard to tell, of course. They both wrote autobiographies, but hers is very reticent about him and his never mentions her at all. After her pictures went out of fashion, he was more famous than her.'

'A sad story.'

'Is it? I wonder. She was the most popular painter of her day, even if briefly. He took part in wars and adventures all over the Empire and became a general with a knighthood. They had five children. They were both devout Catholics. They died peacefully in their beds.'

'There's still something sad about it. Maybe it's her turning into a wife and mother.'

'They weren't living in two rooms. She liked the social scene. She was a keen hostess. He was a garrison commander in Alexandria, commander of the South-East District in England, Commander-in-Chief in South Africa. They owned a castle in Ireland.'

'You think worldly success makes up for everything?' she said.

The slight tinge of mockery in her voice didn't worry him, as it might have done a few minutes earlier. That was because their relationship had already changed: he felt she was basically sympathetic to him instead of the reverse. He looked past her at the crowd of people talking, laughing, changing places around them. Opinions, he now allowed, were expressions of emotion, they didn't have to be interesting in themselves or even rational.

'Perhaps success is the wrong word,' he said, 'since it's associated with fame and money. Satisfaction. You have to get what you want.'

'And if you don't know what you want?'

'Then you're lost.'

'That's a hard philosophy.'

'Everything's hard when you schematize it, take out the flesh and leave only the skeleton. That's why people's lives look hard – or sad – when you pick them up long afterwards and see them as nothing but a set of dates and events ending in the final date and event. And most of us, of course, don't live by some big, single thing we want, but a whole series of little ones which lead us along and keep us smiling.'

'What about you?'

'Me?'

'What keeps you smiling?'

He might have answered that he hadn't been smiling a lot lately, that he was a poor illustration of his own confident statement, since in the absence of any big thing he was less and less amused by the little things; but though he was prepared to tell her almost everything he knew, he wasn't prepared to include what he knew about himself or might find out in the course of articulating it.

'On the whole I have everything I want already,' he said. 'I lead a selfish life, mostly doing what I like. I'd prefer not to have to write articles, but I like having written them.'

'You live by yourself?'

'Yes.'

'Which you prefer?'

'It seems to suit me. Friends come in from time to time. I'm not a misanthrope. How about you?'

Their relationship had ceased to develop. He had put up a barrier and was now suggesting that they move to another site, but he knew even before she answered that there was no opening in that direction. They were back where they started, with polite, guarded conversation.

'No,' she said. 'On the whole I prefer not to live on my own.'

'Ah.'

He made himself sound non-committal, but he'd become so despondent that he couldn't think of anything else to say and when Jack Dillon emerged from the crowd to ask if they'd had anything to eat, Simon stood up to speak to him. He felt as he sometimes did after a poor broadcast, that he'd lost a battle for self-respect and that he couldn't get away from the battlefield soon enough. While he and Jack reminisced about Cambridge, Michael appeared to take Maria home.

'Goodbye,' she said to Simon and then, showing more kindness than he thought he deserved, 'I wish I could see *The Roll-Call*.'

'It's still tucked away in the Royal Collection,' he said. 'I don't have the entrée there.' And, since she was still looking at him, he added without much conviction, 'But maybe you'd like to look at some contemporary art sometime?'

'Yes, I would. Will you ring me?'

He nodded, confused by the warmth in her voice, then returned to the interrupted conversation with his host.

When Simon left the party not long after Maria, the front door was open and he passed Andrew Mowle coming in.

'Have you just arrived?' Simon asked.

'I thought I saw somebody I knew. Been here some time. Got stuck with a frightful bore in publishing. You have to be nice to these people to keep their ads on the book pages. I'm bloody hungry.'

'The food's downstairs in the kitchen. If there's any left. Delicious.'

It was on the tip of his tongue to ask Andrew if he'd seen Maria, perhaps even to boast of his own success with her, but then he recalled that it was a success which he'd somehow turned into a failure. He let Andrew go, closed the front door and walked down the street towards the main road in search of a taxi. It was chilly, with a brisk wind, but dry. Did she really want him to ring her? He couldn't believe it. She'd surely had ample opportunity to see through him – a good-looking fellow, intelligent enough, charming enough, but altogether too cautious and self-absorbed to be more than superficially alluring to someone as spoilt for choice as her. Frankly, he wouldn't wish himself on her. And yet, and yet . . . she'd asked him to ring her . . . it hadn't sounded merely polite, but as if she meant it. Well, of course, she was trained to sound as if she meant things when she didn't. No doubt she counted on his having lost her phone number. Or on his being too lacklustre to bother. What would be the point, even if he did ring her? Another jolt to his self-esteem? As he'd admitted to himself before, they had no interests in common. Except cats and Tolstoy. And now perhaps Elizabeth Thompson. No, he must have bored her rigid with Elizabeth Thompson. He wouldn't dream of ringing her.

6

I

James was in an unfamiliar supermarket. At home he could have collected the things on his list, written his cheque and been out in half an hour, but here he had to search for every item, continually returning to shelves he had passed, crossing and recrossing the whole shop several times like a cat in a new house. Finally he joined a short queue at the check-out, behind an old man wearing a brightly striped anorak and sandals. He was bronzed and stringy, with a few shreds of white hair clinging to the sides of his scalp and he was talking irritably to himself, complaining about the wait, the slowness of the cashiers and the customers.

'Fucking women,' he said. 'Taking their bloody time. Always in your way.'

His voice was getting louder and people were beginning to stare at him, including a black girl at the next check-out desk.

'What's the matter?' he said, raising his voice still more so that she and everyone else could hear clearly. 'Never seen a white man before?'

Almost before James could begin to wonder whether he should intervene, a tall security guard had materialized beside the man's trolley.

'That's enough of that. We don't want any abusive language here.'

'That's not fucking abusive language. I just asked a question.'

'Either you stop that now or you leave. We don't serve people who use abusive language.'

The security guard was leaning right across the trolley now, speaking into the man's face from a few inches away.

'I can bloody buy my stuff elsewhere.'

'Then you do that. We don't want your sort here.'

'You touch me and I'll fucking hit you.'

'You try it!'

A second guard had appeared on the man's other side and the two guards immediately started removing the supermarket goods from the man's trolley. When it was empty except for his own holdall, they handed him that and marched him briskly to the exit. The whole episode was over in a couple of minutes. All the customers and staff suddenly shared a sense of relief, as if a storm cloud had passed over or a bomb had been defused. The old man's lunatic anger had for the time being magnetized all their frustrations and anxieties, collected them together into a single blob and been swept safely out of the shop. Strangers smiled at one another and helped each other with their trolleys and bags. James felt gratitude and loyalty to the supermarket chain for its efficiency and concern for its customers' welfare. A small victory had been won over chaos and evil.

But driving back along unfamiliar roads to the Rutlands' village, he wondered if the victory wasn't a little suspect. The swiftness of the security guards' action was admirable in its way, but it belonged to a new world that might not be so admirable. It represented a new level of public control which might easily become worse than the disorder it was created to eliminate. The guard had seemed neutral, carrying out as professionally as possible orders he must have been given in advance by the management, but perhaps in other circumstances his action would be equally swift and less defensible. Would he, James, and the other customers have behaved differently in that case? Surely not? Once having accepted the need for the security guard and all he stood for, they left the justification to him and his management. In the end, he decided, as he stopped the car in front of the Rutlands' pseudo-Georgian front door and got out to unload the boot, it was probably only a matter of class. In the old society, James's class had had the mastery without question. If he had been born black or working-class he would surely, from birth onwards, have had this sense of alienation from those with power over him? And didn't the old man's semi-insanity consist precisely in still clinging to an old world, in which colour automatically made him superior?

He found Judy, whom he had joined in the Rutlands' house the day before, cleaning the kitchen. She took her duties as a caretaker seriously.

'The boat gets in at 6.15,' she said. 'I said you'd meet her.'

'No news?'

'No news. So we've got till this evening to decide what we're going to do next.'

'Isn't that up to Susie?'

'I don't think Susie will be in any state to decide anything on her own.'

'There's only one thing to do now and that's bring in the police.'
'What about Tony Cass?' she said.
'What about him?'
'You could consult him, couldn't you?'
'I can't see that it would do any good and it might even make things worse.'

James was not sure why he was so unwilling to bring in Tony Cass. He didn't think it was simply his own pride. He really did feel that in some obscure way Tony would make things worse or perhaps only reveal that they were worse. And that might have been the heart of his unwillingness: a disinclination to be dragged into somebody else's melodrama. Ten days or so had gone by since Susie had last heard from David, but still James felt there must be some simple, everyday explanation.

The afternoon was dry and quite warm, so he sat in the garden under the apple tree where he had sat with Tony and David in the summer, lit his pipe and opened volume one of the *History of the Decline and Fall of the Roman Empire* at the first chapter. He had brought it because he expected to have time on his hands, but Susie's decision to return this evening made it unlikely that he would get any further with it than he had on previous occasions. It was extraordinary that a book he had always meant to read still, in his mid-forties, eluded him. Perhaps he would never read it, just as he might never go to China, Japan, Australia, India. In his early twenties at university everything in the world had seemed available and his life infinitely capacious, but he couldn't seriously convince himself that what he'd failed to achieve in the twenty years that had passed he would somehow achieve in the twenty or thirty that remained. He didn't feel regret so much as surprise. Was it possible that he, James Biggar, the centre of the world, would have experienced so little of the world by the time he died? Was it conceivable that books on his shelves would pass on, unread by him, to his children?

'In the second century of the Christian era, the empire of Rome comprehended the fairest part of the earth, and the most civilized portion of mankind . . .'

But his eyelids soon began to droop and, laying his pipe on the table, slipping down in his chair, he dozed pleasantly until Judy woke him with a cup of tea. Gibbon's pages, open on his knees, had fluttered on to Chapter Three, upbraiding him for the appointment he had yet again missed with them. He read on at random, his brain still sluggish with sleep, a passage about the slave mentality of the ancient Persian:

'The Koran, and the interpreters of that divine book, inculcated to him that the sultan was the descendant of the prophet, and the vicegerent of heaven; that patience was the first virtue of a

Mussulman, and unlimited obedience the great duty of a subject. The minds of the Romans were very differently prepared for slavery. Oppressed beneath the weight of their own corruption and of military violence, they for a long while preserved the sentiments, or at least the ideas of their free-born ancestors. The education of Helvidius and Thrasea, of Tacitus and Pliny, was the same as that of Cato and Cicero. From Grecian philosophy they had imbibed the justest and most liberal notions of the dignity of human nature and the origin of civil society. The history of their own country had taught them to revere a free, a virtuous, and a victorious commonwealth . . .'

Sipping his tea and gazing abstractedly down the garden, James contemplated the strange irony by which Gibbon, writing before the creation of the Second British Empire, was transformed two hundred years later into the train of thought of an obscure fellow countryman who had seen the end of that empire and therefore read fresh meaning into his words. Yet 'the education of Biggar, Rutland and Cass,' he might almost substitute, 'was the same as that of Gibbon.'

'Isn't it time you were going?' asked Judy.

She was sitting, reading her own book, in the chair where David had sat the last time James was here. Her cup of tea stood on the table where David's glass of whisky had stood.

'Yes, it is.'

But James was reluctant to move, to disturb the fascinating concordance of so many different timescales. Like the ghostly images of a multiple photograph, pre-imperial Gibbon hovered behind post-imperial Biggar, republican Cicero behind imperial Pliny, summer David behind autumn Judy, the whisky glass behind the teacup. He closed the book slowly and laid it reverently on the table.

'Okay,' he said, stretching and then getting to his feet.

'What are you going to say to Susie? If you still refuse to consult Tony Cass?'

'I'll think about it as I drive.'

But by the time he met Susie, coming slowly towards him out of Customs, he had only confirmed his decision not to consult Tony. Susie stopped in front of him and grounded her suitcase. James, about to put out his hand, remembered that they were on kissing terms, hesitated, and then, seeing how unhappy she looked, put his hands lightly on her shoulders and kissed her clumsily on the left cheek. She immediately burst into tears and clasped him tightly, pressing her face into his chest and sobbing, while other travellers, staring furtively, walked round them. James was not embarrassed. Susie's misery was so wholehearted that he was at once plunged into the midst of it and cared nothing for what the rest of the world might think. He held her and patted her until she recovered her self-control and stopped crying, then he picked up her suitcase and led her gently by the hand to the car park.

On the way back she told him all that she'd been able to find out. David had stayed at his hotel for one night and checked out the next day. The hotel manager thought that a note for him had been handed in that morning, but he had no idea who had brought it. He hadn't seen David with anyone. He had dined alone the previous evening and left the hotel alone. The manager shrugged his shoulders and looked at Susie with vague sympathy but no sense of involvement. He was no more responsible for lost guests than for their lost possessions. In future he would probably put a notice saying as much behind the reception desk.

Without going to the police, there was little Susie could do. She remained in the hotel and visited all the other local hotels to see if David had checked in there; she walked about the town, looking in cafés and restaurants; she went out along the causeway to the small harbour and asked after him there: all without success. Eventually she had simply haunted the town, trudging wearily from street to street, attending the market in the square, sitting on walls or in cafés watching every passer-by, sometimes imagining she saw him and then realizing it was only a stranger with a vaguely similar build or way of walking. It was quite a small town and she didn't think that if he was there she could have missed seeing him, unless he was deliberately hiding from her.

'You don't think he was?' asked James.

'Of course not.'

'Then what do you think?'

But that was more than she wished to reveal, perhaps even to herself. It came down, after all, didn't it, to two equally unpleasant alternatives? David had disappeared against his will – kidnapped or murdered – or on purpose, which meant he wanted to leave Susie and cared nothing for her feelings.

'What do you think?' she asked.

James was struck again by how alike he and Susie were – not, of course, in their tastes or their education or in anything which would show in the ordinary course of their ordinary lives, but in their dislike of facing unpleasant facts when life ceased to be ordinary and became potentially disastrous. Perhaps it was only extraordinary people who were not like Susie and himself in this. The natural instinct was to hope for the best, and if you couldn't quite manage hope, then to pretend for the best. He thought of that memorable passage from Gibbon: a whole nation – or at least the educated, cultivated elite of a nation – could go on believing in their freedom, old-world virtues and liberal values, when all the facts should have told them that they were slaves and that their beloved city and empire were in the grip of madmen, cynics and bullies. And thinking of that, he decided for some reason that he would enlist Tony's help, whatever it might cost his pride.

He didn't tell Susie that Tony had been interested in David's relationship with Rimington, but only that since Tony worked in the Foreign Office he might be able to advise them what to do next. The idea immediately gave Susie fresh hope. James felt pangs of envy, since it was clear that Susie was now preparing to transfer all her emotional dependence from himself to Tony. It was absurd that, having not wanted to become involved in the first place, he now felt aggrieved with Susie for so ruthlessly casting him off and turning to a stronger, better man; but it was as if he had been on the brink of becoming someone stronger and better himself and was now relegated to his old position at the edge of things.

While Judy and Susie were putting supper on the table, he rang Tony at his home.

'I'm speaking from David Rutland's house.'

'What are you doing there?'

James started to explain, but Tony cut him short.

'Right! Okay. We'll meet tomorrow.'

'I shan't be in town till the day after.'

'Don't give me that! I suggest the Hayward Gallery. Half one on the top floor.'

'Look, do you know anything, Tony? I'd like to set Susie's mind at rest.'

'Just tell her not to worry.'

'You mean you've got things under control?'

James didn't know what he meant by that or what he supposed Tony would think it meant, but he found himself automatically falling into this vaguely conspiratorial bureau-speak, as if he were already corrupted by the very fact of throwing himself on Tony's mercy.

'Nil desperandum!' said Tony and put the phone down.

II

Rain, driven by a cold wind, scoured the terraces and walkways and formed puddles in the depressions of unevenly laid flagstones. On the upper parts of the concrete buildings there were dark stains spreading raggedly down the walls. James hated the whole South Bank area even in good weather. To him it represented the unacceptable face of post-war socialism, a dour, joyless environment which contrived to suggest universal contempt – contempt for the arts it housed, for the historic city and river it disfigured, above all for the people it was supposed to serve. People who came here were made to feel their insignificance and isolation, their flesh-and-blood vulnerability next to these abrasive surfaces, their exposure not just to the natural elements, but to those elements exaggerated by bare spaces and buildings that funnelled the wind. Perhaps, once they got inside the buildings, people could recover in music, plays or paintings their sense of themselves and of a world which was not joyless and forbidding, but coming out they were exposed once more to the artificial wilderness and this time reminded that they were unconsidered particles of a crowd, fighting their way in competition with their fellows to car parks, buses or trains.

There were two exhibitions in the Hayward Gallery, when James, chilled and irritable, finally pushed through the heavy, ostentatiously brutal gun-metal doors. He was ridiculously early as usual and he decided to spend the spare half hour or so seeing the big retrospective of Camille Pissarro's work downstairs. He didn't often look at pictures and he had Pissarro docketed as one of the minor Impressionists. Stopping to pass his wet umbrella across the counter to the cloakroom attendant, he found himself beside a board displaying reviews of the exhibitions and began to read Simon Carter's from the *Equalizer*. Headed 'True Socialist, Good Man', it was a paean of praise for Pissarro. According to Carter, his landscapes revealed the sincerity, idealism and modesty of the man, who was always ready to teach what he knew and learn what he did not, remained true to his socialist principles throughout his life and was besides a faithful husband, kind father and loyal friend, but never rich and successful as Monet and Renoir became. 'Pissarro's art has been consistently underrated,' wrote Carter, 'but now all the evidence we need is before us and the proof is there. It is possible for a thoroughly good man to be also a great artist.'

Eager to test this opinion for himself, James hurried through into the galleries. At first he was disappointed. These were pleasant enough landscapes, but ordinary. Gradually, though, he thought he saw the point. Pissarro's was an ideal world at the same time as an ordinary and credible one. 'Ideal' was too grand a word. 'Dignified' might be better. It was a world to which its dignity had been restored. The skill and labour of the artist were part of this dignity, so were the unsentimentalized and individualized peasants who inhabited this landscape not as film extras but almost as co-workers with the artist. They were responsible for the real thing, he for its understanding. Carter was right, this was true socialism demonstrated visually in paint, instead of conceptually in words.

James remembered a little incident related by William Butler in his autobiography. Butler, in the year 1864, when he was still a young subaltern, had visited the battlefield of Waterloo on foot and put up one night in a cottage at Frasnes. He had shared his supper with the head of the village commune, who at the end of the meal had carefully turned the plate of peaches and grapes in front of him and presented it to Butler so that he should have the largest peach.

'It was a simple thing,' wrote Butler at the end of his life, 'but I have never forgotten it. Civility goes a long way, they say; in the case of my peasant friend at Frasnes it has gone more than forty years. Liberty, equality, fraternity, and the greatest of these is fraternity; and perhaps if people practised it more frequently they need not have troubled themselves so much about the other two.' Fraternity was the essence of Pissarro's painting.

James looked at his watch. It was 1.40, he was ten minutes late for his appointment. He found the stairs and ran up them two at a time to the top floor. There were not many visitors to this exhibition and James soon spotted Tony Cass in front of a huge painting of a Scottish landscape. Tony was dressed in a formal suit and tie. James couldn't remember having seen him like that before – he always thought of him as an essentially outdoor type.

'John Buchan,' said Tony, barely acknowledging James's arrival. James wondered if this was a code to which he should reply 'Thirty-nine Steps.' He was still breathing heavily from the fifty steps he had just climbed too fast. He realized that Tony was referring to the painting. It looked thin and scratchily painted after Pissarro and had the insubstantial two-dimensionality of a photograph – an instant click of the tourist's lens instead of the lived-in time and space of Pissarro's landscapes. In the foreground, seen from behind, two men in khaki green tweeds and thick stockings were lying on their stomachs on the top of a grassy bank, while in the middle distance, against layers of bare green hills, a herd of deer ran down a brown slope. The painting was called *Alastair's Day: 2nd Stalk*.

'You like?' asked Tony.

'Not much, after what's downstairs,' said James.

'My favourite contemporary painter,' said Tony, as if he was making a pre-emptive bid at bridge and didn't expect any further opposition.

'Susie is in a state of near-hysteria,' said James. 'Do you know what's going on?'

'I don't think anybody does,' said Tony. 'There are at least three angles to this business, probably four or five. Nobody is seeing the whole picture. My difficulty is that it's not officially my section.'

'Do you know where David is?'

'We're pretty sure he's still with Rimington. The problem is that Rimington's moved – or been moved – and we're still working on his new whereabouts.'

'Why on earth hasn't he been in touch with Susie?'

'Rimington is trying to keep out of touch with people, so if David's with him, he's got no option but to do what Rimington wants.'

'Why is David with him anyway?'

'I've no idea.'

'Really?'

'Really. I assume it's because they're old friends and Rimington wants David's help in some way. If you remember, I asked you to sound David out about that some time ago and you were very hoity-toity.'

'But why is David spending all this time with him? He must be aware of the state Susie would be in by now.'

'I don't know that either. Perhaps he's under some form of duress. Unless he's just permanently smashed with alcohol.'

'Are you sure he's still alive?'

Tony looked round nervously. There was a black security guard a few yards away, but he seemed to be half asleep on his chair. Tony walked away round the screen in the centre of the gallery, James following him, and stopped in front of an underwater painting of fish. A small squad of silver and black barracuda occupied the middle of the picture above blurred sand and weed. They looked to be about to swoop on – or rather torpedo from underneath – a shoal of tuna crossing the top of the painting from the opposite direction.

'Your voice is penetrating,' said Tony. 'Probably an asset in your profession, but in the present circumstances a disadvantage.'

'I'm sorry. I'm not used to these sort of games.'

'It depends what you mean by "games".'

'Quite honestly, I find the whole thing unreal.'

'You live in a very sheltered part of the world.'

'I'm glad I do.'

'Most people don't.'

'All right, but most people in this country do.'

'Most likely because a few people play what you call "games" on their behalf.'

'It sounds more and more like John Buchan.'

'Buchan was not an entirely silly writer,' said Tony. 'In fact he had more experience of politics and of how things actually work than most writers.'

'You haven't answered my question about David.'

'As far as I know, the answer is yes.'

'He is still alive?'

'We hope so.'

'Isn't it time to get in touch with the French police?'

'You must be joking.'

'I'm certainly not joking,' said James, becoming angry. 'As far as I'm concerned, when somebody disappears, you ask the police to find them. I've only not done that so far because I knew you were involved.'

'If anybody's responsible for all this, it's almost certainly the French.'

'Responsible for David's disappearance?'

'For Rimington's. I've told you that I don't know what David's part in the affair is, but I can only presume that it's intimately connected with Rimington's. Rimington disappears because the French want him to. David also disappears – you can add one and one as well as I can.'

'And this is all connected with Balunda?'

'What else?'

'But why are we up against the French? I thought we were partners in the Common Market.'

'Of a sort. We've never been partners in Africa, but always bitter rivals.'

'Weren't we secret partners in the Suez debacle?'

'True, but that was a temporary coincidence of interests and besides, although Egypt is technically part of Africa, it must really be counted part of the Middle East, to which different rules apply.'

'Games again.'

'It's your word,' said Tony. 'But all right. International politics is all games, in the sense that it's concerned with competition and that there are certain rules. What the devil do you think the Empire was, if not our winnings from the last great Imperial Cup Final? Spain, Portugal and Holland were more or less eliminated in the seventeenth century. The eighteenth century saw the final between Britain and France. We won in Canada, won again in India. The French managed to detach the United States from us as some sort of revenge, without much advantage, other than moral, to themselves. The deciding match was played at Waterloo and we spent the remainder of the nineteenth century picking up our reward in India, South-East Asia, Australasia, China, South America and above all Africa. Don't imagine that the French have forgotten or forgiven!'

'We came to their rescue in two world wars.'

'How would you feel about that if you were a Frenchman?'

'But now we're both out of the Cup Final. We have no empires and we're both satellites of the United States.'

'Second-class powers don't stop being competitive any more than second-class people do. They just conduct their rivalry at a second-class level. The Caribbean, Canada and South America have more or less passed into the US Empire. So have the Pacific, Japan, parts of South-East Asia and Pakistan. China has re-established its independence. The Middle East, India and to some extent Africa are still being contended for between the Soviet Union and the US, but there remain areas of Africa where the British and French can continue their second-class competition and Balunda is one of them.'

'It all sounds very depressing,' said James.

'I don't see why. It's just the facts of international life. The facts of history.'

'It's so negative. And unlike ordinary games these games of international politics destroy people's lives.'

'I think your metaphor breaks down there. We have to play them in order to defend our own lives and interests. The reason you're able to sit quietly at home and bury your head in the sand is that other people are occupying themselves with your defence in many different ways.'

James had hardly looked at Tony through this conversation. His eyes had been fixed on the painting in front of them and it was almost as if he had witnessed the six barracuda snapping and mauling their way through the defenceless shoal above them. It was a relief to realize that they had not moved and that, whatever alarming vistas Tony had opened up, he, James, had not moved either. Other visitors were walking round the gallery quite unconcerned, peering and occasionally murmuring to each other, wrapped round with their own private concerns. History, past, present or to come, mattered little more to them than the fact that there had once been an ice age or that the sun would one day burn itself out. Tony and this cold-fish contemporary painter he admired might try to rattle people, but the essential warmth and goodness of humanity persisted. Downstairs was Pissarro. William Butler had survived all his adventures and ordeals and died sane and kindly disposed to his fellow men. Fraternity was the watchword. He turned to look at Tony and found him smiling.

'What I find so odd about you, James,' he said, 'is that it's your job – one of your jobs – to read the news. Don't you believe a word of what you read? Do you think it's all pure entertainment, pure John Buchan?'

James refused to be drawn. 'What I'm concerned about,' he said, 'is how I'm to comfort Susie.'

'You're quite right,' said Tony. 'We have tended to leave Susie's feelings out of account.'

James would like to have protested about that 'we', but he was tired of being lectured and used as a sparring partner, so he only nodded.

'Therefore I think it best,' Tony continued, 'if you do everything you can to calm her down and let her see things in the most reassuring light. David's doing a job, connected with Rimington. Rimington's having to lie low at the moment, so David is too. There are wheels within wheels and one of the wheels, you can tell her, is the FO. The best thing she can do is to simply sit back quietly and wait to be contacted, either by us or by David himself. She'll have to say something to the neighbours and certainly to her husband's partners. She'd better say that he's stayed in France for a particular course of treatment. They'll know David, they'll understand or think they understand exactly what she means and won't want to embarrass her by discussing it. Of course she will be embarrassed by having to mention it at all, but if you stress that that's my advice, I'm sure she'll accept it as the official version and indeed as David's own preferred version for the time being.'

'And the children?'

'Won't be home from school for another month or more. Plenty of time to decide what to tell the children.'

'But isn't all this lies?'

'Since we don't know the exact truth, how can we know what's lies and what isn't?'

'It's suggesting that you do know the exact truth.'

'If you can think of a better temporary solution, let's have it!'

James couldn't and he very much didn't want the barracuda to start moving again. There was no point in worrying Susie unnecessarily. Since the truth might be good or bad, why insist that it might be bad?

'I'll try something along those lines,' he said, 'but I shall tell her that it comes from you and that I don't necessarily believe every word of it.'

'Put the blame on me, by all means!'

'I hope there won't be any blame,' said James severely.

'Better leave separately,' said Tony, with the suspicion of a smile, as if he was pretending to play spies for James's benefit. 'Why don't you have a look at the rest of these for ten minutes or so? There's a character in one of the earlier paintings that looks quite like Ruggles in his better days. See if you can spot it!'

James couldn't; and went back to Pissarro, to cleanse his mind of all the various kinds of pollution he felt he'd been submitted to.

7

'I've done nothing about bringing you abreast of contemporary art.'
'I was afraid you'd lost my phone number.'
'I wondered if, instead of the art, you'd come and have supper. Two or three friends. I can't fit more round my table. One of them might well be an artist, so you'd get the art at one remove, as it were.'
'I'd love to, but I tend to be busy in the evenings.'
'All this week?'
'Thursday's free.'
'Make it Thursday, then. Do you want to bring a friend of your own?'
'He's away.'
'Ah. Then it'll just be you.'

Simon had planned nothing before ringing Maria on a sudden whim and had only mentioned other guests in order not to frighten her off with the prospect of a *tête-à-tête*. Not that he meant to cheat. He had promised her an artist and she should have one. Immediately he'd finished speaking to Maria, he rang Flora Decoud, a distinguished though not widely known painter of abstracts, who was in her early sixties. Flora agreed to come on Thursday and he next tried a literary couple of his acquaintance. They were not free and somewhat at random he rang the Oswalds, near neighbours who were active in local conservation and to whom he was in debt for several dinners. He also remembered that they went in for Burmese cats. The Oswalds accepted and Simon now found himself in difficulty. He needed a single man, but virtually all his friends were married. Another couple would not only leave the numbers still uneven but make the party up to seven, which was one too many for the size of his table. Then he remembered Andrew Mowle's curious interest in Maria. He had never entertained his literary editor, indeed only really knew him in the office, but he thought he recalled that he and his wife were more or less separated. If Andrew came on his own, everything would work out right. He rang the *Equalizer* and spoke to Andrew, saying nothing about Maria, since he wanted to keep her as a surprise.

'Okay,' said Andrew. 'Yes, I'd like that. What's your address?' Simon gave it to him and added: 'Will you both come?'

'I'll see what Liz thinks and ring you back.'

He didn't ring back until Thursday morning, to say that he would be bringing his wife, who was particularly anxious to meet Simon. Simon put the phone down and groaned. Not only had he asked too many people, most of whom were only acquaintances rather than friends, but he remembered now that Andrew's wife ran an art gallery which he seldom visited since he didn't care for her taste in art. He thought of ringing them all and cancelling the whole affair. He even got so far as to dial the Oswalds' number. They were out. He accepted his fate, made a shopping list and went out to buy the things on it.

Maria had said Michael was away, but in fact they had split up soon after the Dillons' party. She had liked him in the first place because he reminded her physically of the guinea pigs she'd kept as a child, but he'd soon proved almost as limited in character as they were. Sex and food were the guinea pigs' exclusive interests; Michael shared those interests but he was otherwise entirely absorbed in making TV documentaries. Maria's own interest in news did not extend to the slow, undramatic processes of ordinary human life. Events, sudden crises excited her and she loved fiction for the way it speeded up the processes and brought them to a head within a definite span of pages. Not that she particularly sought crises in her own life. On the contrary, she preferred to be in control of things, but there was a part of her which enjoyed the unpredictable and almost unconsciously seized opportunities for change. Ever since her first meeting with Simon Carter at the time of Vronsky's accident she had begun to be bored with Michael. She wasn't sure that she necessarily wanted Simon to take his place, but after their second meeting at the Dillons' party she was sufficiently intrigued by Simon to hope that he would ring her up. When at first he didn't she felt vaguely depressed – not as if her life were ruined, but as if a possible treat had failed to materialize – and she had to admit that his invitation lifted her spirits.

His address was only a few streets away and when he had rung off she found the place on the map and sat for some time imagining herself already going there, ringing his doorbell, seeing his face again. Of course she wasn't in love with him, but she looked forward to learning more about him, seeing the inside of his flat, even meeting his friends. Inside his own world, on his home ground, he would no doubt be more relaxed, easier to understand and assess.

She liked the idea of assessing him, as one might a character in a novel whom the author had so far played close to the chest. Simon looked handsome and dashing enough, with an appealing spike of melancholy – a male lead in the Jeremy Irons mould – but if he was attracted to her, as surely he must be since he'd taken the trouble to ring her, his approach was still very measured. This was no Romeo, leaping the garden wall and addressing passionate arias to her bedroom balcony. He didn't even propose to see her alone, but was making sure their third meeting, like their second, would occur in full view of witnesses.

On the other hand, their first two meetings had been entirely due to chance. Simon couldn't rely on their meeting by chance again, and was obviously inviting the friends so as not to force the situation. When he'd talked about Elizabeth Thompson's *The Roll-Call*, the chief impression he'd given had been of the ease and naturalness of its phenomenal success. For two people to have a successful relationship, it was no doubt essential for them to feel the same ease and naturalness. William Butler had only to hear about Miss Thompson's success to remark idly that she might marry him. And eventually she had. The more Maria recalled what Simon had said that night, the more she read into it a meaning she hadn't noticed at the time. Perhaps he hadn't either. The inevitable chemistry, the steady flow of their relationship produced this meaning as it had produced the conversation, the text that contained it. So that the way Simon was organizing this meeting was probably part of the same process, whether consciously on his part or not. She hoped, however, that it was conscious. She hoped he knew what he was doing because although she disliked brash and crudely self-assertive men she didn't fancy naive ones either.

One of the news items she had to introduce that evening was a report from Balunda. A new power figure had emerged there, the guerrilla leader who had swept the dictator, Marius Nakimbi, from power and finally dislodged his corrupt and vicious army. Maria had passed on to Michael the message about arranging an interview with Nakimbi and wondered now whether he had done anything about it. It didn't matter to her either way, but it was odd after almost two years of always knowing exactly where Michael was and what he was doing, to be so completely cut off. She didn't miss Michael personally so much as his place in her life. She had reduced her establishment, was temporarily closer to Vronsky than to any single person in the world. She was fond of her parents and they doted on her, but they lived in Cornwall and she only visited them two or three times a year. She had no brothers or sisters and her school friends had all more or less dropped her since she became a newscaster – conspicuous success cut people off as effectively as conspicuous failure. She had endless acquaintances and knew any number of people who would have liked to start being her friends immediately, but her close relationship with Michael had kept them at a distance. Leaving the studio, smiling goodnight to the rest of the staff on duty, she felt momentary self-pity; who really loved her except Vronsky?

But as soon as she'd left the studio and glanced in the mirror before putting on her coat, she became cheerful again. Her own face pleased her as it pleased others. It was a cheerful face – smiling was more natural to it than solemnity or misery – and though she had sometimes as a child wanted to be able to look tragic, she had long since accepted that she was not the type. The taxi driver waiting to take her home received her with appreciation and as she settled back and the car moved out into the night streets, she remembered that no accounts could be drawn up or identity crises indulged in until after Thursday. When she arrived home she was almost sorry she wasn't paying for the taxi; she would have liked to give the driver a large tip. Then, standing on the pavement getting her door-key out of her bag, she thought that she could perfectly well give him one anyway, but he was already driving away. Inside the flat, she picked up Vronsky and hugged him with absurd over-enthusiasm, as if something wonderful had happened to her.

She had meant to be about half an hour late for Simon's supper party, but although her whole day had been in some sense directed towards the moment at which she could leave so as to arrive neither too early nor too late, she found herself indecisive about what to wear. The blue-striped jersey dress with a vaguely nautical look which she had originally chosen suddenly seemed too countrified and open-air for a winter evening in London and she changed into a severe white blouse and black skirt. That also dissatisfied her, but she tried to pretend her decision was irrevocable and fussed about looking for a suitable handbag until it was already after the time she'd meant to get there. Then she went back to the bedroom and put on the nautical dress again, this time with a belt. That seemed an improvement and she left the flat almost at once, before she could fall into doubts again. It took her less than five minutes to reach Simon's address.

'Don't tell me you got held up in the traffic!' he said, opening the front door.

'No, I'm just late. Sorry.' she said.

'I'd almost decided that you weren't coming at all. However, you're not the last,' he said, standing aside to let her past him into the hall, 'but I really wish . . .'

She crossed the doormat and her shoes clattered on the chess-board floor of the large hall. She turned to look at him as he closed the door. He was dressed casually in a sweater, open-necked shirt and flannel trousers, all in shades of grey, but the newness of the clothes and his tall, straight figure made an almost formal impression. She remembered the elegant jacket he had sacrificed for Vronsky. He was a bit of a dandy, she decided with approval.

'I really wish,' he continued, 'that I hadn't gone and invited all those others.'

He was looking at her with an equivocal expression, as if he might be serious or joking.

'Why do you wish that?' she asked, looking straight at him, keeping her voice neutral and feeling that what she said was hardly spoken by her own will, but belonged to an established litany.

'I don't seem to be able to keep my mind on the important things,' he said. 'Cooking, serving the drinks, making conversation.'

'Why should that be?'

'I ask myself. Usually I'm a relaxed sort of host. That might surprise you, considering how awkward I was the other night.'

'Were you?'

'Do you imagine I always orate in that tedious way? Very embarrassing in retrospect.'

'I enjoyed listening to you. What you told me about the Butlers was all quite new to me. I've thought about them a lot since. I think you're right. They must have had a happy life.'

He was smiling broadly, as if he too recognized that the Butlers had been transformed into a secret code, known only to them.

'But I was afraid if I'd asked you on your own, you wouldn't have come,' he said, joining her at the foot of the stairs.

'Would it have been unsafe?'

'You might have had to put up with another monologue.'

'I dare say you've got other subjects up your sleeve.'

'I've never met anyone as beautiful as you. All other subjects have gone out of my head. And I don't want to share you with other people.'

She continued to look at him, but didn't reply. Her skin felt suffused with blood, sensitive all over. She was drowsy, as if she'd already eaten a large meal and drunk a lot of wine with it, and he looked flushed and heavy-lidded, as if he were in the same state. He moved very slowly towards her and they kissed. The whole thing seemed to have been rehearsed or at least foreseen. It was what they should have done last time they met, but for some reason postponed. It made no difference. In retrospect, the time between had been wiped out. They had lived across a bridge, or over the dots on a page or the space of a scene change in a play, so that the closing of Jack Dillon's door in SW4 was the opening of Simon's in W11.

After a while, without saying anything, but holding each other round the waist as if this scene too had been rehearsed many times, they went up the stairs — two storeys — to Simon's flat.

'We could go out and leave them to eat the dinner on their own,' said Simon in a low voice, as they reached his door.

'It's more fun like this,' she said.

'You're right,' he said. 'It's enormous fun like this.'

The three other guests already sitting with their drinks in Simon's small sitting room didn't seem to have noticed that their host had been absent for hours. Perhaps in their time it had only been minutes. Nick and Mary Oswald, trim, bright-eyed people who must either have been cousins or had grown to look like one another, greeted Maria almost as royalty, both rising to shake her hand and making little bows as they did so. Flora Decoud was a large, blowsy woman with a wide mouth that drooped at one side. She didn't get up, but nodded in an offhand way to Maria, stubbed out her cigarette and immediately lit another.

'Flora is the painter I promised you,' said Simon as he poured out a glass of white wine for Maria. 'England's best.'

'Am I England's?' said Flora. 'I won't argue about the best, either way, because that means nothing, but my father was born in Brazil of French extraction and my mother was Scottish.'

'You're England's now,' said Simon. 'We're not fussy about extractions.'

'I went to school in England,' said Flora.

'That clinches it,' said Mary Oswald. 'An English education makes you really English.'

'Would you count President Nakimbi as English, then?' asked Maria innocently, more to convince herself that she was still capable of ordinary conversation than to be argumentative.

'That appalling black Hitler? No, I wouldn't.'

'I'm sure he went to an English school. Haileybury, was it? Or Harrow?'

'No, I certainly wouldn't count him,' said Mary Oswald rather desperately, unable to say that she had of course meant only white people educated in England, but clearly implying that Maria had cheated in some way.

'Didn't you tell us you'd once been to Balunda, Simon?' asked her husband, diverting the conversation. 'Did you meet Nakimbi?'

'I didn't,' said Simon. 'I had a pleasant time in Balunda, bathing, underwater fishing, playing tennis, drinking long cool drinks and I didn't pay much attention to politics. I probably let the side down. Chap in the area next to mine was frightfully conscientious, discovered a whole lot of voting frauds and gave the local politicians quite a headache. I'm sure my area was all one voting fraud, but I didn't inquire too closely.'

'That wasn't very British of you,' said Flora, holding out her glass for a refill.

'No, I was trying not to be too British at that stage,' said Simon.

His voice was a little too loud and he suddenly looked across at Maria and spilled some of the wine he was pouring into Flora's glass.

'Sorry,' he said, but he sounded delighted and couldn't help smiling.

Maria smiled too and half raised her glass to him. That seemed to recall him to his duties and he frowned.

'Look,' he said, 'I don't know what's happened to the others, but if we don't eat soon, the joint will be ruined. Shall we sit down and start?'

He went out to the kitchen and returned with a tray of avocados, while the rest of them gathered round the table. He had written their names on slips of paper to show their places, but he wouldn't let them sit down until he had switched some of the names round. Maria, who had been placed on his right, was now at the other end of the table facing him. For a moment she wondered why he no longer wanted to sit next to her and then understood that it would have been impossible in their state of mutal excitement. Sitting at the ends of the table they became, as it were, the host and hostess, and of course this was their new status. What a clever, sensitive, quick man he was! Instead of resenting it, as she had when he had taken charge of Vronsky's rescue, her happiness increased almost beyond bounds, so that when Flora said, 'Fancy not wanting to sit next to you and putting me there instead!' Maria had to stop herself laughing by taking a gulp of wine. It nearly choked her. Flora patted her vigorously on the back and they sat down.

'Tell me who all the pictures are by,' said Maria, looking round the room for the first time and seeing that, apart from the bookshelf along one wall, virtually every available space on the walls was covered with paintings or drawings.

'What an order!' said Flora.

'I'm sorry. I didn't mean to make it sound like an order.'

'I think I'll leave the job to Simon. What does a man collect pictures for, except to show them to his lady-friends?'

'That's unfair. He's very keen on contemporary art.'

'Of course he is. He's very keen on ladies too. His interests rub off on one another.'

'He doesn't strike me as a ladies' man.'

'In my experience there are two kinds of ladies'men. The cats – who pursue. And the spiders – who wait at the corners of their webs.'

'You see Simon as a spider?'

'Don't misunderstand me. I'm an arachnophile myself.'

Maria was not sure how to take Flora's remarks. She smiled as she spoke and seemed perfectly relaxed and detached, but everything she said might have had an edge of hostility in a different tone of voice.

'Are there any of your pictures here?'
'Not here exactly. In the bedroom.'
Again she smiled, expansively, leaving her meaning – which might have been just the surface meaning of the words – unclear.
'What sort of pictures are they?'
'Ask Simon! He's the critic. Or better still, look at them and decide for yourself!'
'I mean are they abstract or . . .?'
'Representational?'
'Yes.'
'Representational. But many people see them as abstract.'
The constant ambiguity must be deliberate. If so, Maria decided, it was irritating and meant to irritate. She stopped asking questions and waited for Flora to initiate a topic of her own. Flora applied herself to finishing her avocado. From the other end of the table Simon looked at Maria with half-closed eyes and a broad grin, then turned back to Nick Oswald who, with interjections from his wife – sitting on Simon's right where Maria should have been – was describing their summer holiday in Egypt. The bell rang and Simon, leaving Nick to fill up the glasses, went downstairs to answer the door.
'Simon tells me you have a Burmese cat,' said Mary Oswald to Maria.
'Yes, that's how we met. My cat was hit by a car and he helped me take him to the vet.'
'We have a pair. Both females, though they've been spayed. Terrible adventurers, always getting into trouble, but they're such beautiful, darling creatures. Is yours a brown or a blue, or one of the more recherché varieties?'
'Vronsky is brown. What are yours?'
'Both blue. Ours are called Sonia and Stella. Did you know they were invented at Harvard?'
'No.'
'Invented is perhaps not quite the right word,' said Nick Oswald, giving the impression that he always intervened at this point in a well-practised double act. 'Somebody bought a small hybrid brown cat back from South-East Asia to America and by a process of controlled cross-breeding they arrived at the Burmese.'
'Could it be done with humans?' asked Maria.
'In theory,' said Nick Oswald, 'but cats, of course, are fast breeders. With humans, it would take too long to go through all the necessary generations.'
'Presumably the original humans were black,' said Flora, 'if Dr Leakey was right in believing they lived in the Rift Valley.'
Simon entered, preceded by his missing guests. The first was a small, pretty, fair-haired woman, the second a slight angular man

with an over-large head – or perhaps it was only that his hair was so thick and long. He had a sharp, nervous face, with an almost aquiline nose. Simon introduced them as Liz and Andrew Mowle. He gave Liz the place to the left of his own chair and directed Andrew to sit next to Maria. Both newcomers had looked at Maria with almost comical astonishment as if they could hardly believe she was real, but Andrew sat down on her left without saying anything. In her new capacity as hostess, Maria said brightly:

'I've only just got here myself, though I live round the corner. Did you have far to come?'

'We thought you weren't coming at all,' said Flora, lighting a cigarette and leaning her arms on the table. 'Which of you made the other late?'

Andrew Mowle seemed incapable of speech. He picked up his glass, found it empty and looked round for the bottle.

'Let me guess!' said Flora. 'I think it was you. You stayed late at the office and then insisted on having a bath when you got home. Your poor wife was nearly beside herself, but you were adamant.'

Andrew shook his head, but still failed to speak.

'Adamant,' repeated Flora with relish.

'No,' said Andrew, in a low, half-strangled voice, like a boy justifying himself to a nagging schoolmistress. 'We ran out of fuel.'

'Whose fault was that?' asked Flora.

'Please can I have a drink?' said Andrew to Simon, waving his glass and giving off a distinct smell of petrol as proof of his excuse.

'Aren't you responsible for the car?' asked Flora, as Simon filled Andrew's glass.

'Not really,' said Andrew, still subdued, fidgeting slightly as he waited to repossess his glass.

'Are you the car person, then?' said Nick Oswald to Liz. He was squeezed tightly, because the table was too small, between her and Flora.

'Not exactly,' said Liz. She too seemed distracted and not entirely in command of her voice.

'Well!' said Flora triumphantly. 'We'll have to get to the bottom of this. Who is the car person in this set-up?'

The way she said it made Nick Oswald's awkward phrase sound like a single word with shady associations – carpetbagger, cardsharper, scarper, shirker.

Maria began to suspect that the source of the Mowles' confusion was that they had quarrelled. Conscious of her own unassailable happiness, she felt responsible for their welfare.

'It's bad enough to run out of petrol,' she said. 'I don't see why they should have to be interrogated as well. Why don't we let them eat their first course in peace, since we were so rude as to start without them?'

Liz looked across at her gratefully, but Andrew hardly seemed to have noticed.

'Are you Simon's editor?' asked Flora, leaning further across the table towards Andrew.

'Yes I am.'

'Why don't you give him more space?'

'Our space is very limited.'

'Art has to be noticed to exist. Otherwise it's just masturbation.'

Andrew finished the wine in his glass. It seemed to be reviving him. He glanced at Maria and smiled briefly, then picked up his spoon and dug into his avocado.

'Yes,' he said, 'I agree with you.' He ate a spoonful of avocado and dug out another.

'Art,' he went on, 'is really a communal activity. That's to say, the community wants a certain amount of art and particular members of the community — those with a talent in that direction — specialize in providing it. The difficulty starts when artists become too specialized, when they begin to see art as a separate activity, not tied to the community or the community's needs. The community loses track of what the artist is trying to do and the artist loses track too, because he or she no longer has any valid criteria in other people's judgments. But I'm not sure that masturbation makes a good comparison. After all, that's a simple action with a simple end in view and gives momentary pleasure or relief to the operator, whereas you can't say that of isolationist art. Art has to be noticed, as you say. If nobody notices it, it doesn't even give pleasure to the artist. It's a mess.'

Andrew abandoned his avocado and looked around for more wine. Maria glanced up the table and caught Simon's eye, referring it to Andrew's glass. Simon brought him the bottle and began to clear the plates.

'I don't agree,' said Flora, 'that art is a communal activity. You're thinking of primitive art in tribal societies. In a sophisticated society such as ours, the artist is essentially a loner and usually ahead of the public. The public, therefore, needs guidance and education and the artist needs the support of enlightened people and institutions.'

'I'm not sympathetic to elitist art,' said Andrew and, abruptly ignoring Flora, asked Maria: 'Isn't Michael Arley a friend of yours?'

'Yes,' she said, since that seemed the simplest answer. 'Do you know him?'

'I'm making a programme with him. A series of programmes about the Third World.'

'I remember he mentioned it.'

'*Latitudes South* is the working title.'

He was looking at her eagerly, as if it was somehow important to him that she should have known of the title.

'I don't think I ever heard what the title was.'

She spoke coldly, wanting to keep him at a distance, but he either didn't notice or refused to be discouraged, leaning towards her and speaking rapidly and excitedly.

'I thought of calling it *The World Out There*, he said. 'Suggesting our own insularity, the way we've lost interest in those places, although we so recently treated them as ours, to do what we wanted with. Not just Africa. We're also including the Caribbean and the Far East – Singapore, Malaya, Burma.'

'There must be a title in Conrad,' said Maria, leaning back and glancing at Flora, to try to bring her into the conversation. But Flora was talking to Nick Oswald.

'No, not Conrad at any price,' said Andrew. 'People always want to read Africa as the heart of darkness. It suits their notions of recidivism and despair. Cannibals and voodoo. The whole point of this series is to open people's eyes to the positive side of post-colonialism. That's why I wanted *The World Out There*. It gives the sense of opening out, of a new sort of exploration, not only all of us finding out what they're up to in the ex-colonies, but all of them discovering what they can do, politically, socially, industrially, agriculturally. A plural world with possibilities way beyond this century's East-West obsession.'

'Why don't you call it that, then?'

'Michael was against it.'

'He likes to have his own way,' she said.

'Have you known him long?'

'Long enough to know that.'

She had no wish to talk about Michael. She looked up the table towards Simon, hoping to catch his eye, but he was busy carving a leg of lamb. A dish of potatoes and another of courgettes were steaming in the middle of the table. He was a deft and determined carver: the slices on the plates that Mary Oswald was circulating from under his right hand were complete and even, without ragged edges or small extra pieces. Maria suddenly saw herself and him presiding over a table-full of their own children instead of these motley guests. What an absurd idea! she told herself, but couldn't help finding it delightful. She smiled happily at Andrew as if he were the cause of all her happiness. She thought of telling him what had happened this evening, that she would have no further connection with Michael and that the fate of the programme, of the Third World and of everything except her relationship with Simon meant absolutely nothing to her. But Andrew's face – confused and anxious – deterred her. He was formulating another question, no doubt about Michael. She forestalled him by asking whether he'd written much for television.

'I'm not primarily a writer,' he said. 'My friends see me as a jack-of-all-trades. I've taught in universities, been a folk-singer, a journalist, involved indirectly in politics. Now I'm a literary editor. But I think I'd see myself as an educator, in the broadest sense. Knowledge is what we all desperately need. The last quarter of the twentieth century is about knowledge, its acquisition, its use and its dissemination.'

She looked at him a little mockingly. That snappy identification of himself with the latest quarter of the century seemed somehow typical. He noticed her look and made a smooth transition to a more personal, self-deprecating manner:

'I'm sure I get it from my father. He used to preach controversial sermons, raising all sorts of topics that only had a marginal connection with Christianity – he was good at finding obscure texts to subvert the standard views of the Church. I don't know how he managed to stay out of trouble with his bishop, except that his parish was a small country one and I suppose it was reckoned he couldn't do much harm there. Certainly he never got transferred to another parish and probably he was quite content to be able to stir people up without any practical consequences. No risk of riots on the village green.'

'Are you the same?'

'How do you mean?'

'Do you just like stirring people up or would you like the riots too?'

'I would,' he said fervently. 'I would like a few riots if I felt they'd lead to anything positive. As a matter of fact, I used to be a Maoist. That was when my father was still alive. We weren't on speaking terms for that and other reasons. But of course it became clear in the Seventies that Maoism was a purely Chinese solution to a Chinese problem. I wouldn't call myself a Maoist now.'

He went on at some length to explain where he did stand politically. Maria was beginning to feel trapped. At any other time she would have been more interested in Andrew. She was a little interested in him now, amused by him, but she wished Simon had not shifted the places round. It had seemed the right thing to do at first, now she thought it a strange action, almost a hurtful one. Andrew was a clumsy eater. Perhaps he didn't approve of eating, or at least not of eating meat. On the other hand, it was the courgettes he was pushing to the side of his plate. Several had fallen off it on to the table. He was neither quite a type nor quite an eccentric, she thought. He was full of nervous energy, but it didn't seem to be properly directed. He was like an old locomotive with a considerable head of steam which, instead of turning the wheels, kept escaping in the wrong places. In some ways you could mark him down as a man of the Sixties. He had the free-ranging innocence of that period, the spirit of go anywhere, do anything. He seemed to have radical sympathies, but his desire for revolution was not the dark, conspiratorial kind that belonged to this new age of terrorism. Andrew's was an almost childlike enthusiasm, a response as much to the past as to the future, as though he had just woken up and thrown off the heavy bedclothes of an old way of life and was sure that whatever happened next could only be better. Maria was hardly following what he was saying by now. She looked round the table again. Flora Decoud and Nick Oswald were discussing the evildoings of Kensington Borough Council, Simon and Liz were in earnest conversation about art and Mary Oswald, sitting on Andrew's right, was patiently listening to them. It was time Andrew transferred his attention to her, but Maria saw no immediate way of effecting the handover.

'Thatcher won't last,' Andrew was saying. 'It's a temporary reaction, a necessary swing of the pendulum. One might have seen it coming from all that Victorian nostalgia that was building up in the Seventies. We've been through huge changes since the war. People want to pretend for a little while that they're their own great-grandparents again.'

'What does your wife do?' asked Maria in desperation; and, seeing Andrew's look of surprise at the lack of continuity in her question, added, 'Is she also on the left politically?'

Andrew fell silent and sat staring at his plate. Then he began to stir the discarded courgettes with his fork. Maria wondered if he was annoyed or just taken aback at the way she'd interrupted his lecture. She thought that perhaps if Mary Oswald were to turn towards him now she might be able to divert his attention to some other topic altogether, but Mary remained obstinately concentrated on Simon and Liz.

Andrew suddenly put down his fork and leaned right across the corner of the table towards Maria, almost upsetting his glass of wine. He spoke in such a low voice that she could only just hear him through the other conversations.

'Liz and I are getting a divorce. You're no doubt wondering why we still come out to dinner together. Until tonight we thought we'd patched things up. It's all been a bad mistake. We did run out of fuel, but it was right beside a garage. We just sat there for about half an hour doing nothing about it. That's exactly what our whole relationship was, sitting side by side in a car blaming each other and not caring either to get out or go on. It's completely finished. I shall give her the keys and let her take the car home and I shall see a lawyer tomorrow.'

'I'm sorry.'

'I'm not. I've been a complete idiot, but now I'm a free man. You can't imagine how good that feels.'

Maria tried to imagine it, but couldn't. Her new absence of

freedom seemed to her infinitely preferable. She glanced up the table again to remind herself of what she now possessed and what possessed her. Simon was saying to Liz:

'I don't know why I like her so much. Just ruled lines – an absolutely regular grid of ruled lines. Of course, it's the colour and the texture, as with Mondrian, but Mondrian is almost garish by comparison with Agnes Martin. The bareness and the austerity are ravishing. It's like contemplating an empty sea and sky on a calm day or, for that matter, a piece of sacking.'

Liz, listening to Simon with a doubtful expression, her head on one side, caught Maria's eye. Her expression didn't change, but there was a hostile sneer in her voice:

'In other words, it's all in the eye of the beholder. You attach your feelings to something and then assume that the object created them.'

Her voice cut through the desultory conversation of Flora and the Oswalds and brought everyone into her argument with Simon.

'But the object does create them,' he said. 'It picks out or concentrates certain feelings in yourself, which are then reflected back in the object, heightened in you and so on, back and forth. Surely that's the whole purpose of art, almost its definition?'

'Your feelings!' said Liz. 'Isn't that a thoroughly male attitude, to impose your feelings on someone or something else, and then make out that they were started by the other person? That's the male definition of rape.'

She was looking at Andrew now and it was obvious to everyone that her words were really directed at him. Andrew didn't look at her, but stared carefully at the wine glass in his hand and spoke as if to himself:

'If we're going to be sexist about it,' he said, 'we have to say that most women are incapable of objectivity. They simply don't understand the concept. All their feelings are subjective. For that reason, if no other, it's not possible to have intellectual arguments with women.'

The whole party bristled and grunted with disapproval. It was only a question of who would assume the duty of crushing this monstrous suggestion – one of the men out of gallantry or one of the women out of raw indignation. Nick Oswald was first into the ring.

'I presume you intended to be provocative, but I really can't allow you to get away with such utter nonsense,' he said, smiling and speaking in a jocular way, to show that he didn't mean to cause any personal offence to a fellow guest.

'Nonsense or not, it's what he really believes,' said Liz, refusing to allow the rising storm between herself and Andrew to be diverted or mitigated. 'He calls himself a socialist, he works for a paper which pretends to support feminism, but he doesn't employ a single female contributor on his pages.'

'No, be fair!' said Simon. 'He's certainly had women reviewing books. And what about the dance critic?'

'Pure tokenism,' said Liz. 'The dance critic only reviews once in a blue moon and what about the cinema, theatre, music, art, TV? All men. You'd think all these things were only enjoyed by men, only men's opinions about them were interesting.'

'This argument,' said Andrew, putting the word between inverted commas, 'or rather this stream of abuse, only proves what I said. It has nothing to do with the *Equalizer*, but is simply aimed at me.'

'And you accuse me of subjectivity!' said Liz.

'Excuse me!' said Flora, looking from Liz to Andrew and back. 'Are we getting in your way or are you getting in ours? I believe that in Spain husbands and wives always sit next to each other. One sees why. They have so much to discuss which is not really anyone else's business.'

There was silence and then a movement of relief went round the table. Nick Oswald refilled Flora's glass with a flourish, making it look like a reward for her courage. Mary Oswald leaned across towards Liz and asked her how she'd come to start a gallery. Simon got up and removed the remains of the joint and the plates. It was obviously Maria's task to guide Andrew back into the safety of civilized behaviour, but she could think of nothing to say. She felt tense and slightly sick, as though some of the venom that had shot between Andrew and Liz had entered her bloodstream. Perhaps if she had still been essentially a stranger to Simon, she would have been more detached, but she had suffered with him and for him as much as for herself.

'I suppose you don't know of any spare flats in this area?' asked Andrew, apparently unabashed by Flora's rebuke.

'Not personally,' said Maria, 'but there are plenty of estate agents' boards about round here.'

'I've been searching for some time,' said Andrew, 'one of our problems being that we still share the same flat.'

Maria was struck by the strange, reverse symmetry of the occasion. Would Simon's flat, whose character she'd hardly noticed up till now, become as familiar to her as her own? Her eyes went round the room, as if like Andrew she were a potential purchaser. It was smaller than her own sitting room, much more crowded and piecemeal. Nothing had been chosen to go with anything else. It was not that the furniture and other objects were gimcrack or ugly, but that they retained their individuality and diversity, did not add up to a planned whole. The great number of pictures on the walls added to this sense of random clutter. Maria was reminded of one of those small local museums in which coins and other archaeological finds, dinosaurs' footprints, stuffed birds, agricultural tools, portraits of local worthies, odd pieces of antique furniture, ironwork, pieces of silver and pottery were all displayed together. The binding element there was the locality and its history; here it was Simon and his. She stared at the carpet — faded and worn in places, but richly patterned all over with small, delicately worked motifs of great complexity and variety in blue and green on a crimson ground. No doubt it had come down in Simon's family, perhaps he had grown up with it and known it when it was new, or at least not so worn and faded. The thought gave her intense pleasure. She looked from the carpet to its owner, at that point offering a board of cheeses to Mary Oswald, and tried to imagine him as a small boy. No moustache, of course. But in stripping off his moustache, she somehow stripped off his clothes too and for a moment she saw him sitting naked and chubby in the middle of the carpet, like the cupid in an Italian painting of lovers.

'The Wilson government made two bad social mistakes, both with the best intentions,' Andrew was saying to Flora, who had remarked on the enormous price of flats. 'One was to abolish grant-aided schools without also abolishing private schools, the other was to make it impossible for landlords to let unfurnished accommodation without losing control of their property.'

'Only two?' asked Flora. 'Wilson was an unmitigated disaster in all directions.'

'A disaster for socialism,' said Andrew. 'But if one's to be strictly fair, it has to be remembered that the period was an exceptionally difficult one for this country. Wilson was landed with the adjustment to a post-imperial position at the same time as an economic recession in the rest of the world.'

They drank coffee without moving from the table and then Flora got up to go.

'I start work early,' she said. She nodded all round, moved behind Maria's chair and then stopped and said:

'Do ask Simon to show you my painting! I'd be glad to know what you think of it.'

'Whether I recognize what it's representing?' asked Maria, screwing her head round to look up at Flora. Flora smiled down at her.

'It's not quite as simple as that,' she said and put one hand on Maria's shoulder before making for the door.

Simon followed her out and by the time he returned, the Oswalds, after a brief conversation with Liz about the current repertoire at Covent Garden, were also ready to leave. Andrew was fidgeting with his coffee cup and staring at the table. Simon, pausing near the door on his way out with the Oswalds, looked anxiously at Maria. He was leaving her alone with the Mowles. Could she cope? Could anybody cope, now that Flora had gone? Maria smiled back. She was really not afraid of them, or of anything.

'Can I use your phone?' asked Liz. 'I'm going to call a taxi.'

'Of course,' said Simon, as he left the room. 'It's in the bedroom.'

Andrew threw a set of keys the length of the table.

'Take the car!' he said.

'No thanks.'

'Take the car!'

'I said, no thanks.'

'I'm not coming home.'

'Suit yourself!'

'So take the car!'

'Where are you going?'

'I don't know.'

'You'll need the car to sleep in.'

'No, I won't.'

Maria realized that Andrew was intending to spend the night in Simon's flat. Simon could hardly refuse and they would either have to resume what had started on the doorstep with Andrew on the sofa in the next room, or she would have to go home alone. She couldn't contemplate either alternative.

'I'm afraid you can't stay here,' she said, determined to settle the matter before Simon returned.

Liz, hesitating in front of the keys, understood at once.

'Of course you can't,' she said.

'Why not?'

'You haven't been invited.'

'Simon's not going to throw me out.'

'You won't be welcome.'

'It's no business of yours.'

'I can promise you, you will not be welcome.'

Liz threw the car keys contemptuously back down the table and went into the bedroom to phone for a taxi. Andrew looked at the keys but didn't touch them. He was puzzled.

'Why can't I stay here?' he said to Maria.

Maria looked at him steadily.

'You're not being very bright,' she said.

'How well do you know Simon?'

'Hardly at all.'

'Then how is it you can speak for him with such authority? Why shouldn't I ask Simon himself?'

His obtuseness seemed almost wilful. She got up and began to look at some of the pictures she recognized, a group of etchings by Hockney.

'Unless, of course, I could borrow the sofa in your flat, Maria? Michael wouldn't mind, would he?'

His voice was directly behind her, giving her a shock. She hadn't heard him get up from the table or cross the room.

'Michael?' she said. 'No. Michael doesn't come into it.'

Then, seeing that he'd misunderstood her, thought she was accepting his request, and that his face was beginning to shine with pleasure, added as brutally as she could, so as not to have to discuss the matter any further:

'I wish you'd just go away and leave us both alone.'

Simon and Liz returned at the same moment, but the sharpness of Maria's voice had jolted Andrew enough to make him understand at last and he had drawn back from her almost before they entered.

'I'm sorry,' Andrew said. 'I have been stupid.'

He stood for a moment, half shaking his head, as if he had water in his ears after a bathe, and then abruptly lunged towards the table, took his car keys and went to the door.

'Goodnight, Simon,' he said. 'Thanks for the evening. I'll find my own way out.'

He could be heard getting his coat off the hook in the small entrance lobby and then the front door of the flat slammed behind him.

Liz's taxi came in a quarter of an hour and then Simon and Maria were finally on their own. But the happiness which had enveloped Maria all evening had half blown away. She couldn't forget Andrew's face as she turned on him in front of the Hockney prints. Cringing, wilting? Not quite. Slack, limp, lifeless? She thought of Vronsky lying in the gutter after being hit by the car.

Part Two

8

I

After only one night away, David Rutland already felt reinvigorated. He drank two cups of strong black coffee and ate a croissant for breakfast and then decided to stroll out and see the town. On the way out he stopped at the reception desk to warn the hotel's manager that he'd be out for half an hour or so, in case Arthur Rimington should come looking for him. The manager cut short his halting explanation by handing him an envelope. Inside was a short note from Rimington in his neat italic handwriting:

'Sorry to muck you about, but we have to do this by the book. Go to St Estephe and wait at the café. Half ten. Bring your luggage. See you. A.G.R.'

David obediently packed his things, paid his bill and caught a bus in the marketplace. St Estephe, four or five miles down the coast, was only a hamlet, with a few grey houses along the road and a few more down a side road towards the sea, which at this point was about a mile away. The café presumably served the holiday hinterland of camping sites and villas as much as the residents, though at this time of year it might as well have been closed, for all the business it was doing. David went inside and sat down at a table. After five minutes or so a small middle-aged woman in black emerged through the grimy curtain of plastic streamers behind the counter and took his order. Consciously virtuous, he decided it was too early for brandy and chose coffee, staring out at the empty street while he waited and wondering how he'd been able to resist what he hadn't resisted for years – a stiff drink before eleven. Of course it was because he was on holiday. No one was expecting anything of him and he wasn't even expecting anything of himself. Arthur Rimington wanted something from him, but that only added to his sense of ease and freedom. He was under no obligation. He had come, for friendship's sake, to advise or help if he could, and friends, unlike family or colleagues, took nothing for granted and were grateful for anything you did for them. David had long ago decided that friendship was the true measure of humanity and that every other sort of tie was more or less a mistake.

The woman brought his coffee, took his payment and disappeared beyond the curtain. Sipping the coffee and staring out of the café window, David saw a man in a dark anorak, with the hood up, approaching down the street. The day was cloudy, rather dark, with a coldish wind, but it wasn't actually raining, so that David had already begun to wonder whether the anorak wasn't some form of concealment rather than protection against the weather, when the man drew level with the café window and looked in. It was Rimington. He winked once, turned his head away and walked on. David finished his coffee and then, without hurrying too much, picked up his suitcase and went out.

The street was empty again. Feeling extremely conspicuous now, with his suitcase and his English coat and suit in this out of the way and out of season place, and wondering whether Rimington really needed to make such a performance when his enemies were presumably thousands of miles away in the African bush, David walked on down the street in the direction Rimington had been going. He found him waiting at the entrance to a track just beyond the last house, but as soon as David appeared he went on down the track without stopping to greet him. David followed, picking his way carefully to avoid getting too much mud on his best shoes, and increasingly irritated at the speed kept up by the small, nimble figure in front. The wind here was definitely colder, blowing into his face from the sea and making him regret the lost brandy.

The track continued for at least half a mile and emerged between stone pillars into a railed farmyard. Rimington continued through the yard and disappeared behind the outbuildings, leaving David to brave a furiously barking Alsatian which threw itself at him again and again and was brought up only a few feet short of him by its chain. The house was a handsome one, with the air of a manor, though the yard was quite small and the place was clearly a working farm rather than a rich man's country retreat. In a field behind the outbuildings there was a caravan. Rimington went quickly up the step, leaving the door open. When David reached the caravan, Rimington leaned down and took his suitcase in one hand and his left hand in the other.

'Mind your head!' he said.

Although the caravan was of a standard pattern and its fittings and furnishings were clearly part of the mass-produced ensemble, its tidiness and cleanliness immediately reminded David of Rimington's house in Balunda. That had been in some sense a caravan writ large.

'You'll need a drink,' Rimington said, closing the door, 'after all you've been through.'

'Nothing much,' said David. 'Your arrangements were very efficient.'

He had already forgotten the last stretch down the track and past the Alsatian. The caravan was warm, the drink was coming and he took off his coat and slid his large body down the bench behind the table with a faint sigh of pleasure. Rimington brought a bottle of Calvados and two glasses and slid into the place opposite. His long face had aged a lot in the fifteen years since David had last seen him. The skin was yellower and drawn tighter over jaw and cheekbones and there were deep lines around the eyes and mouth. He had lost most of the hair on the top of his head and what remained round the sides was turning white, as was his British officer's moustache. But his pale eyes were alert and his small, trim body looked as fit and active as ever. Glancing from Rimington to the bottle and back again, David imagined him for a moment sitting on the cork like one of those Alpine bottle-stopper figurines carved out of wood.

'Long time no see,' said Rimington, smiling, pouring out the brandy and pushing one of the glasses across the table to David. David paused only to raise the glass briefly in Rimington's direction and then sank a good part of the contents. It was strong stuff and made him feel momentarily ready for anything.

'Who are we hiding from?' he asked in the manner of a hearty doctor.

'Just about everybody.'

'Do the people on this farm know who you are?'

'Probably not. They're paid to do my shopping and keep quiet.'

'Who are they paid by?'

'The people who are looking after me.'

'So you do have friends.'

'Friends?' said Rimington. 'No, I don't think I'd call them that. They haven't decided what to do yet. Whether I'm a card worth holding or better disposed of.'

'When will they decide?'

Rimington shrugged. 'They'll first have to decide about Nakimbi.'

'He must be a card worth keeping.'

'I don't think so. Nakimbi's finished in Balunda.'

'So you are too?'

'Doesn't follow.'

'Where is Nakimbi?'

'They haven't told me.'

'You're not in touch with him?'

'Certainly not.'

David finished the glass of Calvados. He was beginning to feel confused and the confusion made him feel less friendly towards

Rimington, who, sitting perkily opposite, seemed to be enjoying watching him flounder amongst questions which only raised more questions. He reminded himself that this self-satisfied, superior little man was essentially a criminal, a person who by all accounts had terrorized, tortured and murdered large numbers of people.

'What help do you want from me?' he said, in the stern, neutral voice of a legal adviser rather than a friend.

Rimington took a little sip from his glass, which was still almost full. He looked round the caravan, as if he expected somebody to be concealed there, noted that the windows were closed and that no one was looking through them, then leaned across the table and said in a whisper:

'I want to get into the UK.'

'Is that possible? You're a very unpopular figure there. Apart from the press, the government certainly wouldn't welcome you.'

Rimington sat back and resumed his self-satisfied, enigmatic manner.

'Of course, I couldn't make a public entry,' he said. 'But I'm pretty sure that with what I have to offer, they'd be only too glad to do some sort of private deal. The French have backed Nakimbi all the way along. I can give the British Nakimbi's head, so to speak. That should be as good a ticket as any into the UK.'

'I don't quite see,' said David, with deliberate distaste, 'where that would get you with the British. You yourself say that Nakimbi's finished in Balunda. Stabbing him in the back, or whatever you mean to do, is surely not much use to anybody now?'

'Stabbing Nakimbi in the back! Bugger all you know about it!'

Rimington had become red in the face. David recalled that he had always had a strange capacity to work himself into an instant rage. No doubt it was part of his stock in trade as a successful leader of men. He was like one of the snakes in his glass cases, suddenly raising himself up and spitting with fury. But although David had once looked up to him, he had never been frightened of him and now it was he, David, who was in the stronger position.

'Bugger all. As you say,' he said in a calm, amused tone, as if he found Rimington more ridiculous than alarming. 'But I didn't come here as an expert on Balunda. If you want my help, you'll have to be a bit more helpful yourself.'

Rimington subsided immediately.

'You're dead right,' he said. 'I have to fill you in, David. But don't talk about "stabbing in the back"! If there's any stabbing in the back, Nakimbi's the one that's done it. What does he care about Balunda? He's got millions stashed away in Swiss bank accounts. He's taken retirement and bloody comfortable he'll be, the fat slob!'

Rimington sat back and stared at David as if he expected him to disagree, but David remained silent and looked at his empty glass.

Rimington seemed to have forgotten about the brandy. To take his thoughts off the glass, David turned his head towards the caravan's picture window and the view of dark fields and hedges beyond it. He felt depressed and wished he'd never responded to Rimington's call for help. He wanted to reduce the affair to its simplest dimensions, isolate some small service he could perform for Rimington in token of their old friendship, and go home.

'How about you?' he asked finally. 'Have you got anything stashed away?'

Rimington went red again.

'I bloody well have not,' he said. 'What do you take me for? I never took money for anything, let alone sent it out of the country.'

'Of course not,' said David. 'But it would have made things a lot easier if you had.'

He felt still more depressed. Presumably Rimington wasn't even going to be able to pay the expenses of this trip. The bill was down to friendship.

'Perhaps it would be best and quickest,' he said coldly, pushing his empty glass away as if he had decided to refuse any further hospitality, 'if I were to stop asking questions and you were to tell me, quite simply, how you think I can help you.'

'You're sorry you ever met me,' said Rimington, with a half smile but without any expression in his voice.

David began to feel much too hot and confined. The upright back of the bench seat pressed him too close to the table, he didn't wish to stretch his legs for fear of meeting Rimington's, the seat's plastic covers were uncomfortably rigid.

'It's not that,' he said, though he thought it probably was, 'it's that I'm doubtful whether I can be of any use to you.'

'I take it very kindly,' said Rimington, 'that you came all this way for me. I know you have a wife and children and work to do at home.'

'You were very kind to me all those years ago in Balunda,' David said.

He paused, shifted his legs a little, leaned his head on his hand and felt the sweat on his forehead. He started to take his jacket off, with some difficulty because of his bulk and the imprisoning bench and table.

'The thing is,' he said, 'that I'm just a country solicitor. I don't have access to powerful people and even in England that's what counts.'

'The thing is,' said Rimington, 'that I never had any friends outside Balunda. You were hardly more than a boy when I knew you there. I couldn't really expect you to help me now, but on the other hand I couldn't think of anybody else. And I had a feeling you wouldn't let me down.'

'Well,' said David, flattered more than Rimington could guess, since in the years since they'd met he'd become a person who constantly let people down, 'there seem to be two main problems. Money and getting into the UK. But why on earth do you want to get into the UK? Aren't you better off tucked away here?'

'I'm completely in their hands,' said Rimington, 'and I don't trust them a bloody inch.'

'Whose hands?'

'The Frogs. Frog Intelligence.'

'I see. You mean, this . . .' David waved his hand to indicate the caravan and the farm it stood in, 'is all laid on by French Intelligence?'

'It's not up to Butlin's standard, is it?'

'And how about me? Do they know I'm here?'

'They suggested the arrangements, as a matter of fact.'

'Then why all the secrecy?'

'They didn't want you to give away my hidey-hole.'

'Give it away to who?'

'To the British.'

David rescued the empty glass he'd pushed away. 'Can I have another drink?'

Rimington filled the glass. David drank a little, slowly, and stared out of the picture window again. It looked as if it might have started drizzling, but he couldn't be sure. He wondered if there were watchers hiding in the hedge.

'So what you really need to do is to get in touch with British Intelligence?'

'Maybe, David. Or maybe not. Honestly, I don't know what they're after. The Frogs, as I said, were backing Nakimbi. The British were tied up with the previous regime – General Ozo.'

David noticed that Rimington's hands were all the time busy with one another just below the level of the table. He laid them on its surface now, perhaps conscious that they betrayed his anxiety. The nails were uneven and the quicks torn. After a minute or two he took them back below the table.

'What would be the best that could happen? From your point of view?' asked David.

'I need to explain myself. People have a wrong view of me. Especially the British. I think, if they understood the truth, it would help. In time, who knows? The guerrillas may be able to sort things out. Things may settle down again in Balunda. I might be able to go back. That would be the best that could happen. If not, well, I'd just have to retire to Cheltenham or Tunbridge Wells, wouldn't I, like any other old colonel from the colonies?'

David forbore to say that he was not that sort of colonel – indeed, as far as the British Army was concerned, he might not be a colonel at all, had probably never even held a commission – but Rimington's lack of realism worried him.

'It's going to be very hard to change your image in Britain to that extent,' he said tactfully, aware that most people who had heard of him at all regarded him as a minor version of Himmler or Lavrenty Beria.

'And why is that, David?'

'It's because Balunda has had a particularly unhappy history since independence and, rightly or wrongly, you're held partly responsible for it.'

'And why is that, David?'

'Does it matter why?' asked David, easing himself sideways, wondering if he could manage to cross his legs in the cramped space between the bench and the table and deciding not. 'That's what's happened and it constitutes a major problem for you. For us.'

'It's because,' said Rimington, leaning forward with his forearms on the table, 'underneath all that liberal, brothers-in-the-Commonwealth shit, the British are racists. They don't want to know about a white man who becomes a black man, who loves Balunda better than Britain. Such a man must be evil – he's against nature. Isn't that it? And something else: class. British racism is only another form of British class-consciousness. Black men are at the bottom of the heap. Just above them are brown men and yellow men, Levantines and Jews, Slavs and Latins. Above them are the Northern Europeans and the Celtic races and above all, on the very pinnacle of the human race, are the Anglo-Saxons. Isn't that it? But David, you know as well as I do that when you've disposed of all the races on earth and left the Anglo-Saxons in solitary glory at the top, you still haven't got rid of class. On the contrary, you've entered the citadel of class and the levels of class inside that citadel are even more numerous and complicated than they are in the rest of the world. The working class, that's easy. The upper class, that's easy too. But what about the middle classes? How many levels there? Of north against south, of town against country, and both against suburbia. Of the job you do and the income you earn and what your father did and where you went to school and which regiment you're in and the kind of house you live in and the exact nature of your accent and your eating habits and what you call things . . .'

David smiled.

'You laugh. Of course, it's a joke. At least it's a joke to people of your class. But what about my class, David? Different, isn't it? And that's the point. A man of your class could turn himself into a black man and get away with it. Eccentricity! Love of adventure! Sanders of the River! But a man of my class isn't allowed eccentricity. He isn't allowed love of adventure either, because he's trying to better himself. It could only be love of money or love of power for a man of my class. A man of my class who turns himself into a black man must be either mad or evil.'

'Yes,' said David steadily, not looking at Rimington, 'no doubt you're right, but things have changed a bit since you were last in England. When was that? The Fifties?'

Rimington didn't answer. He was looking at the door of the caravan. He must have had very sharp hearing, since David had heard nothing. A moment later, the door opened and a thick-set, rough-skinned man with a flourishing moustache appeared in it. He looked round the inside of the caravan. David nodded and smiled at him, but the man took no notice. He held out a plastic shopping bag towards Rimington, who rose from the table and took it from him. With another glance at David, but without a word, the man retreated and closed the door.

'Rations,' said Rimington.

'Not a very cheerful fellow,' said David. 'Does he ever speak to you?'

'I can't understand him when he does,' said Rimington. 'My French is good but he has an accent as thick as porridge.'

'You say that it was the French who arranged for me to come and see you,' said David, 'and obviously they know I'm here. But what do they think I'm here for? Not to try and get you into the UK.'

'No,' said Rimington. 'I told them I needed to see you about my business affairs. They naturally think that, like Nakimbi, I've got funds tucked away in safe bank accounts and no doubt they'd be glad for me to have access to them, because then they'd have access to them as well.'

'But now that I know where you are, mightn't I go straight to the British with the information?'

'Yes, but they'll move me somewhere else after this.'

'Then how am I to get in touch with you again?'

'I'll have to get in touch with you.'

'And what exactly do you want me to do, Arthur?'

Rimington checked that the door was shut, glanced round the windows and then lifted the seat of the bench he'd been sitting on. He took out a school exercise book and handed it to David.

'Will you read this, for starters? I'll put together some lunch in the meantime.'

David opened the exercise book. Its narrowly ruled lines were closely packed with Rimington's neat handwriting. It was headed 'Balunda Where I Belong, by Colonel A. G. Rimington'.

'Is there a loo?'

'There's a chemical thing. But if you just want a pee, I generally use the hedge.'

'Watering Africa? Like old times.'

Rimington didn't smile. He replaced the exercise book in the bench before opening the caravan door and letting David out.

II

It wasn't raining, but the air was damp. Perhaps the wind was blowing spray off the sea. The space and cold were luxurious after the inside of the caravan. David walked slowly towards the hedge, not caring how long he put off the moment when he had to go back inside and wrestle with Rimington's insoluble problems; or better still find a way of extricating himself from any further contact with them. He had been foolish to come. He had envisaged, he supposed, a pleasantly nostalgic get-together over drinks and a good French meal, during which he would make friendly noises without committing himself to any definite line of action. This hole and corner set-up in the caravan was meaner and drearier than his imaginings and Rimington's obvious ignorance and helplessness worried him. The Rimington he'd known had always been on top of things, a source of energy and optimism. This Rimington was not exactly crushed, but he was unsure and out of his element, like a spider whose web has been brushed away.

David walked along the hedge until he found the gate into the next field. He was feeling chilly now, since he'd left his jacket and coat in the caravan, but he still preferred to be outside and he wanted to see if there were French Intelligence agents lining the other side of the hedge. There was no sign of anybody. David began to wonder if Rimington wasn't exaggerating his own importance. Did anyone really care whether he lived or died? David zipped up his flies, looked round suddenly, as if he might catch the French agents playing Grandmother's Footsteps, and returned to the caravan. He was shivering and his shirt felt icy as he slid back into his place on the bench. Rimington was slicing a length of garlic sausage with great exactitude, making sure that all the pieces were exactly the same thickness.

'That took a long time,' he said. 'I thought you must have decided to do a bunk.'

David smiled. The thought hadn't occurred to him, but he wished it had.

'Not without my coat and jacket,' he said. 'I was cooling off.'

'You ought to take more exercise,' said Rimington, looking critically at his stomach. 'You were a fine figure of a man when I first knew you.'

He took the exercise book out of the bench and laid it on the table.

'I've gone to seed,' said David, helping himself to another glass of Calvados. 'Inside every fine figure of a man is a fat one struggling to let go.'

'You drink too much,' said Rimington.

'I do,' said David, trying not to sound annoyed. 'That is my number one problem. However, we're not trying to solve my problem, but yours. On the whole, I'd rather have my problem than yours.'

'Mine is temporary,' said Rimington, slicing tomatoes, with the same precision as he'd sliced the sausage.

'Let's hope so.'

David drew the exercise book towards him, opened it at the first page and, after drinking a good measure of the brandy in his glass, began to read:

BALUNDA WHERE I BELONG
by Lt-Colonel A. G. Rimington

This is not an apology but an explanation. I do not say that I have never acted wrongly, but I do say that people have misunderstood me. I have had to kill people and I have had to interrogate prisoners. That is the job of a soldier. But I have never murdered a soul, nor have I tortured anybody.

To those who say that I had no business in Balunda, that I was one of those evil creatures in Africa's recent history, a white mercenary, I say that they lie. In the first place, I did nothing for money, therefore I could not be called a mercenary. In the second place, the colour of my skin was irrelevant. I was not born in Balunda, but after independence I stayed. Not as a neo-colonial exploiter, but as an adopted citizen. Is that so strange? Is not every citizen of the United States adopted in that sense? Or at least his ancestors? What about the German and Austrian Jews and the Indians and West Indians in Britain? Every country in the world accepts adopted citizens and Balunda accepted me. And I soon proved that they had been justified in doing so. Ask any man, woman or child in Balunda who it was that, more than any other, clinched their independence. Not their sham, so-called disgraceful independence handed to them by the British government, but their true dignity of independence that came only by fire and blood and self-sacrifice. I would have died any day for Balunda in that righteous war and died with a glad heart.

After the war was over I was honoured as a true Balundan. I truly believe that people no longer noticed the colour of my skin nor did they think of me in any way as a member of that old colonial race that had once oppressed them. They were free and I was free with them. All the same I was not quite free. I could have been Chief of Staff of the army. President Nakimbi offered it to me, but I refused. I knew that it would be seen outside Balunda as neo-colonialism. People would sneer at Balunda because their army was led by a white man. Therefore I told the President that I would keep my Leopards as an elite unit and as a core of defence against enemies within or without the state, but that I would never accept any rank above my present rank of Lieutenant-Colonel, nor would I become any kind of minister or official, for the same reason. It was not power I wanted, but the best possible future for my adopted country.

Another thing that has been said against me is that I was President Nakimbi's man, his trusted friend, and that I turned treacherously against him. Yes, I was his friend, but I was never his man. I served him faithfully during those years of his first term of office, because I believed him to be on the right path for Balunda. Eventually it became clear that he had been corrupted by power, that he had become a self-seeker and cared nothing for his country, only for lining his pockets and those of his henchmen – not mine, for I would never stoop to take money I had not earned legitimately, viz. my salary and nothing more – and that he would have to go. He would not go by democratic means, since he never held any kind of fair election.

Therefore when I got wind of an army plot against him, I thought long and hard about whether I should support it. I could not bring myself actually to join the coup. I was attached to Nakimbi, I admit it. I had even connived at many of his evildoings and dishonest dealings because he was my friend and because of his early promise and idealism. Finally I told the conspirators that I would not stand in their way or betray them, provided that my conditions were met. These were : 1) that no physical harm would be done to Nakimbi, 2) that he would be allowed to escape into exile, and 3) that elections would be held as soon as possible.

Accordingly on the night of the coup my Leopards and I happened to be engaged on a night exercise in the bush and only a token guard was left to defend the presidential palace. The coup was successful, Nakimbi was put on a flight to Abidjan and Brigadier Ozo became president. Unfortunately my third condition was never met. General Ozo – he immediately promoted himself – never held elections, although he continued to promise them.

My relationship with Ozo was never close, though to begin with I had some respect for him. Ozo has sometimes been compared with General Amin of Uganda, another British ex-NCO who made a bloody mess of his country. Apart from the fact that they had similar backgrounds in the British army in colonial times and that, partly for this reason, both in their early days of power got much more British support and economic aid than they deserved, this is an unfair comparison.

General Ozo was not really an evil man. He was weak and lazy, with sensual inclinations, easily ruled by others. His regime was certainly an evil one, violent and degrading, and it left Balunda with an overmighty and undisciplined army. But that was the consequence of the way Ozo allowed the other officers who took part in the coup to push him around.

I have been accused of being the 'eminence grise' of Ozo's dictatorship. This is a ridiculous charge. In the first place, the main victims of Ozo's purges were people of the Koruba tribe and I have always particularly respected that tribe as well as being a close associate of Nakimbi, who was a Koruba himself. In the second place, I had nothing to gain from Ozo's massacres, since I feared nobody and nothing in Balunda. I was protected as before by my place at the head of the Leopards, I was not seeking to better myself at other people's expense. What had I to gain from torturing and murdering innocent people? In the third place, although I liked General Ozo, I did not like his colonels and they did not like me. They would have been only too glad to do to me what they did to so many other leading figures of Nakimbi's regime – namely cut off my nose, ears, arms, legs and private parts and stuff the latter in my mouth until I choked to death. The Leopards, thank God, protected me and if there is a piece of evidence above all which refutes the charges against me, it is that I and no one else engineered Nakimbi's return to power and overthrew the evil regime of Ozo and his colonels.

I do not mean plotted it. However abysmal the state of the country – and it was by now just about on its knees, what with foreign debt, the shortage of all commodities except basic local food products, the total incompetence of all government departments, whose mainly Koruba civil servants had either fled or been murdered, and the ignorance and stupidity of Ozo himself – however abysmal things were, I would never have agreed to overthrow General Ozo, because as I mentioned earlier, of not being free. No Balundan would have held it against me – apart from the very few profiting from Ozo's regime – but I knew that people outside Balunda would and would no doubt say that I was working for South Africa or the CIA.

Therefore I would have nothing to do with all the plots that were being hatched. I refused to receive Nakimbi's secret agents or the agents of the French, who were still backing Nakimbi and building up an invading force for him in the neighbouring, formerly French territory. However, as it turned out, owing to a series of blunders, I did become involved in Nakimbi's counter-coup and if I had not been, it would have ended in disaster.

On that December night – a few days before Christmas – I

knew something was in the wind and I again took my Leopards on a night exercise, so as to be clear of any involvement either way. By pure chance this exercise was in the vicinity of Tumba airport. It has been said that this was deliberate and that I knew very well that Nakimbi had planned an airborne landing of commandos. This was what they said in the British papers, but that was hardly surprising since the British always supported Ozo's regime and were naturally against Nakimbi's return with French support. As any rate, the story is false. I did know that something might be going to happen and I guessed it would probably be an invasion over the border from the neighbouring ex-French territory. For that very reason I had chosen to carry out the night exercise near Tumba airport. Tumba is a very long way from the border. What I did not know was that there was also to be an airborne landing at Tumba.

Unfortunately, everything went wrong with Nakimbi's plans. In fact, the invasion started after the two aircraft had already landed. They had not landed at Tumba, but back where they started, in their own territory. This was because one of the aircraft had engine trouble and the other had not been properly fuelled before it took off. The invasion meanwhile was also in difficulties. A few villages had been overrun, but part of the force had lost its way, run into an ambush prepared by General Ozo's local commander – I was not the only person inside Balunda who had got wind of what might be going to happen – and retreated hastily back over the border.

Now what was Nakimbi to do? In my view any sensible commander, seeing what a balls-up his plans had got into, would have called it a day. He would have withdrawn that part of his invasion force which was still in Balunda, regrouped, retrained, learned the lessons of the disaster and come again another day. But apparently Nakimbi reckoned that there never would be another day – at least for him. If this attempt failed, the French would abandon him, perhaps find another protégé, perhaps make their peace with Ozo. So Nakimbi went for bust. He ordered the invasion force in Balunda to keep on advancing, he pushed the force that had retreated after them and he packed his commandos back into the two aircraft and sent them to Tumba airport as planned – except that by now it was two days later. A shambles.

The joke was that by the time those two aircraft landed at Tumba, my Leopards had just surrounded the airstrip as part of their exercise. What was our astonishment, as we made contact with the airport officials and informed them that they had just been 'captured' in a purely nominal way and were laughing and shaking hands with them, when two unidentified aircraft in quick succession came bursting down the runway –

literally bursting. The first pulled up with a burst tyre and a lot of smoke, but no real damage. The second narrowly missed the first and ended up on its belly, with one wing through a fence. It was a miracle that it didn't catch fire. The commandos who emerged from these two aircraft were not exactly in fighting shape. And, in fact, although I ordered my Leopards to surround the aircraft and arrest anyone on board, it was more a rescue operation than a military engagement.

At that point the phone rang in the control tower and one of General Ozo's colonels demanded to speak to me. He was panicking. He didn't yet know that the aircraft had landed, but he knew they were on their way. He also knew that I was at the airport and he was determined that I shouldn't be there when the aircraft landed. Obviously he was afraid of my Leopards making contact with Nakimbi's commandos, in case they should join the counter-coup. Now it seemed to me at this juncture – and I had to make my decision on the spur of the moment – that if that was what he was afraid of, it would be better not to upset him with the news that we had already made contact. So I said nothing about the commandos having landed. He then ordered me to get my Leopards to Molo – the capital of Balunda – as quickly as possible and leave the ordinary army to take care of the commandos. I had seen very little sign of the ordinary army at Tumba, beyond a few dozen soldiers and an officer we had 'captured' as part of our exercise, but I didn't argue with him. My main aim was to keep out of this affair, so as not to be accused of masterminding it. I therefore withdrew the Leopards from the airport as instructed and hurried to Molo.

The story that the Leopards, on my orders, killed the Balundan soldiers and the officer we had 'captured' is absolutely false. But I suppose that we were, unwittingly, responsible for their deaths. We withdrew in such a rush that we forgot to return them their weapons, which we had naturally removed from them as part of our exercise. Since, when the phone call came from General Ozo's aide, we had not yet got round to disarming the commandos, it was obvious that once we had withdrawn towards Molo, they would have had no difficulty in taking over the airport, which they did. And it was they, not we, who killed the unarmed soldiers who were supposed to be guarding the airport against them.

When we reached Molo, which is about forty miles from Tumba, we found General Ozo and his staff in total confusion. Their troops were holding the border invasion force pretty well – in fact, they were probably on the point of routing them – but meanwhile they had learned of the commandos taking over Tumba airport and, since they didn't know how large this force was or how many reinforcements might follow it in now that the airport was in their hands, they feared their number was up. The consequence was that when I and the Leopards drove up to the presidential palace in Molo, General Ozo seemed to have lost his nerve completely. He was scrambling out of a back window and trying to get out of the compound without being recognized. He had removed all his insignia of rank and when he was brought to me in the palace by some of my men, who had rescued him from the barbed wire, he was a pitiful sight, bleeding profusely and grey with terror.

The problem for me was now acute. Was I to put Ozo on his feet again and stamp out Nakimbi's counter-coup for him? (It was a big question by now whether I could, even if I wanted to.) Or was I, after all, to support Nakimbi, hold on to Ozo and his capital – which was what fate had put into my hands – and pass them over to the new regime? I was already inclining towards Nakimbi when I learned that he'd landed at Tumba airport and was coming straight to Molo to broadcast to the nation. I ordered the Leopards to prepare the radio station and the die was cast. Of course I had no idea what Nakimbi would do to General Ozo. I assumed that, since Ozo had allowed Nakimbi to escape, Nakimbi would do the same for him. But as soon as he reached the presidential palace, even before his broadcast, Nakimbi ordered us to take the General out into the yard and shoot him there and then. And so from that moment I might have guessed that we were out of the frying pan and into the fire and that all the crimes perpetrated by Ozo and his colonels were going to be avenged and even outdone by Nakimbi's crimes.

There the exercise book finished. David laid it down on the table and drank the rest of the brandy in his glass. Then he looked up. Rimington had finished preparing the lunch and was watching him.

'What do you think?' he asked.
'Gripping stuff. Is that the end?'
'But is it convincing?'
'It's very much *your* story,' David said carefully.
'Of course it's my bloody story. You ask Nakimbi, he'll tell you something completely different. But that's the point. People have to believe that I'm telling the truth.'
'So far as it goes . . .' David said and reached for the bottle of Calvados.
'You can't have any more of that.' Rimington was at the table and snatching away the bottle in an instant.
'Don't be such a bloody scoutmaster!' said David.
'You need a clear head. You're no use to me without a clear head.'

Rimington was thumping the table in his agitation. David remained ostentatiously calm.

'My head is my own affair. So is whether I'm any use to you.'

'I want your opinion, David. I don't want a vague put-off.'

'Did you actually shoot General Ozo?'

'My soldiers shot him.'

'But under your orders?'

'Nakimbi's orders.'

'Were you present at the execution?'

'I was present. It's an unpleasant fact, but it has to go in because it's the truth.'

'I don't believe your story about the airport. I believe you captured the airport for real, allowing Nakimbi's commandos to land, and then pushed off to capture Molo.'

'So you don't find it convincing?'

'I find some of it convincing. I'm convinced you weren't in it for the money, probably not for the power either. You probably did what you did just because you couldn't help wanting to tidy up the shambles.'

Rimington smiled, a very tight, brief smile.

'We'll have lunch now,' he said and began to lay the table. David watched him, wondering why the action seemed strange. He'd so often sat down to meals with Rimington in the old days, at the table surrounded by the snakes in their glass cases. But in Balunda, of course, the table had always been laid by his steward, immaculately dressed in white duck, just as the meal had been prepared somewhere out of sight by Rimington's cook. David had never seen Rimington before as a man without servants or soldiers round him, out of his customary role as a master. His laying the table for David was not the ordinary act of any friend for any other friend in a world from which servants had mainly disappeared. It was a kind of declaration, as if Napoleon were laying the table for a visitor to his exile on Elba: 'Look at me! I am temporarily humbled and patient, but don't imagine that I am not still Napoleon!' It was hard to believe, especially when David recalled the way he had seen Rimington in his days of power gloating over the mysterious disappearance of his rivals in the president's Cabinet, that he had been quite as neutral or as bland a figure in Balundan politics as the exercise book suggested.

III

During lunch, Rimington seemed to relax. It was as if he had cleared one obstacle and didn't want to rush at the next. He had removed the Calvados, but produced a bottle of wine and allowed David a couple of glasses with the meal, though the glasses, David noted, were far from full.

'Why did you give up your sculpture, David?'
'I couldn't make a living at it.'
'That's a pity. You were very talented.'
'I made a hash of Nakimbi.'
'We didn't give you enough time.'
'Portraiture is a matter of getting it right first time. Let's face it, I thought I was a lot better than I was and you didn't know any better than to believe me.'
'We were all optimistic in those days,' said Rimington.
'I can't say I was too optimistic about the state of Balunda,' said David.
'You didn't see it with the eyes of faith.'
'I compared it with what it had been under the British. A quiet, decent place. It might have been boring, but at least people didn't go in fear of their lives.'
'I was brought up in a quiet, decent place,' said Rimington. 'In north London. I wish you could have experienced its quiet decency for yourself.'
He spoke in his peculiar, synthetic accent, a mixture of officer-class drawl with colonial twang laid over what might originally have been suburban London, but as he grew suddenly heated, the drawl disappeared and he sounded more like a sergeant than a colonel:
'It was bloody despair. It was worse than going in fear of your life. You wanted to go in fear of your life. As it was, you went in fear of making a noise or being conspicuous in any way. It was bankruptcy and secret drinking. It was low ceilings. In all senses. The only way to stretch yourself was to get out and never come back. And I did. I got out into the army. National service. I signed up for five years. It was just what I wanted. And I was just what they wanted. Keen, tough, reliable Rimington. Sergeant Rimington, just the man. And wasn't I proud of those three stripes? Until I realized it was just another low ceiling. They begged me to stay. "Not bloody likely," I said. "There are two worlds in your fucking army and I belong to the wrong one." We were in the Gold Coast then, Ghana as it shortly became. I liked the Coast, the white man's grave. I joined the Colonial Service. Well, that was when you met me, you the boy with the silver spoon, straight out of college and already doing the sort of job they'd never have offered me in a million years.'
'Come off it, Arthur! It was a six-month job for callow youths.'
'You know what I mean. A world was open to you, David, a world with high ceilings or no ceilings at all, which was never open to me.'
'I think it's bullshit, Arthur. All this class stuff.'
'What I'm trying to say is not about myself, but about the people in Balunda. You saw it as a quiet, decent place . . .'
'I was only there six months.'

'Exactly. It was the Valley of Despair, David, believe me. Those quiet, decent, subjugated people were pissed out of their minds on palm wine from morning till night. The men, that is. They sat around stupefied in those deadly villages, the trees all round them, frightening themselves and each other to death with diseases and filthy remedies, witchcraft and vendettas. And the women bore their children, grew and picked and cooked the plantains and worked themselves into old age in their twenties.'

'You're not blaming the British for that?'

'I'm saying that anything was better than that sort of quiet, decent life. Can't you put yourself in their place? Can't you imagine for one moment what it might be like not to be a white, Anglo-Saxon, upper-class university graduate? Not for a week or a month or even a year, but for a whole bloody lifetime?'

'I think you're wrong, Arthur. I think you're not putting yourself in their place, but them in yours. Their lives weren't ruined by not being white, Anglo-Saxon, upper-class graduates, but yours was. That's what you're talking about. And it was you that became a colonel, they didn't. They stayed exactly as they were, except that they had to contend with genocidal politicians and homicidal soldiers on top of everything else.'

Rimington's mouth tightened, but he said nothing. After a while he got up and cleared away the lunch things, deftly but a little noisily, as if he was too tense to treat the plates and glasses with his usual care. When he had put everything in the tiny sink, he came and laid a hand lightly on David's shoulder.

'You can't understand. You really can't understand,' he said.

Perhaps it was the gesture, perhaps just the particular way he cleared the plates without piling them, as he had taught his African steward to do it, but David felt himself uncannily removed in time and space to that house in Balunda, where he and Rimington had both, it seemed to him now, been almost entirely different people. He turned his head a little and for a moment allowed himself to believe that the window behind him was the glass case with the green mamba or the rhinoceros viper inside it and that if so, the man sitting where he sat was still in his twenties, a young, handsome, athletic sculptor, flown out to Africa with all expenses paid, to perform his first important commission, from which, no doubt, the rest of his great achievement would grow. And here, sitting beside him was the dashing Colonel Rimington, hero of the civil war, the President's closest confidant, his own good friend. The illusion couldn't be sustained. Rimington was, after all, a small, worried, elderly man with bitten fingernails, trapped in a caravan with no discernible future; and David, next to him, was flabby and tired, his brain fuzzy and his prospects also nil.

'What happened to the snakes?' he asked, yawning and wishing he could lie down and close his eyes.

There was a long pause. David looked sideways, wondering if Rimington had heard the question. He was staring into space.

'I don't know,' he said at last, aware that David was looking at him. His eyes were beginning to water. He stood up suddenly and went away to the kitchen end of the caravan, keeping his back to David.

'Of course I bloody know,' he said, without turning round. 'Those shits left them to starve.'

'I'm sorry,' David said, without much conviction. He still wanted to fall asleep.

'What are you sorry about?' asked Rimington. 'You always disliked them, like everybody else.'

'I'm sorry because I know they mattered a lot to you.'

'If any of those snakes had had any sense,' said Rimington, 'they'd have taken the first opportunity to bite me and escape.'

'I often wondered why they didn't,' said David. 'You held them so carelessly.'

'They didn't, because they liked me stroking them and they were lazy buggers. Got used to being fed and cared for. Trusted me to see to their comfort and welfare.'

'Which you certainly did.'

'No creature should ever trust itself to any other creature. It's not like trusting God, is it? I couldn't save them. In the last resort I couldn't save them, because I put myself first. They should have known that. Nature had taught it to them. They did know it, but they let themselves be conned into trusting me.'

'They had a pretty good life while it lasted,' said David, 'and after all it lasted a good many years.'

He wondered whether they were really talking about the snakes or about their master and it occurred to him that Rimington was now almost exactly in the snakes' position, being kept and fed in his own version of a glass case, only with less benevolent masters. The thought that he too was temporarily in the same confinement roused him a little from his sleepy stupor. He looked at his watch. It was nearly 3 pm.

'Isn't it time I was getting along?' he suggested.

'No hurry,' said Rimington.

'I'll have to find another room,' said David. 'I checked out of the hotel.'

'You can sleep here,' said Rimington.

The idea didn't appeal to David at all.

'I think I'd prefer to be getting along. I want to catch a boat first thing tomorrow.'

'We've still got a lot to talk about.'

'To be quite frank,' said David, shifting in his seat and becoming more animated in his desire to escape, 'I don't think that that exercise book of yours is going to have much effect on the British authorities. Even if I can succeed in getting it into the right hands. You might perhaps sell it to a newspaper and make a bit of money . . .'

'I don't want money. Money doesn't come into it.'

'What *do* you want? I'm still not at all clear.'

Rimington made no immediate reply. Instead he found two clean glasses and brought them and the bottle of Calvados to the table. Then he sat down opposite David again, poured out the brandy and pushed one glass across.

'Most of all, I want to go back to Balunda, David. I told you that.'

'Is that realistic?'

'There's no bloody alternative.'

'Unless Nakimbi gets back, how can you?'

'David, I wish you were still a young man.'

'I wish I were too.'

'Your mind used to be so much sharper.'

'Maybe. I don't think so. I don't thing things were so complicated in those days.'

'I don't know how much to tell you, because I don't know how much you'll take in.'

'Look, if you think I'm too bloody stupid or drunk to be of any use to you, why don't you call it a day?'

David began to struggle his way out of the bench.

'I came to help if I could because of old times. Old times, old ties. But I don't think there are any further obligations on either side. To be franker still,' he added, as he paused, sweating, at the end of the bench, preparatory to standing up, 'I'm not so sure you'd be that much better off if you did find someone else with a sharper mind. They might be even less convinced by your apologia.'

Rimington's colour came up and his moustache twitched, but he controlled himself and said nothing for a minute or so. David reached for his jacket.

'I told you, David, that there isn't anyone else. Absolutely nobody else. If you can't do it, I'm up shit creek. What you have to do is convince the British that I'm worth having, worth saving. If you don't think what I've written is convincing, then don't show it to them. Tell it in your own words or just persuade them to give me a chance to explain myself in person. The British are anti-Nakimbi. Try to keep that in your mind. I mean the British government, the Foreign Office. They backed Ozo and Ozo was toppled. Now it looked as if I was pro-Nakimbi in that business and what followed, but if I was actually anti-Nakimbi and if I'm anti-Nakimbi now, then you see what follows. The British are on goodish terms with the new regime, the guerrillas. If they were convinced that I was and always had been anti-Nakimbi, they could probably convince the new regime of that. I could go back to Balunda. You see how important it is, David? For you to get word through to the British, to the right quarters.'

David sat with his jacket on his lap and thought about this. It seemed to him that the thing was a mare's nest, that whatever the truth or otherwise of Rimington's story, it made little difference. He was clearly no use to anyone and was either hoping to con the British into thinking that he was, or more likely conning himself in order not to lose hope completely. But he, David, was never going to get away from this caravan by telling Rimington to give up hope. He reached for his glass and finished the contents.

'I'll do what I can to get your message through to the right quarters, Arthur. More I can't promise. And now I ought to be going.' He stood up with decision, staggering slightly and bruising his thigh against the corner of the table.

'But you haven't got my message,' said Rimington.

'You just told me it.'

'I told you the outline. Nobody's going to be convinced by that. You have to give them detail, evidence.'

'Where am I going to get that?'

'I'm going to tell it to you now. I couldn't write it down, like the earlier part, because it would be too compromising if it got into the hands of the French. I want you to take the written-down part with you and when they've read that, give them the rest of the story in your own words.'

David's glimpse of freedom, of a leisurely drink in a luxuriously spacious hotel bar, followed by a good dinner and bed, receded. He looked helplessly at his watch.

'But how long will it take?'

'It'll take a while, but in any case it will be best if you don't leave before it's dark. I don't know how closely they watch this place, but we don't want them to have the chance of stopping you.'

David leaned unsteadily against a bulkhead which made his head tip forward. He felt dizzy and almost desperate.

'I can't do this, Arthur. I can't creep out in the middle of the night as if I was involved in something underhand. I'm just a friend and . . . legal adviser. You can't ask me to behave like a criminal.'

Rimington was staring at the table. After a moment he stood up, took David's jacket from the bench and gently helped him to put it on.

'When you were still very young and going to be a sculptor,' he said, 'I gave you a big chance. I didn't know whether you were any good, but I thought you had it in you. And the reason I thought that is that I didn't see any fear in you. People who aren't afraid can do almost anything they set their minds to. Fear is what makes people stumble and give up. Well, the result wasn't as good as all that, so perhaps I was wrong. Perhaps you were more nervous about the sculpture than appeared.'

'I was very nervous.'

'Then you didn't show it. That takes courage.'

Rimington turned and looked for David's coat. When he found it, he draped it neatly over his arm, like a waiter bringing a customer's coat in a restaurant.

'Now I really don't know what you've done since,' Rimington continued. 'Perhaps you've had all sorts of big chances. Perhaps you've taken them. I don't think you have. Perhaps this is only the second big chance in your life. Perhaps I'm fated to be the only person that ever offers you big chances. No, I'm sorry. This isn't exactly a big chance for you, it's a big risk for you. A different thing. But it's a big chance for me, of that there's no doubt at all.'

He held out the coat and seemed to be about to say something more, but didn't. David, still feeling dizzy and troubled by the bulkhead behind, looked down at him with his arms stretched out and the coat, so much too big for him, hiding everything but his head and shoulders and the bottoms of his trousers. David took the coat and threw it along the bench.

'All right,' he said, 'all right. But how am I going to remember what you tell me?'

They agreed that David should take notes of what Rimington told him, but that the notes should be sufficiently cryptic or at least ambiguous that, if they were read by French Intelligence, they would not destroy Rimington's credibility as a supporter of Nakimbi. However, they hoped to evade French Intelligence altogether. When Rimington had told his story, they would have a meal and then a few hours' sleep. While it was still dark, David would make his way on foot to the town and take the first available train back to the Channel ferry.

With his programme mapped out in this way and a definite limit set to his time in the caravan, David immediately felt better. He sat down almost eagerly in his place at the table, found a used envelope in his suitcase and a pen in his jacket pocket and treated his note-taking as a kind of parlour game, trying to condense into as few words as possible the salient facts of Rimington's narrative and finding that the effort to remember and at the same time conceal what he was being told helped him to concentrate better than he usually did. Afterwards he was pleased with himself and sat on touching up his notes and making sure he understood them, while Rimington paid a visit to the farmhouse. He returned with a bottle of wine and a loaf of bread. There was enough left over from lunch to make their supper, but Rimington had wanted to emphasize that his guest was staying the night, so that if anyone was intending to intercept David when he left, it would be thought that no close watch need be kept until the morning.

The meal was a cheerful affair. Rimington no longer stinted the wine and it was as if they had finally climbed back into their old selves and rediscovered their affection for one another. David turned over the buff envelope on which he had written his notes and drew a rapid sketch of Rimington in one corner.

'Not bad at all,' he said, pushing the envelope across for Rimington to see.

'Brilliant!' said Rimington.

'I should have done a bust of you instead of Nakimbi,' said David. 'My whole life might have been different.'

He took back the envelope.

'Now, I'm going to run through my notes,' he said, 'and try to summarize what you've told me. Anything I get wrong you can correct. Okay?'

Rimington was smiling. 'You're a new man, David. This shady business of mine is doing you the world of good.'

'It's more fun than most of my clients' business.'

'One thing I ought to mention, David. I can't pay you for your services. Not in my present circumstances. But of course as soon as I'm better placed, I'll expect you to send me a bill.'

'No charge, Arthur. Now, my first note is ROUND-UP. that refers to your operations immediately after the overthrow and death of General Ozo. Nakimbi put you in charge of catching, interrogating and shooting most of Ozo's associates. He did this, you say, on purpose to make sure that you were compromised, that you were caught up with his regime. Some of these men you were not sorry to have to execute, since they had themselves practised all kinds of cruelty, but you did not use unnecessary torture.'

'Force, David. Torture is always unnecessary, except to sadists.'

'The important thing is that, having dealt with the worst of General Ozo's colonels, you did not, as Nakimbi wanted you to, unleash a general massacre of his opponents. That was done by a man called Obeobubaka. I've written down his name, because otherwise I shall certainly forget it. Your case is that Nakimbi put you in charge of his security operations after his return to power, but that since you wouldn't cooperate beyond a certain point, he set up a second undercover security operation and put it in the hands of this Obeobubaka. And here I've noted LEOPARDS, with a question mark, to remind me that Obeobubaka and his torturers pretended to be a unit of the Leopards.'

David paused and sat puzzling over the buff envelope.

'Two names written here. I've completely forgotten what they signify. OUGU and WALI.'

'Villages,' said Rimington.

'Ah, yes.' David's mind was still blank.

'They were accused of harbouring wanted men. I sent the Leopards to conduct a search, but they found nothing suspicious . . .'

'I've got it. Two days later the villages were destroyed by Obeobubaka's soldiers, posing as Leopards. KORUBAS?'

'The survivors confirmed that the soldiers who came on the second occasion were definitely Korubas and there were virtually no Korubas in the Leopards.'

'Right. The next note I've got is QUEEN'S BIRTHDAY – WAINWRIGHT. Wainwright, you told me, was the British High Commissioner in Balunda. He failed to invite you to the High Commission party for the Queen's Birthday.'

'Deliberately failed. The British were signifying their disapproval of what they thought were my activities as Nakimbi's security chief.'

'You asked for an interview with Wainwright. He refused. so you turned up in uniform in your jeep all the same and were refused admission at the gate. You demanded to see Wainwright in person and the guard said that wasn't possible, you fired your pistol over his head and told your driver to accelerate. He screeched to a halt in the drive, whereupon you jumped out and walked straight up the steps into the High Commissioner's residence. Wainwright himself was receiving his guests just inside the door and you demanded in a loud voice why you hadn't been asked to the party. The guests all fell silent and Wainwright, as you'd hoped, was extremely embarrassed, saying that he couldn't discuss such things in public. You then offered to hear his explanation in private and as soon as you got him to himself, you told him how you were being used by Nakimbi as a figurehead for his massacres and were thinking of seeking asylum. Wainwright wasn't very helpful, but said he would consult his superiors in London. You then left the party and drove away, still giving the public impression that you were furious at the insult of not being invited. The incident, as reported in the British papers, naturally gave you an even worse reputation in Britain than you already had, but Wainwright, wherever he now is – back in England or in another posting – can presumably confirm what you really said to him.'

Rimington first nodded and then slowly shook his head.

'I realize it's all bloody thin,' he said. 'Wainwright either did nothing about it or the Foreign Office told him they weren't interested.'

'And now we come to CHARLIE,' said David. 'By this time much of the country was in chaos. The north was mostly held by the guerrillas fighting to get rid of Nakimbi for the second time. Elsewhere there were roving bands of soldiers, nominally belonging to Nakimbi's army but actually just bandits and killers, looting and burning the villages, raping the women, stopping vehicles at random and murdering the passengers for their possessions. Your Leopards were virtually the only disciplined unit left and Nakimbi kept you in Molo for his own protection. I suppose he was afraid you'd go off on one of your famous night exercises at the crucial moment?'

David smiled disarmingly, but got no smile back from Rimington.

'Charlie,' he continued, 'was a young captured guerrilla brought to you for interrogation.'

'He was about fourteen,' said Rimington, 'but more like a veteran than a child.'

'He refused to say anything except that you had murdered all his relations, would no doubt murder him, but would soon be punished for your crimes. When you asked him when and where he thought you'd murdered his relations, he gave you a very circumstantial account of how the Leopards had attacked his village and how he'd escaped by shamming dead among a pile of bodies, including his mother, his uncle and two – was it? – brothers. You then told him that the Leopards had never visited that part of the country and you called in several of your officers to confirm the fact. He was convinced, but said it made little difference since you were just as much his enemies as the people who had murdered his relations. You said he might be wrong about that.' David paused and thought for a moment.

'Did you say this in front of your officers?'

'No, I sent them back to their duties.'

'You asked Charlie if he'd take a message back to the guerrilla leader. To the effect that you might be thinking of changing sides. Charlie agreed and that night you released him and let him disappear into the town. However, you had no message back from the guerrillas and you've no idea whether Charlie ever got through to them; if he did, whether he delivered your message; or indeed whether he lived or died. Are those the main points?'

Rimington appeared not to have heard. He was sitting with his elbows on the table and his hands over his face.

'Is that the gist of CHARLIE?' asked David.

Rimington removed his hands and stared down at the table.

'When you tell it back to me like this,' he said, 'it sounds hopeless.'

'I'm sorry. I was doing my best to remember.'

'Your memory's fine. It's not your fault. It's just that I realize – hearing it objectively – there's no weight to it.'

'I'll try to make it a bit more substantial when the time comes. Obviously presentation is important. This is a rehearsal. If I believe that you were anti-Nakimbi, that will make a considerable difference to whether they believe it. Or at least believe in the possibility, which is all that's required at this stage.'

'Do you believe it, David?'

'Yes, I think I do. I wasn't so sure at first and of course when I arrived I saw you as the person I'd read about in the papers. It didn't entirely fit with what I knew of you in the past, but I could only conclude that I hadn't known you very well in the past. I assumed the worst, put it like that! But gradually I think I've come to see that it was as you say it was.'

'Thank you, David.' Rimington raised his head, 'Thank you all the more for making this journey to see me. I wasn't wrong about you, was I? Whatever you have or haven't done with your life since those days, you're the same . . . terrific chap. With the same loyalty and courage.'

'My final note,' said David, partly warmed, partly embarrassed by Rimington's fervour and aware that he had somehow crossed a bridge and was now committed to do everything possible to help Rimington, whatever it involved, 'is AIRBORNE. Nakimbi's regime is collapsing, his troops being driven back on Molo by the guerrillas, he orders you and the Leopards to escort him to Tumba airport for the last possible flight out. When you reach the airport, the plane is revving up on the tarmac. Nakimbi goes straight on board, while you and the Leopards guard the runway. And then Obeobubaka appears on the aircraft steps – he was already on board waiting for Nakimbi, it seems – and shouts something. You run across to the steps. Obeobubaka shouts again. You still can't hear him. You go to the top of the steps. Obeobubaka says that Nakimbi wants a last word with you. You step inside the cabin door. Somebody hauls you in and pushes you down into a seat, the door is closed, the plane takes off, leaving your Leopards to face the guerrillas without their leader, leaving you, when the aircraft touches down, an exile with Nakimbi and the appalling Obeobubaka and henceforth dependent on their French friends.'

'Do you think that rings true, David?'

'Only too true. Obviously your next move, if Nakimbi hadn't tricked you, would have been to seize the airport, as you did the time before, and make your peace with the guerrillas.'

'It sounds treacherous.'

'Not in the context of your previous relationship with Nakimbi and Obeobubaka. And the fact that you didn't, as you could have done, seize Nakimbi on the way to the airport to use as a bargaining counter with the guerrillas, shows how fair-handed you really were. You wanted him out, you didn't want him strung up or shot. You were trying to behave, just as you did in the previous changes of power, with as much neutrality as possible.'

'Will you make one further note, David?'

'Certainly.'

'I want you to make it clear to the British that where Nakimbi's concerned, I'm no longer neutral. I'm willing to reveal anything and everything about his actions as president – his corruption, his sexual perversions, his personal responsibility for individual murders and tribal pogroms. I feel now that the big mistake I made was to try to be neutral. That was because of my white skin and my British origins. When Nakimbi ordered me to shoot General Ozo, I should either have shot Nakimbi as well or put them both on the next plane out of the country.'

'And ruled it yourself?'

Rimington snorted, then smiled and nodded his head, putting his hand out to touch David's arm.

'You've understood, David. You've understood completely. There was no way I could do the right thing.'

David hesitated for some time and finally wrote NEUTRAL at the bottom of the buff envelope and drew a line through it. Then, feeling the need to pee again, he hauled himself to his feet and went out into the darkness. He didn't go as far as the hedge this time, but relieved himself in its general direction. There was a light in one window of the farmhouse, but otherwise no sign of life. The wind had dropped, but the sky was thick with clouds, hiding the moon and stars. If it stayed like that, there shouldn't be any difficulty in slipping away unseen. Back inside the caravan, Rimington was still sitting at the table. He looked up and indicated the bottle of Calvados, now three-quarters empty. David smiled and shook his head. He was extraordinarily tired and, apologizing, lay down on the bench.

A little later he was dimly aware of Rimington covering him with a blanket and removing his shoes. He dreamed that he was back in Balunda, making the bust of Nakimbi. But instead of working in clay, he was carving a hard, black wood. The face he was chipping out with enormous difficulty was grotesque and frightening, a tribal mask, not a likeness, but he felt great energy and excitement. This was what he had been searching for. He kept turning to Rimington who was standing somewhere behind him and telling him, 'It's a breakthrough, Arthur, it's a breakthrough.' But after a while, the face of the carving seemed more and more to resemble Rimington's, though it was still undoubtedly a tribal mask and still black.

IV

Trudging along the top of the beach, with the low tide somewhere out of sight to his left and the dune immediately above him to his right, David wished he had not accepted Rimington's plan. Surely it would have been more sensible to strike inland and use a road? Rimington had said he might lose his way in the darkness and end up walking in the wrong direction and that going by the sea, even if it was slower, made that impossible. But there were worse things than losing the way and one of them was to be walking in dry loose sand in town shoes and carrying a suitcase.

Other people's plans, David reflected, were seldom satisfactory; indeed, people's plans in general, including one's own, were nearly always either too simple or too complicated. They were attempts to impose a pattern on future events, when events had their own organic pattern. Just as if you settled down to make a portrait of somebody with a fixed idea in advance of what sort of person they were or how you meant to depict them, the result was always a disaster. Because Rimington's chief anxiety had been that David would lose his way and not be far enough out of the neighbourhood before it became light, he had simply not considered that the one advantage of walking along the beach was cancelled by its several disadvantages: it was slow, exhausting, ruinous to his shoes and he wasn't at all sure he'd be able to continue with it.

He wondered if he should perhaps ditch the suitcase. There was not much of value in it. Rimington's exercise book and the buff envelope with his notes would go in his pockets. His passport and return ticket were already there. It would only be a few personal items and the suitcase itself that he would lose. He decided against it, partly on the grounds that he might arouse suspicion in Customs if he had no luggage, but mainly because the suitcase had been given him by Susie and he felt sentimental about it.

He smiled at himself. He had hardly once thought of Susie since he left England and here he was soldiering on with a piece of old leather she had given him many birthdays ago, as if it was some sacred bond between them. The moment he saw her again he would stop thinking about her and he didn't imagine she would be wasting many thoughts on him. Suddenly tired out, he mounted the dune, slipping and exhausting himself further in the steep slope of sliding sand, felt about for a tuft of coarse grass and sat down. He opened the suitcase and took out Rimington's bottle of Calvados, nearly empty now but given to him as iron rations when they parted. He drank from the bottle and felt momentarily better. It was perhaps slightly less dark now than it had been. Once the dawn came, his walk would be easier and pleasanter. How far had he come? A mile? How far to go? Another four or five? Better not to think about that. But as soon as it got light he would look out for tracks leading away from the beach and take one until he reached a road. Wouldn't it be better, in fact, simply to sit here until it did get light and then go inland without any more beach-work at all? Much better, of course – an instant improvement on Rimington's unrealistic plan. He took another sip from the bottle to celebrate this inspired improvisation, this piece of organic planning, and then shifted himself about a bit until he found a more comfortable, partly recumbent position in which to wait for the light. It would come, he reckoned, roughly from the direction he was facing, across the fields over Rimington's caravan. He closed his eyes and allowed himself to doze a little. The only trouble was that it was cold. He decided to finish the bottle. He needed its warmth and comfort more now than he would when it was no longer dark. Besides, his load would be that much lighter when he started to walk again.

Lying with his head back to get the last possible drop out of the bottle, he imagined a disapproving Rimington dancing up and down in the sand like an angry gnome. He threw the dry bottle as far as he could in the direction of the caravan and chuckled. What a ridiculous business! What an absurd interlude in the respectable career of a middle-aged Sussex solicitor! People wouldn't believe a word of it. You didn't go to France to get involved with the secret service. That was Berlin or Vienna. You went to France for French farce, adultery. All their friends – Susie too, no doubt – would assume that was what he'd been up to. If he told them how he and Rimington had crept out of the caravan door at 4 am, avoided the farm track for fear of alarming the Alsatian, struck into the fields without so much as a torch and hugged the edges in a semi-crouching posture in case anyone should spot them crossing the open spaces, they would roar with laughter. 'And who do you say you were running away from, David? Invisible agents of French Intelligence?'

David himself had ceased to believe in the invisible agents long before they reached the sand. Indeed, he had begun to wonder afresh whether Rimington wasn't suffering from delusions.

'I think we've made it, David,' he said, as they shook hands at the top of the beach. 'I think we've fooled the bastards.'

'I hope so,' David said, looking forward to being rid of him. Rimington let go of his hand and put an arm round his shoulder as if he, on the contrary, couldn't bear to part with David.

'You're the best friend anyone ever had,' he said, 'the best chap I ever bumped into. I knew it from the first moment I set eyes on you and you haven't let me down.'

He took his arm away and David, unable to think of a suitable reply, picked up his suitcase and began to walk.

'The best chaps don't get medals,' said Rimington, still just visible in the gloom, 'but they don't need them. Medals come from bureaucracies. The real thing is man to man.'

David had turned a little and waved cheerily, but without stopping. His relief at being finally on his own had carried him some way, until the clogging sand had gradually transformed his mood to irritation.

There was still no evidence of dawn and it was too cold to remain inactive any longer. Perhaps it would be possible to find a track even though it was dark. But after stumbling about over the dune for a while, David abandoned the idea and slithered back down the slope on to the beach. Suppose he walked further down towards the sea, where the sand was damp and firmer, he would surely make better progress. He splashed through a shallow pool left by the last high tide and found he was right. His socks were sodden now, but he could stride along at a good pace with his arms swinging. His body was warmer again and he could almost have recovered his cheerfulness, if he hadn't felt that something was obscurely wrong. His mind was too hazy to concentrate on the problem and he kept moving for some time with a sense that whatever the problem was it hardly mattered beside the fact that he no longer felt so tired and discouraged. Even his arms had stopped aching.

He remembered then that he had left the suitcase on the dune. The blood rushed to his head and he came slowly to a halt. He was trembling all over and would have liked to sit down and give up altogether. It occurred to him that perhaps he had carried out his original intention. He searched all the pockets of his coat and jacket. His passport and tickets and money were there, but not the exercise book or the buff envelope. He could easily go on back to England, abandoning the suitcase wherever it lay, but he would have to abandon his mission for Rimington with it. No doubt he could remember much of what Rimington had told him, but would that be any good without at least the exercise book to convey some idea of Rimington's desperate need to justify himself? He felt no conviction that anything could be done for Rimington in any case, but he had undertaken to do what could be done and this act of carelessness made the undertaking as valueless as if he'd never meant to keep it. There was no alternative but to go back and find the suitcase. Of course he wouldn't find it in the dark, therefore he would, after all, have to hang about until it was light.

He turned round, pushed his hands into his coat pockets, hunched his shoulders and began to walk slowly and doggedly back, with the sea on his right. 'The best chaps don't get medals,' he told himself sourly, 'but then the best chaps don't leave the precious documents on a sand dune either. Rimington's biggest mistake was ever to get mixed up with a best chap who wasn't a best chap and my biggest mistake was ever to get mistaken for a best chap by Rimington.'

After he had walked for some time and stumbled over a small outcrop of rock which he thought he remembered from the way out, he decided he'd better move up to the dune, however tiresome it was to walk there. Otherwise he could so easily overshoot the place where he'd rested. In fact, having reached the dune, he stopped where he was. Nothing whatever could be found in the dark, but as soon as it got light he would surely be able to discover his footprints and they would lead him more or less to the place where he'd left the suitcase. He didn't try to climb the dune this time, but flopped down on its slope and closed his eyes. His wet feet were numb, but the rest of him was temporarily warm from walking and from the agitation caused by the mishap. He managed to sleep a little.

When he woke it was distinctly lighter, not light enough to see footprints in the sand, but enough to pick out the outline of the dune behind him. The sea had come in some way. His face was damp and he was shivering, but he was reluctant to move. Instead, he burrowed himself into the sand, crossed his arms more tightly round his chest, closed his eyes again and slept a little more.

The next time he opened his eyes it was properly light, though the clouds were low and grey and it was beginning to drizzle. The sea was now quite high. On such a flat beach it came up quickly, but it was very calm, with only miniature breakers at the edge. David roused himself, sat up and beat his body with his arms to get warm. Then, slowly and stiffly, he got to his feet and went up the dune for a better view. The dune was much broader on top than he'd imagined and full of hummocks and hollows. Looking roughly north-westwards, the the way he'd been going, he thought he could see a track running inland in the distance. The metalled road he'd travelled yesterday in the bus couldn't be more than a mile or two down that. He even though he could hear a car. He turned round to look back the way he'd come. Visibility was very poor and the drizzle was increasing. There was little to be gained from stumbling back along the top of the dune in the hope of meeting the suitcase – it was too large and uneven an area. The best course was to retrace his footprints on the firm sand, provided the sea hadn't already covered them, and find the point at which they turned back towards the dune. Hurrying now, he ran down the dune and out towards the edge of the sea. His prints were still there, stretching back the way he'd come, though the tide was close to wiping them out. He walked back as briskly as he could beside them, sweating with anxiety and exertion, the rain saturating his hair and running down his face.

All this while he'd been vaguely aware that he could still hear the car, indeed that it seemed to be closer, but it was not until the noise had become very distinct that he mentally transferred it from the road somewhere inland on his left to the beach immediately in front of him. When he looked up from the line of footprints, he saw a grey, jeep-like vehicle with the hood up coming straight towards him, one wheel almost in the foam where the sea was breaking. David stopped in surprise and then drew aside up the beach since the vehicle was still coming on and didn't seem to have seen him. At once it altered course in his direction. Again David paused for a moment, his responses not very rapid, his mind still partly occupied with the problem of finding the suitcase. Then, almost too late, it occurred to him that the vehicle was not there by chance, but had come on purpose to find him. He jumped aside, the car braked to a halt only a few feet from where he'd been standing and he began to run towards the dune. He heard a door being opened and a man shouting at him in French. He took no notice. The great thing, he felt, was to reach the dune and be out of the way of the car.

'Stop!' the man shouted in English.

David had reached the loose sand at the top of the beach and was floundering and staggering in his efforts to keep running. He didn't think he would stop, not until he had the advantage of the slope and the broken ground. But as he wrestled with the slope, he heard a shot and saw a little puff of sand just in front of him. Not quite believing his own eyes and ears, he did stop; then turned to see what was happening behind him. His foot slipped in the sand and it must have looked to the man standing on the beach as if he was still trying to get away. The man fired again, and this time David was hit. He collapsed sideways into the slope, feeling relieved that at least there was nothing more he needed to do.

Part Three

9

Liz Mowle ran a trim and successful gallery near Mornington Crescent. She specialized in smallish works – prints, watercolours and drawings by British artists who were mostly still living and many of them young, but who had remained impervious to the experiments of the twentieth century. Gentle English landscapes were what she liked best herself, preferably with some element of the visionary, the mysterious or at least the misty. When a new artist came into the gallery with a portfolio of work to show her, it was a new Samuel Palmer or David Jones she always hoped to find and sometimes almost thought she had. In the early days of her marriage to Andrew Mowle, he had been charmed by this gentle, poetic side of her nature and entirely overlooked the efficient, hardheaded element that made her gallery work as a business. But then Andrew only ever saw in other people what related to himself at a particular moment.

After the dinner party at Simon Carter's flat at which they had finally parted, Liz almost immediately regretted that public quarrel and felt guilty about it. On the other hand, she was relieved that Andrew made no attempt to move back into the flat. He took away his bicycle and the bare minimum of his books and personal possessions and went to stay with an old university friend living in North Kensington.

'Now Ben Brooks can move in permanently,' Andrew said. 'I shall like to think of his socks draped over the wash-basin.'

But in fact after Andrew moved out she saw much less of Ben, as if she had only encouraged him to irritate Andrew. The real reason was that now she was free to have the person she did love in the flat. Matthew was a young landscape painter she had recently taken on at the gallery. He signed his works M. Davies and she was sure that if ever there was an heir to both Samuel Palmer and David Jones, M. Davies was the man.

Nevertheless, she still felt distantly responsible for Andrew and after a few weeks rang him up to see if he'd found somewhere more permanent to live and whether he wanted the rest of his books and some of the furniture.

'I really don't care,' he said. 'You can sell the books and anything else that might or might not be mine. Possessions are a bore. We'd all be much happier if we lived like monkeys, picking what we needed out of the trees and dropping anything we didn't need as we went along. I think I'm probably happier now than I've ever been in my life.'

'What about the trees?' she said.

'The trees?'

'Your friends.'

'Their name isn't Tree, it's Maddon.'

The next time she rang him he was in a different mood. He'd had a slight accident on his bicycle, was still limping about with a stick and had evidently got on the nerves of his host – or more likely his host's wife, whom he'd never liked.

'I've got to go,' he said. 'They're chucking me out. In any case, their children are more than I can stand. Children I'm sure, are solely intended by nature to wear out and destroy their parents. So as to leave the field clear for themselves. Then the trap falls on them in turn and they give birth to their own assassins. That's the real meaning of the Oedipus myth. Oedipus was the one who managed to have it both ways, destroying both his parents and his children at one fell swoop. We'd all like to do that.'

'Didn't he also destroy himself in the process?'

'Only his eyesight. I'm sure he felt it was worth it.'

'Where are you going now?'

'How should I know?'

'Why don't you get a flat of your own?'

'What would I use for money?'

'My offer still stands. I'll lend you a thousand. Didn't your brother say he'd chip in? You can surely get a mortgage for the rest?'

'Will you help me look for something?'

'Honestly, Andrew, I haven't got time.'

'Well, I certainly haven't. I've got to finish the TV treatment.'

All the same, she did give up one Saturday to helping him. They collected lists of flats from two or three estate agents and visited eight or nine likely places in various parts of Camden and Islington. About half of them seemed possible to Liz, but none raised the faintest flicker of interest in Andrew. It was Liz who put polite questions to the owners and thanked them for their trouble. Andrew hobbled grimly round, made a few disparaging comments without attempting to spare the feelings of the owners and stalked out to the car afterwards with the air of someone who had proved his point:

there were no flats he could afford that he could also conceive of living in. By the end of the day Liz felt anxious as well as irritated, understanding that the sort of help Andrew wanted was much more than she was prepared to offer.

'You need a holiday,' she said, as she dropped him off at Kentish Town tube station.

'A holiday!' he sounded furious.

'I don't mean a Caribbean cruise, I mean a change. You must be able to take a week or two away from the *Equalizer*. Couldn't you go down to the country – stay with your mother or your brother? Then you could perhaps finish your TV thing and that would be one less anxiety.'

He grunted, slammed the car door and began to limp away. She flicked down her indicator, put the car into gear and prepared to join the stream of traffic down Kentish Town Road. A moment later Andrew was back, banging on the near-side window. She wound it down a few inches.

'What do you want now?' His sullenness and rudeness were catching.

'Sorry, Liz. Sorry. And thanks for all you've done.'

'That's all right,' she said, grudgingly, still unable to throw off the mood he'd passed on to her.

'I wasn't wrong to marry you. You're the nicest person I know. But you were wrong to marry me.'

He turned away before she could reply and disappeared into the underground. Waiting at the lights further down the street, she felt a qualm. Had he been saying goodbye? Surely he wasn't so badly depressed that he'd jump in front of the train? Ought she to go back? The lights changed to green and she drove on, thinking for a few minutes that if there was an easy way to circle round she might go back. There wasn't and she didn't.

She saw him again a few weeks later when he came into the gallery. He was still limping, but had discarded the stick and his depression seemed to have lifted completely.

'I was passing,' he said, 'and I thought you'd like to know that I've bought a house.'

'A house?'

'I realized that what got me down about all those places we saw was that you couldn't swing a cat in them. It was staying with Donald that made me realize how necessary space is to human beings. Not just large rooms, but plenty of them.'

'Sounds elitist.'

'I don't mean that every single person – or couple – has to occupy a whole house to themselves. I mean they need access to a whole house. The answer is communities, not units.'

'Is there going to be a community in your house?'

'I'm working on it. I shall let out rooms to students and there'll be several communal spaces – the kitchen obviously, but also a library, a living-room and perhaps a games room in the basement.'

'It's a large house?'

'Ten or eleven rooms. Depending on whether you count the bathroom.'

'Only one bathroom? That will be very communal. Where is the house?'

'Near Finsbury Park. Handy for the tube and the park. Good bus services. The house needs a certain amount doing to it, but I'll get round to that gradually. The students will have to muck in, of course, but we don't want anything very sophisticated to start with – there's a cooker already there, some heating – all we need really are a few beds and the rest is decoration. I don't know why I didn't think of this before.'

'It sounds splendid,' Liz said, thinking that Andrew was really, when you came down to it, less a socialist than a vicar manqué. 'And the rents will pay the mortgage.'

'I shan't charge much in the way of rent. Just enough to cover the bills and contributions to the improvements perhaps. The point is for everybody to feel they're equally involved in making it work.'

'And you'll be able to afford it?'

'It's cheap. Forty-five thousand. With the money from my brother and some more from my mother and your money, the mortgage only needs to be twenty-five thousand, say two-fifty a month, which I can afford out of my salary. And that's not counting what I'll get for the TV series, which incidentally I've finished.'

'Congratulations!'

'Only the treatment, of course, so far. But that will bring in something and once the real thing is given the go-ahead, we're into the real money.'

'I couldn't be more pleased.'

'If you could make it fifteen hundred or even two thousand, that would be best of all.'

'No, I couldn't, Andrew, I'm sorry. I promised you a thousand and I can do just that.'

'Super! Thank you, Liz.'

He began to walk round the gallery, viewing the pictures without much attention. He had never been interested in visual art, so she was surprised when he stopped in front of the group of landscapes signed M. Davies and examined them closely.

'I like these,' he said, sounding surprised himself.

She wondered if he knew that Matthew had moved in with her, but thought it unlikely, given Andrew's lack of curiosity about relationships in general and his ignorance of the art world's in particular.

'I like them too,' she said.

'Can I have one?' asked Andrew and when she looked at him without knowing what to say. 'I don't mean as a gift, I mean, are they for sale?'

'You *are* in the money.'

'Well, of course I'd have to pay later, since it's all earmarked for the house, but I would like one of these pictures to put in it.'

Andrew left the gallery with an M. Davies landscape of Lulworth Cove under his arm and her cheque for a thousand pounds in his pocket. Liz had not managed to tell him that M. Davies was more than just one of her stable of artists.

In early June, Andrew held a housewarming party. It was fortunate, as Liz remarked to Matthew, that summer had come or the guests might have been required to warm the place with their own bodyheat, since there was little sign that the house could be heated any other way. The two main interconnecting rooms on the ground floor, where the party was based, contained Andrew's possessions: a few odd pieces of furniture, books piled along the walls in the absence of shelves, a portable typewriter, an elderly record player, a black-and-white TV set and a much worn and grubby Turkish carpet covering part of the floor. There was a gas fire in front of a crudely boarded-in fireplace and the walls were decorated with two or three kilims, a poster advertising an exhibition of Trades Union banners and, over the fireplace, Matthew's watercolour.

The guests divided roughly into two groups. There was a number of young people of both sexes – Liz assumed that these were students from Andrew's classes and were the pool from which he hoped to form his community. But the majority of the guests were middle-aged, well-off and successful. Any pair of them in isolation might have been visiting a grown-up child or other young relation in such a place, but gathered together, behaving as if Andrew's new house, like their own or those of their other friends in some smarter district, only needed a few touches to give it the elegance and refinement to which they were accustomed, they seemed unreal and even absurd. They were like a first night audience at the Royal Court Theatre which had suddenly changed places with the actors and found itself on a set intended to convey dereliction.

Andrew, darting about enthusiastically with a bottle in each hand, seemed not to notice the discrepancy between his guests and his house. He made some attempt to bring the students and the social lions together, but the incompatible groups fell apart again as soon as he moved on. When he first encountered Liz and Matthew – they had been let in at the front door by a short, plump girl with dark hair – Andrew assumed that Matthew belonged to the student group.

'Have you been introduced?' he asked.

'We arrived together,' Liz said, to make their relationship as clear as she felt it needed to be, 'and I'd like to introduce you to Matthew.'

Andrew smiled and nodded.

'He painted the picture over your fireplace,' said Liz.

'Good Lord, did you?' said Andrew. 'Don't you think it makes the room?'

'Matthew's paintings always hold their own extraordinarily well,' she said quickly before Matthew could say anything ruder.

But Matthew was flattered and Andrew was so delighted to meet the artist he admired – perhaps the first he'd ever admired – that it didn't seem to occur to him that there might be any other reason for Matthew to have come with Liz.

'I know the place well,' said Andrew, drawing them over towards the picture, 'and you've got it spot on. In fact, more than spot on, because it not only looks exactly like that, it feels like it. You know Lulworth Cove, don't you, Liz?'

'I'm not sure I do.'

'Of course you do. That time we stayed with my mother, we went over there one evening. My mother lives in Weymouth,' he explained to Matthew. 'The thing about Lulworth Cove,' he went on, without allowing either of them to break his train of thought, 'is that it doesn't seem quite real.'

'It's an almost perfect circle,' said Matthew.

'Exactly. It's not natural and yet at the same time it seems quite perfect, quite precisely what a cove ought to be. It's like the dream of a cove. The archetype of a cove. That's what's peculiar. It has that Platonic feeling. Instead of, as you usually do, seeing the imperfect, imprecise shadow, you're seeing the original idea. And that's the feeling your picture conveys. I can't tell you how important it is to me. It's an inspiration.'

'I'm glad you like it,' said Matthew, flushed with pleasure and mesmerized by the force of Andrew's enthusiasm, as Liz recognized that she had once been herself. She should have been pleased on Matthew's behalf and felt sure that she would have been if the enthusiasm had come from anyone else, but Andrew's had somehow lost its value. Not that she thought it was insincere or valueless in any absolute terms, but that she had learned, in the painful process of their drawing apart, to discount the sparkle in his eyes because it never seemed to light up anything beyond an idea and the words that expressed it. But that was unfair. Ideas were what excited Andrew, what he lived for, and if she had wanted something else from him, that was an error on her part, not a misrepresentation on his.

She turned away and looked for someone to distract her. A group of students, standing in a defensive circle near the drinks table in the window and making mocking comments on the middle-aged contingent of Andrew's guests, suddenly fell silent and stared at the door. Most of the people in the room, indeed, appeared to be aware at the same moment of who had come in, though the momentary hush was immediately followed by an increase in the noise of conversation, as though the social lions, at least, didn't wish it thought they were impressed or surprised. The students, however, were clearly impressed, for here at last was a successful person they all knew by sight and could approve of, if only because she was even better to look at in reality, in this incongruous setting, than on the screen.

Liz saw Maria Dobson with astonishment. Had Andrew's obsession with her not been in vain? Had he, after all, surmounting so many obstacles, won through to her? Yet Andrew himself, still in animated conversation with Matthew, was almost the only person in the room who hadn't seen her come in. Then, just behind Maria, Liz saw Simon Carter. That was the explanation, of course. Maria and Simon must still be lovers. Simon was Andrew's art critic and might naturally expect to be invited to his housewarming. Liz went over and reintroduced herself.

'You're not living here too, are you?' asked Maria.

'Certainly not.'

Simon nodded politely to Liz and slid gracefully sideways towards the drinks. He had only once visited Liz's gallery and obviously hadn't cared for what he saw there. No doubt he was afraid she would reproach him and try to hustle him, so she was amused to see that as he crossed the room he was spotted by Andrew and drawn towards the fireplace to view Matthew's picture and to be introduced to the artist. Simon would have to pay at least nominal respect to his editor's new taste in art.

'Does Simon do anything apart from criticism?' she asked Maria, meaning to make the question sound neutral, but in fact quite clearly expressing her irritation with him.

Maria was surprised and responded defensively.

'Should he? It seems to take up most of his time.'

'Really? I don't think he's one of the critics that gets round the smaller galleries much,' said Liz.

The conversation was controlling her. She felt as if she were driving down a road she had never meant to take.

'He seems to have very strong views about what's worth seeing and what isn't,' said Maria.

'How does he know until he's seen it?' Liz flicked back.

'You'd better ask him.'

Maria was offended by her aggressiveness and turned to talk to one of the two or three men who had gathered round her. Liz watched in silence for some time, trying to detect what Maria was really like. She must surely be tougher and more knowing off-screen than she appeared on it, if only to have got on to it in the first place? Or did she owe everything to her appearance? Was it all completely natural, in other words – the wholesomeness, the charm and the face? Without coming to any conclusion, but confused by her own instinctive hostility, she went to get herself another drink, meeting Andrew, who had left Simon and Matthew together, on the way.

'Your *princesse lointaine* seems to be still with Simon Carter,' she said.

'She does pick unsuitable men.'

'I think it's just as well you didn't make it with Maria. She's not at all your type. I've been observing her. All that innocence, that naturalness. It's very, very controlled. She's absolutely ruthless for her own interests.'

Again Liz felt that she was being dragged along by her own words in a direction she didn't wish – or only half wished – to go.

'You're jealous,' said Andrew.

'Why should I be jealous?'

'I've no idea.'

He darted away, leaving Liz angrier with herself than him. Why was she behaving like this? It must be the place – she was very sensitive to her surroundings and everything about this house and Andrew in it jangled her nerves. She went straight back to Matthew, helping himself to another glass of wine at the table in the window, and suggested they'd had enough. Matthew was surprised. He was elated by Andrew's admiration for his painting and by the conversation they'd had. Andrew, if he took the trouble, always cast a particular spell over people much younger than himself, because he was himself still essentially a twenty-five-year-old, exuding brilliance and promise without the wariness and complacency that usually come over those who have confirmed their brilliance and realized their promise in middle age.

Matthew was also surprised by Liz's dislike of the house and suggested that at least they ought to see the rest of it before they could judge it properly. The window they were standing by looked on to the patch of back garden. Apart from thistles and dandelions and the straggling ghosts of plants such as Michaelmas daisies and irises which somebody must once have planted deliberately, it was mainly a rubbish tip for rusting pieces of obsolete machinery – at least two washing machines, a cooker, a lawn mower, etc. The small, grimy kitchen, occupying an extension built out into the garden, looked as if it had been equipped with what could be saved from the garden. The large basement, the two upper floors and the attic were almost entirely empty, uncarpeted and depressingly dilapidated. There was obviously a bad damp problem in the basement and the state of the ceilings at the top of the house suggested that the roof leaked in several places.

None of this upset Matthew – he was delighted with the space – and his good humour gradually altered Liz's perception. Not that she ceased to find the place squalid and alien, but that she started to detach what she saw from her own feelings. Why should it matter to her any longer what conditions Andrew lived in, if he was satisfied? Matthew teased her about her reactions and she responded by exaggerating them, until they were both laughing at the idea of her being the one that had to live here. Leaning weakly against the window frame in one of the empty rooms, she suddenly found it spongy and yielding and a few bits of rotten wood fell on the floor as she quickly took her weight off it. Matthew pretended the floor too was about to give way and led her out round the edges with elaborate precautions that made her laugh even more. Going down the stairs, he warned her against the banister and pointed out a lavatory without a door. At the bottom of the stairs they had to sit down to calm themselves before returning to the party. As they did so, they heard somebody sweep a chord or two on a guitar and the whole roomful of guests suddenly grew quiet.

Entering the doorway, they saw that Andrew was the guitarist. Seated sideways on the edge of the table against the light, surrounded by wine bottles and dirty glasses, hunched up, with his large head seeming to grow forward rather than upward from his shoulders, he looked like a figure from a Dutch tavern scene.

'Jan Steen?' whispered Liz to Matthew, but before he could reply, Andrew addressed his audience:

'My latest song . . .' He seemed about to say something more, but struck another chord instead.

Some of the guests made polite noises, but most were clearly embarrassed. Liz had enjoyed Andrew's songs at the time they first met – several of them, after all, were inspired by her – and the others – the protest songs – had good, cutting words, even if the tunes were second-hand. But she didn't even know he still wrote songs and could hardly believe this was the right audience to sing them to. She crossed her arms and found she was gripping her chest almost too tightly to breathe.

'It's called "Troubadour",' said Andrew, striking the guitar again and dropping his head still further over it. His voice, falling into a mid-Atlantic accent, was very light, not unpleasant, but too constrained to command a large audience. The tune was hopelessly banal, a country-style piece which Liz felt she had heard countless times before. The words were excruciating.

'This is my fate,
To be shown your door.
This is my state,

> To love you all the more.
> Early or late
> I have to be your troubadour.'

The guests shifted and muttered, needing even more of the drink they couldn't now get at. Liz wondered how many of them knew who the song was aimed at, whether indeed Maria herself knew. Andrew had sung another verse before Liz spotted her, standing with Simon in the middle of the room. Her colour was perhaps a little higher than normal, but that might have been the heat of the room.

> 'Who can tell me that I'm foolish?
> Who can tell me that I'm wrong?
> You may think I'm being ghoulish,
> You may think it's just a song.
> You'll never love me,
> So you say,
> But listen, believe me,
> It won't go away!
> No, believe me,
> Not even for a day!
>
> 'The more you're seen,
> I want to touch you more.
> There on that screen
> It's you that I adore.
> But what have I been?
> Only your troubadour.'

Maria certainly understood now. As people applauded without warmth and many of them, following the direction of Andrew's gaze, turned to stare at her, she took Simon by the hand and pushed her way towards the door. Liz caught her eye, but looked away. Matthew put his hand out for Liz's glass.

'No, I think we'll go too,' she said.

Out on the front step with the bewildered Matthew beside her, she found she was still holding her empty glass. As she paused, wondering what to do with it, the door opened behind her and Andrew said; 'Where is she? Did she like my song?'

'She hated it,' Liz said. 'That's why she left. What did you expect her to do? Really, what did you expect?'

She handed Andrew her glass and walked away without looking back.

10

The Biggars had Susie Rutland, her two sons and her mother to stay for Christmas. The two sets of teenage boys, who had never met before, got on well with each other, mainly because William and Stephen Biggar, like their parents, were determined to make up to their visitors for David's disappearance. Susie Rutland and Judy Biggar had long conversations together. Each seemed to admire the other for being what the first was not. The outsiders in this otherwise harmonious gathering were James himself and Susie's mother. Mrs Chamberlin found the house too cramped and the boys too numerous and noisy. Her opinions on almost every subject were directly opposite to Judy's and James was not the sort of man she admired. She was polite, but too often pained. The truth was she disliked accepting what she thought of as charity on her daughter's behalf. She also, alone of them all, believed that David had disappeared deliberately, so that when any reference was made to him, she tended to show disapproval. The rest behaved more as if they had been bereaved. On the whole they kept off the subject of David, perhaps because of Mrs Chamberlin's attitude. And if so, James thought, that was probably her best contribution to the household. No doubt David was uppermost in all their minds, as he certainly was in James's, but there was nothing more that any of them could say to one another on the subject and they had no idea whether they should really be mourning him or hoping for his return.

James felt anger and guilt. His anger was directed at the Foreign Office, which had taken responsibility for the whole affair, assured Susie that it would do everything in its power to discover what had happened to David, but demanded in return that she do nothing and above all say nothing publicly herself. The official she saw at the Foreign Office was not Tony Cass. He had bowed out altogether, explaining that he'd only taken an interest in the first place because of his one-time connection with Balunda and his acquaintanceship with David. His own area of operations, he pointed out, was Latin America, not Africa, and he hinted that the problems of Balunda were beginning to look quite trivial beside those blowing up on the other side of the Atlantic. Susie had accepted all this with too much complacency, James thought. But since he couldn't suggest anything for Susie to do other than rely on the Foreign Office, he was more or less reduced to vilifying it and that, as Judy told him privately, was worse than useless. It could only increase Susie's distress. His guilt was for his own failure to make contact with David at the time Tony Cass first asked him to. Perhaps he wouldn't have prevented David's disappearance, but he might at least have gained some clue which would have helped the search for him. Tony had been right to call him a drip.

On Christmas Day they all went to matins at the parish church. It was quite a large building, built between the wars in an ersatz Gothic style, and was packed with vestigial Christians like themselves, paying tribute to the notion of Christmas as a set of pleasantly reassuring observances – presents, roast turkey, tree, plum pudding, choirboys, carols – rather than to the supposed founder of Christianity. James immediately recognized the vicar – a mild, wispy man with long sideburns and a permanent look of astonishment which came from his arched eyebrows and exaggeratedly open eyes – as a creature like himself, a fellow drip. Indeed, the Reverend Toomin conducted the service and delivered his sermon exactly as if he were an announcer employed by the Church of England instead of the BBC. James had never renounced his half-belief in a creator god, though he very much doubted the divinity of Christ and thought the Church's one foundation was really the literary genius of its Elizabethan and Jacobean translators. On this occasion, however, in his state of discomfort with himself, he made a conscious effort to identify with the service, to arouse in himself a kind of religious lust. Christ's message certainly seemed to be that only by recognizing yourself as a drip could you be redeemed by faith; and perhaps an announcer-style vicar came nearer to being a true Christian than the self-advertising thunderers and converters. On the other hand, Christ himself, divine or not, had definitely not been a drip. He had not practised what he preached – or only for demonstration purposes, as in the riding of the ass and the washing of the feet. James could easily imagine Tony Cass washing somebody's feet if he wanted to rattle him.

Everything about the church and the service conspired against James's desire to be caught up in a holy cloud. The windows were neither multicoloured nor clear, but a dispiriting, dirty amber; the choir was minimal and unambitious, attempting no more than to lead the congregation in a steady slog through the hymns and canticles; the churchwarden who read the lessons didn't listen to what he was reading; the congregation was dutiful but without enthusiasm; the vicar made even the blessing sound like a back-announcement. As they shuffled slowly out of the church, James promised himself that he would not go through this pointless ritual another Christmas. At lunch his frustration broke out in a sharp exchange with Mrs Chamberlin, who approved of the vicar and had found the service exactly to her taste.

The Rutlands left three days after Christmas. The day before they left James, at Susie's request, had a talk with her elder son, Tim. Nearly eighteen now, he had suddenly decided to join the army and Susie didn't want him to. She hoped that James, drawing on his own experience as a National Serviceman, might be able to dissuade him, but James felt equivocal on the subject. True, he hadn't much enjoyed his own two years' service, but he still harboured a romantic admiration for soldiers in the abstract, as his interest in General Butler revealed.

'I hear you're thinking of going into the army,' he said to Tim.

'Not thinking of it. I've definitely decided,' said Tim.

'Have you always wanted to?'

'I used to think more of the navy.'

'Did your Dad approve of that idea?'

'He didn't know about it.'

Should they be speaking in the past like this? James wondered. Grammar and the strange limbo to which they had consigned David became confused in his mind.

'Why have you decided against the navy?'

'There aren't any ships, are there?'

'If you were in the army, you'd almost certainly have to go to Northern Ireland.'

'Yes, I'd hope so.'

'The main trouble with the army,' said James, 'in my limited experience, is not the danger so much as the boredom.'

'I don't see that as a problem,' said Tim. 'There's plenty of sport, there's the training, which could be interesting, especially if you got into something like the Paras or the SAS, and there's a lot of social life. Also it's decently paid.'

James was silent. He felt that Tim was probably right – the army might be just the job for him.

'Do you think Dad would be against it?' asked Tim.

At least they'd got into the right tense again.

'I simply have no idea.'

'There have been soldiers in our family,' said Tim.

'You wouldn't think of being a lawyer, like your father?'

'That would be boring,' said Tim. 'Anyway, I'd never pass the exams.'

'If you thought your father was definitely against it,' said James, picking his tenses carefully, 'would that make a difference to your decision?'

'He probably would be against it,' said Tim, 'because Mum would persuade him to be.'

'But underneath? What would his real opinion be?'

'I don't think he'd have one. I should think he'd say go ahead and try it. But mainly because he wouldn't want to be bothered thinking about it.'

James murmured soothingly. Tim's candour took him aback. But why? Didn't he expect children to be aware of their parents' selfishness? No, it was surely what Tim's candour implied, that the unsatisfactory relationship with his father still existed and therefore that he expected to see his father again. Indeed, why not? Away at his boarding school, he was used to not seeing him for months at a time. It was he, James, who had been conducting the conversation on the unspoken assumption that David wouldn't return to express his own opinion.

'If it's really what you want to do, then I think you should,' he said.

'Well, I shall anyway,' said Tim. 'Mum's not going to physically stop me and Dad . . . do you know what's really happened to Dad?'

'I wish I did.'

'Is he a hostage? Or has he been murdered?'

'I should think that's most unlikely.'

'I know Dad's had other women,' said Tim, quite casually but still sounding like an inexperienced actor speaking a line he'd learned. 'Is it something of that sort?'

'I doubt it. But honestly, your guess is as good as anyone else's. It's all very distressing and very mystifying.'

James felt stiff and unhelpful. He had begun to warm to Tim, to see in him something of that bold, relaxed physicality he'd always envied and been warmed by in David, but Susie and David himself complicated the relationship. James was in a surrogate position. He couldn't simply make a friend of the boy. Perhaps if David were really dead, if he knew David to be dead, it would be possible, but as it was he was playing his customary role, being neutral, keeping the drama at arm's length, avoiding involvement, reading the announcements.

Two or three months after Christmas James's father had a stoke. He was a large, energetic man who, since his retirement from managing a chain of hotels, had kept fit by playing golf and gardening. But his years of companionable good living as a hotelier had made his complexion as sanguine as his temperament and if particular deaths went with particular lives, James supposed that they could all have foreseen this one for his father. Not that he was dead yet, but paralysed down one side and his speech affected, so that when James visited him in the hospital he found it strange to have to do most of the talking to a person who had hardly ever listened to him before for more than a couple of minutes at a time. When his father did speak – and it was not for want of trying or from any new-found willingness to listen to James chatting on that he didn't – he was difficult to understand and had to repeat the same short sentence several times, growing more irritated and urgent with every repetition. Finally he got his message through:

'Prune the roses!'

As James drove away from the hospital, he felt that irritation and his own sense of inadequacy blotted out every other aspect of their relationship. Yet although his father had always had a dominating personality, James had never been crushed by it, had been allowed to go his own way and make his own decisions. If the relationship was unsatisfactory, it was rather because his father had not expected anything of him, had given him what was necessary in the way of food, lodging, education, advice and funds, but demanding nothing in return, not even much account of himself, let alone respect or love. He did love his father, he was sure of that, and he certainly respected him for his cheerfulness, worldly wisdom and strength of character. He would have liked to believe, perhaps he had hoped for some sign – now that his father was brought low – that his love and respect were returned. It didn't seem that they were.

James visited his parents again in the spring, after his father had come out of hospital. His speech was better, though still slurred and uncharacteristically subdued. Physically he was completely altered, drained of energy as well as bulk, passive and half frozen, confined to a wheelchair instead of striding about filling a room. For some time James couldn't pin down the oddness of the visit and then understood that it came from nearly always looking down at his father. Because it was now he who had to lead the conversation – his mother had never been a great talker and spent much of her time shopping, getting meals and keeping the house tidy and efficient – James for the first time told his father about David's disappearance. His father was briefly interested and paid close attention especially to James's fulminations against the Foreign Office.

'You think they're hiding something?'

'I'm certain of it. I think that just as politicians of opposing parties have more in common with each other than they do with the voters, so governments have interests in common with other governments which they put before the interests of their own nationals. I simply don't believe that David couldn't be found or the truth about his disappearance discovered if it suited the government.'

'You feel strongly about this.'

'Yes, I do.'

James's mother interrupted them to wheel his father into the dining room for a meal and the topic didn't recur until later in the evening, when his mother was out filling the hot water bottles. His father began to speak in his new, toneless, muffled voice:

'Glad you feel strongly about your friend, James. Never noticed you feel strongly about anything. Of course you must have done and I should have noticed. Strange people we are. Two sides to us. Two instincts. One tells us to have children or we can't survive. The other tells us only we matter, only our own lives are important and children are irrelevant. Our world stops, who cares about theirs? Especially if they don't care. You fight a knife-edge war for the survival of civilization and your children don't even notice. Water under the bridge. Why don't you write a letter to the papers? I always did that when I felt strongly about something. It's your world, no one else's. Until it's your children's.'

Next day, when James left to go home, his father was still in bed. James bent down and kissed him – he couldn't remember if he'd ever done so before – and said goodbye. His father said nothing, but as James paused at the door he saw that his father was still looking at him and might perhaps be smiling. A few weeks later he suffered a second stroke and was taken back to hospital. James arrived at lunch-time, having stayed to complete his early morning stint at the BBC, and was taken aside by one of the hospital staff. His father had died an hour earlier. Did he wish to see the body?

It was lying, covered with a sheet, on a hospital bed in an otherwise empty cubicle. The male nurse pulled the sheet back to expose the head and went out quietly. James looked at the face for some time. Except in photographs he had never looked at it so steadily before. He felt extraordinarily little emotion, only annoyance with himself for having arrived too late to find him alive. That was absurd, of course. They had been virtual strangers for the best part of half a century, living almost as separately in their separate generations as if they had been grandfather and grandson instead of father and son. And when William was the one standing on his feet and James the one on the hospital bed, would it be much different? James wanted it to be different, but he feared it was already too late. Relationships, like characters, were set from the beginning, because they were aspects of the characters involved in them. With conscious effort you might modify both characters and relationships a little, but human beings really were mostly mechanical. It was just that we only partly understood the mechanism and therefore assumed the operator – free will, conscious choice – had more control than it did. How could he expect to miss his father now, when their characters had decided all along that they wouldn't miss each other?

But finally he kissed his father's forehead, as if to deny such a bleak conclusion and remind his father's ghost, if it still hovered, of their brief and unexpected rapport last time they'd been alive together. Then he walked slowly and numbly out of the hospital, emerging to a gloriously clear, sunny afternoon and a view of the sea below the cliff on which the hospital stood. Seagulls floated, banked and squealed. His father had been a month short of his seventy-fifth birthday. James had perhaps a quarter of his life left. He felt he would like to be able to give it to his father, to show that he had loved him in spite of appearances to the contrary, but he was immediately aware that such a feeling couldn't be trusted since it wouldn't be tested.

11

On a warm, cloudy day in early summer James met Simon Carter coming out of Broadcasting House. They nodded and smiled and were about to move on, James through the swing doors and Simon towards Oxford Circus underground station, when both at the same moment had second thoughts and stopped to speak to one another. Simon, James noticed at once, was jaunty and pleased with himself. His cheeks glowed, his black moustache shone like the fur of a well-groomed cat and his light-coloured casual clothes looked as if they were new that day.

'What have you been doing in BH?'

'Reviewing a show of Bridget Riley's.'

The mention of a woman artist made James think of the one he was interested in.

'What about Elizabeth Butler? Did that exhibition ever come off?'

'I'm afraid it didn't. My fault partly. I didn't press, because I got caught up elsewhere.'

'Oh yes?' James felt absurdly relieved, as if the secret of the Butlers had reverted to his keeping.

'The thing is, I've got married.'

'Congratulations!'

'It's something I should have done long ago,' said Simon. 'Except that I hadn't happened to meet Ms Right.'

'How did you meet her?'

'Her cat was run over. I sprang to the rescue.'

James wasn't sure he liked this new, ebullient Simon. In fact, he'd always found him a little too cocky and glossy, as though he lived in a world more weightless and effortless than the normal one.

'Well,' he said, moving slightly towards the doors, 'I ought to be checking a few pronunciations. Give my best wishes to your new wife – what's her name?'

'Maria,' said Simon, and unable to contain his pride, added, 'You may have come across her. She's a sort of colleague of yours, I suppose. Maria Dobson.'

'Good Lord!' said James, feeling immediately and stupidly envious, as Simon's tone seemed to require him to feel, though without any proper reason, since it had never occurred to him that he might want to marry Maria Dobson himself. 'I see. I've never met her. TV newscasters and radio announcers don't meet. They're personalities and we're just friendly voices. I do congratulate you.'

He passed through the doors and took the lift to the second floor with an unaccountable sense of gloom. Surely he wasn't so mean-spirited that he was made miserable by somebody else's happiness? What was the matter with him? Then he remembered that at least Maria Dobson had replaced Elizabeth Butler in Simon's affections and felt better.

Simon went on down Upper Regent Street without being at all conscious of having upset James. He wasn't normally insensitive to other people's feelings, but at the moment he was so saturated with happiness that it was as if he only had to shake himself for drops of it to fall on any bystander and make him happy too. His marriage to Maria was the primary ingredient, of course, but mixing a little in her world had also given him a new source of patronage. He had been asked to do a TV series on contemporary British art. In winning the princess he seemed to have won half her father's kingdom too. It wasn't just the money and the addition to his reputation. He had strong views about contemporary art and looked forward to sharing them with a wider public than he'd ever been able to reach through the *Equalizer*.

The marriage had been very hole-and-corner, with only Flora Decoud and a cousin of Maria's as witnesses. They were able to escape the notice of the press because Maria's real surname was not Dobson but Hinks and she had entered and left the registry office disguised in a blonde wig. Their honeymoon was a long weekend in Amsterdam and she returned to work afterwards without telling any of her colleagues that she was now Mrs Carter. However, the day after Simon met James they were going to Cornwall to stay with Maria's parents and they had agreed that after that they would gradually let their secret out.

Dr and Mrs Hinks lived in an old vicarage next to the church in a Cornish village called St Craw. The village was in a heavily wooded hollow about three miles from the sea, though it was more like five miles along the twisting single-track roads. The house, Simon thought, was a little too organized to be comfortable. Every polished surface shone, every cushion was plumped up and spotless, every piece of furniture positioned as if with the sticky tape on the floor used for stage furniture. The one element that seemed out of character was their collection of pictures. Simon guessed it was the doctor's collection more than his wife's, since it was he who eagerly took Simon round it as soon as he showed interest.

'Of course, we couldn't conceivably afford them now,' he said. 'They've suddenly come back into fashion again and are beginning to fetch ridiculous sums.'

The pictures were nearly all from the so-called Newlyn school, named after the village next to Penzance on the south coast of Cornwall where artists had congregated towards the end of the last century. Simon had never much cared for their work – what he'd seen of it. The Newlyners were too Victorian for him, too academic and melodramatic in style. He suspected them of being sentimental about the fisherfolk and the call of the sea in a way calculated to appeal to affluent members of the *fin-de-siècle* middle classes who liked sometimes, in their well set-up townhouses, to be reminded that they belonged to an island race. But as Dr Hinks conducted him round, Simon modified his attitude. The pictures were stagey and their style was antediluvian when you considered the way Pissarro, Monet, Gauguin, Van Gogh were painting at the same time just across the Channel, but to condemn them for that was to miss their point. Their appeal was in their unreality, in their telling a story you wanted to hear – at least he found that he wanted to hear it now, even though he hadn't before. The island race was a potent myth for the island race. He was temporarily prepared to accept it, especially since he was on holiday and had no wish to disagree with his father-in-law.

Yet the oddity remained, that these pictures were to Dr Hinks's taste. Their prevailing mood was pathos. True, it was robust, heroic pathos – the faces were tough, weathered, inured to pain, and there was usually a strong, comforting arm round the shoulders of the new widow as she stared out of the window towards the empty sea or bowed her head in her hands – but disaster and despair were paramount and were treated with a kind of relish. Frank Bramley's *A Hopeless Dawn*, belonging to the Tate, was the best known and perhaps the most tearful image produced by the Newlyn school, but Dr Hinks had a sketch by Walter Langley showing an old woman comforting a young one in front of a calm sunset view of the Lizard, whose title, taken from Tennyson's *In Memoriam*, was the bleakest Simon had ever come across: 'Never morning wore to evening but some heart did break.'

There was nothing melancholy about the doctor. He was a trim, fit man with a soft voice and a smile that flashed along his lips as he talked but was disconcertingly switched off altogether when you talked to him. He seemed to enjoy every aspect of his life, as why shouldn't he when it was all planned and selected to suit himself? He enjoyed his paintings too, pointing out details and technical touches and offering information about the artists' lives with the enthusiasm of a true collector. Simon asked him why he'd originally been drawn to this particular school.

'Of course, we didn't live in Cornwall then. Only came once a year. I hankered after the place, I suppose. Couldn't get enough of it.'

'Souvenirs?' suggested Simon.

'More than that. Therapeutic. That sounds too clinical. Restorative. Refreshing.'

'Rather gloomy, though, some of them.'

'Yes? I suppose so. Not more than real life in Lincolnshire, where I used to practise, you know. And I so much prefer the Cornish scenery.'

That was perhaps the straightforward explanation. What Simon saw as a preternatural emphasis on human suffering in the paintings, the doctor simply took for granted. The ostensible subjects were no more important to him than the mythological goings-on in the foreground of landscapes by Claude or Poussin.

After tea, Simon and Maria strolled round the village and into the broad, clear-windowed church. There was an ancient font near the door, but not much else of special interest. The churchyard, however, on its northern side set against the steep hillside under a screen of big trees and thick undergrowth and on its southern sloping gently towards the stream that ran through the middle of the village, was delightful – a place for the living more than the dead. Wild flowers grew in the long grass at the edges, butterflies and birds came and went and the evening sun raked the whole area through a gap in the trees on the southern side of the vicarage. Simon and Maria sat on an ancient box-tomb which listed slightly and had sunk into the ground. She let her head rest on his shoulder while he put his arm round her.

'Tired?' he asked.

She had driven them down in her car. Simon had never learned to drive.

'Fairly tired,' she said.

'Happy?'

'Fairly happy,' she said, meaning she couldn't be more so.

It occurred to him that, with a slight adjustment of Maria's position and a change in his sex and age, they could easily model for one of the groups in the foreground of a Newlyn school painting. His mind went to Hardy, master equally of exquisite moments of happiness and despair. Novelists didn't generally bother much with ordinary, even-tempered lives. They needed to keep their own and their readers' interest engaged with steep ups and downs.

'Never morning wore to evening,' he said, 'but some heart did break.'

'What?' asked Maria indistinctly, half asleep with the warmth of the sun.
'The title of one of your father's pictures.'
'I thought it was familiar.'
'Will ours, do you think?'
'Our what?'
'Our hearts break.'
'Surely.'
'You really believe it?'
'Nothing ever stays the same,' she said. 'And the only way our hearts would not break would be if we stayed just as we are for ever.'
'I'm afraid you're right. So we've had it.'
'Not yet, though.'

Her eyes closed again. Of course, Simon thought, feeling her hair tickle his cheek and pressing her side gently with his hand, neither of them believed a word of it. They had spent their first weeks after Simon's dinner party exploring each other's bodies, minds and memories. Their two separate pasts had merged, like the two rivulets twisting down round the steep slope on which St Craw was built to become the single, slow-moving stream in the bottom of the valley. It was inconceivable that the stream would divide again. Superstitiously, as if by attaching their relationship to the landscape in his mind he had made them really identical and laid a sort of topographical bet on their marriage, Simon decided he would not inquire into what happened to the stream after it left the village. He assumed it fed directly into the sea, a few miles to the west, and he didn't fear obliteration, if that was what the sea stood for, provided they went into it together. All the same, they weren't truly one person. They were two merged people who had agreed to accept each other's assets – or at least the assets that each coveted in the other – and treat the rest as irrelevant and disposable. Even the assets were not necessarily solid, consisting largely of what each thought the other possessed. Simon was not worried about this from his point of view – he considered he knew exactly what Maria was like. But he already detected misapprehensions in her view of him. She thought, for instance, perhaps because of the circumstances of their first meeting, that he was more of a man of action than he was. His Walter Raleigh-style sacrifice of his jacket to her cat had given her a fixed image of a Walter Raleigh character. Indeed, he liked to see himself in that light. The elegantly casual clothes he wore, his Kipling moustache, his disdainful, unflappable, imperial-expeditionary manner were part of the role. It was not a false role, it corresponded in many ways to natural characteristics he had inherited or learned as a child, but it was consciously cultivated and therefore partly artificial. He could see that he only fitted the role some of the time, that the Walter Raleigh of the street, as it were, dwindled into somebody more shapeless and uncertain in private. Perhaps the real Walter Raleigh had too. Perhaps a person wouldn't cultivate such an image at all – throw his cloak in a puddle and make a theatrical farewell speech on the scaffold – if he weren't deeply unsure of his own reality. But Maria looked for Walter Raleigh off the street as well as on. Because he didn't want to disappoint her, because part of the pleasure of their relationship for him was in playing this role for her, he occasionally felt, as at this moment, a sense of strain and disturbance. How long could he keep it up? Would he lose her if he failed to? His body was beginning to ache from holding the same position under her weight. He shifted a little and she sat up and looked at him.

'Are you going to be bored here?' she asked. 'Do you really like the country?'

'A book of wine, a glass of verse and thou beside me in the wilderness . . .'

'I couldn't get out soon enough.'

'We don't have to stay if it upsets you,' he said. 'We could go to Timbuktu instead.'

'Could we?'

'Or the Hindu Kush or up the Orinoco,' he said. 'But for me it's much more exotic to visit St Craw and glimpse your childhood.'

'I was never a child here. That was Lincolnshire. Here, only a disaffected teenager.'

He laughed.

'I'm trying to imagine it. The flashing eyes, the sulky mouth, the vicious retorts, the slammed doors.'

'Weren't you ever like that?'

'It was so many years ago.'

Superior age was one of his assets and he flourished it recklessly on many occasions, getting the most out of it while he could.

'You seem to have a good memory of what it's like.'

'I've seen the films and read the books.'

'You're always making out that nothing's real.'

'For an art critic,' he said, 'only hedonism is real.'

He leaned across and kissed her. She put her arms round him and he pulled her on to his lap and, holding her masterfully with one hand behind her head, swung her sideways and downwards. Then, parodying some great lover of the screen, he bent towards her and kissed her passionately on the mouth. When they disengaged, Simon saw a man standing near the door of the church watching them.

'Evening!' the man said.

'Good evening!' they both said.

The man started down the path towards the gate into the road, passing nearer to them as he did so. Then he hesitated, stopped and turned to Maria.

'You know, I'm sure we've met somewhere,' he said.
'No, I don't think so,' she said.
'You don't live here?' he asked.
'No, just visiting.'
'We couldn't have met at one of the summer concerts?'
'No, we haven't met,' she said.
'My name's Mitten,' he said. 'Brian Mitten.'
'How do you do?' she said abruptly and turned away.
'Well, it's very strange,' he said, lingering in the hope of further conversation.

Finally, getting no encouragement, he went on down the path, but stopped again at the gate to look back with the same puzzled expression. Then he disappeared along the road.

'Why didn't you put him out of his misery?' asked Simon.

Maria shrugged.

'He was polite enough,' Simon said.

Maria shrugged again and then got up and walked towards the vicarage gate. Simon followed her. He felt upset not by the man's seeing them in a clinch, but by Maria's attitude. Her contempt – if that's what it was – could so easily extend to him. Why, after all, should she have picked him out from so many? No doubt he was better-looking than Brian Mitten, who gave the impression of being undernourished and badly proportioned. Brian Mitten's ears stuck out, his nose turned up clownishly and his clothes needed to go to the cleaners. But was there really such a gulf fixed between that man and this, that she could hardly be civil to the one and had married the other? It wasn't that he was surprised by or condemned her attitude to Mitten. Men pressed towards her wherever she went – they knew who she was, they thought they knew or they wanted to know – and she must often feel like a solitary cow in a world hopelessly overstocked with bulls. No, it was his own anomalous position that he was suddenly aware of. He identified with Mitten and felt separated from her.

At the gate she stopped and turned towards him. He stopped too. She wasn't looking at him. She seemed to be staring at a gravestone to his left. He looked at her as if she had become a complete stranger. She was not even the woman he had seen running to save her cat. She was someone who seemed to be visiting the old vicarage and was undoubtedly more beautiful, more exactly his idea of a desireable woman than any he had ever seen. His finger went up to his moustache, as if to convince himself that he was not the clean-shaven Mitten. Then she stopped staring at the gravestone and looked straight at him. After a moment she smiled.

'What's the matter?' she asked.

'I can't believe you married me,' he said humbly, forgetting that he was the reincarnation of Sir Walter Raleigh.

'Did I?'
'Maybe there's some mistake.'
'Is your name Carter?'
'You're not by any chance Maria Mitten?'
She shivered and became serious.
'I really didn't fancy him,' she said. 'I hope we don't meet him again.'

They turned in at the vicarage gate and met Vronsky, who had come with them to St Craw, looking for his supper.

During their own supper, Simon asked the Hinkses if they knew Brian Mitten. They didn't, but when the pudding was being served, Mrs Hinks passed the question to their cook — a woman from the village who came in to do the evening meal when they had visitors.

'He lives in Padstow,' she said. 'I don't think he's lived there long. He comes here to play the organ on Sundays — Mr Winter's been in hospital for nearly a month. But nobody cares for this Mitten.'

'Why not?' asked Mrs Hinks.

'He plays the hymns and psalms all right, but his voluntaries are purgatory. Very loud and no tune at all.'

'Is that the only reason you all dislike him?' asked Dr Hinks.

'He's sly. You know Mrs Champion puts pots of marmalade and chutney outside her gate — for people to help themselves and leave money in the box. Well, she saw this Mitten stop there — his head came over the hedge and she was quite sure it was him — and when he'd gone she went out to collect the money — there were three pots gone, but no money.'

'Did she go after him?'

'He'd ridden away on his bike by then. Next time she saw him at the church, she didn't like to mention it.'

'Perhaps he found he had no money and meant to pay later,' said Mrs Hinks.

'Not him. And if he did mean that, why didn't he? No, the sooner he goes back where he came from — Bristol, I think it was — the better.' She returned to the kitchen.

'The evidence seems a little slender,' said the doctor. 'Mrs Champion might have been mistaken about the head she saw over the hedge, or indeed about the number of pots she put out in the first place.'

Maria laughed. 'It sounds like Miss Marple,' she said.

After supper, the four of them played Scrabble. Simon was no match for the others, but he was beginning to feel more relaxed with Maria's parents and didn't mind. He found Mrs Hinks warmer and more interesting to talk to than he'd suspected from her slightly forbidding appearance. Perhaps it was only that she seemed genuinely interested in him.

'How did you come to be a critic?' she asked, while her husband was scratching his head over a combination of letters.

'When I came back from Africa,' Simon said, 'I got a job working in a gallery. I started to write introductions for some of our catalogues and then I gradually realized that I was more interested in making sense of what was going on than in selling it. So when a critic I knew told me he was resigning, I asked him if he'd recommend me for the job.'

'Rubella,' said the doctor, laying his letters down the board so as to reach the triple word score at bottom right.

'That won't do,' said Maria, 'it's Latin.'

'Latin naturalized into English,' said her father. 'It's a perfectly acceptable usage.'

'Nonsense!' said Maria. 'It's a scientific word in Latin.'

'I should have thought it would count,' said Simon. 'It's fairly common currency, like "influenza" or "sinusitis".'

The word wasn't in the small Oxford Dictionary they had to hand, but Dr Hinks insisted on consulting Webster, which was allowed as a fall-back, and found it there. Maria was annoyed. She had had a word ready to capture the triple score. She was still cross with Simon after her parents had gone to bed and left them downstairs with glasses of whisky.

'You don't have to curry favour with my parents,' she said.

'Don't be ridiculous!'

'I didn't bring you down here to be nice to them.'

'It was only a game,' he said, smiling to show that he didn't take her or the cliché seriously.

'My father always cheats,' she said. 'He can't bear to lose.'

'Perhaps you're like him in that,' he said.

'Perhaps there's something about you that's like him,' she said, sounding still angrier. 'Always superior, never flustered, never letting go.'

He sipped his whisky and made no reply, thinking that she was both right and wrong. He was often flustered, but could never let go.

'I've always hated these pictures,' she said, standing in the middle of the room and waving her arm violently at the walls. 'Sentimental gloom. Did you say you liked them?'

'I like them better than I used to.'

'Shall we go home tomorrow?'

'If you want to.'

'It would be awfully rude to my parents, wouldn't it?'

He nodded and looked at her without expression, alarmed by her childish destructiveness, but also excited by this clip of her as she must have been before she left home and became a public figure.

'But you needn't worry. They wouldn't blame you. They know what I'm like. They gave me a happy home life and I wanted none of it.'

You exaggerate, he thought, getting up and going to the window. When the millions watch you on the screen they see a happy home life. This display of temperament is the unconvincing part. He drew the curtains and looked out into the darkness, seeing his own reflection and hers over his shoulder.

'What *did* you want?'

'I just wanted out.'

'You got it,' he said, turning towards her, seeing with relief that she was beginning to calm down and wondering if Walter Raleigh had ever had this sort of scene with Lady Raleigh and if so, what his technique for riding it had been.

She finished her whisky and said defiantly, 'But I don't want it back. Not in any form.'

'Have I ever offered you a happy home life?'

'I wish we hadn't married,' she said, sitting down suddenly on the sofa.

'I forced you into it.'

'Don't let's tell anyone we are! I'd rather it was a complete secret.'

'Fair enough. As long as you're still *my* secret, let them all think they can still have you.'

He remembered that he'd already boasted of his secret to James Biggar and hoped he hadn't passed it on.

'And I don't like that picture by Flora Decoud that hangs over the bed in your flat. What does it mean?'

'I don't think it means anything. It's an arrangement of lines and colours.'

'She said it represented something.'

'Then ask her what.'

'I find her disturbing. I'm not sure I like her.'

'We'll move it anyway. It probably represents a plant of some sort. Flora used to be a surrealist when she was very young. Her subjects then were always plants – plants you might meet in nightmares. That painting is called *Tanglewood Tail*, which is a reference to Nathaniel Hawthorne's book of Greek legends.'

'I've read it.'

'Given the way "tail" is spelt, I should think there's a sexual reference too. Flora's paintings are always to do with sex, I think. And she insisted I hang this one over my bed, so it's probably fairly explicit if you know how to decode it. It's probably absolutely disgusting.'

'But you've never asked her about it?'

'I also find her disturbing.'

'Is that all abstraction is? An elaborate code for something else?'

'That's what art is.'

'And you have to have critics to decode it, of course.'

'Of course. Artists paint solely for critics, didn't you know? Just as people start wars and murder their wives solely for newscasters. You and I are both in the retail trade.'

'Give me some more to drink!'
'I've got a better idea,' he said. 'Let's go for a walk!'
'It's completely dark.'
'Not by any means.' He peered through the window.
'All right.' She put out her hand. He went across and took it.
'You're not too tired?'
'No. Why should I be?'
'After all that driving?' He pulled her off the sofa. 'But I really meant that I thought you might be tired of me.'
'I thought you *were* tired of me.'

They let themselves quietly out of the house and walked down the road away from the village. The full moon was very large and bright, the air pleasantly warm. Vronsky, who had been out hunting in the garden, followed them, warily and with dignity, his thin tail curved tautly in the air like a ceremonial sabre. They crossed the stone bridge over the stream, when the road began to rise again, and passed between woods on either side. The trees were large and well spaced without much undergrowth. When they came to a gate on the right-hand side, Maria climbed over it. Simon followed. The moonlight wasn't much help in the wood, but Maria knew it well and they made steady progress in spite of the uneven ground. Vronsky had either not ventured so far or was invisible in the deep shadows.

'Vronsky won't get lost, will he?' said Simon.
'You worry too much about that cat.'
'What if he met a fox or a badger?'
'He likes adventures.'

Simon doubted if he did. In his experience, animals only liked the sort of adventures in which they pursued and destroyed other creatures, not those in which they themselves might be worsted. He suggested this to Maria.

'Maybe,' she said. 'But humans are different, aren't they?'
'Some humans.'

They were far into the wood now and suddenly found themselves in a small clearing, dimly lit by the moon.

'What a stunning place!' said Simon.
'I'm glad you like it.'

They stood side by side with their arms round each other's waist. The light made the clearing look artificial – it seemed to have been prepared for some formal event, a play, a ballet, a duel.

'What should happen, do you think?' asked Maria.
Simon turned to look at her.
'Well?' she said, turning her head towards him, so that their noses almost touched.
'I think you should take all your clothes off,' he said.
'A floor show?' she said. 'What a vulgar idea!'
'It's a very select audience,' he said.

'You've already seen the show.'
'Not in a natural setting.'
His hand moved up her back, searching for the zip of her dress. She disengaged her arm from his waist and stood back out of his reach, then walked away to a tree some twenty yards to their left. It had been broken by lightning or some other accident – a large branch growing out of the main trunk from quite low down had fallen horizontally, though still attached raggedly at the break. Maria went behind the tree and after some moments her arm appeared and hung the dress over the fallen branch. Simon stood without moving exactly where she'd left him. The rest of her clothes joined the dress on the branch. Maria stepped out from behind the tree and stood only a foot or two away from it, partly shadowed by it. She wasn't very distinct. Simon took a step forward and then another, cracking a twig, making an unbelievably loud noise in that still place. Maria moved quickly back nearer to the tree.

'It was me,' said Simon. 'I can hardly see you.'

Maria seemed to take courage from his voice. She strode out boldly into the moonlight and stood there facing him, her weight on one leg, with the other slightly bent and thrust forward, her arms folded under her breasts. Of course Simon had seen her body many times before, but never, as he said, out of doors, nor in such a dramatic light, at such a spectatorial distance. She didn't look like a Greek goddess, he thought. The ancient Greeks – or at least their sculptors – liked their goddesses with small breasts, sloping shoulders and narrow hips. The scene was not the naked Diana surprised by Actaeon in some Renaissance masterpiece by Titian or Veronese: Maria's pose was too modern, there were no rich draperies, no supporting chorus of other naked ladies or cherubs. Nor was she a fairy-tale princess. Princesses one imagined to be ivory white and delicately petite, almost two-dimensional, perhaps because of Persian-style illustrations to *The Arabian Nights*. Maria was not exactly large, certainly not fat, but she was sturdy. What did she remind him of?

From the other side of the clearing there was a yowling sound and Vronsky appeared, walking towards her like a dancer crossing a stage between two passages of pirouettes. Maria turned her head to her left to look at him and it seemed to Simon as if he had known the pose and the moment long before. Vronsky reached her and rubbed his fur against her legs. Maria bent to stroke him and then looked up again at Simon.

'Do you want me to do a dance?'
'I'd love that,' said Simon.
'I don't think I'm in the mood.'
'What sort of mood are you in?'
'I feel isolated.'

'May I join you?' asked Simon, removing his own clothes as he went towards her. 'It's a good act, but it needs a clincher.'

'Have you got a clincher?'

By the time he reached her, he too was naked. After a while they lowered themselves with some care on to the scratchy, uneven ground. When they had temporarily finished moving, Vronsky came and settled himself against Simon's back.

'I'll bet you've never done that before,' Simon said.

'What do you bet?'

'Have you?'

'Not here.'

'Where then?'

'I think it must have been grassier,' she said. 'I don't remember having all these sticks embedded in my bum.'

'You probably imagined it, then. Reality is always sticks embedded in the bum.'

They got up and went to repossess their clothes. The moon had moved on and it was much darker, so Simon's, scattered along the way between his viewing and his closing points, were not easy to find. He had just stooped for his trousers when he was aware of a flash of light to his right. He looked up and saw Maria recoiling from the tree. There was another flash. It came from behind the fallen branch where her clothes were and was unmistakably a flashbulb. Clutching his trousers, Simon ran towards it, shouting:

'Who's that? What do you think you're doing?'

There was a third flash and then the sound of someone running away through the trees. Simon caught his foot in a hollow and fell down, twisting his ankle. Maria came and helped him up.

'That was bad,' said Simon. 'How long had he been there?'

'Who knows?'

'You were quite close to the tree when he opened up.'

'At first I thought it was a shot.'

'What a bugger!'

'I'm sorry,' she said.

'Why are you sorry? It's him that should be sorry.'

'It was my idea to come here.'

'But the floor show was my idea.'

'Mine too.'

'Was it?'

'I think so. At any rate it seemed the right thing to do.'

'It was. In spite of that bastard.'

She dressed and then, since his ankle was still painful, found his clothes for him and supported him back through the wood to the road. Vronsky greeted them in front of the vicarage door.

'Cats!' said Simon. 'Useless creatures! Why couldn't you have barked?'

12

I

Lulworth Cove was swarming with holidaymakers. Andrew's mother parked half across somebody's drive in West Lulworth, then she and Andrew and Matthew walked round the edge of the hill and settled for their picnic high up on the slope overlooking the cove and the bay beyond. It had rained earlier, but the warm wind had dried the grass and the view across to Weymouth was especially clear: they could see tiny warships anchored in Portland Harbour. Groups of people walked round the path above them from time to time, but the mass of trippers was on the beach round the cove and there was a constant stream of them coming and going on the slipway down to the right.

After tea, Matthew moved a little down the slope to the left and began making sketches, using a small pad and a soft pencil. Andrew and his mother sat in silence for a while, observing the scene, then she reached into the picnic basket for her book and lay back with a sigh against the steep slope.

'I don't know why you read that rubbish,' Andrew said.

'Because I don't find it rubbish,' she said.

'Romantic tosh,' he said.

'Iris is a very intelligent woman. Her characters are extremely realistic – I've met nearly all of them at one time or another – and she deals with serious moral issues.'

'Pfff!' he said and then remembered that he'd not come here to argue with his mother, but to ask her for money.

'Okay,' he said, 'I'm probably wrong. I gave up reading them in the Sixties and anyway I don't much care for novels.'

'You're a very arrogant person,' she said. 'Just like your father. Luke, I think, is more like me.'

'You mean he's not arrogant?'

'I shouldn't tell you this, Andrew, because he particularly asked me not to, but Luke is in some difficulty over money. Owing to the Common Market cutback on dairy produce, he's having to reduce his herd. I do think you should try to pay him back at least part of the money he lent you.'

'Surely the government's making some recompense?'

'I've no idea. But it's bound to be inadequate. How could it be otherwise, since the purpose of the cutback is to save the government money?'

'Nevertheless, the government's responsible.'

'I don't see why.'

'Because,' said Andrew, drawing his legs up and resting his chin on his knees, 'it was the government that encouraged farmers to produce more milk.'

'You always think everything's down to the government and nothing to individuals.'

'I'm a socialist.'

'In any case, I suppose you don't deny that you, an individual, borrowed money from him, another individual, and that the government doesn't come into it.'

'I shall do everything I can to repay him.'

'He does need something now.'

Andrew looked out to sea. Then he got up and went down the slope to where Matthew was.

'How's it going?'

'Not much good,' said Matthew. 'Too many people.'

'Maybe if we took a walk,' said Andrew, 'and came back later when most people have gone home . . .'

They left Mrs Mowle reading her book beside the picnic basket and followed the path round the hill. They were cut off from the top of the hill by a barbed-wire fence.

'Military,' said Andrew, in a knowing tone, as if one expected on a country walk in England to have to make detours round military installations.

'How do you mean?' asked Matthew.

He had never had any interest in the contemporary world as it appeared in newspapers and on TV. He'd always lived in London and accepted the daily round of noise, crowds, buses, tubes, fast foods, street lights and, until recently, education at school and art college as the basic facts of his life, but his interests since he was ten or eleven years old had lain elsewhere: in a pastoral England which was more mythical than historical, an invention mostly of his own imagination, stimulated by a passion for English Romantic watercolours and partly endorsed by selective visits to real countryside where he could make his sketches.

'I mean this is one of their no-go areas from which the public is excluded. Thousands of acres of good land kept for this useless purpose: training soldiers to fight the last war. The vanity of generals.'

Matthew looked at him with surprise and stopped to stare through the fence as if he expected to see the generals and their armies materializing over the hill, their boots scattering the brown, yellow, white and black-spotted butterflies and trampling the multicoloured stipple of blue cornflowers and harebells, white cow-parsley, purple bugle, pink clover and yellow coltsfoot and rock-roses that covered the short windbeaten grass. It was Matthew's extraordinary innocence and literalism that appealed to Andrew and had prompted him to invite Matthew to use the top floor of his new house as a studio. Matthew had accepted immediately and, singleminded about his work as he always was, had hardly even listened to Liz's objections. He continued to spend the nights with Liz at her flat, but he was in Andrew's house all day. He didn't pay rent, but was invaluable to Andrew for his talents as a carpenter, electrician, plumber and general handyman. He'd already replaced most of the rotten window frames and floorboards, put a new door on the lavatory and a new toilet bowl inside it, shored up the banister and made temporary repairs to the roof.

Their friendship had grown as Andrew's relations with the other members of his would-be community had soured. The idea of everyone contributing freely and equally had quickly proved unworkable. Nobody seemed to have the funds to pay the bills or the time to shop, cook, clean or clear up. He had drawn up a roster of duties and specified a minimum weekly payment, but by the end of the month both systems had broken down for lack of proper supervision. The more conscientious students left, the others stayed and the community decayed into a system of everyone for him- or herself, with Andrew reduced to the status of landlord, demanding but not always receiving rents, harassed by squabbles over the use of stores and amenities. Matthew – present only in the daytime, aloof from all the bickering and making small but steady improvements to the building – was the only positive gain.

Their joint visit to Dorset to stay with Andrew's mother had been arranged on the spur of the moment. The bank manager wanted something done at once about Andrew's overdraft and Matthew had decided that he needed another encounter with Lulworth Cove. He paid no attention to Liz's objections, resolutely refusing to see that there was anything awkward about his friendship with her ex-husband.

'You still like him yourself,' he pointed out to her. 'It was only being married to him that was the problem and I'm not married to him.'

'Do you think he's homosexual?' she asked.

'He may be, but I'm not,' said Matthew.

Andrew's mother also seemed in doubt about the nature of their relationship. In her usual forthright way she broached the matter as soon as she'd let them into the hall of her small house on the west side of Weymouth.

'I haven't made up the beds,' she said, 'because I didn't know how you wanted to sleep.'

There was silence. Andrew raised his eyebrows, Matthew left the question to him.

'In one room or two?' she said.

'Doesn't matter,' said Andrew, not seeing it as his problem.

Mrs Mowle looked at Matthew.

'Two,' said Matthew.

'Thank you,' she said, liking him immediately.

'But we can make the beds,' Matthew added.

'I was hoping so,' she said.

Andrew and Matthew walked on, following the path. Andrew was still thinking about the fence and the militarism it symbolized.

'Oh Christ!' he said, suddenly stopping so that Matthew, walking half beside and half behind him as the path allowed, nearly banged into him. 'Look at this!'

The path and the fence beside it, following the contour of the hill, ended at right angles to a much higher barbed-wire fence, mounted on rusty iron posts, which ran straight down from the top of the hill to the bottom. There was a stile set at this point in the original fence and Andrew hurriedly and angrily climbed it and stumped off towards the top of the hill. Red flags were flying on tall white poles at intervals inside the fence to his right and there were triangular white noticeboards reading 'Danger. Unexploded Shells. Keep Out'. In the distance a series of promontories descending into the sea looked, with their notched, scaly outlines, like a row of sleeping dinosaurs.

At the crest of the hill the fence was interrupted by a gate, with tangles of barbed wire across its top. A notice read 'Lulworth Range Walks – Closed'. A smaller swing gate set into a framework beside it was padlocked. Andrew seized it with both hands and shook it violently.

'Doesn't it get on your wick?' he said.

'Um,' said Matthew.

'Let's climb over!' said Andrew, returning to the fence, which was lower and less well defended than the gate.

'Is that a good idea?'

'The thing is a provocation,' said Andrew. 'And the more we question whether it would be a good idea to climb this fence, enter that building, object to this government decision, probe that secret, the more we learn to wear our chains.'

He was putting his foot on the wire as he spoke and, using the post to steady himself, clambering up from strand to strand. Then he jumped down the other side and waited for Matthew. They joined a path running along the ridge past a separate enclosure containing a low brick building and what looked like an antique radar scanner. For a while they walked cautiously, looking all around them, expecting they weren't sure what – a dog, a sentry, a minefield, a burst of machine-gun fire or an angry general. But the place was deserted. Down below on their left were the outskirts of West Lulworth and the buildings of what was clearly an army camp. Southwards, to the right, the land dipped into a small plateau before ending in the sea. There were more clouds than before, but the sun still shone intermittently, throwing their shadows ahead of them.

Walking now more confidently, they reached the highest point of the ridge and found themselves looking down into a kind of natural stadium, with a little wood near the centre and patches of low scrub. The hillside below them was scored with tracks and white scars where the chalk had been exposed by shellfire. Giant letters on boards were propped up to denote target areas.

'There you are!' said Andrew triumphantly. 'The Armoured Corps' firing range.'

Matthew looked blank.

'Tanks,' said Andrew. 'We've seen their secret.'

There was no sign of any tanks. Andrew began to descend diagonally, shading his eyes and peering about in the hope of spying a tank hiding in the bush. Matthew stayed where he was.

'What's that?' he called, pointing across the valley.

Andrew paused in his descent. On the far side of the range was a small car park. Two or three cars had stopped there and their occupants were just visible staring across at the firing range from the opposite side. Several small children emerged from one of the cars and began to chase each other in zigzags. Andrew came back and rejoined Matthew.

'Doesn't seem all that secret,' said Matthew.

They returned in silence the way they'd come. The sun was in their eyes and they were grateful for the intervals of cloud. The fence seemed more difficult to climb than on the way in and Andrew snagged his trousers as he negotiated the top strand of wire. When they got back to their picnic-place overlooking the cove, Mrs Mowle was asleep, with her book spread open across her face to shade her eyes. Andrew lay down on the slope near her and stared out to sea. Matthew opened his pad and began to draw. The cove was nearly deserted now and the tide had come up a long way. A couple of fishing boats were heading for the mouth and another was bobbing near the slipway. After a while Mrs Mowle sat up, put a blade of grass in her book to mark the place and closed it.

'Did you have a nice walk?' she asked.
'All right. We went over the fence and into the MOD bit.'
'Was that interesting?'
Andrew grunted noncomittally.
'Why have you split up from Liz?' she asked.
Andrew shrugged. 'It's been coming for a long time,' he said.
'You haven't been married all that long. She's a nice girl.'
'I know she is.'
'It's a great sorrow to me. I'd have liked a grandchild.'
'We should have thought of that.'
'It's all very sad,' said Mrs Mowle.
'Of course it's sad. Life is sad. Life is very, very sad indeed.'
'I entirely disagree with you. Some people have sad lives, that's true. But I don't see why yours should be sad.'
'What about Father's?'
'He didn't have a sad life,' she said, sounding injured. 'On the contrary. Much of the time he enjoyed himself hugely.'
'Then why did he commit suicide?'
'He did not commit suicide. You've no right to say that. There was an open verdict at the inquest and I am absolutely convinced that there was no question of suicide. He was not an unhappy man.'
'He'd stopped believing in Christianity. That must make a vicar unhappy.'
'He was always full of doubts. Faith, he used to say, was like a long cliff walk. You were always going right up and then right down again, wondering if you could face the next climb up and then doing it all the same. He loved cliff walks. He also loved his job. In between hating it – or rather fearing it.'
'If it wasn't suicide, why did he have the garage doors shut?'
'Because, as I explained at the inquest, he forgot to open them. He had gone into the garage by the side door, got into the car and started the engine and then fell asleep.'
'It's not very likely.'
'It was Easter Monday. He was exhausted.'
'Not a happy phrase.'
'You are intolerable, Andrew!' She spoke very loudly and harshly, so that Matthew looked up from his sketchpad in alarm. 'I sometimes seriously doubt whether you have any true feelings at all, whether you care or even think about anybody but yourself. I'm not surprised Liz didn't want to go on living with you.'
'Well, at least you've reached a satisfactory explanation for that.'
'And I think that if you find life sad, it's entirely your own fault. You've never done anything but throw it away. Throw away all the wonderful chances and openings offered to you. You were so

clever as a boy. Your father and I admired you so much. Perhaps that was the trouble. You weren't content to be admired. You wanted to irritate and provoke.'

Andrew's mood changed suddenly. He moved closer to her, put his arm round her shoulder, patted her.

'I'm sorry. I know I drive you up the wall. But I don't think you're right about me throwing everything away. On the contrary, you could just as well say that I live life to the full. I don't rest on my laurels. I climb the next peak. Excelsior! For instance, this telly series on the Third World I'm working on, that's a very important thing. I mean, compared to teaching at Oxford, consider the number of people I can influence and stimulate with this series!'

'Of course,' she said. 'Of course I'm still proud of you. When will the series be shown?'

'It's got to be made first. In fact I'm going to the South of France next week with the producer and a camera team to do the first interview.'

'Is France part of the Third World now?'

'We're going to interview the ex-President of Balunda. He's living there temporarily.'

'Is he going back to Balunda?'

'I should think it's unlikely, but he's been back once already, so I suppose it's still possible.'

'Africa seems to have become just like South America since we stopped governing it.'

'That's exactly the sort of attitude my programme is designed to change.'

'I don't think my attitude matters either way, does it? I may not be alive to see your programme, let alone to feel more sympathetic towards African dictators.'

It was getting late and chilly. Andrew helped his mother to her feet and supported her while she writhed and groaned with pins and needles. Matthew was still absorbed in his drawing.

'Can we see what you've done?' asked Mrs Mowle.

He had covered page after page. In the early drawings there was a giant emerging from the water at the slipway, later there was a vast albatross-like bird at different angles, with its wingtips extending across the circle of the cove, as if they were the needles of a compass. But the last ten or twelve pages were dominated by an enormous tank. Sometimes it was right in the middle of the water, with only its turret appearing, lapped by waves; sometimes it was driving up the slipway or on to the beach, but in the last drawing it was transparent, covering the whole page, with the cove forming through it, as though it was the tank that had been there first and the cove was slowly eroding and negating it. They all agreed that they liked this last drawing best.

When they got back to the house and Mrs Mowle was putting together a cold supper, Andrew broached the question of a loan. His problem, he assured her, was only temporary. Within a month at the most he would have a substantial advance from the TV people, out of which he could pay back both his mother and some of Luke's loan. He didn't mention the loan he'd already received from his mother. She promised to sell a little capital and let him have three or four hundred pounds within the week.

II

The two cars turned off the road and stopped in front of high iron gates. The drivers switched off their headlights and men appeared with torches. After a few words with the driver of the first car, they retired and opened the gates. The cars went slowly down a short gravel drive round a clump of trees and pulled up in front of a square stone house with lights showing behind the shutters at the windows. Andrew Mowle, Michael Arley and his team of five, with their camera, lights and sound-recording equipment, had flown to Nice two days before and driven in a hired minibus to a hotel in Avignon. They had hung about there, sightseeing and enjoying the mild sunshine at pavement cafés, until word arrived that ex-President Nakimbi would see them tonight and that cars would be sent for them. They had set off after dark and the journey had taken about two hours, but Andrew and his companions, seated in the backs of the cars, with curtained windows, had little idea where they were. They had passed through the town of Uzès and in the last half hour had seemed to climb a little, so that Andrew guessed they were in the foothills of the Cévennes, but it hardly mattered so long as they really were going to get an interview with Nakimbi.

Andrew, Michael and his assistant, Shirley Dunn, got out of the first car and waited for the driver to unlock the boot for their equipment. Ricky Brigstock, the chief cameraman, with the assistant cameraman, the sound-recordist and the lighting man joined them from the second car. A few moments later a short, taciturn Frenchman appeared and, after checking them and their equipment perfunctorily for hidden weapons, conducted them up narrow stone steps to the front door. At the door they were met by a lean and grey-haired black man, who introduced himself as Nakimbi's Finance Minister and led the party through a large, bare hall with a stone-flagged floor into a moderately-sized room with a high beamed ceiling and a wooden floor, the floor partly covered by a thick white carpet. This room too was somewhat bare. There was a table in the window, one or two cupboards round the walls and a few upright chairs, all in the same dark wood. They looked like antiques of local workmanship. There were also two modern armchairs. The sound-recordist glanced round and murmured apprehensively about the acoustics. Andrew and Michael sat down at the table with the notes Andrew had prepared for the interview. The two cameramen and the lighting man found the power plugs and then began to shift the furniture round, but the Finance Minister stopped them.

'The chair cannot go in the window. I'm sorry,' he said.

'A little more towards the window, then,' said Ricky, the chief cameraman, accustomed to getting his own way.

'I am afraid the chair stays right here, on this spot,' said the Finance Minister, sitting in it, crossing his legs elegantly and smiling in a friendly way.

Ricky looked at Shirley, who looked at Michael. Michael shrugged, as if he thought it reasonable that ex-presidents on the run should object to sitting in front of windows.

'We'll do as he wants,' he said.

'It must be understood,' said the Finance Minister to Michael, 'that the President does not want to talk about recent events in Balunda. He will discuss only the post-colonial situation in Africa in general.'

'Of course,' said Michael. 'But it is specifically Balunda's experience of the post-colonial situation we want, so I hope we'll be able to go into some detail.'

'That will depend,' said the Finance Minister warily.

The two lights came on suddenly and made him blink.

'Ah-ha-ha-ha!' he said, the loud, ribald African sound making a strange contrast to his polished English. 'This is too bright.'

'If you insist on having the chair in the middle of that black space,' said Ricky, 'the lighting has got to come close in.'

The Finance Minister bounced springly out of the chair and out of the light.

'Too bright,' he repeated.

Ricky looked again at Shirley and she at Michael, who avoided her eye.

'Is there any chance of a compromise?' he asked in a tired voice, staring down at the notes on the table.

'Either you photograph this geezer,' said Ricky, 'or you do it for steam radio. If he can't stand a bit of light, he shouldn't have grown a black skin.'

'Is this fellow a racist?' asked the Finance Minister, apparently with amusement.

'I'm a photographer,' said Ricky. 'The only difference I can see between one colour and another is how it picks up light.'

Michael took no further part in the argument.

'We may have a problem with what Nakimbi's prepared to discuss,' he said in a low voice to Andrew.

'I don't see why. If he's willing to talk about post-colonialism, that's all we want.'

'It's all *we* want,' said Michael, 'but it's not all we were sent here to get.'

Andrew looked at him suspiciously. Michael put his elbows on the table, clasped his hands together, leaned his chin on his hands and stared back earnestly at Andrew.

'This is a bloody expensive jaunt, as you must have noticed. Camera crews don't swan about Europe making pilot interviews for projected series. Nakimbi has refused to be interviewed since he was overthrown. What the bosses want from us is some news footage. In other words, they *do* want Nakimbi to talk about recent events. Now obviously you don't begin with that or you'll frighten him off, but it shouldn't be too difficult, once you've got him relaxed and talkative, to slide in a few provocative questions. I'd guess he'll be only too keen to justify himself, once he feels, as I'm sure he will, that he's got a sympathetic interviewer with a genuine interest in Africa's problems.'

'Why didn't you tell me this before?'

'It didn't seem all that earthshaking. And you don't need to make a meal of it now. I'm only pointing out that we need to take something back with us that'll pay for the trip.'

'I'm not a professional interviewer.'

'That's the beauty of it. You're a left-wing literary journalist presenting a series on post-colonialism. As long as Nakimbi sees you as that, he won't be worried.'

'If you'd told me this before I'd have refused to do it.'

'Maybe. Maybe that's why I didn't tell you. Come on, Andrew! Shit to all that conspiracy theory stuff! I just didn't think it mattered, okay?'

'I don't like it and I've a bloody good mind to cry off.'

'What kind of world do you live in, Andrew? Making TV programmes is not some pure scholarly activity. It's about showbiz basically. It's about filling the air with entertainment and occasionally slipping in something a bit less bland. Now you could look at what we're doing the other way round. *We* want to get to grips with the Third World. But nobody else wants to. Right! So we have to play down what we're doing. We have to steal camera crews and make compromises with the people that own them, in order to get the material we want. No news value, no series.'

'That's the threat?'

'It's not a threat, for Christ's sake! It's the basic economics of this trade.'

'I haven't got any of that sort of question prepared,' Andrew said.

'It will be better that way. More spontaneous. Just remember to bring the subject round when the moment seems good. But in case you get really stuck, I've jotted a few things down.'

Michael took a piece of paper out of his pocket, unfolded it and pushed it across the table. His schoolboy handwriting was easy to read and the questions seemed to leap off the page as if they were too dangerous to be committed to paper: did the guerrillas have outside support? would they have any chance of reconciling the old tribal differences within the country? how much support remained for Nakimbi? what did he think was the main cause of his downfall? did he hope to return? Andrew looked up to find the Finance Minister standing beside their table and guiltily slid Michael's notes under his own.

'We are all sorted out now, Mr Arley,' said the Minister. 'How about you?'

'Yes,' said Michael.

'I will inform the President, then,' said the Minister and left the room jauntily. He had not given an inch. The chair remained exactly where it was, the lights were set further back.

'Okay, Andrew?' asked Michael.

Andrew made no response. He found Michael's piece of paper again, crossed out one or two of the more direct questions and tried to re-phrase them as general observations, but they only seemed more dangerous, like gun-barrels inadequately camouflaged with leaves. He looked up resentfully at Michael, but he was yawning and stretching as if he already took Andrew's acquiescence for granted. The rest of the team, sulky and tense during their abortive squabbles with the Finance Minister, had also relaxed now that he had left the room. Shirley offered a mint to Ricky and his assistant and took one herself. Ricky flung himself down in the interviewee's chair. The sound-recordist and the lighting man were taking nips from a hip flask. They were like a band of marauders which had been temporarily cowed by an unexpected brush with authority, but was now re-asserting its independence and mutual solidarity. The lights were switched off, but the camera on its stand, aimed straight down at Ricky, was the symbol and source of their power. When the door opened and ex-President Nakimbi came in, they all instinctively closed round the camera, as if determined this time not to be scattered into submission.

Nakimbi was much larger than his Finance Minister, not gross, but altogether smoothed and rounded. From his bald crown and shiny cheeks to his brand new shoes he was like a highly finished and polished sculpture. He gave no impression at all of decline or hardship; on the contrary, he seemed entirely at ease with the world, a millionaire on holiday (which, in a sense, he was), rather than a king in exile. His voice was soft and soothing and his accent an attractive blend of African vowels with Oxford drawl. He shook hands with every member of the team and repeated their names as if he meant to make a personal friend of each of them. He pretended to be about to sit in the wrong chair.

'Oh, is that the hot seat? But will we see nothing of you, then, Mr Mowle?'

Andrew explained that his questions would mostly be edited out in order to leave the President's replies as statements on their own.

'But surely this arrangement of the chairs will make us too confrontational? It will be better if we sit side by side and talk like friends.'

'This is how we found the chairs,' said Michael.

'Good heavens, they can be moved! The chairs are not nailed down, Mr Arley.'

The members of the team exchanged glances. The Finance Minister had followed Nakimbi into the room, closing the door behind him and seating himself on one of the upright chairs in the shadows near the door. He made no attempt to intervene.

'We got the impression they were nailed down,' said Ricky.

'Why don't we try them over there?' asked Nakimbi, pointing towards the shuttered windows. 'Or would that make difficulties with the lighting?'

There was silence. Ricky looked dazed. Shirley turned to Michael with a completely straight face, as if the idea were new to her. Michael smiled politely.

'Why not?' he said.

They moved the chairs, while Nakimbi looked on benignly and the Finance Minister remained quietly on his chair by the door, his expression, so far as it could be judged in the comparative darkness, neutral. Then, while the technicians re-sited their equipment, Nakimbi joined Michael and Andrew near the table.

'I understand you want a general discussion of Balunda's problems,' he said. 'Not too much detail.'

'We're not against detail as such,' said Michael. 'In fact, I don't see how we can avoid it altogether.'

'Nor do I, Mr Arley. From the cook's point of view, a lamb pilaf is all detail. The pieces of lamb, the different spices, the yoghurt, the onion, the rice. Only when it comes to the table does it seem to be a lamb pilaf. I have always been in the cook's position, not that of the person at table. But I leave it to you. Ask the cook for his recipe! The cook will answer to the best of his ability.'

Was this, too, like the business with the chairs, meant to be a direct contradiction of the Finance Minister's previous instructions or was it simply a more emollient way of saying the same thing? But Andrew felt encouraged. The Finance Minister obviously belonged to a world of bureaucratic restrictions and devious manoeuvres to which Andrew always took particular exception. Michael had turned out to be a bird of the same feather. Although Andrew distrusted Nakimbi's smoothness – he could have fitted snugly into a Tory Cabinet – he was at least a sophisticated, self-confident and intelligent man. There would be no need to cover anything up. If he didn't like the questions he was asked, he would simply turn them aside or refuse to answer them. There could be nothing underhand about asking them. Andrew's own self-confidence returned and with it his relish for the job in hand. He liked nothing better than a serious discussion of important issues and as last-minute adjustments were made to the positions of the chairs, the lights switched on and the microphone tested, he sat forward eagerly, leaning sideways, with one elbow on the arm of his chair, so as to be able to look Nakimbi directly in the face, and smiled as if he had found a true friend. Nakimbi smiled back with equal warmth and when the camera began to roll he suddenly laid his hand on Andrew's arm and said:

'You can ask anything you like, Mr Mowle.'

Andrew was thrown for a moment. Did this mean that the Finance Minister had overheard his conversation with Michael, perhaps even seen Michael's secret questions, and reported as much to Nakimbi? He glanced uncertainly at Michael, seated near the camera, but he looked stern and gestured impatiently at the camera's red light.

'When you became President of Balunda, Mr Nakimbi,' Andrew began, 'you were not in the same situation as any other leader of a newly independent African state. Balunda was not handed to you ready-made on a plate by the retiring colonial power, it was forged in the furnace of civil war. Do you think this gave you more options than other founding presidents?'

'It did not give me more options, no,' said Nakimbi. 'And I will explain why not in a moment. But it did remove one great burden or obstacle to our progress, namely the imposition from the start of a quite inappropriate British parliamentary system. Now nobody is to imagine that we Africans are against democracy or that we don't understand or don't want democracy for ourselves. Of course, we have always been democratic – probably more genuinely democratic in our traditional institutions than any country in the West. We have always run our affairs, at both village and tribal level, through councils and mutual agreement. No, the burden was Britain's own semi-mystical belief in the institution of Parliament, with its built-in system of confrontational politics. For Africans, that is not a helpful way of arriving at the best policies.'

He stopped and smiled disarmingly, but continued before Andrew had a chance to break in.

'The options, however, even though we were not saddled with parliamentary government, were still extremely limited. They were limited by our disadvantaged position in a world organized for the benefit of a very few rich and powerful nations. Basically, the options were to belong to one of the two great economic empires as an uncomplaining, forelock-touching retainer; or to be a little bit more rebellious, to walk the path between the two empires and perhaps gain a little more from both of them than could be gained from either separately.'

'Would you say that that option – that non-aligned policy – worked?'

'It was always a risky option.'

'Why risky?'

'It encouraged confrontation. It imported the confrontation of the superpowers and their satellites into our little country. It encouraged the old European rivalries and hostilities to break out again on our soil.'

'You mean that it was not internal hostilities that broke up your government, but outside interference?'

'Now just a moment, Mr Mowle! Don't let us be superficial! No one is saying that my government was universally popular. I have certainly not said so. My policies were quite radical, you know. I was trying to make an African nation and a modern nation, both at the same time. Of course many people opposed that. And of course I made mistakes. All this had to be worked out. It had to be tried out. It had to be debated and agreement reached, so that everybody would be content to pull together in the same direction.'

'But that agreement was impeded by European interference?'

'It was made impossible. Totally impossible.'

'Why was that?'

'Because in the existing system no solution can be allowed which does not favour and support the existing system. In a world ruled by Europeans – of course I include Americans, who are only transplanted Europeans – there is no place, except a subordinate one, for Africans.'

'You're saying that independence did not bring an end to imperialism.'

'I would like to avoid these catchwords. But you are right that the Europeans have not changed. Their greed for land and natural resources and their need for expansion are as great as ever. They still want to enslave the Africans and have their living space, but for reasons of history and propaganda, they cannot any longer do it by direct conquest. Their method is first of all to turn Africans into Europeans – inferior Europeans – and then little by little to recover what they have temporarily lost – all that great expanse of Africa – by helping the Africans to ruin themselves.'

'You mean economically?'

'Yes, economically. But also by civil wars.'

'You mean that the Europeans are deliberately creating civil wars?'

'I didn't say that. But the inevitable outcome of forcing Africans into a wholly inappropriate European mould is to produce insecurity and instability. Such conditions very soon result in civil war.'

Andrew paused before asking the next question. His initial feeling of solidarity with Nakimbi had been replaced by irritation with his glibness. Andrew didn't disagree with what he said, but he began to see him as an operator and to recall his chequered record as leader of his country.

'When you became president for the second time . . .'

Nakimbi smiled and wagged his head.

'No, I never ceased to be president. No one else had been elected in my place.'

'When you returned to power the second time, it was the result of a military operation. Wasn't that with European assistance?'

'What do you mean?'

'Weren't you armed and generally assisted by a particular European ex-colonial power?'

'The soldiers were my own countrymen, Mr Mowle. As for their weapons, I'm afraid we don't make modern armaments in Africa. Perhaps we should. Isn't that exactly what I have been saying. Let us not talk vaguely about "a particular European power"! The reason I had to go into exile was that the British stirred up instability in my country by turning elements of my army against me. General Ozo was a British stooge.'

'But you came back with French help. Mightn't General Ozo's supporters say that you were a French stooge?'

It was Nakimbi's turn to pause. For a moment Andrew thought he had gone too far and Nakimbi would walk out. The Finance Minister in the far corner was half on his feet, as if he expected that to happen. But Nakimbi settled back and smiled more reassuringly than ever.

'General Ozo's supporters would say anything about me, of course, but I must remind you, Mr Mowle, that although my own people, the Koruba people, are a minority in Balunda, I was not elected president by a minority. I did not rely on military force to keep me in power, as General Ozo did, nor did I rely on the support of European powers. I relied on the people of Balunda.'

Andrew thought this was a good moment to introduce one of Michael's questions, albeit in a modified form.

'You mentioned being yourself a Koruba, Mr Nakimbi. Balunda is, of course, like most African countries, built out of a great many different tribes. Isn't this a problem?'

'Of course it's a problem.'

'Isn't it a major problem? Nothing to do with the Europeans, I mean.'

Andrew felt himself floundering at the very moment when he should have sounded most confident. His question had somehow lost its edge. He had been congratulating himself on finding an opening for the question, instead of concentrating on how to phrase it.

'I'm glad you put it like that, Mr Mowle, because it makes very clear what you really mean. Like all Europeans, you are delighted to be able to talk about tribalism, because you think that is the great African vice. Nothing to do with the Europeans. These poor Africans are just football hooligans who don't know any better than to go and beat up another tribe. For once the Europeans can feel superior again instead of guilty about Africa . . .'

'No, that isn't what I meant at all,' said Andrew, annoyed at the way Nakimbi was trying to make him out a blimp, when his sympathies lay all with the Africans. 'I simply asked you to agree that it was a problem.'

'It's a problem only because of the Europeans.'

'You mean, because they made artificial countries out of disparate tribes?'

'Partly because of that.'

'But you yourselves created Balunda in the same way, out of disparate tribes.'

'Not disparate, Mr Mowle. Please allow me to put you right on this point without interruption. This word "tribes" is very emotive, very special to Africa – to peoples that you like to think of as primitive. You don't speak of the Scots as a tribe – or the Welsh or the Walloons or the Basques or any of the very diparate peoples that make up Europe and America. Let us use another word – "communities". Balunda and other African nations are made up of many different communities, each with its own peculiar customs and histories. Nobody wants those differences, those varieties of human social organization to be lost. On the other hand, they can hardly – in the modern world created by Europeans – exist as completely independent groups. That is obvious to you when speaking of the different communities within your own nations, but not apparently when speaking of African communities. Now how is it that you in Britain cannot solve the problem of Ireland? The answer is very largely because of outside interference. The IRA receives arms and money from Libya, from the Irish element in the United States, from anybody who wants to make trouble for Britain. That is also what happens in African countries.'

'But there are genuine grievances that boil up and lead to the outside interference.'

'You're talking about Ireland, of course.'

'I wouldn't defend any British government's record in Ireland.' said Andrew hotly. 'Nor am I trying to suggest that the British are morally superior to Africans. Quite the contrary. The whole purpose of this series is to reveal the Africans and other Third World peoples as genuinely independent entities, with their own moral imperatives.'

'Every community has grievances, every person has grievances. It's just a question of whether somebody else makes use of them for his own evil ends. Otherwise grievances need not become insoluble problems.'

They were at cross purposes. Nakimbi was not only refusing to recognize Andrew as a sympathiser, he was beginning to sound as if he himself was more on the side of the oppressors than the oppressed. Perhaps he was not so intelligent, after all. Perhaps he didn't want to discuss the issues seriously but, like any second-rate politician, simply justify his own record. His smug generalizations were beginning to make Andrew very angry.

'We're talking of grievances,' he said, 'but isn't that a rather inadequate way to describe the kind of killing that's been going on in Balunda?'

'Totally inadequate. I would never describe killing as a grievance.'

'But you don't deny that there has been a great deal of killing in your country? Not only killing, but torture, rape, violence of every kind.'

'Why should I deny it? My country has been destroyed by the military. I myself have been twice driven into exile by the military. This is not an interesting question. The question is why my country has fallen into the hands of the military.'

Andrew hung on grimly. He felt that Nakimbi was too slippery for him, that he would change the shape of the discussion as often as his interviewer tried to pin him down, but that if he could only be caught off balance, it would be a small victory.

'You yourself came to power the second time by means of the military. Presumably you were no longer able to control them?'

Nakimbi shook his head slowly several times. He was smiling.

'We are giving a false impression,' he said. 'This is quite off the point. Have you ever disturbed an anthill and watched the result? It is very hard to know exactly what the ants are doing or even to follow the movements of a single ant with any accuracy. How much harder when the anthill is a whole country and you are not even watching it in person, but receiving the reports of the press who are not themselves particularly well-informed.'

'Would it be off the point to say that when your supporters – mainly Korubas – came back to power in Balunda, they took revenge on the people who had been persecuting Korubas?'

'It would be much too simple, Mr Mowle.'

'Are you saying that it wasn't a tribal conflict? In no way a tribal conflict?'

'I'm not saying that. I'm not saying anything at present, because it's difficult to describe to a blind man who will not stop asking the wrong questions what is happening in an anthill.'

'The wrong questions from whose point of view? Yours?'

'Of course. But it's my point of view you are asking for. If you want my enemies' point of view, you can easily go and ask them.'

Suddenly he waved his hands, palms outwards, in front of his face in a regular rhythm like windscreen wipers. 'Can we stop, please? Can we stop and talk this over?'

Shirley looked at Michael, who gave the signal to stop the camera. The Finance Minister left his chair and came forward as if to support his chief and escort him out of the room if the interview was over. Andrew felt defiantly pleased with himself. Perhaps he'd lost the chance of getting any more out of Nakimbi, but at least he'd stung him.

'You see,' said Nakimbi, addressing Michael and the technicians rather than Andrew, 'we are fencing with each other. This interview is in the Western style: hostile questions and confrontation. Now I am very used to this style. Please don't imagine that I'm afraid to answer his questions. They are quite predictable and easy to parry. If you like, we can go on all night like this, but shall I suggest a better method? I will tell you the true facts of Balunda's history, as I understand them, and you can all ask me questions whenever you need clarification. It's up to you.'

Nakimbi rose from his chair and walked over to his Finance Minister. They conferred in the background, while the television team waited for Michael's decision.

'If he wants it that way,' Michael said, 'I can't see it will make much difference to the end result. All right, Andrew? You put in some valiant efforts there, but I'm afraid we've got nothing much to take home with us yet.'

Andrew shrugged and affected a relaxed detachment, but couldn't help feeling humiliated. Michael clearly thought that the failure of the interview was his fault.

'It's a bit of a gimmick really, isn't it?' said Shirley, understanding how he felt. 'I've often noticed that powerful people much prefer to make statements than answer questions.'

Nakimbi returned and the Finance Minister brought his chair and placed it near Nakimbi's.

'I've asked Mr Obeobubaka to join our discussion,' said Nakimbi. 'To correct my account if necessary. He is very well informed, of course.'

He sat down and smiled at them all in turn, ending with Andrew, as if forgiving him for his inadequacy and reinstating him as the official steward of the occasion.

'When you are ready,' said Nakimbi, lying back in his chair with his legs stretched out and his hands linked across his chest.

Andrew looked at him with distaste. He had always disliked wealthy and privileged people and Nakimbi was wealth and privilege incarnate.

III

'Blather!' Michael said.

Andrew, carrying their third cups of coffee since they'd arrived in the airport lounge at Nice and been told their flight was delayed, sat down beside him. The rest of the team were on the benches nearby. Used cups and glasses, torn cellophane, chocolate wrappers, cigarette packets, overflowing ashtrays and other debris covered the tables. They were all tired and disinclined to talk, except Shirley. She could appear fresh, interested and efficient almost indefinitely. She was talking to the lighting man about dentists. One of his back teeth had been troubling him and she had once worked briefly as a dentist's receptionist. She was pointing out the startling improvement in dental equipment and techniques since the war. There might be other things wrong with the modern world, but in dentistry we had made true progress. She was particularly impressed by South African dentists. Anybody who still thought of Afrikaners as heavyhanded farmers should try a South African dentist.

Michael was not listening to her. He was talking about the events of the night before.

'Reels and reels of blather,' he said.

Shirley had been right. Nakimbi's 'democratic' interview had been nothing but an excuse to perform to a captive audience. He had lectured and exhorted them, used their occasional questions as further pegs on which to lash down his great marquee of self-justification and selfless striving for the good of his people, expertly reduced them by a mixture of flattery and guilt-by-association to a kind of five-person movement for the better understanding and restoration to power of Marius Nakimbi. The sixth and seventh persons, Andrew and Michael, were pariahs, but since they couldn't be excluded from the marquee, they were forced to participate in the performance. Whenever they attempted to sharpen the questioning, Nakimbi cited them as examples of the vested interests and received thinking of the domineering European world and its tame media. Gradually they both lapsed into silence and Michael conveyed to his team by the sullen way he sat in his chair his strong disapproval of the proceedings, but they took no notice. One couldn't deny that Nakimbi had charisma. The team warmed to that shining sun, temporarily abandoning the inferior leaders they came out with.

Even more irritating than the interview had been its sequel. The team were packing up their equipment, while Nakimbi stood jovially by, when the assistant cameraman, a small and usually silent Welshman called Colin, said:

'What about this Colonel Rimington, then? We forgot to ask you about him.'

Nakimbi looked at Colin carefully, as if suspecting this might be some new ploy on the part of his adversaries, Michael and Andrew, but Colin's naive sincerity was obvious. He had read scandalous stories about Rimington in the papers and was simply curious. Who better to satisfy his curiosity than the great man who was condescending to be his friend?

'An interesting question,' said Nakimbi finally, 'but if you really want to know about Colonel Rimington, I suggest you ask Mr Obeobubaka.'

Colin obediently turned towards the Finance Minister, who was standing with his hands resting on the back of the upright chair he had occupied during the 'democratic' part of the interview.

'It would take a long time to tell you everything about Colonel Rimington,' he said and closed his eyes, as if summoning up memories. 'He's a bad man, a very bad man,' he added, opening his eyes again and noting that they were all listening attentively. 'You would be ashamed to hear of the things he did.'

'The last Englishman in Balunda was worse than the first,' said Nakimbi.

Michael was signalling to the sound-recordist to switch on his microphone, but Nakimbi saw him.

'Please, no!' he said. 'The interview is finished. If you want to hear about Rimington that must be off the record. If you had remembered to ask me earlier, I should have said the same. The history of Balunda, of Africa, is not affected by Rimington. He is not relevant to your programme. Of course, he is relevant to my personal history. I put trust in him, which he betrayed, and I have been accused of many crimes which were perpetrated by him without my knowledge. But although I would say that Rimington tried to wreck Balunda for his own selfish ends, I would not say that he succeeded.'

'Isn't it true,' asked Andrew, 'that he ran your special security service?'

'Address your questions to Mr Obeobubaka, please,' said Nakimbi.

'He was not to be trusted,' said Obeobubaka, 'but there were many people who did trust him. He was a good leader of fighting men, that must be said, and had built up a reputation in the civil war, so that he had many loyal followers. Unfortunately he left them in the lurch. He jumped on a plane and left his soldiers to face the enemy without him. True! In front of them all, he ran across the airfield and forced his way into the aircraft. That was the action of a coward. I was surprised then and I cannot account for it now. I don't know whether he had suddenly lost his nerve. Earlier on he had been treacherous and ruthless, but not cowardly.'

Once launched on the subject of Rimington, the Finance Minister hardly needed prompting. He seemed to be fascinated by the man. Nakimbi, meanwhile, had seated himself a little away from his new admirers and was watching their reactions closely.

Some of what Obeobubaka said seemed to contradict directly Nakimbi's claim that Rimington's actions had not affected Balunda's fate. For example, when Nakimbi returned to power after his first exile, Rimington and his soldiers were still protecting the presidential palace in Molo, the capital. Nakimbi and the small force of commandos that had accompanied him from the airfield to seize the capital were not in a position to storm the palace. They would have to wait a day or two until the main body of their troops came up. Nakimbi, therefore, asked for an interview with Rimington and the two men met alone in the large gravelled space in front of the palace, while their bodyguards watched them from cover. The interview was in a sense presided over by General Ozo, whose large bronze statue stood in the centre of the space. The discussion was long and often heated since, after all, Rimington had once been Nakimbi's right-hand man, but had gone over to General Ozo at the time of his coup. Nakimbi offered to forget the past if Rimington would return to his former allegiance and hand over the palace without bloodshed. Rimington eventually agreed to this. He had no real alternative except to make a last stand, but he was still worried about what would happen to General Ozo. Nakimbi assured him that Ozo woud be unharmed and would be flown out as soon as possible to any country that would give him asylum. Rimington seemed dubious about this and paced about restlessly considering it. Then he suddenly stooped, picked up a handful of gravel and flung it at Ozo's statue.

'All right,' he said, 'Ozo is dead. Long live President Nakimbi!'

Whether this was a prearranged signal or whether General Ozo, watching from one of the palace windows, drew the obvious conclusion from the gesture, though he couldn't hear the words, the effect on him was instantaneous. He left the palace by a back door, flung away his gold-braided and heavily medalled uniform jacket and tried to escape into the town over a high wall topped with barbed wire. He was a fat and lethargic man and it took him some time to get on to the wall. Rimington, meanwhile, finding him gone, ordered a search and the soldiers caught up with him as he was trying to struggle through the wire. When Nakimbi entered the palace a few hours later, Ozo was dead, shot, according to Rimington, by over-zealous soldiers as he was trying to escape. Mr Obeobubaka's opinion, however, was that he had been brought to

Rimington more or less unharmed, except by the barbed wire, and that Rimington had then had him murdered in cold blood because he didn't want another man he had betrayed escaping to tell the tale to the outside world.

Michael put the obvious question to Obeobubaka. Why, if Nakimbi had so many good reasons to distrust Rimington, had he put him in charge of his own security service?

'I questioned that myself,' said the Finance Minister, smiling and looking sideways at Nakimbi. 'The President told me that he wanted Rimington under his eye. I replied that he who sups with the devil needs a long spoon, but President Nakimbi laughed and told me that the devil himself invented that saying, since it gave him a much better chance of putting poison in the pot. President Nakimbi – I hope he will forgive me saying so – is a very clever man. If you have a tame scorpion in your house, you don't let him go about stinging your faithful dogs. You put him to watch the other scorpions.'

The mention of scorpions reminded Colin that there had been sinister stories in the British press about Rimington's collection of snakes.

'Those snakes!' said Obeobubaka, in a pained voice. 'What stories have you read?'

Colin couldn't elaborate. They hadn't really been stories at all, but hints of unspecified horrors. Obeobubaka nodded gravely, but seemed to prefer to drop the subject. Rimington, he said, was thought to have been at some time a British agent. Certainly he seemed to have funds and weapons for his own particular soldiers which were not available to anyone else. But it looked as though he had eventually quarrelled with his paymasters. Probably he had become too conceited and demanding. Nobody could remain on the level with such a man for long. He either let you down or trampled you underfoot.

Obeobubaka told them that, as Rimington's cruelties and acts of tyranny increased, President Nakimbi realized that he must somehow neutralize the wild beast he had himself nurtured in his own compound. It was not easy, since Rimington's hold over his own soldiers made him in effect an independent leader, a bandit chief with great power for evil in the country. As long as it was a question of dealing with the remnants of Ozo's regime, it was necessary to allow Rimington some latitude in his security operations, but President Nakimbi freely admitted that these had gone too far, that innocent people were suffering and that a constant cycle of violence was being kept in motion. If it had not been for Rimington's activities, he was sure that the guerrilla movement in the north would never have received the support in the villages that it did.

So Rimington *was* more important than Nakimbi at first admitted? But nobody asked the question and Obeobubaka hurried over the point as if he too understood that he was contradicting his superior. He himself was given the job of limiting the damage done by Rimington. Rimington's sphere of operations was gradually confined to the capital and it was then, when Obeobubaka and his team assumed responsibility for security in the bush area, that the full extent of Rimington's reign of terror began to come to light.

'Excuse me,' Andrew interrupted, 'but I thought you told us you were the President's Minister of Finance?'

'I am now, Mr Mowle.'

'When you say "reign of terror" . . .' Colin said and broke off, since he only meant to steer the story back to what interested him, not to ask a question. The team were all sitting down again now, caught in mid-activity like children by a Pied Piper, oblivious of how late it was and how tired and thirsty they were.

'Of course we don't often know exactly what Rimington did to his victims,' Obeobubaka said, 'because very few survived, but I can tell you what happened to a boy called Charlie. He did escape. He was somewhat incoherent, somewhat traumatized by his experience. He was working for the guerrillas – probably as a messenger – when Rimington's soldiers captured him. A boy of about thirteen years old. Rimington took this boy home with him and showed him that collection of snakes you mentioned. The boy was frightened, but fascinated. Rimington picked them out of their cages, one by one, and explained all about them: how this one gave you a bite which could be cured and that one was deadly poisonous, how this would run away and that would not, how this was slow and that could move faster than a bicycle. Then the boy was stripped of his clothes and shut in a toilet. Quite a large room, but pitch black and with no furniture but the toilet-bowl and a hand-basin. He remained there a long time – he didn't know how long, perhaps a day or more. He was given no food, but he was able to drink from the basin tap. At last Rimington came and spoke to him through the door. "One of my snakes has escaped," he said, "you remember the Gaboon viper I showed you? This is not a very close-fitting door and I'm afraid it may have crept in there with you. Please keep absolutely still or it may bite you. I am just going to find my torch." And the boy heard his footsteps going away down the passage. He did not come back for several hours. You can imagine what condition the boy was in by that time. In his terror and weakened state he had been holding himself tense for all this while. Then he heard the door softly opened and Rimington came in with a torch and a long, thin stick. "Keep still!" he whispered to the boy, "I know that viper is in here somewhere." He began to play the beam of the torch slowly round the floor and brought it finally on to the boy, sitting on the floor against the wall and shaking uncontrollably. Suddenly Rimington shouted "Move, move, I see it!" and, as the boy struggled to get up, began to hit him with the stick, many times, beating him viciously all over his buttocks and legs. After that he snapped off the torch and went out again. But this pretence about the snake, this psychological nightmare, followed by the vicious beating in the torchlight happened several times more, until, in fact, the boy lost consciousness. After that he didn't see Rimington again. He was taken by the soldiers back to Security headquarters and on the way escaped.'

'How could he escape in such a state?' asked Andrew, wishing somehow to counter the half-nauseating, half-prurient effect of the story with the objectivity of doubt and logistics.

'I would not be surprised if the soldiers helped him,' said Obeobubaka. 'They were human beings, many of them fathers. Could they see this kind of thing and not begin to believe their colonel was mad?'

'You mean that he was not trying to get information out of the boy, but only to indulge his own sadistic tastes?' asked Michael.

'It is time for me to go to bed,' said Nakimbi, standing up. 'Mr Obeobubaka has told you more than enough about a man whom all Balundans would prefer to forget. We are not blaming Britain for him. All countries contain such people. But ask yourselves why you should only want to hear about atrocities when you turn your attention to Africa!'

After that, subdued and silent, Andrew and the others had returned through the night to their hotel in Avignon and from there to the airport this morning.

'We can surely use some of it?' Andrew said, stirring his coffee, touching the cup to his lips and then deciding he didn't want to drink it after all. 'Some of the purely historical stuff is very relevant to the African experience as a whole.'

His animosity towards Nakimbi had mostly evaporated. He had reverted to thinking of him as a representative of his abused country rather than as one of its abusers; he was sure this was the juster assessment, since the social and historical circumstances were responsible for the man, not the other way round. Andrew now began to blame himself for the way he had allowed himself to be riled by the personal, dictatorial element in Nakimbi. He had gone to use him as a witness and had unforgivably turned to treating him as an accused.

'Relevant, no doubt,' said Michael, screwing up bits of silver foil from his most recent bar of chocolate and trying to lob them into an empty cup two tables away, 'but bloody boring.' His dislike of Nakimbi had, if anything, increased since the night before, perhaps because of the way he had temporarily hijacked Michael's team and made him look ineffectual.

'What really worries me about last night's fiasco,' he continued, 'is that it calls in question the whole enterprise.'

'Because we didn't get anything they could use on a news programme?'

'Not just that, though I'm certainly not going to be flavour of the week back at the office. I'm thinking of all the other fat-cat fathers-of-their-people we're going to be interviewing. Are they going to be any different? Or are we going to can reels and reels more of this blather all over the Dark Continent?'

'I didn't think we'd ever envisaged the series consisting mainly of interviews with African presidents.'

'No, well, for God's sake, let's cut them right out! As soon as we get back, I'd like you to have another look at your treatment. Work towards something much sharper and less open-ended. I'd prefer it if you wrote a lot more of the script yourself. If we have to use interviewees, we'll nail them down to extremely specific questions.'

'But my whole idea was not to prejudge the issues – to let the people of the Third World speak for themselves and hopefully open our minds to new ways of thinking about them.'

'You didn't get any of that last night, did you?'

'I think that was my fault.'

'Look, Andrew, it wouldn't have made the slightest difference if you'd lain on the floor and let him shit in your face. I'm not criticizing your performance or even Nakimbi's, when it comes down to it. That's the way he is, that's his message – "we're poor and you're rich and it's your fault" – and there may be a lot of truth in it. Sincerity or lack of sincerity is not the issue. The issue is: does Nakimbi's message have any appeal for TV audiences in the rich countries, which is where we have to sell the bloody programme? The moral self-flagellators are a very minority audience these days. Go away and think about it, Andrew, and we'll meet for a chat in a week or two. Okay?'

13

Horatio Cass was screaming. He was crimson in the face and wouldn't eat his food. Diana stood with a plastic bowl of pap in one hand and a spoon in the other and felt like screaming too. She had no urge to hit the baby, perhaps because she knew it wasn't him she was angry with. After a moment, finding she was too inhibited to scream, she threw the bowl at the sink. It hit the outer edge, bounced off, deposited most of its contents on the cork floor and rolled towards the radiator under the window. She threw the spoon after the bowl. That went nowhere near the sink, but slid across the wooden table in the middle of the kitchen and fetched up near the cooker. Horatio's attention was briefly diverted from himself and he stopped screaming. Then as Diana left the room to fetch the Calpol he started again.

From upstairs came the angry voice of Christian: 'For Christ's sake, Mum! Can't you make him stop that bloody noise? I'm trying to do my homework. It's going to take me all night as it is.'

At the same time she heard Martha and Tricia in the sitting room turning up the sound on the TV. Jack was out of the house playing tennis with a friend or he would have made the worst fuss of all.

Since 9.30 that morning when the daily phoned to say she couldn't come, the day had been a disaster. Indeed, the disaster had really started earlier in the week when the Spanish au pair suddenly walked out. Now, after a day of coping with Horatio and his tooth, shopping, cleaning the ground floor rooms and bathroom, collecting the girls from school and preparing one meal for the children and another for the six guests invited to dinner at 8.00, she could scarcely believe that Tony was late home from the office. Screaming was not at all an adequate response. For the twentieth time that day she imagined walking out altogether or rather imagined the effect of her walking out on those left behind, particularly Tony, when he finally returned to the screaming baby, the angry and hungry children, the half-cooked meal, the unlaid table and the six goggle-eyed guests. What she couldn't imagine was where she'd go after she walked out. Therefore she stayed, gave the baby his painkiller, finally got him to lie down and go to sleep, pulled together a meal for the rest of the children, exiled them to the upper parts of the house, tidied up the sitting room after them and was mounting the stairs to change and make up, when Tony let himself in. She stopped and looked at him in silence, savouring the moment, waiting to find the most suitable expression for her bottled-up, foaming resentment.

Having dropped his briefcase, hung up his jacket and loosened his tie, he finally noticed her watching him from above.

'Such a bloody hoo-ha!' he said. 'You wouldn't believe it unless you'd been there.'

'What are you talking about?' she said in a low voice, still holding back the moment of release, but sounding savage enough to herself.

'I must have a drink,' he said and moved towards the sitting room. 'How about you? Gin?'

'Gin!' she said, her voice still low, but trembling with sarcasm. 'You haven't got the faintest idea, have you? You breeze in at a quarter to seven when you know that people are coming at eight. If you had a houseful of servants, if this was the Embassy which I'd have thought it should have been by now, given your age and your supposed brilliance at your job, then I suppose a quarter to seven might be just about the right time to turn up and help yourself to a drink and change into a dinner jacket or maybe a white tie and tails, with your KBE round your neck, and tell me about the hard day you've had. But, as a matter of fact,' she said, losing her way and muffing the climax, 'you haven't even got a CBE yet.'

'What's all this about?' he asked in an even, medical tone, recognizing that she needed help, but admitting no liability.

'The only servants in this house are me!' she shouted.

There was another pause, during which they could sense that the faint noises coming from the children upstairs had stopped. Tony crossed the hall, sprang up the stairs and put his arm round her.

'We do need drinks,' he said.

'I've got to change,' she said, 'and lay the table and finish cooking the meal. But you'd better have a drink because you've had such a hard day.'

'We'll have drinks upstairs,' he said, still holding her. 'You go and change. There'll be plenty of time to lay the table and all the rest of it. Don't worry!'

She supposed, as she began to go through the dresses in the wardrobe, that like Horatio it was only a controlling hand she'd been asking for and when he came up and joined her in the bedroom and clinked glasses with her, she felt even more like the baby. Tony sat patiently while she related the horrors of her day, but they no longer seemed very impressive horrors. They were too trivial in themselves and even when they were pushed together in a pile they appeared, like the sweepings of an apparently filthy kitchen floor, curiously scanty. She could see that, although he showed sympathy for her and took her state of mind seriously, he thought nothing of the objective evidence.

'I'm sorry,' he said. 'We'll get a new au pair as soon as we can and if Mrs Thing can't come again tomorrow, then what the hell? Just leave the house and I'll give it a proper clean over the weekend. Surely Horatio's tooth will be through by then and that'll take some of the pressure off?'

His brisk disposal of all the problems that had brought her to the edge of hysteria made her feel worse not better. Her anger had been a kind of pleasure. She had never meant to accuse him of not being an ambassador yet – that was something they both looked forward to and which in large measure justified their lives, but because it was of such crucial importance it was not a subject to introduce into quarrels. He made no reference at all to her jibe. That was proof of his superior wisdom and strength of character.

'It wasn't that I hadn't remembered about the dinner party,' he said. 'It's been a red alert day and the meeting went on and on and on.'

He started to remove his clothes.

'No time for a bath,' he said, 'though I've been looking forward to one from about four o'clock on.'

He filled the basin with water and washed his face, neck and torso.

'What was it all about?' she asked, a little grudgingly.

'Highly classified,' he said, half muffled by his towel. 'Not to say for your ears only.'

He threw the towel at the rack with a fine backhand gesture and it landed precariously over the top rail.

'I hope you're leaving the bathroom as you found it,' she said. 'I spent at least an hour making it fit for the visitors.'

He went back and wiped the steam off the mirror over the basin, then carefully folded the towel and put it on a lower rail of the rack.

'Far away down the world,' he said, taking a clean terracotta shirt out of his drawer – he always liked to emphasize his sporting, outdoor persona at dinner parties – '52 degrees south of the Equator, 480 miles north-east of Cape Horn . . .'

'The rough one?'

'The very rough one.'

He had got his shirt on now and stopped to take a sip of his whisky.

'Down in that godforsaken spot in the South Atlantic, there's a group of small islands which most people have never heard of . . .'

'The Falklands.'

'Well done, Diana! Top of the class!'

'Doesn't it have stamps?'

'It does. Stamps are one of its main sources of income. And, of course, they have HM's head on them, because the Falklands, believe it or not, are still part of the British Empire.'

'I should think they just about are the British Empire, aren't they?'

'More or less. However, according to the Argentinians, the Falklands shouldn't be part of the British Empire, but part of Argentina.'

'And should they?'

'That's not really the question. Or at least it's only a subsidiary question, though a very vexed one. From our point of view the problem is that the Falklands are inhabited, though they weren't when they were first discovered. The first man to land was probably British – at the end of the seventeenth century. But the first inhabitants were undoubtedly French – they started a colony on the main eastern island in the middle of the eighteenth century. Two years later the British left some Marines on the west island, but in the meantime the French had sold their colony to Spain. Are these trousers too shabby, do you think?'

'They look all right from here.'

He put them on and pulled up the zip.

'In 1770 the Spanish sent a fleet from Buenos Aires and the thirteen British marines surrendered and departed, leaving behind a cabbage patch and a stock of coal. There was a frightful outcry in Britain and very nearly a war with Spain. Dr Johnson was called in to write a pamphlet for the government against having war and a secret agreement was signed with Spain. Or probably was. Since it was secret, it's hard to prove. Anyway, the practical outcome was that the British moved out. Our scene now shifts to the 1830s, the age of Palmerston and the Strong Arm of Britain. What had happened in the meantime was that Argentina had got free of the Spanish Empire and installed a penal colony on the Falklands. The British sent a sloop, pulled down the Argentinian flag, put up the Union Jack, sent the Argentinians home to Buenos Aires, and soon afterwards installed their own colony, run by a public company with a royal charter, which made its way by raising sheep and selling the wool. But ever since 1833, when Palmerston's sloop chucked them out, the Argentinians have been trying to get back and the more disastrous their economy becomes and the worse their military regime is hated, the keener they are to make some nationalistic capital out of repossessing the lost domain. Yes, you look terrific. If only they chose ambassadors by the way their wives dressed, we should not now be living in W12.'

'I'm sorry I spoke like that.'

'I'm sorry you haven't got your Embassy yet, Lady Cass. Shall we go down and see how the chefs are doing with the banquet and whether the butler has laid the table?'

Carrying both their empty glasses, he followed her down the stairs and into the kitchen. His good humour and flattery and the way he had set her comfortably on a kind of hilltop, while history unrolled like a map at her feet, had restored her sense of being superior to events and with it her dignity and self-respect. But in the kitchen the baby's pap still lay on the floor, an unpleasant spread of what looked like vomit between the table and the sink.

'Oh Christ!' she said, losing countenance immediately, the horrors of the day returning to overwhelm her again.

'What is it?'

'Horatio's food. He wouldn't eat it.'

'Little bleeder.'

She stooped to the cupboard under the sink to find a floor-cloth, but he took it from her.

'Not in front of the servants,' he said.

While he was gathering the mess up in the cloth, he noticed the plastic bowl still lying under the window and, recovering that, caught sight of the spoon near the cooker.

'That boy's going to be a terrific cricketer,' he said, 'with a throw like that at hardly a year old.'

'It was me that threw them,' she said miserably.

'Not at him?'

'No, not at him. Perhaps at you.'

He dropped the spoon in the sink, rinsed and wrung out the cloth and returned it to its cupboard. Then he came and put an arm round her waist.

'You have had a horrible time, poor old thing!'

She began to cry, more for her lost dignity than out of self-pity, but he comforted her, lent her his large white handkerchief and then looked at his watch.

'Action stations!' he said and went off into the dining room to lay the table. He was back in a few minutes with Christian, who had come downstairs on some errand of his own and been deputed to open the wine bottles. Then he was bounding upstairs to settle a quarrel between Martha and Tricia and order them to their joint bath and back in the kitchen again to ask if Diana would like him to make the salad.

'You must be exhausted,' she said.

'Not at all. I was exhausted, but I've got my second wind. What do you want? Just lettuce or a cornucopia?'

'Whichever you like.'

'Right! Tomatoes, cucumber, green pepper, spring onions – what's this?'

'Fennel.'

'Just cut it up, do I, like the rest?'
'Only a little.'
The joint was in the oven now, the artichokes laid out, each on its own plate, with a small jug of vinaigrette standing nearby, the potatoes peeled, the spinach washed, the sorbets in the freezer. She began to assemble the cheeses on a hand-carved platter, acquired during their tour of duty in Yugoslavia ten years ago.
'So what was your meeting about? Are you going to give the Falklands back to Argentina?'
'Are we hell? Those benighted colonists won't let us.'
'How many of them are there?'
'Two thousand. Roughly the population of Chipping Campden or Soho, rather less than Aldeburgh.'
'So how can they stop you?'
'Promises. Politicians' promises.'
'Those don't usually amount to much.'
'No, I think this is really a matter of national honour, unfortunately. The Argentinians are serious this time. Our man in BA was at the meeting and he was insistent that all the signs point to exacerbation.'
'Exacerbation?'
'The Argentinians are going to sharpen and sharpen the issue until they've got a climb-down on our part or an invasion on theirs. The best idea, which has been around for some time, is for what's called 'leaseback'. Something like Hong Kong. We concede the islands belong to Argentina and then we lease them back for the next generation or two to satisfy the colonists. But the colonists are going very cool on the idea and you can imagine that a Tory government isn't going to press it very hard.'
'What did the meeting decide?'
'Play for time with the Argentinians, put gentle pressure on the colonists to settle for leaseback. In a nutshell, nothing.'
He was mixing the salad with excessive vigour.
'So there's bound to be trouble.'
'No question. That's what was so incredibly upsetting about the meeting. One and all agreed that there was bound to be trouble. Not a single person could say how to avoid it. And the upshot will be that the government will not have its mind concentrated for it, will just be given the opportunity to push the whole thing back into the same dusty corner where it's lain for the last 150 years.'
'So what should be done?'
'The islands should be handed over to Argentina, of course. That's what everybody really wants – except those two thousand sheep people. We shall lose the islands eventually. It would be better to hand them over with dignity.'
'Is there nothing you can do? You personally, I mean. To concentrate the government's mind?'

She was starting to make a *bearnaise* sauce now, simmering chopped onions, chervil and tarragon in white wine, adding pepper and watching carefully for the wine to evaporate before straining the mixture and setting it aside to cool. Then she turned to look at him, wondering if he'd said something she'd missed while she was preoccupied. He was dipping his finger in the jug of vinaigrette. He put his finger in his mouth and walked to the window.

'I think I shall play a deep game,' he said.

'How do you mean?' she asked, assembling the butter and eggs and making sure the whisk was handy.

'I shall work on the assumption that the government wants to ignore the warning signs. I shall do everything in my power to encourage them.'

'To ignore . . .?'

'That's right. To make it obvious to the Argentinians that they're not bothered in any way.'

'Well, then, surely the Argentinians will . . .?'

'They surely will. And then, since we shall have done bugger all to counter them, made no preparations of any sort, we shall have to give way.'

'Hand over the islands?'

'Arrange leaseback, at any rate. Solve the problem in the only way it can ultimately be solved. The whole thing is vintage Gilbert and Sullivan and therefore ought to be dealt with on the principle of a Gilbert and Sullivan plot. A territory we don't want and can't let go is really no different from an executioner who's due to be boiled in oil for beheading an heir apparent he only pretended to behead to please the heir apparent's father.'

'And what about the national honour?'

'I think Dr Johnson said the last word on that.'

'What did he say?'

Horatio had begun to cry again, but she was still involved with the sauce. Tony sat down at the kitchen table and suddenly looked tired.

'Basically that such a childish concept as national honour wasn't worth the trouble and expense of possessing this particularly unattractive and unproductive piece of the earth's surface.'

'I'm afraid I'll have to get him up again. He must be hungry.'

Tony grunted. He was drawing islands with his fingers in some water spilt on the table.

'And of course it might just bring down the government,' he said. 'That would be a tremendous bonus.'

14

'In 1890 I exhibited *An Eviction in Ireland*, which Lord Salisbury was pleased to be facetious about in his speech at the banquet, remarking on the "breezy beauty" of the landscape, which almost made him wish he could take part in an eviction himself.'

Since meeting Simon Carter outside Broadcasting House and receiving as it were, the freedom of Elizabeth Butler, James had switched his attention from the husband to the wife. He had borrowed her autobiography from the London Library and was reading it now, as he sat in the garden after breakfast.

William Butler's lifelong compassion for oppressed peoples had been formed at the age of eight when he was taken by his father to see an eviction in the Irish village where they lived. More than forty years later there was another spate of evictions and since the Butlers happened to be staying in Ireland, Elizabeth went to see one for herself. On her way she met the police coming away, 'armed to the teeth and very flushed'. The cabin had already burned down, though the ruins were still smouldering and the ground was hot underfoot. She had set up her easel and begun work on an oil sketch, when the woman who had been evicted returned to search through the ashes in case any of her belongings had survived. Lady Butler expressed her indignation, but the woman didn't respond. She was, as Lady Butler put it, 'philosophical'.

James sat in an arbour surrounded by climbing roses, puffing at his first pipe of the day in the warm sunshine, and looked at his own house with its freshly painted white walls, trimly slated roof and black-beamed porch. 'Philosophical.' It was inconceivable. Less than a hundred years ago the British government sent its police to burn down one of its own citizens' houses and the owner – no, of course, she was only the tenant – the tenant was 'philosophical'. That was always the difficulty with history: to understand what was acceptable and what was beyond the pale.

On the other hand, although the eviction might have been acceptable to her, it obviously wasn't to Elizabeth Butler, nor could it have been carried out in that way at that late date in any part of the British Isles except Ireland. History was not a long thin line in time, it was more like overlapping layers. Twenty years ago, in a village in Balunda, James had been able to experience an early morning in pre-Roman Britain. Balunda today was – what? – fighting its Wars of the Roses. With late twentieth-century weapons, though. That was the extra twist. And watched by millions of late twentieth-century TV voyeurs, just as Lady Butler could take her paints and canvas and turn the wronged woman and her ruined home into an Academy landscape for the entertainment of comfortable people in late nineteenth-century London. She was pleased with the result too: 'it has the true Irish atmosphere.' Yet what else could she do? She was a painter, not a politician. She was using her art to draw attention to an evil. It was simply the nature of the world and of history that she was looking out from behind the canvas, while the other woman was picking through the ashes – both in the same landscape, but belonging to different layers of time as well as class.

James's thoughts veered suddenly to his father, as they often did since his death. It was a sort of emotional indigestion, he supposed. His feelings about his father were still unresolved, lying close to the surface. And the chief feeling was discomfort, a sense of inadequacy and waste. It wasn't that he felt sorry for his father, who had lived a fairly long life, after all, and never seemed a dissatisfied person. No, it was James himself who had suffered loss, not only of the physical person but of a whole area of potentiality. Some day, at some time in the last forty years or so, the relationship of father to son, son to father should have ripened, but it never had. A whole area of himself and his own life had been lost. Worst of all, the same thing was going to happen with his mother. It was like a nightmare in which you knew you had to run, but couldn't move a limb.

Increasingly he suffered the same distress from encounters with friends. He never seemed to get any nearer to them, to know them more deeply. It was like going on the dodgems at a fairground – you bumped and parted, bumped and parted. He tried to recall his friendships when he'd been younger – surely they were deeper and more intense? They'd all had more time to spend in each other's company then, as well as more energy. On the other hand, they'd also been more unrealistic, especially about the future, especially about time. It was naive to expect that your relationships with your friends would go on developing and expanding. By the time you were old, no doubt you took it 'philosophically'.

James's pipe was beginning to burn his tongue. He put his book on the garden seat beside him and propped the pipe against it. What was he going to do about the Butlers? He was sure that somehow they stood for something, typified something which it was important to examine and understand. The optimism and disillusionment of the Victorian Age perhaps, but was there anything special about that? Didn't every notable period have its rise and fall, its energetic beginning and its tired disintegration? Yes, but surely the Victorian Age was different, at least for people in Britain? It coincided more or less with the rise and fall of the First Industrial Age, with Britain's position between Waterloo and the First World War as the leading world power, with the gradual shift from aristocratic to middle-class government, with the most significant developments in transport since the Romans, with the spread of literacy, the invention of photography and mass-circulation newspapers, and the crude origins of recording and wireless, embryos of the media. Ten years after Wolseley and his Gang had failed to relieve Khartoum, Kitchener built a railway through the desert and took revenge on the Mahdists. His mythical reputation, eclipsing Wolseley's overnight on the strength of one battle, was a media phenomenon. When his famous First War recruiting poster was resuscitated in the Sixties as an advertising gimmick, it was as if history had finally allotted him his true value. James's thoughts became clouded and his attention wandered to a bee at work on a clump of tobacco flowers. He stood up and went indoors. In the dining room he picked up *The Times* and took it with him to the loo, so as to glance through the inside pages he had not had time to read at breakfast.

There was nothing much of interest on the home news pages. Somebody called Lord Trefgarne, speaking for the government, had announced the scrapping of *HMS Endurance*, the navy's last warship patrolling the South Atlantic. Tim Rutland was right, James thought, not to have gone into the navy. It was obviously becoming a purely ceremonial force. Remembering his conversation with Tim at Christmas, James groaned. He felt partly responsible for the way Tim had behaved afterwards, refusing to go back to school and, since he was now eighteen, ignoring his mother's protests and joining the army immediately as a private. Susie had certainly blamed James and indeed, having written to the Biggars to tell them what Tim had done and to add that he seemed to have made his decision on the strength of his interview with James, she had cut all communication with them. He turned on to the foreign news and saw a brief paragraph headed 'Ex-British Officer For Trial'. Apparently Colonel Rimington had returned to Balunda and was to be tried for a long list of crimes, including murder, torture, rape, child abuse and sorcery. He had pleaded not guilty and was to conduct his own defence. The BBC's news bulletin at lunch-time had a few more details: Rimington was claiming that he'd chosen to return and face possible execution rather than allow the history of

Balundan independence to be 'distorted by the ignorance and lies that suited scoundrels'. That word 'scoundrels', James thought, had almost as much of a period flavour as 'philosophical'. Both somehow seemed innocent, implying a world which still had a grasp of moral values and expected them to be generally admitted, even if often flouted. The radio news also mentioned that Balunda's ex-president, Marius Nakimbi, had left France and was thought to have been granted asylum in an unnamed African country.

James spent the afternoon mowing the grass. Judy's passion for flowers had led to the gradual encroachment of small flowerbeds at the edges and sometimes in the middle of the lawns. The day stayed warm and sunny and when Judy got back from school they both sat in deck chairs on one of the newly mown lawns and drank tea.

'I still have to clip the edges,' James said, when Judy complimented him on his mowing, 'that's the really heavy job, with all those beds.'

Judy smiled, ritual acknowledgment of a ritual grievance.

'I know you only do it for my sake,' she said. 'If you lived alone I suppose you wouldn't bother with a garden at all. How would you live, I wonder? In a bachelor pad somewhere near the BBC, I expect. But what would you do on your days off? Maybe if you'd lived alone, you'd have written your epic.'

'Maybe I would.'

'And you'd have preferred that, wouldn't you?' she said.

James thought about it. The question was half mocking, but it suddenly seemed wholly serious to him. It suggested not only that he'd chosen the wrong life, but that there was now no other choice. It further suggested that if he had chosen the wrong life, he'd done so the moment he fell in love with Judy, or at least when he married her.

At the time, it hadn't seemed a matter of choice. They'd met on a train. He was travelling to Sheffield to stay with an old Oxford friend. She was returning to her teacher-training college after the summer holiday. She had opened the conversation but he'd done most of the talking. When they parted at the station, they arranged to meet for lunch the next day and by the end of James's stay they knew they were in love. They married a year later when Judy got her Dip. Ed. After that first encounter from opposite window seats, the whole thing had been as inevitable as the journey itself. You got into a train to Sheffield, the train followed the rails and, two hours or so later, you stepped out at your destination. You were sexually and intellectually attracted to someone and she to you; you both kept working at the jobs you'd learned to perform efficiently and which brought in a sufficient living; you did not step out.

That was where the analogy failed. There was no destination in a relationship. You might of course suddenly get out at any station along the way and start in some other direction, but the relationship, as long as you stayed with it, was constant. You could shift inside it, the scenery outside would change too, but arrival played no part in it. And surely strange consequences flowed from that simple fact? If there was no arrival, then the whole notion of time was suspended. A relationship was always in the present. Again, without arrival, there could be no ultimate success or failure. The relationship continued or stopped. Success or failure was a matter of quality, of present quality – having nothing to do with your successes or failures in the past, let alone whatever might transpire in the future. And again, if you were involved in such a relationship, in the midst of it, travelling without destination, it was obviously not possible to travel in other relationships at the same time.

James couldn't quite make the image of the train combine at this point with his earlier image of the dodgems, but he felt that only served to emphasize the fact that the two kinds of relationships couldn't be combined. He bumped and parted, bumped and parted with his friends and even his parents because he was squeezed into his own dodgem with Judy.

He'd been staring all this while at a patch of the mown grass and looked up to find Judy staring at him. Her face was both the same face he had first seen opposite him in the train and also the face of a quite different person. He'd come to know that first face very well – he could once have drawn it from memory if he'd had David's talent for drawing – but this face he didn't know in that way. It was more complex, not so much because it had aged, acquired lines and lost or gained outline, as because in his eyes it was a blur of all the faces that had intervened and all the occasions on which it had been placed opposite him. His own face in the mirror was equally blurred for the same reason. They were neither of them static, describable objects, but sequences of exposures in slow motion, processes, overlaps. The brain was well equipped to gather and store first and even second and third impressions, but it stalled on the familiar. James could no longer recall his father's familiar face, only his paralysed and dead ones. Now he searched Judy's face as if to shake his brain into action, force it to recognize what mattered: the present, living, only face in front of him.

At the same time he wanted to find the exact thing to say, the expression in a nutshell of what he'd been thinking. In a way, this moment now seemed more important to him even than the moment when she'd first spoken to him on the train, because like her face it was composed of innumerable moments at which their relationship had changed and ramified. But the expression in a nutshell eluded him. They were not in the habit of discussing their relationship, however much they might discuss other people's. To try to crystallize it now would be to falsify it. The present moment could never be pinned down or it became a dead butterfly. It could only be experienced and then perhaps pinned down afterwards, when it had ceased to be alive and present.

'No,' he said.

'No . . . what?'

'No, nothing could ever have been better than here and now and what we are. If there was ever a choice – which I tend to doubt – I couldn't have chosen better.'

She began to say something, but it was drowned by a train going past in the cutting next to their garden. They sat smiling at one another until the train had swished away into the distance.

'What were you going to say?'

'It took you a long time to decide,' she said.

'Not to decide.'

'What, then?'

'I was making a momentous discovery.'

'Yes?'

He felt it was already going out of his head.

'A journey without destination, that was the nub of it. Nearly all the things we do have a purpose: to get food, earn money, finish a book, get to a place. Therefore we think life ought to have a purpose too: to get richer or more successful or improve ourselves morally or whatever. And life does in a sense have a purpose for us: to reproduce ourselves. So it makes us fall in love with each other. But the relationship which emerges from that moment of falling in love is quite different. Or can be. And I think ours is. It has no purpose and it makes everything else that does have a purpose look tawdry and timebound. Because a purpose implies a fulfilment and a completion and therefore a moving on to something else with another purpose. Whereas . . .'

He paused, searching for a grand, positive peroration, saw her smiling at his efforts to construct an instant philosophy of life, and began to smile himself.

'Whereas we just go on sitting in the same old train,' he said and added quickly, 'Which is very much preferable, if you see what I mean.' She leaned forward in her deck chair and touched his hand.

'I thought you were going to say the opposite,' she said. 'That you'd have preferred to remain unmarried and write your epic.'

Another idea struck him.

'I never realized till now why we took this particular house.'

'We took it for the garden,' she said.

'No, we took it because it was next to a railway.'

An hour or so later, when he'd finished clipping the edges and was going indoors, he remembered that he'd left his pipe beside Lady Butler's autobiography on the garden seat. His back was stiff and his hands and forearms still trembling from the concentrated tension needed to work the edgers, but the weakness, the temporary simulation of old age was curiously pleasant. James put the book under his arm and knocked out the ashes from his pipe. He stood and surveyed the lawns and the well-trimmed edges with complacency. Had the Butlers, like him, discovered that their relationship was the thing they cared about most, more than her painting, more than his military career? Of course it was a kind of withdrawal, an exclusion of the rest of the world, but wasn't that what all the great religious teachers and most of the philosophers recommended? True, they didn't generally envisage a domestic relationship with another human being, but that was probably because they weren't usually the marrying type and had to invent invisible substitutes in another dimension. Unlike himself, the Butlers had done notable things in the world and made themselves public figures before they withdrew into their private relationship with one another. So had the British people. That withdrawal was generally seen as a decline, but suppose one saw it as a virtue and a strength. Epics were celebrations of nationalism and aggressive masculinity. Couldn't he celebrate the Butlers and by implication the Empire they served in a sort of reverse epic whose climax was withdrawal?

James went into the house, filled and lit his pipe and zigzagged excitedly about the kitchen, explaining his new idea to Judy. Dodging him as best she could, she prepared their supper.

15

The photograph of Maria naked in the wood appeared in a Sunday paper the week after she and Simon returned to London. The picture was dark and blurred, but the face was recognizable. The accompanying paragraph was headlined 'A BIG SURPRISE':

'If you were down in the woods near the sleepy village of St Craw in North Cornwall recently, you could have met lovely newscaster Maria Dobson on holiday with her friend Simon Carter, an art critic. They were staying with Maria's Mum and Dad, Dr and Mrs Hinks, who live in St Craw, but nothing could keep Maria and Simon indoors on such a balmy night and when it comes to nudes by moonlight, Simon definitely prefers real life to art. Maria is back on your screens now, but we're afraid you won't be able to see much of her moon-tan.'

Maria was immediately given a week's holiday, so that her employers could consider whether she should continue in her job. A statement was issued regretting the newspaper's action and announcing that the couple had been married some weeks earlier. Public interest in the affair lasted a few days and then died away when it was clear that everybody without exception thought Maria had a perfect right to go naked in the woods and that only the photographer and the newspaper deserved censure.

While her employers debated her case, Maria and Simon were concealed from the press and public at a house in the Thames Valley. It belonged to a TV executive and his wife and had been built in the Twenties beside a small tributary of the Thames. The large lawn at the back of the house sloped from French windows down to the river's edge and was partly shaded by a big horse-chestnut tree, a beech and, along the bank, weeping willows. There was a well-maintained boathouse containing a skiff, but Maria and Simon were advised not to risk being seen by going out in it. The whole place – especially the spacious hall of the house, with its oak-banistered staircase – suggested the setting for a Ben Travers farce.

Tom and Laura Glenny (she worked for a company making TV commercials) commuted to London every day, leaving Maria and Simon on their own, except for the resident cook-housekeeper, Mrs Huggett. She was a thin, faded, work-worn person, who seemed at first terrified of her new charges, avoiding their eyes when she served breakfast or lunch, keeping to her kitchen most of the time and only entering the other parts of the house to clean and tidy them when she was sure Maria and Simon had definitely settled elsewhere. But when, on the second day at lunch, Maria insisted on speaking to her, she proved surprisingly talkative. She came from Hull, where her husband had been a trawlerman until the fishing business began to collapse – he had died soon after being laid off – and, since her children were all grown up and had left home, she had answered an ad in *The Lady* and come south. No, she didn't mind the work – it was what she was used to, since she'd been her husband's and children's housekeeper all her adult life – but she didn't care for the place. It was lonely and alien, all these big houses set apart from one another, so that you hardly ever saw anyone and never spoke to anyone except the shopkeepers. Her only friends, she said, were the people on the TV screen and although they smiled and chatted to you, there was no way you could chat back to them.

'Well,' said Simon, 'now at last you've got one you can chat back to.'

Maria, admitted Mrs Huggett bashfully, not daring to look at her, was one of her favourite personalities and she could hardly believe she was really here in the flesh in front of her.

'I feel the same,' said Simon. 'Too good to be true.'

'You're a lucky man,' said Mrs Huggett. 'But won't it be terrible if they don't let her back on the news?'

'People will be shooting themselves,' said Simon. 'For that very reason I don't think there's much doubt about their decision. However, speaking for myself, I shouldn't mind at all.'

'You wouldn't?'

'I've always resented having to share her with others and besides, she's always out appearing on the box when I'm in and want to watch it with her.'

'You mustn't be selfish,' said Mrs Huggett, shyly touching Maria's arm, as if she too now owned a share in the national treasure.

When they were alone, Maria asked him if he'd really prefer her to stop working as a newscaster.

'In a way. In a way not.'

'Because of the photograph?'

'No, that's nothing to do with it.'

Whenever the photograph came up in their conversation, Simon discounted it, so that, without deliberately avoiding the subject, they never really discussed it at all. He felt that, quite apart from the increased notoriety it had given Maria, it had had a strange effect on her which he was reluctant to explore with her, probably because he suspected it was something she wanted to explore. He shied away from admitting to himself that it was an experience she didn't regret, since if she actually liked the idea of appearing naked to the whole nation, it became almost tantamount to a betrayal of him. Was it simple jealousy, then? He could hardly be jealous of millions of people. No, it was to do with her feelings towards him, not his or others' towards her. The photograph crystallized an anxiety that already existed, from the moment he fell in love with her: that being in the public eye was what she really lived for and that he was only a passing fancy.

Nevertheless, they enjoyed their secret days in the Glennys' version of Rookery Nook like a second honeymoon. Simon had brought a pile of art books and catalogues with him, so as to begin the research for his TV series on contemporary art, and they went through them together, working out how the material might be divided into programmes, which artists should figure most prominently and how the whole subject should be most alluringly presented, so that the public might once and for all be won over and disabused of the idea that all modern art was a con. Maria herself stood for this putative public and Simon's desire to convince his one-person audience of the value of contemporary art was inextricably tangled up with his desire for her.

'But what is the heart of the problem?' Maria asked, on one such occasion, when they were lying in each other's arms in the bedroom armchair, with books and papers scattered round them. 'Why is there such resistance to contemporary art, if it's really so easy to enjoy?'

'Nothing's easy to enjoy without a little knowledge and practice. Not even sex. Not eating or drinking. Look at the difficulty children have with that. Look at the tasteless, dreary things they have to be weaned away from. The eye has to be trained to appreciate visual sensuality. Particularly when it's already learned a bastard kind of visual sensuality consisting in the simple equivalence of images. I know I enjoy looking at a tree, so I also enjoy recognizing a tree in paint, because it reminds me of the real tree. But that's only a surrogate sensuality, a reminiscence or shadow of the real thing. True art is real sensuality, direct enjoyment through the eye of the thing in front of you.'

'As good as sex?'

'Why not? Or better. If it's good art and bad sex.'

'How about talking about art? Where does that fit in?'

'Anything done with passion is a kind of sensuality. Or at least a prelude or invitation to sensuality. Wouldn't you say?'

'Reading the news?'

'Othello won Desdemona by describing his battles.'

The honeymoon was interrupted each evening by the return of their hosts. Tom Glenny was a well-built, energetic man in his early forties, with a florid complexion, a handsome head of fair hair and bright blue eyes. Simon disliked him unreservedly, no doubt because he never stopped flirting with Maria in the most blatant way and treated Simon as an awkward and mainly contemptible appendage. He could do this more easily since he shared Maria's professional world, knew all the same people and was himself an influential figure in that world. Despising intellectuals in general, he made it almost impossible for Simon to open his mouth without giving rise to a jibe about 'you aesthetes' or 'people with arty-tarty tastes'. Maria didn't seem to mind his flirting with her nor to notice how he humiliated Simon. Laura Glenny, meanwhile – thin, pale and dark with a shy, girlish manner that sometimes made her seem more like Tom's daughter than his wife – spoke very little and observed all that was going on with a little ambiguous smile. She treated Simon politely, almost deferentially, and was herself, he thought, inclined to be intellectual, but she made no attempt to counter her husband's aggressive self-assertion and perhaps even encouraged it by her acquiescence.

Maria showed little interest in the Glennys when she and Simon were alone. Tom, she said, was well-known for thinking himself a Don Juan and nobody took him very seriously in that role. As a TV executive, however, he was thought to be hot stuff and likely to rise to the very top, so that there was no point in offending him, particularly since she didn't find him offensive and they were stuck with him for these few days. No, she didn't find him the least attractive, but if he found her attractive she couldn't help it and anyway, as Simon knew, she liked being admired.

'What if I were to flirt with Laura?'

'Go ahead!'

'You wouldn't mind?'

'I probably would.'

'There seems to be some inequality here,' said Simon.

'Tom flirts indiscriminately – it's his natural method of expression with women. But if you were to flirt with Laura, it would be different, because you're not that sort of person. It would be serious and personal.'

'I can't make out Laura's attitude to Tom's behaviour.'

'Ask her!'

'But what do you think?'

'Since she's been married to him for some years, I should guess she accepts it as normal. As I said, nobody takes Tom's show-off behaviour seriously. Least of all, I should imagine, his wife.'

'Do you like him?'

'He's just a person I know and see around. Liking doesn't come into it.'

'It always does for me. If I don't like somebody I avoid them.'

'But you're a critic. Your whole life is sorting out sheep from goats.'

'Tom's certainly a goat.'

'He can be quite entertaining. I'm not as fussy as you about who I mix with.'

By the end of the week the strain of spending the evenings with the Glennys was telling on Simon. He felt that however lightly Maria treated his complaints, she was accepting too much attention from Tom and that a gap was opening up between himself and her. His response was not to redouble his own attention to her, but to withdraw; and he settled down to work by himself at the table in the bedroom, leaving her to sit in the garden reading one of the novels from the Glennys' shelves of mostly Fifties' and Sixties' paperbacks.

The Glennys returned from London that Friday evening with the news that Tom's colleagues had passed Maria as still fit for her old job.

'After all,' he said, as he spewed champagne into her glass before supper, 'half the punters must have undressed you in their imagination long since and no one's going to complain because it turns out there's a real woman with a real body under that demure expression.'

Pausing with the bottle in his hand and looking her up and down, he seemed to be illustrating his thesis. His wife watched both of them with her opaque smile and Simon had the uncomfortable feeling that she didn't just acquiesce in her husband's sexual overtures to other women, but probably enjoyed them.

'As a matter of fact . . .' Tom put down the bottle and raised his own glass to toast her, 'I'm convinced this is the best thing that could have happened to you. For why? Because now you'll be a personality in your own right, instead of just another newscaster. Believe me – I'm telling tales out of school now – one or two of my colleagues were chiefly worried they might lose you to another channel.'

Maria responded by raising her own glass. Her face glowed with pleasure. Simon pretended to be smiling when she glanced at him, but he felt leaden.

After supper, Tom asked what they wanted to do the next day. Simon supposed that if they couldn't yet go home, they would have to keep their heads down as usual and that he personally would be working on his notes. Tom immediately suggested to Maria that he take her out for a spin in the skiff.

'I thought you said that was too risky,' said Simon.

'Oh, I think we can get away with it,' said Tom in his loud, boisterous voice. 'Maria can wear a very large hat. Laura's got a large hat. You'll lend her your hat, won't you, Laura?'

'Of course,' said Laura, her voice seeming to get smaller and softer as his swelled. 'But Maria hasn't said whether she wants to go or not.'

'Yes, I'd love to go,' said Maria, smiling at Simon's stony face. 'But what about you, Laura? Won't you come too?'

'No thank you,' said Laura. 'I'm not mad about boats. We'll have lunch here, shall we? Or will you take yours with you, Tom?'

'No need,' said Tom. 'If we go upriver, there's that very charming pub that does delicious beef sandwiches. We'll have a bite there.'

'I don't quite understand how that's possible,' said Simon, trying to keep his tone neutral, but sounding aggressive. 'For Maria to go swanning off to pubs when apparently it's still too soon for us to go home.'

'It's entirely up to you, of course,' said Tom. 'This isn't a concentration camp. You can go back to London when you like. Except that, firstly the announcement about Maria being back on screen on Monday will probably appear in tomorrow's papers, so you might be wiser, if you want to avoid a mob of hacks round your door, to stay away at least until Monday. Secondly, on a personal note, I'd rather hoped we could make up this weekend for having to leave you so much to yourselves during the week.'

There was silence. Simon shrugged and looked at Maria, leaving the decision to her.

'Do stay! Won't you?' said Laura.

'Of course we'll stay,' Maria said. 'But why don't we take our lunch, instead of going to a pub?'

'Splendid!' said Tom. 'We'll do that.'

'In that case,' said Simon, 'I think I'll change my mind and come too.'

Tom looked put out, but Maria smiled across at Simon with obvious pleasure. His whole mood changed immediately, from sulkiness to a happiness reflecting her own.

'Maybe I'll change my mind too,' said Laura. 'I'll go and ask Mrs Huggett to make us a picnic for four tomorrow.'

'Right!' said Tom. 'Are you good at rowing, Simon?'

The expedition upriver went reasonably well until lunch-time. Tom did most of the rowing, though Simon took a clumsy turn or two. Tom made many references to the weight of the boat, the fact that there might be room for four but a skiff was really better for two, the difficulty of rowing when you couldn't rely on the steersman and so on, which, though apparently tongue-in-cheek, were too often repeated to be amusing. Laura held the ropes from the rudder and did the steering, but she didn't concentrate very well and the boat often veered from side to side of the river and sometimes narrowly missed other boats coming in the opposite direction. Simon did much of the talking and was mainly responsible for Laura's lack of concentration on the steering, since he was explaining to her the importance for the French Impressionists of the new lower middle classes in mid-nineteenth-century Paris, with their Sunday excursions to the new suburbs along the Seine and their particular pleasure in boating.

'Impressionism was really the celebration, the apotheosis of a way of life which was then quite strange and sudden, but has since become commonplace. Then they just went out and enjoyed themselves on the river. Now we enjoy ourselves partly because we see ourselves in a sort of Impressionist painting.'

The day had been intermittently sunny while they were on the river, but when they had tied up, sat down on the bank and laid out the picnic it began to spot with rain. The sandwiches were stodgy.

'We'd have done better at the Moorhen,' said Tom, raising a large coloured umbrella and moving closer to Maria so as to shelter her with it. The rain came on harder and, since there was only one umbrella, all four of them huddled together under it. Simon found himself crouching at the edge of the group, with the rain wetting his left shoulder, while Tom, on the other side, had his arm round Maria's back and Laura sat across her legs.

After a while, when the rain had eased off to a light drizzle, Maria pulled herself away from Tom and stood up.

'I'm going for a walk,' she said and began looking for a gap in the barbed-wire fence along the towpath.

'I'll come with you,' said Tom, handing the umbrella to Simon.

'Somebody has to look after the boat,' said Laura mildly and, looking up at Simon who was on his feet but still awkwardly holding the umbrella at a steep angle so as to shelter both of them, 'You go and join the others. I'm quite happy to stay. I hate getting wet anyway.' Simon, torn between politeness to her and anxiety not to lose sight of Maria, ended by staying where he was.

Maria and Tom scrambled through the fence and struck off across a field away from the river. They walked fast, in silence at first, the rain wetting Tom's face but kept off Maria's by the man's boater that Tom had lent her as some sort of disguise when they set off that morning. At the far side of the field they found a gate and Maria climbed up it and sat on the top while she negotiated her skirt, suitable for sitting in a boat, but too long and full for walking in the country. Tom slipped the gate off its fastening and swung it gently open, then playfully pulled it back again and let it go so that she rode it back towards the hedge at increasing speed. He was there to catch it, though, before it bounced against the post, and put up a hand to help her down. She ignored it, but waited while he latched the gate and then set off along a narrow track at a slower pace. The rain was coming down harder again. Tom's hair was sodden and his elegant pale blue shirt and faded jeans had turned dark and clung to his body. Maria's summer dress, light green with a thin red stripe, was in the same state, but showed it less.

'Getting soaked isn't normally my idea of fun,' said Tom, 'but on this occasion I wouldn't be anywhere else. I can't deny that I find you irresistible.'

Maria said nothing. She was wondering how on earth she came to be getting herself extremely wet in the company of this man she hardly knew and wasn't much attracted to. Particularly when the man she was attracted to was patiently sitting out her whim on the riverbank with this man's enigmatic wife, who might be capable of anything. The fault, however, was largely Simon's. He should have come with her. She began to feel angry with him.

They were passing a barn and there seemed to be a farm not far ahead. Tom put his hand on her shoulder, but did not attempt to keep it there when she moved away from him.

'You're really wet,' he said. 'Wouldn't it be a good idea to take shelter while this cloud goes over? Look, it's surely brighter behind?' He turned aside to explore the barn without expecting a reply. She waited on the track.

'It's perfectly dry,' he called, 'and very commodious.'

Standing there, she began to feel chilled and went over to join him inside the barn. It was a large, corrugated iron structure, with one end entirely open. There were bales of hay left over from the winter at the back, but most of the space was empty. Tom sat down on a stray bale, found a packet of cigarettes in his shirt pocket and offered her one. She refused.

'Damn!' he said. 'I left my matches in the picnic basket.'

Putting the cigarettes away again, he added, 'The thing is that Laura likes intellectual gibberish of the sort your husband was talking and I don't. Does he always go on like an article in a colour supplement?'

'I think his ideas are usually more original,' said Maria, trying to keep her teeth from chattering.

'You are a body with a mind,' said Tom. 'He is a mind with a body. That's to say he lives mostly in his head and you, I should say, mostly around your solar plexus. Or am I wrong?'

The notion seemed to her crude and uninteresting and she hardly bothered to acknowledge it. She felt she'd had more than enough of his company, not so much because he didn't attract her as because she began to sense that his reputation as a Don Juan was not just talk. He was entirely singleminded. He meant to have her and did not expect to fail.

'I'm going back to the boat now,' she said, but hesitated under the drips falling across the open end of the barn as she saw that the rain was still heavy.

'You're shivering, Maria,' he said and in a moment had left his bale of hay and was pulling her back into the dry with his arms round her.

'Please!' she said.

'Please what?'

'Please let go!'

'You need warmth.'

'Maybe. But not from you.'

'Why not from me?'

'Please let me go!'

She struggled and he did let her go, but stood very close, as if he might grab her again if she tried to move.

'I want you, Maria,' he said. 'I can't let you go. What's the harm? Life is for living.'

What he said was absurd. She despised it. But the urgency of his voice, his closeness, his insistence – all physical rather than rational pressures – overrode what she thought of him. Gradually he began to touch her, almost as if he were administering some sort of medical treatment – that, after all, was the original excuse for his contact – her hair, her neck, her shoulder, her arm, her hand. Then he began to kiss the same places, very lightly, and at the same time to touch her body lower down – her breasts, her stomach, her thighs, her buttocks. In a way she felt anaesthetized, her mind noticing that it had no control over her body, but her body was also experiencing pleasure, sending signals to that effect to the mind, so that it was more likely that her mind saw no good reason to exercise control.

After some time they moved together to the back of the barn where the bales of hay were stacked – she was not very concious of the ground under her feet, so he was probably more or less carrying her – and he took off her wet clothes with the same slow, concentrated precision as he had used to touch and kiss her – it was like being dismembered by an expert butcher, but without the pain. He didn't take off his own clothes – that would have broken the thread of concentration which was all that prevented her, she thought, running screaming out of the barn – but at some point while undressing her he had loosened the top of his trousers and finally entered her quite undramatically, as though he were still only touching her with his fingers.

It was not rape, she thought afterwards, as he lit a cigarette with the matches which he had after all found in his trouser pocket and she lay, still naked, half buried between the bales of hay, but it was a kind of ruthless assertion of one person's will over another's which she had never really believed possible – not at least in any world she inhabited.

16

Susie's instinct was always to cut her losses. She believed in happiness as other people believed in Christianity or socialism. Life made no sense without it, so she could never understand the school of thought which said you had to be realistic, to face facts. It was always best, in her experience, to sweep unpleasant facts aside – not under the carpet, but out of the house. In the case of David's disappearance, the facts were so unpleasant and obtrusive that the only sensible course was to sweep the house itself away, with all the painful memories it contained. She accepted that David was dead and threw herself energetically into finding a new home and reorientating her life.

She began by concentrating her search around Oxford, so as to be within easy reach both of her mother and her younger son John's school. Tim's defection to the army she treated as she treated his father's disappearance – an event it was better to exclude from further consideration. She broke off relations with the Biggars more because they were associated with David and the dreadful time of his first loss than because she really blamed James for encouraging Tim to be a soldier. Meanwhile, until Tim should discover the error of his ways, she turned all her attention to John. Previously overshadowed by his brother, he responded eagerly and became, as she said to her mother, 'a tower of strength'.

The house she eventually found was in a neat Cotswold village, a place almost entirely inhabited by well-salaried executives working in Gloucestershire or Midland industries and by equally well-heeled weekend refugees from London. Susie's new house was much larger than she needed for practical purposes, but it corresponded perfectly to her image of herself in being spacious, gracious and set back from the road, with proper gateposts, tall iron gates and a little curve of drive. Also, quite by chance, it gave her a new occupation. She had intended anyway to give more time to her painting, but this house had been occupied by a couple of professional potters who had scraped a living for some years but finally been forced to move to humbler quarters in a less affluent area. After attending some classes in Cheltenham and getting her predecessors' kilns modernized, Susie settled down to a busy regime of potting as well as painting, gardening and improving the house. She was soon, too, involved in all the activities of the village, dining out with her neighbours, regularly attending the Sunday service at the church, taking part in fêtes and flower shows – her light, sociable, optimistic personality flowering and expanding in a way it had never been able to do in the shadow of David's.

When John came home for the long school holiday, he at first helped his mother with operating the kilns and then quickly became absorbed in making pottery himself. He was keen to turn it from a hobby into a business and quite soon they did begin to sell their wares to people in the village and even beyond it. Susie made the more ambitiously aesthetic objects – large bowls with broad flower patterns, generously shaped jugs and vases, pretty one-off plates in bright checks or stripes – but John preferred the less noticeable, everyday things in simple brown or grey glazes – mugs, cups, plates and saucers – and liked turning them out in quantity.

Tim wrote to them from time to time and on one occasion – when he had leave after his basic training – came to stay, but their relationship remained guarded and unsatisfactory. His letters, characteristically inarticulate and uninformative, contained a new element of enthusiasm – he was now training with the paratroopers – which might have suggested to Susie that her opposition to his army career was pointless, but she could find no glamour in the idea of her son being an ordinary soldier.

In the late summer reports began to come out of Balunda of the trial of Colonel Rimington. Susie was never much interested in news and would probably have missed the reports altogether if John hadn't been at home. He was keeping an eye on the foreign pages of the newspapers because his school holiday task was to produce an up-to-date account of Britain's former West African colonies. He had written for information to the various High Commissions in London, but Balunda was one of those that didn't reply and he had been wondering if he'd have to leave it out. Susie had got up from the breakfast table and was stacking the dirty crockery in the dishwasher when John, still lingering over his coffee and idly running through the paper, called out excitedly:

'I say, Mum, here's one of the ones I've been looking for.'
'One of the whats you've been looking for?'
'Balunda.'
'What about it?'
'A bloke called Colonel Rimington is being tried there.'

'Are you sure?'
'That's what it says.'
'What for?'
'All kinds of things.' John read out the list from the paper: 'Murder, treason, corruption, robbery, witchcraft, torture, conspiracy, embezzlement, spying, sexual offences.'

Susie was shocked. Her mind had been pleasantly occupied with her plans for the day – some tidying in the garden, a batch of pots to be fired, some flowers to be taken to the church, shopping, a drinks party to attend in another village in the evening. She felt her heart thumping alarmingly and sat down on the nearest chair, scraping the legs noisily on the red tiled floor.

'Are you all right, Mum? What's the matter?'
'Colonel Rimington?'
'That's right. Do you know him?'
'I don't. But he was the person your father went to meet in France.'
'Good Grief! Well, he's in Balunda now. You don't think Dad . . . ?'
'I've no idea, no idea at all.'

John read rapidly through the short column again.
'There's no mention of Dad here. Do you want to see?'
'I'm sure it's nothing to do with your father. Just the name gave me a shock.'
'But if Colonel Rimington is being accused of all these things, maybe Dad . . .'
'No, I don't think so.'
'Maybe he murdered Dad.'
'I'm sure he didn't. David was very fond of him and he of David. They met originally in Balunda.'
'That must be the answer. The people in Balunda that are accusing Colonel Rimington must have got Dad. For being his friend.'
'I really don't want to talk about it, John. I don't think this is anything to do with David. It's nearly twenty years since he was in Balunda.'
'But . . .'
'Please, John! Leave it!'

She sat quietly for a minute or two until she felt that everything inside her had returned to normal. Then she got up, cleared away the rest of the breakfast things, wiped the table, swept the crumbs off the floor and went upstairs to make the bed. She was sure that it was as she said: the name had momentarily shocked her, but she was not really upset, she didn't feel any pangs for David any more. She switched her mind to thinking about this evening's party, at which she hoped to see again a man called Geoffrey Patterson who ran a successful small business in Bristol, was recently divorced and had been attentive to her when they met at another party a fortnight ago.

But during the next three weeks Colonel Rimington wouldn't go away. He didn't rate much space in the papers and the details of the trial and of his alleged misdeeds were scanty, but John gathered them eagerly whenever they appeared and took a teasing pleasure in drawing them to his mother's attention, though he knew it upset her.

'It says here that he kept a lot of snakes in glass cases in his living room. He would collect the poison and use it to get rid of his enemies. Also to practise witchcraft.'

'Well, maybe.'

'That's what it says here.'

'You don't have to believe what it says there.'

'It also says that he murdered General Ozo, the president. He'd been overthrown in a coup and was trying to escape over a barbed-wire fence.'

'I don't want to hear about it.'

'Ozo had got caught in the wire and was all torn up and covered with blood. Rimington ordered his soldiers to help him down. Then just as Ozo was getting over his fright and beginning to thank Rimington, he took out his revolver and started to shoot him, first in the arms and legs and then moving inwards. Apparently Rimington had always taught his soldiers that they had to shoot their enemies in one or two particular spots to be sure of killing them and he was using General Ozo as a dummy to demonstrate how many times you could shoot somebody without killing them. But Ozo died rather soon and Colonel Rimington was very annoyed. He said it was because Ozo was so fat and had died prematurely of heart failure.'

Susie covered her ears and went out of the room before he'd finished, but a few days later he had more grisly details.

'Apparently he used to burn villages. And he'd take people's children away and flog them and give them the snake torture – unfortunately, it doesn't say what that is – until they handed over their money. This money he stashed away in Swiss bank accounts and it's still there. It says he was also a spy for the British . . .'

'*It* says!'

'Don't you think any of this is true, Mum?'

'It doesn't sound like the man David told me about.'

'It was Colonel Rimington's friend, President Nakimbi, who persuaded the French to send him back to Balunda, because having trusted him for so long he finally realized what Rimington had been up to. So maybe Dad was wrong about him too.'

Whether it was the effect of hearing these disturbing details about a man whom David had liked and admired and who was almost certainly involved in some way with his disappearance, or whether it was just finding herself alone in a house that was far too large for one person, Susie became depressed after John had gone back to school. Her usual remedy of turning towards happiness and away from unpleasantness didn't seem to work, perhaps because the unpleasantness was so amorphous and seemed to come from inside instead of outside. It was not sufficiently real – you couldn't see it to sweep out of the door. Geoffrey Patterson was certainly keen to support her, both morally and physically, but she didn't want a new intimate relationship – or not at any rate with him. Her painting and pottery seemed her best resort and she spent most of her time alone in her studio, listening as she worked to the music on Radio Three.

Music, she decided, was almost entirely concerned with happiness. Not modern music, of course. She didn't know what that was after and was quick to switch it off. But the older composers were somehow able to contain all the human moods in an envelope of pleasure, so that you were never abandoned to ugliness and discomfort. Music of that sort, she felt, was like believing in God – it offered encouragement and protection. Naturally, in the course of her listening, she often heard James announcing the programmes. This too she found a comfort, because he had such a kind, civilized voice, epitomizing the same values of sanity, reliability and good living as the old composers. She knew that in person he was indeed kind and civilized, but also less firm and self-assured than he sounded, and she had no inclination to re-open their relationship. His radio voice belonged less to himself than to the public service he was performing. It was the personification of Radio Three.

Nevertheless, in her present condition, spending so much of her time alone when she was by nature gregarious, obscurely haunted by the mystery of David's disappearance and Colonel Rimington's part in it, neither her Sunday God nor her daily diet of music was enough to raise her spirits. Her mother, when she came to stay at the beginning of November, found Susie suffering from a long-drawn-out cold and persistent headaches, looking pale and run down. Mrs Chamberlin was not herself a cheerful person and she was almost entirely absorbed by her own needs, but since she usually relied on Susie as a source of energy and was no longer able to, she was forced to recognize that something required to be done.

'What about a holiday?' she suggested. 'We could go to Morocco or Egypt – somewhere nice and sunny.'

Susie resisted the idea – she didn't fancy her mother as a travelling companion. Mrs Chamberlin would do nothing but find fault with the arrangements and the service and between eating and sleeping they would sit and stroll about aimlessly having no fun at all. However, since she no more wished to be pitied by her mother than by the Biggars, she made a determined effort to pick herself up for the duration of her mother's visit and evaded any further discussion of what might be wrong with her or how it might be remedied. Various neighbours were invited round to meet Mrs Chamberlin, invitations were received in return, they made several expeditions in the car and her mother was finally put on her train back to Birmingham in the comfortable conviction that Susie was restored to health. Susie almost believed it herself, but when her mother had gone she found she was still not sleeping well and still felt lethargic and downhearted. Even looking forward to Christmas, when she would have John and her mother in the house again and would certainly enjoy setting up all the traditional festivities in her new surroundings for the first time, didn't lift her spirits. She began to wonder if there was something physically wrong with her.

Then, a week after her mother's visit, she received a phone call from Tony Cass in London.

'Did you see yesterday's *Telegraph*?' he asked.

'No,' she said. 'I don't take the *Telegraph*.'

'I suppose you haven't forgotten Colonel Rimington?' he said.

'No,' she said guardedly. 'No, I noticed that he was being put on trial in Balunda.'

'Ah, you did. Well, the prosecution has now completed its case – a pretty damning one I must say, in quantity if not quality – and Rimington has been defending himself. The *Telegraph* carried a longish report of it yesterday and David was mentioned.'

Susie couldn't answer. The news made her feel so weak and dizzy that she almost fell down. She sat on the arm of the chair and held the telephone receiver with both hands to stop it shaking.

'Are you there, Susie? Did you hear what I said?'

'Yes, I'm here. What did it say about David?' Her voice was shaking too, but she tried to keep it even and noncommittal.

'Not a great deal, I'm afraid. Nothing hopeful. Nothing absolutely final, but I don't want to raise your hopes.'

'I don't have any hopes now.'

'No, well, that's wise of you. Look, I'm ringing because I thought it might possibly be of help if I came down to see you.'

'Yes, I'm sure it would,' she said eagerly, though she hadn't thought she'd want to see Tony Cass again after the way he'd simply dropped all interest in her and David a year ago.

'Good. Then are you free tomorrow?'

'I am free, yes.'

'Good. I'll bring the cutting from the *Telegraph* with me, but of course you may be able to find somebody round about who takes the rag and hasn't yet used it to light the fire. I'll come by train. Can you meet me or shall I get a taxi?'

She arranged to meet him and give him lunch and he rang off. She knew the vicar took the *Telegraph* and found that he'd not yet thrown it away. At first when she skimmed through the column headed 'RIMINGTON ACCUSES FRENCH', she couldn't see anything about David. His name didn't seem to be there. She went back to the beginning and read the whole thing quite carefully, forcing herself to understand it paragraph by paragraph, her heart beating almost audibly, her hands sweating and trembling and her arms aching as she held the pages open.

Colonel Rimington was indeed accusing the French. According to him or according to the *Telegraph* reporter's precis of his speech, he had dedicated himself from the moment of independence to the welfare of Balunda and its people. He had given up his British citizenship and taken Balundan nationality and, he said, he would have given up his colour too and become black, if only the doctors could give you a colour-change operation like a sex-change one. All the accusations of cruelty, perversion, and wholesale murder were lies invented by those who wished to divert attention from the crimes of the real villain of the piece, ex-President Nakimbi. And who were those people? The very nature of the charges against him provided the clue. He was accused of spying for the British. Yet General Ozo was well known to have been supported by the British and President Nakimbi by the French and it was he, Colonel Rimington, who had helped Nakimbi back to power for the second time and, on Nakimbi's orders, been forced to execute General Ozo. He, Rimington, had always tried to remain strictly neutral in the Balundan power struggles, since although he thought of himself as a Balundan, he knew that others could never ignore his white skin. Therefore he had done his best to support Nakimbi during his second term of office, as he'd supported him in his first and also supported Ozo. Perhaps this was a rather British way of looking at things – the notion of supporting whoever turned out to be the people's choice of government – but he was after all born and brought up in Britain in that gentlemanly tradition. This did not mean, however, that he was a British spy. The notorious incident with the British High Commissioner, Mr Wainwright, would surely suggest the opposite and if the prosecution maintained that that was rigged, then he would like to know how it was that the French in collusion with the British had made sure that he was brought back to Balunda to face all these terrible and utterly false charges.

And here Rimington did mention David. Not by name, but the reference was clear. How did Rimington know the French were in collusion with the British? Because in an unguarded moment – or perhaps simply to deprive him of any hope of escape or redress – they had told him so. When an old friend, a British lawyer, had come to see him in France and had taken away his own written memoir of the truth about events in Balunda during his years of power and influence, that man had been intercepted on his way back to Britain by the French Intelligence service. And if, they told Rimington, he thought the British would kick up a fuss about that, he was making a big mistake. The British MI5 was aware of what had happened and accepted that it was entirely a French affair and would not warrant their own interference.

Susie read the paragraph again, but there was nothing specific about what had happened to David. Only that vague and threatening word 'intercepted'. She read on into the next paragraph, but it was concerned with the long history of French and British rivalry in Balunda and contained no further reference to David. She threw the paper on the floor and sat staring into space, letting her mind slowly explore the implications of what she'd read. Either Colonel Rimington didn't know what exactly had happened to David or he was only interested in the loss of his memoir, not of his friend. Surely that wasn't possible? Besides, he wasn't trying to curry favour with the French or the British Intelligence services. On the contrary, it would have made his case sound so much stronger if he'd said 'murdered' instead of 'intercepted'. So either Rimington didn't know or David wasn't dead. She couldn't allow herself to build anything on that, but she couldn't altogether keep her mind from recognizing it as a strange, unlooked-for possibility.

And now she remembered that Tony Cass was coming to see her, had suddenly demonstrated a new interest in the whole affair. Had he known the answer all along? She got through the rest of the day automatically occupying herself with various activities – collecting the dead leaves in the garden, tidying the house, driving into Cheltenham to buy tomorrow's lunch, cleaning the silver – while her mind processed and reprocessed the information she had got from the paper and what she could remember of the events surrounding David's disappearance and its aftermath. She worked late on a painting to tire herself out, but slept badly and dreamed of being pursued round her own garden by evil, gnome-like figures, uniformed like French policemen.

When she met Tony at the station next day, she half expected to find him accompanied by sinister Frenchmen. But she'd forgotten what a strong and reassuring person he was. He spent the drive questioning her about her move, her new house and her children and told her about his own family. By the time they'd settled down in the sitting room for a drink before lunch, Susie felt more relaxed than she had for months. Oddly enough, considering the news he came to discuss, she felt as if life had suddenly returned to normal.

'Did you manage to see the paper?' he asked at last.

'Yes, I did.'

'There was more of Rimington's defence yesterday and today. His line seems to be that all Balunda's troubles are down to the ex-colonial powers and their black puppets and that he, Rimington, is the real champion of black Africa. Quite bold and clever. Clearly a remarkable man, whatever horrors he's perpetrated. However, there was nothing more about David. We'll have to see if anything comes out in the questioning. I doubt it myself, because this is obviously just a smokescreen of Rimington's and doesn't affect the main issues.'

'You mean it's untrue?' she asked. 'David wasn't intercepted by the French Intelligence service?'

'That may well be true,' Tony said. 'Of course they've denied anything of the sort from the beginning, but it seems the likeliest explanation. But as for his allegations about the British colluding with the French, that of course is complete nonsense and the main reason I've come all this way to see you is to assure you of that. Both officially and personally. The idea that we might have connived in the disappearance of one of our own nationals in order to protect what are essentially French interests is not only incredible, it's ludicrous. It fits nicely into Rimington's line of defence but into no other conceivable scenario. I'm most anxious for you to understand that in the real world there's just no grain of truth or sense in that.'

Tony sat back in the armchair and sipped his vermouth. Susie looked at the floor near his feet in silence. One of his legs was crossed over the other. She noticed what very large shoes he had, strong, handsome, old-fashioned brown shoes, with a distinctive pattern on the uppers – they were probably handmade. She had no doubt that what he said was true. She was silent not because she doubted him, but because she was savouring the relief of his certainty. Sitting so confidently in the armchair, slightly swinging his upper leg, he made everything come right. She even felt proud of her new house again, looked forward to the lunch and expensive wine she was about to share with him, saw herself through his eyes as still young and with a life to live.

'Yes,' she said. 'Of course. I do understand that.'

'Well,' he said, smiling as she looked up and he caught her eye, 'I'm afraid that brings us no nearer to knowing what did happen to David, but I have to say that the substance of Rimington's accusation against the French rings true. David's suitcase was found on the beach – it contained what were obviously the notes of a conversation with Rimington on the subject of his life and times in Balunda – it's not likely that David simply took a bathe and didn't come back.'

'You found his suitcase?' she said.

'The French police found it or had it brought to them. They got in touch with us about it, but I don't think they knew any more than we did. They weren't in collusion with their Intelligence people.'

'Why didn't you tell me about the suitcase?'

'It got us no further,' Tony said. 'No further at all. We saw no point in distressing you all over again. But I think, Susie, you should recognize,' he added, putting down his glass and leaning forward in his chair, 'that if David was intercepted on that beach by persons unknown – who may or may not have had a connection with French Intelligence – it's extremely unlikely that he's still alive.'

'I know,' she said.

'Why this should have happened to him we shall probably never know for certain. I'd say it was more likely an accident than a deliberate order to eliminate him. But neither the why nor the how is particularly important. What matters is that he's gone and that you have to cope with that. You've already coped with it. You've done magnificently. You've moved to this splendid new house, you've made a completely new life for yourself. It would be fatal if you allowed anything that was said far away in Balunda – by this dubious character Rimington or any of his accusers – for their own purposes, to settle their own scores – to affect your equilibrium.'

'Yes, I see that,' she said.

'What I'm really saying, I suppose, is: don't, for God's sake, hope for the best. Don't look back, don't let yourself be damaged by it any more. And now what about lunch?'

'I think it must be nearly ready.'

'I'm sure it is. I can smell something delicious.'

'I'll go and bring it to the table.'

'We'll both bring it to the table.'

'All right.'

She walked ahead of him into the kitchen and heard him chuckling behind her.

'You know, I can't help being reminded – even though I said you shouldn't look back – of that unforgettable occasion when I last saw David, at your old house, and he was quite plastered from the moment we arrived and there wasn't any lunch.'

'Oh, dear, that was my fault. I'd made a mistake with the day. You had to eat at the Brown Bull.'

'It was ghastly. But funny in retrospect. That's the advantage of ghastly occasions, they do add to life's amusement afterwards.'

Unhappiness too, Susie thought, as she handed Tony an oven glove and watched him carry the asparagus quiche to the table. Unhappiness made the happiness you experienced afterwards far greater than before.

17

Andrew was sleeping badly and went to see his doctor. They had only met once before. Andrew seldom had trouble with his health and wouldn't have bothered to sign on with the local GP at all if he hadn't still needed treatment for the aftermath of his cycle accident. His new doctor was a regular reader of the *Equalizer* and during this second encounter they spent most of the few available minutes discussing the magazine's recent change of editor. The tablets the doctor prescribed helped him to sleep for longer periods, but they didn't make him feel any less jaded when he woke and they did nothing, of course, to remove the anxieties which had caused his sleeplessness in the first place.

He was hopelessly short of money. His mother's loan and the prospect of payment for his abortive interview with ex-President Nakimbi had temporarily calmed the bank manager, but his current account had already plunged back into the red, his deposit account was long since closed and he had borrowed up to the limit of his credit card account. He lived extremely frugally, but the new house – with its inexorable instalments of mortgage repayments and rates and its huge bills for electricity, gas, water and telephone run up but seldom paid for by the students – was like an elephant being nurtured by a sparrow. He had revised some of his ideas for the Third World series, but had heard nothing further from Michael Arley. He kept meaning to ring Michael himself to ask what was happening, but the longer he waited and the more it became clear that nothing but the TV series could begin to meet his financial needs, the more he hesitated to make the phone call that would put the matter to the test. He preferred to believe that help was on its way than to take the risk of knowing for certain that it wasn't.

At the end of the autumn he received a letter from his brother Luke.

Dear Andrew,
　Mother tells me that you did manage to get yourself a house and that you're pleased with it. That's splendid. She also tells me that you're in no position to pay back any of the money I lent you. That's not so splendid, but of course I didn't mean it to be a short-term loan. The problem is, as she may have told you, that there's been a change of policy over farm subsidies and people in a small way like me are getting squeezed. So, since I can't really make ends meet on the new quotas, I'm going to have to sell the farm. I shan't do badly out of it, I hope, so I don't want you to think that I'll be begging in the streets or anything like that. In fact, I'm really writing to say that if anyone's at fault in this business, it certainly isn't you and you mustn't think it. I've tried to explain that to Mother, but I know she blames you, so I want to make it quite clear that I don't and that she's wrong. Times change and we have to change with them. Nothing lasts for ever and spare money is really only a sort of camouflage. Maybe if I'd had that extra money I could have lasted here a bit longer, but so what? The change would have happened and I might have ignored it for a while. Eventually it would probably all have come out the same. In any case, the money wasn't wasted because it bought you the house you needed. Maybe I'll do a bit of travelling when I've sold the farm. And I'd like to call on you if I happen to be travelling via London. I enjoyed your company the other day and wished we saw more of each other.
　All the best meanwhile, from your affectionate brother
　　　　　　　　　　　Luke

'The other day!' Andrew thought. 'He does live out of the world. It was at least a year ago.' Then he read the letter through again slowly, looking for irony, doubting if it really meant exactly what it said. He was forced to conclude that it did, that his brother truly didn't want him to feel badly about the loan, that he was not obliquely urging him to save the farm. And having concluded that, Andrew did feel badly about the loan. He was a selfish sod and his brother was wrong about change. Times changed, circumstances changed, but people didn't. Once a selfish sod, always a selfish sod. It occured to him for a moment that he'd just denied the whole basis of his faith in human progress, but he was distracted from that line of thought by the sound of Matthew letting himself in at the front door with his own key and starting up the stairs to his studio.
　In the last two or three months Matthew had abandoned his delicate, poetic watercolours for large, crude oils in shouting colours and with subjects half way between contemporary protest politics and mythology. Andrew found them childish and repulsive. According to Matthew, Liz held the same opinion, but he was

undeterred, convinced that he was following his own true line of development as well as becoming part of the Zeitgeist. What made the change worse from Andrew's point of view was that Matthew had become so absorbed in his new work that he no longer had any interest in or time for his previous role as house-handyman. He didn't refuse to mend the hinge on the sitting-room door, put a new pane of glass in the kitchen window, investigate the sinister smell in the cupboard under the stairs; he simply never got round to them.

Andrew called out to Matthew, intending to ask him at least to attend to the bathroom tap which had become almost unusable. But Matthew either didn't hear him or didn't want to and continued upstairs. Andrew felt too tired to pursue him. Instead he went to his desk in the window and laid Luke's letter beside the photograph of Maria, which he had cut out of the paper, and a clutch of unpaid bills. One of these was a final demand, but Andrew had nothing to pay it with, so he pretended it wasn't there and stared instead, as he did every time he came near the desk, at the photograph. The body —caught half between moving forward and turning away, with one breast fully lit, the other in deep shadow, the belly a white area, the pelvis and legs shades of grey – could almost have been read as some kind of plant or small tree. The face was just recognizable, although with its shocked expression and mouth open, it bore little resemblance to Maria's self-confident, collected image on the TV screen. Try as he would, Andrew couldn't bring to mind the three-dimensional, flesh-and-blood Maria he had met only twice. But of the two images left to him – the head-and-shoulders, coloured, animated newscaster and the blurred grey naked figure frozen in front of the flash – he rejected the newscaster as false and treated the moment of the flash as if it were still taking place in front of his eyes. Somehow he could believe he was in the presence of this vulnerable, half-mythological Maria, the other was for ever out of his reach.

Thinking of Maria he remembered that Simon would be coming in to the *Equalizer* with his copy today. He had seen Simon on several such occasions since the photograph appeared, but had never referred to it. The fact was that he hardly associated Simon with his Maria. It was as if, in cutting her photograph out of the paper, he had cut her out of her connection with life.

It was time to leave for the office. He wandered about irresolutely for a few minutes, debating whether to go by bike or tube. If it was good weather he nearly always went by bike. Today the weather was equivocal, cloudy and a bit dark with some wind, but not as yet any rain. He decided to go by bike and wheeled his machine down the front steps. Then, as he went back for his pannier bag and to close the front door, the wind began to rise and bring spots of rain.

'Fuck!' Andrew said aloud and, suddenly filled with anger, threw his bag inside the hall, wrestled his bike up the steps again and pushed it in after the bag. Then he slammed the front door and set off for the tube station.

It was only when he reached it that he realized he was still wearing his cycle clips and had nothing to read. He stuffed the clips into his pocket and bought a paper. He didn't have to wait long for the train, but his anger persisted. He couldn't account for it. Luke's letter? Matthew's failure to mend the bath tap? The uncertain weather? None was really a sufficient cause for this sharp inward fury that possessed him. It must, he decided, be lack of sleep or a side effect of the doctor's tablets. The train seemed to jolt more than usual and to stop with too much of a jerk in the stations. In a perverse way he enjoyed being thrown from side to side and seeing the other passengers suffering equal discomfort. 'A Subway Named Anger,' he thought, and for a moment wondered if there might be a song in it. But he had given up writing songs – he was too old for that kind of syrupy simplification. The students had made him realize how out of touch he was and being in touch was the name of that game – it was like wearing the right clothes and using the right code words, you had to belong or you got it wrong. Maybe that was what the song should be about, the herd instinct, the mindless rushing through tunnels into lighted stations which represented sudden changes of style, mini-historical periods – the Fifties, the Sixties, the Seventies, the Eighties – each with their walls tiled in different patterns and colours, so that you could make believe you had arrived somewhere and left somewhere else behind, instead of being what you actually were, a nothing going nowhere.

Still seething with his strange, directionless anger, Andrew got out at King's Cross. He wished now that he'd come by bike. He'd forgotten that the worst aspect of the tube journey was that you had to change lines and scurry round a maze of corridors, part of a tide of other people, joining, meeting and crossing other tides. The next train took longer to come and Andrew started to read his paper. A short item on the front page announced that a court in Balunda had found Colonel Rimington guilty of a whole list of crimes and sentenced him to death. 'Serve the bugger right!' thought Andrew. He had read some of the previous reports of the trial and assumed from the start that Rimington hadn't a leg to stand on in his defence. You couldn't expect a white colonel who stayed on in a black country after independence to be up to any good.

Andrew spent the morning looking through the proofs of the books pages and receiving, correcting and marking up his contributors' copy for the arts pages. The theatre critic was going to be late as usual – he'd been in the job longest and couldn't be persuaded to get in before 4 pm. The TV critic also tended to be late, but today he arrived before lunch, hoping to grab 200 words more than he'd been allotted. Andrew was ruthless and offered him the choice of deleting his first two paragraphs or his last item. He went away grumpily to think about it, while Andrew dealt with Simon Carter. Simon's copy was immaculate as always, though Andrew thought it dull, little more than a straight description of a large exhibition at the V & A devoted to the court of the Gonzagas at Mantua.

'Surely the most interesting thing about the Gonzagas,' he said to Simon, 'is not what they collected, but how they used art to aggrandize themselves?'

'Perhaps,' said Simon. 'But the art they commissioned is actually rather good.'

'Can it be separated from the purpose for which it was commissioned?'

'I think it can. Of course, historically it had that political purpose, among others, but now we just enjoy it as art.'

'Do we? For whom is this exhibition intended? Isn't it reassurance for the Tory middle classes?'

'I'm sure it's going to be a popular show.'

'It may appear popular – like the Royal Family, like state occasions – but its effect is to encourage elitism, to reinforce hierarchies.'

Simon made no reply, but his closed expression showed that he didn't accept Andrew's argument. Irritably Andrew played with his ball-point. Then, as if a locked compartment of his brain had suddenly sprung open of its own accord, he asked:

'How's Maria?'

'She's well, thanks. At least, fairly well.'

'What's the trouble?'

'Nothing serious. Quite normal in fact. She's pregnant.'

Andrew felt much as he had at the time of his cycle accident. He had been riding quite fast with his eyes on the surface of the road when he'd suddenly collided with a parked car. Now he sat behind his desk staring at Simon and feeling just as if he were lying on the road tangled up with his damaged bike. The only difference was that the pain wasn't in his leg but in the lower part of his chest. Simon was also silent, his head turned slightly sideways, looking down at the floor. His face had a naturally morose expression in repose and the news seemed no more cheerful to him than to Andrew.

They had been sitting like this for some time when the phone rang. It was answered by Andrew's secretary in the room next door and a minute or two later she came in. She was a young, bright-eyed but not very pretty girl, new to the job and still enjoying the glamour of being in touch with people whose names appeared in print.

'It's someone who wants to review a book,' she said.

'I'm busy!'

'I've told him that. He's very persistent.'

'He can leave his number and I'll phone him back. Simon's just told me he's going to have a baby. Rather, his wife is.'

The secretary was immediately delighted.

'Congratulations!' she said to Simon. 'You must be thrilled.'

'Well, I suppose so,' said Simon.

'We ought to celebrate,' said the secretary.

'Of course we ought,' Andrew said.

'Shall I go out and get a bottle round the corner?'

'Certainly,' said Andrew and put his hand in his pocket.

'It's all right,' she said. 'I've got some money. You can pay me back.'

She smiled at Simon and went out, first to deal with the caller on the phone, then to buy a bottle of white wine and fetch glasses from the cabinet in the boardroom.

Under the influence of the wine and her uncomplicated pleasure, both Simon and Andrew became more cheerful. The particular reasons that had made the news so difficult to deal with between the two of them now sank beneath the surface of something universal and unequivocal – Christmas, a marriage, a birth – which outweighed personal reservations and transformed both of them into temporary believers in the ordinary reasons for human happiness. The secretary, filling and refilling their glasses, taking it for granted that the prospect of a first child must be among the greatest joys available, additionally delighted by the thought that she liked Simon and that the mother was beautiful and famous, was the priestess of the celebration. When the TV critic returned with his altered copy, he too was brought into the celebration and when the wine was finished all four of them went out for lunch to a cheap Italian trattoria a few streets away.

Andrew was in excellent spirits throughout the meal, allowing the TV critic to dominate the first part of the conversation with an account of the latest shifts and displacements in the BBC's hierarchy, then delivering his own assessment of the weaknesses in the Tory government and remarking that it would almost certainly not last for a second term. When the bill came, Andrew again found he had no money, but Simon took the bill to himself and the other three, remembering who he was married to, were satisfied he could afford it. Outside the trattoria they went their separate ways, Simon and the TV critic to the tube station, Andrew and his secretary back to their office.

'Please give Maria my very best wishes,' Andrew said, as he shook hands with Simon, using both hands as an extra gesture of affection, then added, 'Give her my love!'

'You must come to supper,' Simon said.

'Terrific! Look, I'll give you my home number.'

He scribbled down the number, banishing the thought that it was the phone bill for which the final demand lay on his desk next to Maria's photograph and Luke's letter and that, unless he discovered some unexpected fresh source of income, his phone would be cut off before Simon got round to ringing the number.

Once back at the office, Andrew's good spirits slowly evaporated. His head felt heavy and woozy, incapable of concentration. When the theatre critic came in Andrew was short and pernickety with him. They were still arguing over one of the critic's favourite, overused adjectives, when Andrew was summoned to the editor's office.

The editor was a new broom, determined to find new readers for the magazine and less interested in political principles than in stirring up controversy. He was a heavily built man with a pale, greasy skin, lank black hair which he wore over his forehead to resemble Augustus John's portrait of the young W. B. Yeats, and extremely hairy arms. His shirt sleeves were always rolled up and his shirt collar open, with the tie pulled down, so that, even if he hadn't constantly invoked 'Journalism' as if it were a mystic faith, he would have been immediately recognizable as the stage or movie version of a journalist. Up to now he'd been too busy reshaping the main political part of the magazine to bother much with the literary and arts sections and he and Andrew, though not much liking each other, had remained on polite terms. The proofs of the books pages were on his desk and as soon as Andrew entered the room, without asking him to sit down, the editor burst out:

'Who's going to read this stuff? I want to know who you think you're aiming at?'

If he hadn't drunk so much wine at lunch, if he'd been feeling more himself, Andrew would have accepted this challenge with pleasure and explained at some length that a paper which specifically catered for left-wing intellectuals had a duty to review serious left-orientated books which were seldom reviewed anywhere else, at least anywhere with more than a few hundred readers. As it was, he went red in the face and became angry.

'What do you think is wrong with it?' he demanded.

'It's bloody unreadable, that's what's wrong with it,' said the editor, thumping both his hairy arms on the desk and leaning forward aggressively.

'By what standards?'

'By mine, of course. By anybody's standards who wants to know what's being published and to read an entertaining reaction to it.'

'That's begging a good many questions,' said Andrew, too angry to capture the initiative, but aware that his feeble parries simply allowed the editor to keep up the attack.

'It's begging only one question as far as I'm concerned. Are you or aren't you prepared to do something about it?'

Andrew sat down on an upright chair with arms that stood to one side of the desk. He placed his own arms carefully on the chair's, closed his eyes and made an intense effort to clear his brain and overcome the thudding in the temples.

'If what you're trying to say,' he said, 'is that you want a completely different sort of literary section – something more like other people's – more conventional – "entertaining" was your word, I think – then, yes . . .'

He paused and opened his eyes and noticed that in order to face him, the editor had had to shift round in his chair and abandon his aggressive pose across the desk.

'Yes,' he went on, 'I accept that that's what you want and we had better discuss it. But does it have to be at this moment? I've still got work to do upstairs on the arts pages. You've given me no notice of this fundamental readjustment of priorities. Frankly, I've had a tiring day. Can't it wait till tomorrow – no, that's press day – the day after?'

The editor seemed temporarily speechless. It was as if Andrew's wave of inarticulate anger had transferred itself to him. Then, with a ridiculously stagey gesture, he raised one of his hairy arms and pointed his finger straight at Andrew.

'You've had a tiring day! So that was why you took two hours off for lunch!'

'Barely two hours, I should have thought.'

'You were not in your office at 2.30. You were still not there at 2.45. If that's barely, I'm bloody well sitting here in my underpants. One hour is the allowance for lunch.'

'I wasn't aware that I was required to keep typists' hours.'

'You're paid to work here. Not to have drinking sessions with your friends. Not to take yourself off for long lunches, leaving the office unmanned. Not to say you can't discuss your lousy books pages because you've got too much work to do. What is this? A gentleman's club or a bloody paper? Well, I can tell you, with people like you working for it, it's not going to be a paper much longer. We've got to have work done on this paper and we've got to have readers and I'm just informing you that I don't care a fuck about any discussion. I want these books pages changed and I want them changed by next week's issue.'

The crude savagery of the attack overwhelmed Andrew. He now saw for himself what other members of the staff had already told him, that there was no point in arguing with this man, he was simply a bully, acting out a scenario of his own in which the rest of the cast hardly mattered. Feeling suddenly quite cool – his anger replaced by contempt – Andrew rose from his chair and walked to the door. He meant to leave without saying another word, but as he turned the handle, the injustice of something the editor had said stirred his anger again.

'As for what I'm paid, which you were kind enough to mention,' he said, 'it's derisory. As long as I was working for something I believed in, I was prepared to put up with that. But if you want typists' hours and a hack review section, then I want the rate for the job.'

He went out leaving the door open and stalked past the editor's secretary's desk without allowing her to catch his eye. Climbing the narrow, dusty stairs to his own office he found himself shaking and covered with sweat. The throbbing in his temples had become a heavy lump of pain at the back of his head.

'I'm not well,' he muttered to himself and, not wishing to be seen by his secretary until he was in better condition, sat down on the bend of the stairs and put his head in his arms resting on his knees.

After a while he heard a creak on the landing below. Raising his head he saw the editor standing there staring at him, for a moment nonplussed by his apparent collapse.

'Since you were so uncivil as to leave without waiting for my reply,' said the editor, 'I thought I should make it clear that there's no question of any rise in salary for any member of the staff of this paper, until the paper starts to make money instead of losing it. Your alternatives, therefore, are to do the work you're paid for and accept editorial instructions or . . .'

'I resign,' said Andrew in a very low voice, standing up and grasping the banister.

There was a pause and, in case the editor hadn't heard him, he said again, 'I resign' and turned away to go up the stairs.

'Perhaps you'd put that in writing,' said the editor and returned briskly to his office.

Sitting at his own desk, Andrew took a sheet of notepaper out of the drawer and wrote slowly, 'Dear Editor, I resign, Yours, Andrew Mowle.' He put the date at the top of the sheet and pushed it to one side of the desk. He sat staring into space for some minutes, not thinking so much as wiping his thoughts clean – of the editor, of the desk and the office, of the whole building and all it contained. Then, almost automatically, as though one action flowed from the other without conscious decision, he found his pocket diary and looked up a phone number at the back.

Michael Arley's secretary answered. Michael was away, she said, could she take a message?

'This is Andrew Mowle. I want to know what's happening about that series on the Third World.'

'I'm sorry, I'm not with you. Which series?'

'You must know what I'm talking about. We made a pilot interview for it, not all that long ago, in France.'

'What was the title?'

'The working title was *Latitudes South*.'

'Now I remember. But surely we wrote to you about that?'
'No, you didn't. Or if you did, I never got it.'
'I'm sure we wrote. Or maybe Michael was going to phone you himself first.'
'Well, if he was, he didn't.'
'Oh dear! The thing is . . . Perhaps it would be best if I waited until Michael gets back and then he can contact you himself.'
'When does he get back?'
'Probably next week.'
'That will be much too late. I've cleared a space to start work right away.'
'Oh dear! The thing is, they decided it was too expensive. They felt it would be too large a commitment at the present time. We should have written to you, of course. I was almost certain we had written to you. I'm awfully sorry, Mr Mowle. Have you got an agent? Perhaps we wrote to your agent?'

Andrew put the phone down and called out to his secretary through the open door:

'Tania! Is there anything I have to finish?'

He left the office an hour or so later and walked to the tube station. Putting his hand into his pocket for the tube fare, he encountered his cycle clips. The day was still overcast, but it had never rained. He could perfectly well have come by bike. On the other hand, he was quite relieved now not to have to face the physical effort. The station was crowded and so was the train. Andrew stood, wedged into a solid mass of people, in the central section of the carriage. When the train stopped at stations, they all stumbled about together and smiled and apologized to one another. Andrew's head was still aching a little, but otherwise he felt physically better. He liked being in the press of people. They none of them had anything or could look forward to anything special. They were typists and office-workers who did a job for its wages and went home afterwards to relax in a pub or watch TV. They earned and spent, married, had children and died, enjoying what they could, putting up with the rest, not expecting too much, not suffering too much frustration. Andrew didn't feel he was patronizing them so much as identifying with them, casting off his own foolish attempts to be a noticeable individual and merging his essential ordinariness with theirs.

It was difficult, because of the crowds, to see the names on the stations and Andrew had been too absorbed in his sense of himself as simply another face in the crowd to count the stops. He'd forgotten to change on to the line for Finsbury Park, but had travelled on as if he were going to his old flat with Liz in Belsize Park. He thought for a moment that he would go there after all, see if Liz was in, talk to her and tell her what had happened to him. But when the train stopped at Kentish Town he got out and crossed to the return platform. There were far less people travelling in this direction and he got into an almost empty carriage.

Now, as he sat through the stops to King's Cross, he seemed to be coming round from an anaesthetic that had so far numbed his feelings about the interview with the editor and the phone conversation with Michael Arley's secretary. He didn't regret the interview – that outcome had surely been inevitable. The other was growing very painful. Had he really expected anything different? Surely he hadn't counted on it? But he must have done. It had been the basis of his whole immediate future. At any rate there had been no other basis. That was the real pain: it removed the future.

He got out at King's Cross and followed the signs to the Piccadilly Line. There were a lot of people on the platform. The lighted sign hanging overhead said 'Cockfosters 2 mins' and below that 'Cockfosters 5 mins', as if one might choose to have three minutes extra on the platform. He threaded his way through the crowd to the far end, where the train would appear. It was strange to think that Maria would never be able to travel by tube – not at least until she was much older. Because she was so successfully the people's girl-next-door, she could never mix with the people at all. How excited and pleased they'd all be when she had her baby! But why was Simon so gloomy about the prospect? Had he already taken against the role of prince consort? Andrew told himself that he was no longer the least envious of Simon. His own life would have been swallowed up in Maria's just as surely as Simon's.

The train could be heard now in the tunnel and a few moments later shot out into the station. The doors opened, but Andrew didn't get in. He had nothing to hurry home for. He would wait for 'Cockfosters 3 mins', as it now appeared on the board. The doors closed and the train pulled away. 'Cockfosters 3 mins' went to the top of the board and 'Arnos Grove 6 mins' appeared beneath it.

Now that he'd missed the first train, Andrew felt a pang. His house was there waiting for him. It wasn't a beautiful building, but it was the first he'd ever owned and he was childishly fond of it. The trouble was that he couldn't now keep it. If he sold it, he'd be able to pay most of his debts and he'd have to do that. The house wasn't really his at all. It belonged to the building society, the bank, his mother, Luke, Liz – all the people and institutions who'd foolishly invested in his optimism about the Third World. He began to feel angry again. It was not himself that Michael and his minions had rejected, but all those struggling peoples, all those latitudes south, all that vast real world beyond their own little fortress of flimflam, self-esteem and false values. And as he thought of Michael and his cocky expression, the conceit in his voice, he felt extremely sorry for Simon, his new friend. Michael was Maria's sort of man, Maria was

Michael's sort of woman — both of them would have been wholly at ease with the editor and at one with him in his views of the sort of reader the *Equalizer* should now be aiming to attract. He spat on them all and, as if they were there on the line beneath the edge of the platform, he went and did so. Out of the corner of his eye he saw a middle-aged woman, with greying hair, a long nose and a sour face, turn away in disapproval. The line was vibrating gently. The next train for Cockfosters was imminent. Looking at the dirty, litter-strewn bed on which the shiny rails were laid, Andrew suddenly remembered the verse that used to hang on the wall of the vicarage nursery:

> Matthew, Mark, Luke and John,
> Bless the bed that I lie on . . .

'What about Andrew?' he'd once asked his father, somehow imagining that it was Luke and the others who were lying on the bed rather than blessing it. His father had patiently explained that it was Andrew who was lying on the bed. 'I' meant Andrew, he said, confusing his son even more. The next part of the verse had gone out of his head. In any case the train was visible in the tunnel. Andrew swayed for a moment on the edge of the platform and then let himself fall forwards, hearing the woman standing near him scream, remembering just too late that he'd never made a will and that the house which ought to be used to pay his debts to everybody, but especially Luke, would probably go to Liz.

Part Four

18

'Why am I here? Why are we here?' It sounded like the title of a Gauguin painting, Simon thought. The rest of the passage was less heaven-storming, more ill-tempered:

'Somebody remarked when I was in Delhi a few weeks ago that we shouldn't expect anything but ingratitude on the part of the Indians. We are living through their adolescence and adolescents always bite the hands that feed them. They are only waiting to be free of us and have forgotten the childish days when they looked up to us and were grateful for our protection and advice. Well, no doubt that time was long before my time. Looking back on my work in India, I realise that I have had little pleasure from it, little but wear on the nerves, chores, crises and a perpetual groundswell of resentment and even hatred from those whose interests I came here to serve. When the Recording Angel asks me what I have done for humanity, I shall truthfully answer "Damn all!" Not for want of trying, but because I was so foolish as to adopt a career which was all waste and water under the bridge.'

Simon put Uncle Percy's diary face down on the carpet beside his chair and sat staring at the empty fireplace, seeing the cracked, blackened firebricks behind the grate only momentarily before his mind switched off them to analyse what was wrong with the passage. Apart from the histrionic opening, why did it strike such a false note? Was Uncle Percy genuinely perplexed by Indian resentment? Surely he hadn't really thought of himself as no more than a kind father? Of course his first important job in India had been to tutor a young maharajah. Badi's charming, flirtatious manner of circumventing every effort on Uncle Percy's part to concentrate his mind on sterner things than polo and picnics, tennis and tiger-shoots, new ponies and motorcars, was fully charted in the earlier sections of the diary. It could have been no surprise to anyone, least of all his former tutor, that having attained his majority he proved a hopeless ruler. To the day of his death he remained Uncle Percy's devoted friend, admirer and gracious host for any number of luxurious entertainments and sporting events. But his death came prematurely – he was barely thirty – and he had by then already retired to his holiday house in Simla after resigning his princedom at the command of the authorities in Delhi. He was not supposed to have had any direct hand himself in the appalling state of corruption revealed in the financial affairs of Dehrapur, but his chronic laziness and love of pleasure had given his ministers *carte blanche* to ruin him. Uncle Percy, though he had long since been posted elsewhere, must have felt that some part of the blame for the failure of the handsome boy to turn into a wise ruler lay with him.

One of the high points of the diary – from the reader's point of view – was the occasion when Uncle Percy was shot at on the steps of his Commissioner's house in Awara. The gun had first failed to go off and then wounded the Commissioner's accompanying policeman, who had courageously tackled the would-be assassin. Uncle Percy escaped without injury and the whole affair was dismissed by him as the work of a fanatic. But it was clear from other entries in the diary that political unrest was becoming endemic to Awara and that though Percy Carter was personally well liked, he was certainly not seen as the father of his people so much as the tool of an alien bureaucracy. In a way to be shot at conferred more distinction on him than he actually possessed, for, except in purely local and ceremonial matters – judgments in court, the hiring and firing of local officials, the laying of foundation stones and opening of fêtes – he had very little independence at all. Only a fanatic, as he remarked himself, would have thought it worth trying to blow off one paltry Commissioner's head as a way of altering history.

Perhaps, then, what Uncle Percy was complaining about was that he didn't have enough power. He had gone out east to rule an empire and found himself, after all, little more than a superannuated nanny whose charges had long since left the nursery.

Yet he was surely overstating the case? Indian nationalists might wish the British to leave as soon as possible, but what if they had actually left, there and then? Somebody had to hold the place together, cover the retreat, hand over working institutions to properly constituted authorities. Somebody had to be the Commissioner of Awara, even if it didn't much matter who or whether he was shot down by a fanatic and had to be replaced. That was Uncle Percy's mistake. The romance of India for the old imperialists consisted in the extraordinary exploits of individuals – Napier, Nicholson, Sleeman, Lawrence. The reality was a steady stream of soldier and civilian ants, most of whom might well feel they had achieved nothing individually, but whose lack of individuality was indispensable to the proper working of any system of government on such a vast scale. Uncle Percy need not have chosen to be an ant for the rest of his life; but having done so, it was not for nothing. Furthermore, he had not returned to England after independence, but retired and died in India. That suggested that his bitterness was only partial, that having made his bed, he was content to lie on it.

Now Simon began to turn the investigation on himself. Why was he conducting it? Was he interested in penetrating the character of his Uncle Percy or in understanding the nature of the British Raj? Perhaps the answer was obvious: Uncle Percy was his own collateral relation, part of his personal history, and the British Raj was his country's collateral relation, part of his national history. Both might be ignored – entirely forgotten even – by an Englishman living in the year 1982, when to the outward eye there was no more British Raj and no more Sir Percy Carter. Yet to ignore them was to say with Uncle Percy that it was all water under the bridge, 1982 as much as the years of Uncle Percy's career in India. In reading and thinking about the diary he was redeeming Uncle Percy in some measure from his sense of waste and nothingness. He was seeing him as a person who had lived and had feelings and wanted not to be wasted.

Simon heard the front door being opened and went to meet Maria in the hall. The baby was due in a month or so but she was still doing her job as a newscaster. Left to themselves, her bosses would probably have preferred her to take a holiday – there was no precedent for a pregnant newscaster – but the nation willed otherwise. Maria had become the nation's archetype of the young mother-to-be and it not only wanted to see her as often as possible, it also wanted her to behave like every other working woman in the same position, to go on doing her job to the last possible moment. Nobody, of course, except Simon and Maria – and perhaps Tom and Laura Glenny – doubted that Simon was the father and, although the incident in the woods had happened perhaps a little too early for the conception, it was generally assumed that there must have been other similar incidents and that the whole story combined nature, passion and married respectability in the most touching way. It was, as it were, *Lady Chatterley* rescripted for family viewing.

All this was hard for Simon to bear. True, it would give a tremendous fillip to his series of programmes about contemporary art, which was scheduled for the early summer, but he often wished the baby would die. He didn't say so to Maria. The baby, after all, was certainly hers. It could also, of course, be his. She had taught herself to believe that and sometimes he himself felt convinced that it was, but the conviction never lasted. He still loved Maria, but he couldn't love the baby. After she had told Simon what had happened in the barn on that rainy day with Tom Glenny, insisting – what she herself believed – that it was virtually rape, Maria no longer felt guilty and indeed they agreed that the incident was closed and that they should go on as if it had never happened. But the pregnancy reopened the incident and altered the agreement. For Maria the baby itself was more important than the question of who conceived it. For Simon it made that question more important than anything else.

'I haven't been watching tonight,' he said, as he made coffee for himself and cocoa for her and she sat down carefully on a kitchen chair. 'I was reading Uncle Percy's diary. Anything interesting in the news?'

'I don't think so,' she said, looking happily round the room, which was still both new and familiar – recently painted and furnished, but already a place she felt as an extension of herself and her child. They had sold their separate flats in Holland Park and bought this house in Hammersmith some months earlier. 'Didn't you say you were finding Uncle Percy a bit of a bore?'

'I go off and on with Uncle Percy,' said Simon, dropping two spoonfuls of cocoa into the hot milk and stirring it vigorously. 'A lot of the time he's just enumerating the details of his day. Then he suddenly lets his defences down and you catch a glimpse of something moving behind the poker face. He's a sort of crustacean, I suppose. He'd certainly go bright red if you popped him in boiling water.'

Simon felt obscurely disloyal to his uncle as he said this. In the privacy of reading his diary, he took him more seriously, treated him as a fellow human being, almost as a confidant. Why, then, did he feel it necessary to throw him across to Maria as a stereotype, a joke figure?

'There was something odd in the news,' said Maria. 'Let me try and remember what it was.'

'It can't have been much if you can't remember it.'

'It was odd. It hardly seemed to be a news story at all – very trivial, but also faintly ominous, if you know what I mean.'

'No I don't.'

'Like Watergate – when it began. But it wasn't anything to do with the United States. No, I remember now, it was South America. Actually, more like Antarctica – that sort of area. A tiny island called South Georgia. A party of scrap metal merchants has landed there.'

'So what?'

'Exactly – so what?'

Simon brought the two cups and sat down at the table opposite her.

'You wouldn't think there was much scrap metal on South Georgia,' he said.

'It's an old whaling station.'

'Rusty harpoons and that kind of thing.'

'The point is that these scrap metal people come from Argentina and they've run up an Argentinian flag.'
'Go on.'
'That's all.'
'How odd!'
'Yes, that's what I thought.'
Vronsky came clattering through his new cat-door and looked about for food. He was closer to Simon than Maria these days, so he came and rubbed himself against Simon's leg first. When that failed, he tried Maria's, but then jumped on to the table and sniffed at the hot drinks from a safe distance. Simon stroked him.
'South Georgia belongs to us, does it?' he asked.
She nodded. The subject had ceased to interest her. She could feel the baby moving about inside. She put her hand on her belly and smiled. Simon looked away and concentrated on Vronsky.
'What would you say to "Anna"?' she asked.
He refused to be drawn. When they were out with friends or had friends in, he would play this naming game briefly, so as not to show his real feelings, but it sickened him. 'It' was the only name he thought appropriate and he meant to leave the final choice entirely to Maria. He drank his coffee and pulled Vronsky's ears and his thoughts began to revert to Uncle Percy's diary. Then he looked up and found her watching him.
'I remember so well,' she said, 'something you said when we first met. Apropos of having to cope with Vronsky after his accident. "Life has a way of searching out people's weaknesses."'
'Sounds second-hand. I should think it was a quote.'
'Maybe. But true, don't you think?'
'The whole structure of Greek tragedy is based on it. Most drama for that matter. But I wonder if life is.'
'Your weakness, you said, was your sentimentality about animals.'
'Yes, I think that's perfectly true. One of my weaknesses.'
'No, I don't think it is true. Your weakness is not being at all sentimental about people.'
'Is it a good thing to be sentimental about anything?' he said, fiddling with the spoon on his saucer.
'I really mean, to have strong feelings.'
'Sentimentality means excessive feelings, I'd have thought. Feelings in excess of what's justified.'
'I'm not trying to get my English right. I'm trying to get you right.'
'Improve me?'
'Understand you.'
'I thought you did already.'
'I begin to understand that your feelings are only aroused by things weaker than yourself. Things over which you have control.'

'No, that's not true. I have passions for all kinds of works of art and literature.'

'That's it. You love art because it's at one remove. You love animals because they inspire your pity. But what – who – do you love directly? That's outside, beyond yourself?'

He balanced his spoon across the coffee cup and pushed it gently until it fell on the table.

'Who do you?' he asked.

'I love you.'

'I suppose I don't really believe you.'

'I also love this,' she said, touching her belly.

'Yes, I believe that.'

They sat in silence for a while and then she went up to bed. He kissed her at the bottom of the stairs and turned away towards his study.

'You probably are right,' he called up to her as she reached the landing. 'But I don't see what I can do about it. Every day in every way I feel more like my Uncle Percy.'

'I don't think I'd have cared for him,' she said.

What he'd wanted to say was that he did love her. But he couldn't say it in the context of that conversation. It would have sounded trite and therefore untrue. He couldn't say it because it was true. Did that make sense? Wasn't that exactly what happened to Cordelia in Act One of *King Lear*? He was taking refuge in art again. But that was Maria's way of looking at it. For him art was not a refuge – more a kind of computer, in which all experience was stored. Knowing which keys to press to release it, though, depended on your own experience. Hence he'd suddenly understood Cordelia's behaviour which had always seemed incomprehensible. Art, therefore, was not a substitute for life, hardly even a preparation for it, but only a back-up, a recognition. He laughed. Maria was right. Here he was again, retreating into an analysis of art instead of facing what she'd really been saying to him. But he knew that. He knew what he was like. The pain came from his not being able to change, from his not being able to be more loving, rather than from being faced with the truth.

Uncle Percy's diary still lay on the floor beside his chair. He picked the volume up, closed it and slid it into the shelf beside the others. He didn't think he'd read any more of it. He'd solved the problem. Uncle Percy was himself. Not literally, but in so far as he was interested in Uncle Percy, wanted to probe his life and motives, it was because he was searching for aspects of himself. The potency of the image of the Raj was its supremacy, its control over millions of lesser beings for whom Uncle Percy and his like felt pity and responsibility, as he, Simon, felt pity and responsibility for animals. But in Uncle Percy's time, those lesser beings had begun to re-emerge as people. That was why he felt such a sense of waste and impotence. He had no love for people, could do nothing for them. No, that was unfair – to himself as well as to his alter ego in the past – it was not that they didn't love people, but that they couldn't. The love was locked up inside themselves, there was no key to it. They could see its reflections in mirrors, in works of art and books. That was Tennyson's Lady of Shalott, of course, walled up in her tower room, with only the shadows of real life outside for company. Then in the mirror she saw Sir Lancelot riding along the real road beside the real river. She opened the window and looked out, broke the mirror, broke the spell, but also destroyed herself.

Uncle Percy had probably loved the boy maharajah, but had surely never said so, never dared break the spell of the impeccable, superior Raj, which would certainly have destroyed him. He himself loved Maria. Why hadn't he been able to say so? Because of the child? Because of the abominable Tom Glenny? Or still because of the Raj?

19

Susie had taken to visiting London once or twice a week. Tony would occasionally meet her off the train at Paddington, but more often at a rendezvous arranged the previous week when they parted. They would lunch together until it was time for him to go back to his office, then she would fill in the afternoon with a film or shopping and make her way at about six to a flat in Marylebone which belonged to a friend of his. She had never met the friend, but the name under the doorbell was G. Pontefract and Tony always referred to him and the flat as Graham. It was an anonymous place containing a sitting room, bedroom, kitchen and bathroom, barely furnished, with only a few pictures on the walls – mostly topographical prints of European cities – and a single shelf of Reprint Society books. There was nothing personal at all, nothing to flesh out Graham's character or interests and Tony would tell her nothing about him except that he was often abroad and they had known each other at Oxford. Susie and Tony each had keys to the flat – which was always clean, with the bed freshly made for their visits – and he would arrive there as soon as he could get away from the office, sometimes before her, but usually half an hour or so later. He could never stay much beyond eight and would find her a taxi to take her back to Paddington and wave to her briefly before turning away to look for another himself. It was an unsatisfactory and inadequate way of being with and making love to the person around whom her whole life now revolved, but there seemed no alternative. His career was extremely important to him and he had a wife and five children in Shepherd's Bush. Susie didn't suppose that he loved her as much as she loved him but for the moment she was content to accept whatever time and love he could spare her.

Their rendezvous for Thursday, 1 April, was the Serpentine Gallery in Kensington Gardens. When Tony had still not turned up at 1.30 and Susie had had enough of the works by Australian artists on display, she went outside and wandered slowly and anxiously towards the road. Suddenly she saw him paying off a taxi and ran to put her arms round him.

'Hardly any time, dear heart,' he said. 'We'll just have a quick snack over there,' indicating the cafeteria below the bridge, 'and then I have to get back.'

'I thought it must be an April Fool,' she said, as they crossed the road, 'except it's after midday.'

'Anything but,' he said. 'Big, big problems and plenty much trouble, but I'm afraid it's not for little ears like yours, so you'll just have to forgive me and believe that it's all for the best.'

The problems didn't seem to trouble him much. His mood was buoyant and although he tried to look sad when he told her that they would not be able to meet at the flat that evening, he was almost rubbing his hands. Susie's disappointment made her angry.

'Why couldn't you have rung me before I left home? It's a completely wasted journey.'

'Are you only interested in sex? Just seeing me isn't enough?'

'I wouldn't mind if you weren't so pleased about it.'

'No, I'm not pleased about it. Not pleased about only seeing you for half an hour. I admit I'm a fraction pleased about the other. Much depends on what happens in the next few days. It could be a disaster, of course.'

'And you can't tell me anything about it?'

'Nothing whatever. But you'll know by tomorrow, I think. Everyone will know.'

'And when shall I see you again?' she asked.

'Shall we say Wednesday? Things should be resolved one way or tother by then.'

When Tony's secret became public late the next day, Susie was not only horrified and scandalized like everyone else, she was also even more puzzled to account for Tony's mood of the day before. The Argentinians had invaded the Falkland Islands. After a brief gunfight with the invaders, the small force of Royal Marines at Port Stanley had surrendered and the governor had been evicted and was on his way to Britain. 'It could be a disaster,' Tony had said. Surely it was a disaster? In what way could it not have been? He must have known the invading force was on its way. Did he expect the Marines to be able to repel it? No one else seemed to have expected that. The general view was that they had done well to put up a token resistance. But Susie's overwhelming feeling was of shame at the affront to British pride and anger with the incompetence of the government. How could Tony have been so jubilant?

The next day, Saturday, there was a special session of Parliament to debate the issue. Susie took some comfort from the Prime Minister's firm statement that 'the government have now decided that a large task force will sail as soon as all preparations are complete. HMS *Invincible* will be in the lead and will leave port on Monday.' On the other hand, the government in general and especially its chief spokesman, the Defence Minister, gave a very uncomfortable impression of having been taken completely by surprise and being still, for all the bluster about the task force, in a state of confusion bordering on panic. The only really forceful and satisfyingly belligerent voice in the House of Commons was that of the Leader of the Opposition, who was more noted for marching in CND rallies for peace than castigating 'foul and brutal aggression' against outposts of the British Empire.

But there was almost more anger, both in Parliament and the press, against the Foreign Office for their failure to foresee the invasion than against the Argentinians for their success in mounting it. When it was announced on Monday that the three Foreign Office ministers had all resigned, Susie wondered if Tony too might not be caught up in their ruin and lose his job. She'd heard nothing from him since they parted on April Fool's Day, but he rang at last on Monday, from a call box, and confirmed their arrangement for Wednesday. He sounded now not at all jubilant, but almost chastened.

'I think I can make lunch,' he said, 'but I'm afraid we'll have to skip Graham. Too much going on.'

'Why did you sound so pleased?' she asked. 'I simply don't understand, if you knew what was going to happen, how you thought . . .'

'I can't go into that,' he said. 'It's a total cock-up.'

'That's what I'd have thought. Except that we do at least seem to be sending the task force. If that can really do anything.'

'We have to hope for something at the United Nations,' he said. 'Or through the US. The rest is fantasy.'

'You mean . . .?'

'I really can't talk about it now, Susie. See you on Wednesday at the Minstrel Boy.'

The Minstrel Boy was a pub near St James's Square with an upstairs dining room. He was there waiting for her when she arrived a little late. He looked tired, but he had partly recovered his customary buccaneering manner. The room was crowded and noisy, so it was easy to talk without being overheard.

'I've ordered steaks,' he said, as soon as she sat down. 'I hope you've no objection.'

'Why should I?'

'The Argentinian national dish.'

'Is it?'

He smiled his slow, teasing smile and poured her a glass of red wine.

'Things are looking slightly better,' he said.
'Are the EEC going to support us?'
'I don't know about that. But the US may be able to get the whole thing called off.'
'Make the Argentinians leave, do you mean?'
'My dear girl,' he said, 'I'm tremendously fond of you, as you know, but I wish you weren't such a jingo. You really should understand that to fight a war for these godforsaken islands which are quite useless to us, thousands of miles from anywhere, inhabited mainly by sheep, would be absolute madness. It would be far madder than the Suez business and that was idiotic enough.'
'But they belong to us,' Susie said, feeling her whole face flushed and tense, deeply upset by his unexpected attitude.
'Of course they don't belong to us. If they belong to anyone, it's the penguins. All sorts of people have occupied them at various times, including us, including the Spanish, but we've done nothing whatever for them, virtually ignored them all these years and really the time is long past when we can sit about on bits of the world and say they're ours just because we once planted a flag there. Suppose Argentina laid claim to the Shetlands or the Channel Islands – do you suppose that would be reasonable, even if there had been Argentinians living there for several generations?'
Susie refused to be trampled underfoot in this way. She was not usually much moved by world affairs, but like so many other people in Britain she had become passionately involved in this issue.
'Are you really saying that the Argentinians should have them? You wouldn't say that if you lived there. If you were one of the people who had just been overrun and had to live under those brutal military dictators, those people who torture and murder anyone that doesn't agree with them.'
'Any Falkland Islander that wants to, can leave. Several of them have. It's only a couple of thousand we're talking about. We could give every one of them a fat cheque as a present to go and start sheep-farming again in New Zealand or wherever and still it wouldn't cost us what it's going to cost us if we try to get the islands back, let alone the lives that are going to be lost on both sides.'
'I shan't feel particularly sorry if the Argentinians lose a few lives. They deserve anything we can do to them.'
'Why, Susie, why? They believe just as strongly as we do that the Malvinas are theirs. They've warned us for two years that they want the islands back. We've hummed and hawed and put them off and refused to take the matter seriously. What else could they do, in the end, but go and take them? And, surely, if you try to see the thing without prejudice, it's far the most sensible arrangement that these islands off the coast of Argentina should be administered by Argentina? If anybody's in the wrong, we are. For not making a

peaceful, fair settlement with Argentina in the best interests of the islanders long ago.'

Susie could no longer speak for emotion. She pushed her chair back noisily, got to her feet and began to look around for her handbag. The people at the nearest tables broke off their conversations and watched with interest as Tony stood up, went round the table and took her arm, urging her to sit down and they would talk about something else. And at that moment the waitress arrived with their steaks. She hovered uncertainly while Susie refused to be mollified.

'No, no I don't want to talk about anything else. No, I want to go. I don't want anything to eat. I certainly wouldn't touch the Argentinian national dish.'

She found her handbag, stooped to pick it up, shook Tony's hand off her arm and made for the door.

He caught her up in the street and tried to put his arm round her waist, but she shook him off again, quickened her pace and turned into Jermyn Street, making for Piccadilly Circus where she would catch the tube for Paddington and go straight home. She was aware that Tony had slowed and dropped behind and she slowed a little too, but still went on walking away from him.

'Susie!' he called after her, 'Susie, please! I'm sorry.'

She stopped and turned round. He had stopped some way back. They stood there like that for some while, looking at each other with set faces, while irrelevant passers-by hurried through the space between them like shadows or wisps of smoke. Her anger began to give way to pleasure. He really did look anxious, he really was sorry, she had made him see how much it mattered to her that Argentina's actions should be punished, not condoned. And for the first time in their relationship she was in control. In case she should smile and he should see it, she turned aside and began looking into the window of a shop. Very quietly and almost deferentially he came and stood beside her, a couple of feet away, and they both stared exhaustively at the impressive collection of different cheeses laid out in the window. The sight made her suddenly very hungry and he must have sensed it, for after a moment he left her and walked into the shop, emerging with an elegant bag which he offered her with an ironic bow. She accepted it and allowed herself to smile, just a little, conditionally. He smiled back, showing his relief. She was immensely happy. For the first time she felt that she really mattered to him, that he didn't want to lose her.

'I'm very sorry,' he said. 'I had no idea you cared so much about the Falk . . .'

She put her finger over his lips. They bought a couple of dark red apples at a stall in Piccadilly and ate them with the cheese in St James's Park on the way back towards his office.

'I wish we had time to visit Graham today,' he said, as they sat touching legs on a bench near the lake.

'Couldn't we?'

'No way. No way at all, my darling. But next week we will, even if Spain invades Gibraltar. I promise.'

He was nervous, however, of their staying too long together so near his office. Allowing her to accompany him to that particular park had clearly been a kind of concession, a sign that he was putting himself out for her. They parted without kissing and he strode off without looking back.

Their relationship had shifted again when they met the following week, after Easter. He had had most of the long weekend at home with his family and was no longer suffering from lack of sleep. She had received the news that Tim's parachute battalion was to sail from Portsmouth in a week's time to join the task force assembling at Ascension Island in the South Atlantic. Tim himself had written her a short letter, containing no details, but almost incoherent with delight at the prospect.

The news completely demolished all the defences she had built up against contemplating David's disappearance and Tim's defection to the army. It seemed to her that she had been picked out by fate as a target, that somehow she was paying for all the happiness she'd had when she was younger and that she couldn't now expect anything but disaster, the death or disappearance of her son to follow on that of his father. When Tony met her at lunch-time in the entrance to the National Portrait Gallery, her eyes were red and she was only waiting for him to take her in his arms to break down completely. He seized her by the hand, hurried her out on to the pavement and looked about for a taxi.

'He was going to Belize,' she kept saying. 'His battalion was going to Belize and now they've changed the plans at the last moment and some other regiment is going to Belize. Why should they do that? Why should it be Tim that has to go to the Falklands?'

'We're going straight to Graham,' he said. 'Let's talk about it when we get there.'

A taxi stopped and took them to the flat in Marylebone. Once inside, he allowed her to cry for some time, holding her tightly and making no attempt to interrupt her repetitive monologue about the blows of fate and the way she had been singled out. Eventually, when she became quieter, he relaxed his hold a little and gave her his handkerchief to dry her face and blow her nose, but still said nothing.

'It all goes back,' she said, 'to that day when you came to lunch in Sussex and I wasn't there.'

He looked surprised.

'Somebody had committed suicide in the Underground and I knew it was a bad omen.'
Do you believe in omens?'
She had stopped crying. He carefully released her and moved away from her to the other end of the sofa.
'Shall I tell you what I think?' he asked.
She nodded.
'I shall only tell you if you promise to listen carefully, without crying and without getting angry and without flinching – by which I mean not trying to slide away, either physically or mentally.'
'All right,' she said.
'I think you're a very silly little girl. Your experience in the Underground has nothing whatsoever to do with David's disappearance or the Argentinian invasion of the Falklands and they have nothing to do with each other. There are thousands of other mothers whose sons are going out to join the task force and there are hundreds whose sons were going to Belize, but are now going to the Falklands instead. However, I think the odds are now very high against anyone having to fight for the Falklands at all. We've got a good result in the Security Council, we've got the whole of Europe, much of Latin America and above all the US trying to effect a fair settlement of the dispute and I do believe that even our own banana-state government is prepared to do a sensible deal rather than thump any more tubs or rattle any more sabres. And I will add that this is exactly the result I hoped for all along and that if you'd allowed me to explain myself properly last time we met, I should have suggested that if governments, like certain people, didn't constantly prefer to pull the bedclothes over their heads and refuse to acknowledge facts, they wouldn't have to wake up one day in a frenzy and talk about 'blows of fate'. We should have sorted out the Falklands with the Argentinians years ago. Well, better late than never. This is something good that's happened to us, not something bad, and I'm rather proud to feel that I've had some small responsibility for it.'

He didn't elaborate on what his responsibility was and she didn't ask him, since, although she still didn't understand or sympathize with his political stance, she was chiefly grateful for what he'd said about there not being any fighting. She didn't want the Argentinians to keep the Falklands, but even less did she want Tim to be involved in getting them back.

Tony and she went to bed together for the rest of the lunch break, until he had to go back to his office and, meeting again in the early evening, saw an American film called *On Golden Pond*. It was an elegiac and skilfully sentimental view of old age and family solidarity which Susie adored and which had her crying again.

Tony's optimism about there being no fighting in the Falklands persisted for two or three weeks. The US Secretary of State's well-meant attempts to achieve a settlement by shuttling between Britain and Argentina ended in failure the Monday after Tony's and Susie's meeting and that same day the task force left Ascension Island and moved southwards towards the Falklands, detaching a small invasion force of three ships and about 200 Marines and special services men to recapture South Georgia, where the trouble with the scrap metal merchants had first broken out. By the following Sunday evening South Georgia was again in British hands and the Prime Minister, besieged by reporters in Downing Street, was turning away their questions about the details with the very words Susie felt she would have used herself if she'd been Prime Minister: 'Just rejoice at that news and congratulate our forces and the Marines. Rejoice, rejoice!' Tony, however, squirming at the memory of how Mrs Thatcher had said it for the cameras, with that false softness in her voice and that winsome twisting of her head to one side, refused to admit that the cause of peace and settlement was lost. South Georgia was a side issue – it was too far away from the Falklands to be used by the British as a base for launching a re-invasion and its possession was not especially important to Argentina. Diplomacy was still going on and he could still more or less guarantee to Susie that Tim, whose battalion had set out a week after the rest of the task force and hadn't yet reached Ascension Island, would be returning home disappointed but unscathed.

Susie at this time was in an ambiguous state of mind. On the one hand, she welcomed and depended on Tony's assurances that there would be no battle and that Tim would be safe. On the other hand, she was utterly against a settlement and wanted to hear of the task force overwhelming the Argentinians on the Falklands with the same apparent speed and ease as it had overwhelmed those on South Georgia. When, on 30 April, the United States abandoned its policy of even-handedness between the opponents and declared its support for Britain and when, in the early hours of 1 May a Vulcan bomber from Ascension Island succeeded in making a crater in the airstrip at Port Stanley, Susie, almost permanently seated in front of her TV set or beside her radio, clapped her hands and shouted aloud for joy. By the following Tuesday, when she next saw Tony, the warrior-patriot side of her had entirely ousted the anxious mother. These days a strange robot-like civil servant from the Ministry of Defence had displaced such familiar conduits as Maria Dobson and her colleagues and become the face and voice of the news. The bulletin, read by this man with icy objectivity and slow, synthetic delivery, that the Argentinian cruiser *General Belgrano* had been torpedoed and sunk by a British nuclear submarine with the loss of up to 400 lives, convinced Susie that all would be well in the way she wanted it rather than the way Tony wanted it – that the British would pulverize the Argentinians without the slightest damage or even danger to themselves.

Tony, confronting her shining, joyful face over pizzas in a chain restaurant near Leicester Square, was like the full bucket at the other end of her empty one. She danced in the air, he lay at the bottom of a dark well. Very gradually, as she consumed her pizza with appetite and he toyed with his and at last left most of it on his plate, he succeeded in bringing her down nearer to the level of his own mood.

'I have to tell you, Susie,' he said, 'because you'll find out any day now, that I've been wrong. There will be fighting and Tim will probably be in it. The sinking of the *Belgrano* makes it almost certain.'

'Why should you say that? I should have thought it would mean that the Argies would cave in.'

'I doubt it.'

'But you could also be wrong about that.'

'Argentina is ruled by a junta of military officers. This particular junta is only newly established, very vulnerable, very liable to be overthrown. The invasion of the Falklands was a great patriotic act, which has made the junta wildly popular, but still more vulnerable. Because, if they don't succeed in holding on to the Falklands, they're lost. This sinking is a bad setback for them. But they don't have the option of caving in. Their only option is to do something just as bad or preferably worse to us. And we can't cave in either, can we?'

'I should hope not.'

'Because having sent the task force down there, having drawn the sabre, we can't just put it back in the scabbard and go home. Well, yes, we could, on one condition – that the PM resigned.'

'That's not possible.'

'No, I see now that it's not. She should have resigned at the time of the invasion, but she let the Foreign Secretary do it instead. She's not the man I took her for.'

'What do you mean by that?'

'I mean that if she had been a man, I think she would have resigned. I would have resigned in those circumstances. And even if I hadn't, I'd have made sufficient concessions to ensure a sensible settlement. This woman is going to have a war to prove that she was right not to give way and your son Tim is going into the fire to pull out the chestnuts for her.'

Susie smiled nervously, hoping to elicit a smile from him, some sign that he was exaggerating, indulging in argument for argument's sake, but not really meaning to frighten her. But he only stared steadily at her, his heavy jaw clenched, his mouth tight, his eyes unfriendly.

'You want to hurt me,' she said, 'because you can't hurt her.'
'That's not true,' he said. 'I don't want to hurt you, but I'm telling you now that you may be hurt and that it's better to be aware of that, to have some conception that it might be so, than to let it come at you with a bang out of a blue sky.'

Susie woke up the next morning at home to discover that if he'd been wrong before, he was right now. The very afternoon of their pizza lunch, perhaps as he was walking back to his office and she taking the tube to South Kensington to see an exhibition of Indian art at the V & A, two Argentinian fighters, flying south-east of the Falklands, each launched an Exocet missile. One missile fell harmlessly into the sea, the other hit and set fire to the British destroyer HMS *Sheffield*. Both the fighters and their missiles were French, sold to Argentina well before the invasion of the Falklands, but fitted and tested by a team of French technicians who were still in Argentina in spite of France having come out in support of Britain. There was, therefore, considerable anti-French feeling in Britain, but for Susie in particular the French connection seemed to confirm and redouble her original belief in 'the blows of fate'. The French had somehow deprived her of David; now they had made it certain that the Argentinians would not go under easily and that Tim's battalion would have to fight in earnest. She began to hate the French almost more than the Argentinians and, shopping in Cheltenham a few days later, loudly demanded that the greengrocer get rid of his stock of Golden Delicious apples. He didn't take her very seriously, but her friends in the village did, when they noticed that she was drinking far more than usual and generally behaving like someone on the edge of a breakdown. To encourage Susie, take her out of herself and calm her fears about Tim became the village's war effort and it was made easier by the fact that she now spent most of her time there.

Her last visit to London to be with Tony had coincided with the news that Tim's battalion had reached Ascension Island and was now continuing south to join the fleet standing off the Falklands. Tony seemed to be more than ever sunk in his own gloom. He wouldn't discuss it, though it was obviously involved with his miscalculations over the Argentinian invasion and therefore perhaps meant that his career and prospects had been damaged. The form his gloom took, however, was a refusal to comfort her, indeed almost a deliberate attempt to discomfort her, as if he'd begun to blame her for his own misplaced optimism. Without his buoyancy and cocksureness, she didn't find him lovable and no doubt the feeling was mutual. They went to the flat in Marylebone as usual and made love there, but it was an act more of irritation than passion and when they parted and he closed the taxi door on her, she realized that they hadn't arranged their next meeting. She was about to pull down the window, but he'd already turned away to look for another cab for himself and she sat back bitterly in her seat, determined to leave the next move to him, assuming that he'd ring her at home. He didn't, and she didn't ring him. Their affair, like the chance of a settlement in the Falklands, seemed to have been sunk by the Exocet.

20

Not a single member of Tim Rutland's parachute battalion regretted the last-minute switch from Belize to the Falklands, though the long voyage south in a converted North Sea car-ferry was tedious. It was mainly occupied with physical training and shooting practice, together with special instruction in first aid to the wounded, including the use of drip-feeds and enemas to restore lost body fluid. Tim took this more seriously than some, perhaps because he believed more wholeheartedly that it would come to a fight. The possibility of the Falklands' affair being solved peacefully did indeed seem less likely as they neared Ascension Island – the news of the sinking of the *Belgrano* and then *Sheffield* coincided with the colder weather, shorter days and the issue of Arctic clothing – but for Tim it was less a matter of weighing up the objective evidence from the real political world somewhere beyond the horizon than of his own passionate conviction that this was it. He had been born to fight for his country and here, almost the moment he was ready for it, the opportunity offered. It couldn't be a mistake, they couldn't now all go home and be peacetime soldiers again. His destiny had landed him in this battalion and diverted it to the South Atlantic, his destiny made it sure that he would really see action.

Tim's destiny, though not his sense of it, wavered a little in the middle of May, when there were last-minute attempts by United Nations diplomats to effect a reconciliation between Britain and Argentina, but by 20 May, when senior officers on board the command-ship HMS *Fearless* received from London the single code word 'PALPAS', ordering a landing on the Falklands, it was confirmed. That same evening, assembled in the Continental Bar of their ex-car-ferry to sing hymns, say prayers and listen to a short address from the padre, the 450 men of Tim's battalion at last fully shared his belief. The padre, less confident that they shared his in an omnipotent and beneficent God, referred to it as 'an insurance policy'. By dawn the next morning – a clear still day – after a confused but fortunately unopposed night landing, the battalion was climbing the steep hill called Sussex Mountain, overlooking San Carlos Bay; and once up there, exhausted from the climb with their overloads of extra rations, ammunition and radio batteries, their feet still cold and sodden from standing in the landing barges and wading ashore through three feet of water, they began to dig in and come to terms with their new environment.

At first, Tim found it less easy to come to terms with than anything he had experienced so far. On the one hand, the bare, treeless, windswept landscape and the steep, but not high or mountainous hill they sat on were absurdly familiar. They had travelled half way down the globe and arrived not at some exotic, outlandish location, but at an errant fragment of British moorland. It was peat they dug out of their trenches and turves of peat they built up as walls against both the wind and a possible ground attack by the Argentinians. On the other hand, the ancient Celtic view they looked down on, with its long low spits of land merging into glittering sheets of water and more bare hills rising beyond, included a fleet of modern warships; and this hilltop itself was covered all over not with scattered groups of peacefully grazing sheep, but furrows of heavily armed men, visible mainly as helmets and gun-barrels bristling out of the ground, like some nightmare crop sown and springing up in one day. Tim had never been much of a reader, but when he was fourteen or fifteen his father had persuaded him to attempt a story called 'The Island of Sheep'. He had struggled through it and come to enjoy it enough to read one or two others by the same author. John Buchan's specialty was to take a landscape like this one over San Carlos Bay and the Falkland Sound and fill it with action and adventure: the extraordinary happening in the midst of the ordinary was his almost invariable technique. Tim recognized that he had walked into a kind of Buchan landscape and that it was probably this he had wanted all along, to take part in a real Buchan adventure instead of just reading it.

The action began almost as soon as they got up on Sussex Mountain, even before they'd dug themselves in. The platoon commanders were suddenly blowing their whistles and shouting 'Down . . . get down . . . get down!' There was nothing yet to get down into, but they lay flat on the ground as the first Argentinian aircraft – light, propeller-driven Pucaras – came over the back of the hill from the south-east so low that they seemed almost to be racing down over the grass. But in fact they were too low and came too suddenly over the hill to do much harm to the troops. For that purpose, they had to bank and make a run from the other direction, but in doing so became themselves more vulnerable. Two were shot down almost at once, probably by missiles from the ships, since the battalion's hand-held Blowpipe missiles were still at the bottom of the hill and their more substantial, radar-controlled Rapier systems would take even longer to instal.

More Pucaras followed, mostly going for the ships, and Tim was just beginning to recover from his terrible initial feeling of exposure and helplessness, when the first jets from the Argentinian mainland – American Skyhawks and supersonic French Mirages – swept in on the same course. To begin with, the mere sound of these aircraft, ripping over the hill and down at the ships, was worse than anything else they might do. It was as if, somewhere at the base of your spine, a thread was cut which loosened the whole backbone and paralysed you with instinctive, unavoidable fear. Gradually, though, as it became clear that the ships in the Sound were the main target and that the troops on the hill simply happened to be positioned at the start of the attacking aircraft's run, that personal fear was replaced by a more generalized horror of what might be the outcome. Tim and his companions could see the lines of waterspouts and hear the explosions as the aircraft dropped bombs which missed or hit their targets. Sometimes an aircraft might be hit and they would cheer as it burst into flames, but situated as they were on the enemy side of the arena and too far away to be able to pick out the details of what the ships were flinging back at the planes in terms of missiles and machine-gun fire, it looked a hopelessly one-sided affair. The huge cloud of black smoke rising from a stricken frigate suggested that it was only a matter of time before the rest of the fleet went the same way. Their horror was that of partisan specatators unable to do anything to influence or alter the life-or-death struggle below them. Occasionally the battalion machine-gunners would try to bring down an aircraft as it roared over the hill, but it was not much more than a gesture.

The battle between air and sea went on intermittently all that day, Friday, and then, after a respite the next day, rose to a crescendo on Sunday and Monday. By this time the paratroops were dug in and the Rapier anti-aircraft missiles installed and making some contribution to the defence, but the reckoning was heavy: ten British ships sunk or hit for perhaps twenty-five Argentinian aircraft, some claimed by the ships, one or two by the troops on shore, others by the Harriers scrambling from the two British aircraft-carriers lying out to sea and intercepting the Argentinian jets on their way home. On Tuesday the Argentinians, celebrating their National Day, sank the destroyer HMS *Coventry* with a flight of Skyhawks and sent their last two Exocet missiles into the huge cargo ship, *Atlantic Conveyor*, believing it an aircraft-carrier. With this ship went down seven helicopters and many of the supplies vital to the troops' advance on Port Stanley.

Tim's 'destiny', though he didn't realize it at the time, was directly affected by the loss of these supplies. While he and his companions sat uselessly in their water-logged slits in the hilltop, suffering more from the cold wind and perpetually wet feet than from enemy action, the senior officers down below at Brigade Headquarters in San Carlos were making new plans. They had been ordered by London to break out of the bridgehead immediately – no doubt this would be a good thing for everyone, for the troops themselves, for the British public around its TV sets which wanted some sense of progress after the disasters of the past few days and above all for the politicians and military chiefs whose reputations and careers were entirely staked on this desperate gamble 8000 miles from home. But with the loss of so many supplies and especially all but one of their main troop-carrying helicopters, there was no question at present of starting the main advance on the capital. What remained? There was known to be a concentration of Argentinian troops at Goose Green, some twelve miles to the south. It was from the airfield there that most of the Pucaras flew to attack the ships. In military terms it was not strictly necessary to knock out Goose Green before attacking Port Stanley. Once the capital fell, such outlying strongholds would probably surrender. But even if it achieved nothing else, a victory at Goose Green would improve British morale and shake that of the Argentinians. The match was so far more or less even. This would be like scoring a goal in the first half. The decision was taken to send the Parachute Regiment's 2nd Battalion to score the goal.

When this decision finally reached the paratroops themselves, it was received with jubilation. It was not suggested to them that it might really be an unnecessary diversion, nor would they have accepted it as such. For them, the main purpose of being in this uncomfortable place at all was to clobber the 'spics' and send them home to Buenos Aires with their crests fallen and their insolent flags wrapped round their heads. Therefore if there were spics at Goose Green, let them by all means be the first to take their medicine. Nor did Tim and his comrades inquire into the wisdom of sending a single battalion against what was reckoned from the reports of SAS patrols and other sources to be at least equal if not double numbers of enemy, entrenched and fortified in well-prepared positions, with minefields and with air and artillery support. The paratroops were to be given no armoured support – the Royal Horse Guards' light tanks were mysteriously required elsewhere – and, as it turned out, virtually no air support either. As for artillery, there was to be a battery of three light 105mm guns, three 81mm mortars and three Milan anti-tank weapons with a total of seventeen missiles. During the hours of darkness there was also to be artillery cover and starshell illumination from the 4.5-inch gun of the frigate HMS *Arrow* standing of the coast to the west. But like a spirit from another world *Arrow* would have to disappear before cock-crow or it would itself become an easy target for enemy aircraft.

None of these factors for or against the attack was of much interest to the soldiers, any more than the details of lighting, scenery or sound effects in a play are of interest to actors unless they go wrong in the middle of a performance. But the odds stacked against making the attack and known to the producers of the performance, the senior officers at Brigade Headquarters, were as nothing to the true odds, known only to the enemy. They were not defending Goose Green one to one or even two to one. Four hundred and fifty men were setting out to snatch a propaganda victory from sixteen hundred.

Tramping steadily with the rest of his company along a muddy track in darkness, Tim had no sense of taking part in an action which might turn out to be the Falklands' equivalent of the Charge of the Light Brigade. Goose Green lay to the south-east of a narrow isthmus about a mile wide and six miles long with a spine of high ground down the middle. Half-way down the isthmus a line of gorse ran across from coast to coast, between a farm called Boca House on the west and a small settlement called Darwin, tucked under a steep gorse-clad hill, to the east. It was known that the enemy were defending both Boca House and Darwin in strength.

Tim's company was in reserve for the first part of the operation, while the other three companies cleared the approaches to the isthmus. The frigate, moored somewhere off Boca House, had begun firing at 2.30 am, but the first engagements on the ground had not been fought until about 7.00. The noise and flashes somewhere ahead urged the company on. The real test of all their training and endurance up to now was only just ahead. Tim felt that he'd never in his life covered a stretch of ground with so little idea of its solidarity. His mind was like an alarm clock set for say an hour hence: the immediate present, the minute hand moving slowly round the face, was already a kind of past, swallowed up in his constant expectation of the moment when the bell would go off, when he would be running forward firing and being fired at. Every so often, as his nervous tension gave him a pain in the shoulder, the arm, the hand, the thigh, the stomach, he told himself to relax and managed it for a few minutes, until his mind again forgot about his body and projected itself forward into the first attack. It was something like waiting to go in to bat in an important cricket match at school, a mixture of the desire to be doing it and the fear of not doing it successfully. There was no fear of death or injury or, if there was, it was covered up and contained by the much greater fear of not turning out to be good at the one thing a soldier was intended for and could never rehearse in advance. That was the big difference from playing cricket or any other game: you really had no notion whatever of your form, of how you'd react in the heat of the moment.

An hour passed and then another. The column was still moving ahead at a steady pace and the ground was descending slightly. They must already have passed the places where the first engagements had been fought and for the moment there was no sign of anything happening ahead of them. The two companies in front were presumably now striking down along the east coast towards Boca House on the west. Then the column halted and the officers were called up to the front to confer with the company commander. They returned to say that there'd been a mistake. The company was going in the wrong direction, they'd have to retrace their steps. There was a certain amount of muttered swearing, somebody suggested that at this rate they'd probably never even see a fucking spic, but on the whole the news was received in silence, with a kind of nervous resignation. They all felt diminished by the mistake and slightly panicky, as if something irretrievable had happened. Soldiers, like actors, depend on a tightly organized and precisely understood framework of the known in order to be able to cope with the unknown.

By the time they made their rendezvous with the colonel and battalion headquarters, they'd lost an hour on their excursion and there was barely an hour of darkness left. B Company, it seemed, had already carried out the first task orginally assigned to Tim's company – clearing the top section of the west coast – and the company was now directed to continue forward on to the spine of the isthmus, covering both sides of the track. HMS *Arrow* was still contributing the occasional starshell, but mostly it was pitch black. The company was no longer marching in column, but deployed in a defensive formation, Tim's platoon scouting in front, with another directly behind it and the third behind and to the left. The going, off the track, was rough and unreliable – you could easily catch your foot and stumble – and in some ways that was preferable, since it kept your mind on the simple matter of moving forward without falling over instead of on whether or when the great moment would come.

The first shots came from the right instead of in front and were directed at the platoon behind Tim's. Tim could see the streaks of tracer and hear the firing getting heavier and their own men returning it and then suddenly, as his platoon mounted a small ridge, he too was under fire. He dropped down with the others and began to fire back. It was all right. You did what you'd been taught and it was the officers who had to decide what to do next. Somebody slid up beside him and moved on looking for the platoon commander. It was the company commander. 10 Platoon was fully engaged with the trenches to the right, but 11 Platoon was moving round to outflank the trenches in front and while it did so, Tim's platoon was to try to go straight over the top. The company commander withdrew, the platoon commander waited until they could see that somewhere over to the right front 11 Platoon had made contact with the enemy; and then he was up and running forward and they were all running after him, trying to keep their distance from one another, as they'd often practised, but also trying not to catch their feet in a tuft or a hole and above all not to waste any time in this target position. Then, almost immediately, the roles were reversed, for they were looking down the first trench at the same moment as the lieutenant threw a phosphorus grenade into it and there was time to see the shocked, terrorized faces of the Argentinians as they fell or tried to leap away from the burning, clinging stuff thrown out by the explosion. Tim did not feel compunction as, for the first time in his life, he fired his rifle at a living person only a few yards away and brought him down. He did not feel exhilaration either, though he was certainly in a high state of excitement. It wasn't that he wanted to kill the man or enjoyed it, it was only that he had to – as if he were fighting a fire or getting his blow in first at a lethal snake. Savagery was the only possible mode of behaviour, anything else would have been suicidal. The soldiers had been urged on many occasions to accept surrenders and take prisoners whenever the opportunity arose, but there was no such opportunity when storming trenches whose occupants you could only see in the light of explosions.

The momentum of the platoon's attack carried them on to other trenches. In the darkness, noise and confusion they were like swimmers dealing with a steady succession of breakers. They no longer operated as a platoon or even as sections, but in groups of two or three, the machine-gunners covering while the others got up to within twenty yards of a trench and sent in a grenade or sometimes a rocket. They were taking casualties themselves – the man beside Tim suddenly fell, holding his stomach – but Tim had little sense of danger or even hesitation. Each new trench was another obstacle to be cleared and passed. It was because it wanted to stop him, not because it wanted to kill him that he rushed on time and again to neutralize it. The excitement was extraordinary: wholly physical, wholly without goal or memory, a continual combustion of effort and exhaustion, effort and exhaustion, so that each time the effort was greater and the whole body seemed to stretch to a new crescendo, with the five senses all confused, the hand seeming to see the gun-barrel, the eyes to smell the explosions, the roof of the mouth to vibrate with the rattle of machine-guns. And then it all stopped. There were no more trenches. All around the immediate racket died away and Tim became aware for the first time that enemy artillery was pounding away in front and their shells passing overhead. They seemed to be landing some way behind, aimed presumably at a fire burning in the distance there. Then, not far to the left, in the area of trenches they had just cleared, flares went up. The corporal of his section loomed up beside him.

'Wake up, Rutland! We're regrouping.'

Dazed, hardly able to stay upright, Tim staggered towards the flares. But it still wasn't time to rest. The major sent them through all the trenches again, to make sure that none had been missed. After that it was time to collect the casualties, their own and the enemy's. The doctor had set up his aid post near Battalion HQ, just behind their company's position. The injured had to be carried in the soldier's folded capes, since there were no stretchers. It was a slow, arm- hand- and back-aching business and the enemy artillery, four miles away at Goose Green, was dropping shells along the way. But now Tim was grateful that it was still dark. The Argentinian soldier he was helping to carry had lost half his face. He was hardly even as old as Tim. It was impossible to think of him without feeling sick. Perhaps they should never have attempted to move him; at any rate, their tedious labour was wasted, since he was dead by the time they laid him in front of the doctor. At least three of their own company had been killed, but Tim was astonished to find the man who had fallen beside him back on his feet near the aid post. The blow to his stomach had been from a bullet which hit his belt and the bullet itself, which he showed to Tim, had bounced up and lodged in his navel. He was bruised, but not out of action.

'Bloody ridiculous!' he kept saying, meaning his luck, the chance that any bullet fired by an enemy in anger could end up pocketed like a pebble in your tummy-button. Tim agreed with him, though it wasn't exactly what he felt about luck. It didn't just settle on you like a fly, at random, it was part of some larger pattern of your life. His father's disappearance, his own participation in this incomparable experience which was denied to so many others, were not, as he saw them, isolated chances, but somehow linked. After all, if his father had not disappeared, Tim might never have been in the army or if he had, then probably still as an officer cadet at Sandhurst, eagerly training for an action like this, which might never happen again.

'Bloody ridiculous!' said the man, rolling the bullet in his palm, and after all his own luck turned out to be more like a fly settling than a pattern. Less than three weeks later he was killed in the final assault on the ridge above Port Stanley, caught in an inaccurate barrage of covering fire from his own side's artillery.

As it began to get light, Tim's company moved forward and settled on their bellies in the short grass near the edge of a minefield. It was not a comfortable position, since there was scarcely any cover and the enemy's artillery seemed to know where they were. Luckily the soft ground absorbed most of the shells and there were few flying splinters. But no further advance could be made until the other companies, attacking the trench system above Darwin to the left and in front of Boca House to the right, had broken through. The morning, grey and dreary, though not cold, brought no further progress and no relief from the enemy artillery. They could see their own mortars vainly trying to loosen up the enemy defences on Darwin Hill, but it was obvious that the attack had stalled and the euphoria over the night's successes ebbed away. About mid-morning they were ordered to crawl back behind a low hill where they were less exposed to the artillery. Here at least they could brew themselves tea on their small solid-fuel cookers. While they were doing so, three Pucaras flew over to attack their gun-lines, but their own Harriers, which might have opened up the way to Goose Green for them and silenced the Argentinian guns there, couldn't operate because of the persistent low cloud.

In the early afternoon there was a rumour that the colonel had been badly wounded and then they heard for certain that he was dead. Tim asked the lance-corporal lying near him if this meant the end of their operation.

'Why should it?'

Tim didn't know quite why it should, but though he'd hardly ever spoken to the colonel himself, he felt bereft and on the verge of panic. This particular colonel had been a charismatic, high-profile leader, whose personal energy and passion for his job seemed indivisible from the battalion's. If they had been fighting a war on a larger scale, this personal element might have been less important, but here, surely, it counted for more than anything else – the will of one man and of the one unit that acted as body to his head to overcome everything that stood in their way. Without the head, the will was gone and the body must collapse. But Tim was wrong. Somehow the colonel's desperate and apparently irresponsible action in personally attacking an enemy position overlooking the gorse-covered clefts on the far side of Darwin Hill broke the stalemate. The company that had been launching abortive attacks on that position all day now at last overran it. Not that the colonel had intended to sacrifice himself, he had simply been exasperated by the resistance to his plans and determined to overcome it by any means available, including the gun in his own hand.

The capture of Darwin Hill wiped out the damage to morale caused by the CO's death. The battalion's second-in-command took over and all efforts were now concentrated on taking Boca House, the strongpoint on the other side of the isthmus. While B Company and the artillery continued to attack the Argentinian trenches in front of the farm, Tim's company was given a new task, a modification of the dead's colonel's original plan. Crawling on their bellies, they made their way to the beach off which HMS *Arrow* had been anchored during the night. So long as they kept right up against the low cliff that edged the beach, they were out of sight of the enemy. The sand was quite firm, since the tide came all the way up the beach and indeed it was almost high tide now, so that as they crawled and crouched along the narrow space that remained they were often wetted by the spray and, cut of from all but the sounds of battle away to the left, felt themselves to be in a race with the sea more than the enemy. Perhaps it was this that gave Tim a sense of disorientation. They had returned to the ordinary, the unchanging. Because it was so ordinary it asserted itself immediately and made everything that had just happened – the night battle among the trenches, the lying all day with shells raining round them, the sudden deaths of their comrades and their colonel, and the corpses of the enemy – seem quite unreal. Yet at the time all those events had seemed more real, more significant than any previous experience. Tim allowed himself to think that he was still a child, running along a beach with his brother to surprise their parents in a pretended attack by camouflaged paratroops. Any moment now they would rush out from cover making the noise of machine-guns which, to keep his imaginary game alive, he pretended he was only imagining in the distance up there over the slope of the hill.

But he was far more exhausted than he could ever have been in games with his brother. Everything was hurting: his helmet, his pack, his belt, his boots, his chest, the muscles in his arms and legs. When the major finally halted his column on the seaward side of Boca House, most of the men flung themselves down on the damp sand, panting and gasping as if they were fish thrown out on dry land by the sea. They were given a few minutes to recover and then formed up in their platoons in long lines for the assault on the house. This time there was scarcely any resistance. A mine went off as they ran up the low slope from the beach, but it injured nobody, merely increased the terror of their arrival for the defenders. Already pounded for hours from in front by rockets, shells and machine-guns and now inundated on the flank by these waves of wild men from the sea, the Argentinians put out white flags and surrendered. Having rapidly cleared the defences round the house and left the prisoners in the charge of the sergeant-major and a section from one platoon, the company passed on into the open ground beyond, towards the high ground which overlooked their final goal, the airfield and settlement of Goose Green. It was now after 4 pm. The colonel's plan had envisaged their being at this point some six hours earlier, but then the colonel had believed that if you hit them hard enough the enemy would run. The spics were more numerous, better positioned and less despicable than he'd believed.

Tim's company paused below the high ground while their commander received further instructions from Battalion HQ and passed them on to his own platoon commanders. The day was still dull and cloudy, though the cloud had risen and showed signs of breaking up. And now, lying on the damp ground again, waiting for the order to go down and take the airfield, Tim was overcome by lassitude. He wanted to turn over on to his back and go to sleep. He couldn't imagine why the Argentinians should have wanted to possess these unremarkable lumps of peaty pasture or why it was necessary for him personally to go forward and offer himself as a target yet again to drive them out of it. He had done his fighting and come through it. His destiny was fulfilled. He was a real soldier. His mind was full of pictures of the appallingly torn-up corpses – some of them like the contents of a butcher's window – they had briefly seen in the defences of Boca House. Now it was all to see and do again and probably much worse, since they had only so far been dealing with the forward defences.

The corporal was handing out more ammunition and getting each man to check his weapon. Tim responded sluggishly, unwillingly.

'Come on, you dozy bugger, wake up!' said the corporal, but Tim still felt as if every movement had to be made against a huge weight.

'Get back down there to the sergeant and tell him this section's ready!' said the corporal, and as Tim began reluctantly to pull himself off the ground, 'Not like that! Keep your fucking head down! And take your weapon with you! What are you going to do if the spics come over the hill? Strangle them with your bare fucking hands?'

Full of resentment, still struggling with sleep, Tim crawled down to the sergeant and delivered his message.

'All right, lad, well done!' said the sergeant, and reaching into his breast pocket, found a packet of mints and offered it to Tim. He didn't particularly care for mints, but he took one and found that, absurdly, his eyes were full of tears, in gratitude for the sergeant's kind tone and gesture of understanding. He felt ashamed and tried to brush the water away without the sergeant noticing, getting the blacking from his face on to his sleeve. How ludicrous he must look, a blacked-up paratrooper in full combat gear, surreptitiously crying because his sergeant had given him a sweet!

The order came to move forward again, first to the high ground and then downward, keeping to the lee of the slope so that they would be invisible from the airfield until the last moment. Well away to the left they could see C Company also going down the slope in a line with bayonets fixed, like figures in a First World War film, making for a building called the Schoolhouse which was thought to be well defended. Indeed soon afterwards C Company stopped advancing and went to ground under heavy fire. But Tim and his company were racing down the slope now towards the airfield, with Tim's platoon out in front, still protected from the enemy's artillery and trenches by the shallow valley they were in. At the south-east of the airfield, where the ground rose again, was a flagpole with the blue and white striped Argentinian flag flapping sluggishly in the light breeze.

That was what they were after, that was, in a way, the whole object of the exercise. Killing spics might be necessary, making them prisoner or driving them out of their trenches were moves in the right direction, but to haul down their flag was to score the goal and Tim, who had up to now wanted nothing better than to be an indistinguishable member of his section, his platoon, his company, his battalion, was determined to be the first to get his hands on the rope and win that distinction. He had been a good runner at school and it was as if the run down the hill and the sight of that obvious winning post had reawakened his suppressed officer-class upbringing and education. Exulting in his fresh energy and unbeatable speed, Tim surged past the five or six men in front of him, drew level with the lieutenant leading the platoon and, with no effort at all, overtook him and raced away in front. He heard his name being shouted but took no immediate notice. Only when he found himself on more level ground with a clear view of the flagpole and the airstrip, did he pause and look behind, suddenly feeling isolated and unsure of himself. The lieutenant and the corporal were waving at him angrily.

'Get back!' shouted the lieutenant.

'Get fucking back!' shouted the corporal.

Tim turned towards the flagpole, now hardly a sprint away. The whole area seemed to be deserted, though down to the left, round the Schoolhouse, there was fantastic bedlam and black smoke billowing out of the top windows of the building. Uncertainly, half inclined to run for his prize and face the consequences afterwards, but more and more aware that he'd made a mistake, that soldiers did not run ahead of their officers unless told to do so and that in any case the flag belonged to all of them, not to him alone, he stepped sideways and was blown backwards into the path of his angry platoon commander by a mine.

That was the end of Private Rutland's part in the recapture of the Falklands. He lay near where he'd fallen, first concussed and then in excruciating pain from his mangled leg. He was only dimly aware of the final destruction of the Schoolhouse in an explosion which incinerated all the Argentinians inside it. He was not aware that soon after his own disaster both the lieutenant and the corporal had died in a burst of firing near the flagpole, when several of the enemy had come out under a white flag. At one point, just before dark, he thought the whole hillside had caught fire – it was napalm dropped by a Pucara. He saw Argentinian Skyhawks fly one way to strafe the British and, at last, the cloud having lifted, Harriers fly the other way to drop cluster bombs on the enemy artillery behind Goose Green. But this belated aerial activity in the last half hour before dusk was confused in his mind with those first days as a helpless spectator on Sussex Mountain.

When it was dark the battalion broke off the fighting and withdrew up the hill, taking with them their dead and wounded. Tim was evacuated that night by helicopter to San Carlos and from there to the hospital ship SS *Uganda*. The following night, after he'd come round from an operation to remove the lower part of his right leg, he was told that the Argentinians at Goose Green had surrendered and that the blue and white flag near the airstrip had been ceremonially hauled down.

21

The climax had arrived. A week ago, on duty in the continuity studio, James had had the wretched task of reading the news of the disaster at Bluff Cove, when the two landing ships *Sir Galahad* and *Sir Tristram* had been bombed by Argentinian aircraft, with the loss of fifty-three lives and many appalling injuries from the firestorm that followed. The disaster overcast the wonderful sense of good fortune and British military genius in which everyone had bathed since the news of the capture of Goose Green the previous week. The very names of the two ships, James felt, added to the desolation, as if not just two flat-bottomed troop-carriers but Britain's mythical heroes of the Round Table themselves had perished with the Welsh Guardsmen in the flames. But now the whole British infantry force assembled on the Falklands – paratroops, commandos, SAS, Gurkhas, Welsh and Scots Guards – with supporting armour, artillery, naval guns and Harrier jets – was advancing on Port Stanley.

James was at home this weekend and, temporarily unhooked from his addiction to the news by the depressing lull that followed the disaster, had intended to bury himself in his work on the Butlers. The theme had been constantly modified by his immersion these last two months in the Falklands saga. He still wanted to celebrate the idea of withdrawal and somehow to draw a parallel between the exemplary domesticity of the Butlers in their retirement and the return of Britain, after it had laid down its imperial burden, to being a private nation. But he recognized now that he had not paid enough attention to the military element in the Butlers – the fact that they were both in love with the heroism of battle, the glamour as well as the unselfishness of being prepared to lose your life on behalf of your tribe. Of course this idea had been wholly out of fashion until two months ago. James thought of himself as a liberal, with a small 'l', but the Falklands War filled him with national pride and made him a partisan of the Prime Minister, if not her party. Lady Butler in her old age in the twenties – the narrative voice of his poem – was now to express her unambiguous admiration for her husband's military skill and courage in addition to her sympathy with his compassion for the underdog. And this did, after all, seem much nearer to the truth. She had only painted one *Eviction*, but any number of military subjects. The difference was mainly one of tone. No longer the Tennysonian or Elgarian dying fall, the long, melancholy trumpet call as the flag was hauled down slowly in the sunset, but a brisk assertion of rugged independence and historical realism. Not 'might is right', rather 'might is necessary to defend the right'.

The news of the advance on Port Stanley destroyed any chance of progress with the Butlers. Restless with excitement, James went out into the garden. The roses were in full bloom and James walked about sniffing them and reciting their names to himself: Peace, Eroica, Albertine, Crimson Conquest, Honorine de Brabant, Mme Isaac Pereire and Zephirine Drouhin. According to Simon Carter, someone had asked Maria if he could name a new rose after her. Strange to think that in a hundred years' time people might be walking round their gardens in summer sniffing a flower called Maria Dobson and not thinking of her as a person but solely as a rose. It was almost a modern version of one of Ovid's metamorphoses – the nymph or dryad transformed into a fountain, tree or flower – but Ovid was not one of James's favourite classical authors. He was too much of a city smarty-pants. For many years James had thought the same of Simon Carter, but since their recent meeting he'd revised his opinion.

They had met in Bond Street. James was looking in a shop window for a handbag for Judy's birthday and wondering if he would splash out on something really expensive, something that would make her go pink with amazement. Simon had crossed the road through the dense stream of taxis, Porsches, Bentleys and Mercedes to say hello. Having done so, he seemed to have nothing more to say and to be embarrassed by the encounter. To give him an excuse for breaking away, James remarked that he was looking for a handbag for his wife.

'You're not in any particular hurry?' asked Simon.

'No,' said James warily, looking at his watch.

'What about a drink or some coffee somewhere?'

'Why not? But I think I ought to get this handbag first.'

They went inside together, looked at a selection and inquired the prices. Although he had wanted to buy something expensive, James now felt he had stepped into water too deep for him and began making noises of withdrawal.

'Be a devil!' said Simon, not as Tony Cass would have said it, mockingly, derogatorily, but with sympathy and encouragement. 'Honestly this is nothing. You don't know what spending is. I used to count the pounds until I got married.'

His mood, James realized, was ebullient. He had not been silent from embarrassment but because he was holding himself in. James braced himself and bought one of the cheaper bags, convincing himself that he preferred its design anyway. It was still three times more than he'd ever spent on a present before, but having bought it, he felt proud of himself and full of pleasure at the thought of how it would please Judy. For that feeling alone it was worth every pound.

'Wasn't it overspending that killed your literary editor?' he asked, as they left the shop and walked northwards.

'The inquest didn't come to any very definite conclusion,' said Simon. 'I had lunch with him a few hours before it happened and there was no sign that he was in a state to kill himself. But apparently he went back to the *Equalizer*, quarrelled with the editor and resigned. He owed money to his wife, his mother and his brother, as well as to the bank and the building society and most of the utilities, but he could easily have sold his house and paid them all off. His brother was at the inquest and produced a rather farfetched explanation. Apparently Andrew had been commissioned to do a TV series on post-imperialism, which had fallen through. That's always a depressing thing to happen, but I wouldn't have thought enough on its own to drive someone to suicide. However, the brother suggested that it wasn't the loss of the job or the blow to his pride that upset him, but that he cared so deeply about the disadvantaged and the miseries of the Third World in particular. The TV series was to be his great crusade, his attempt to awaken the people of the West to their duties and responsibilities. I didn't see Andrew like that at all – he never seemed to me to care too much about anyone beyond himself. And surely you don't jump in front of a train because you've been balked of a chance to save the world? You set about saving it some other way. Jumping in front of a train is a way of saying you want someone to save you, isn't it?'

'It couldn't have been an accident?'

'Well, that was suggested too. He'd been taking some kind of drug in random quantities and his doctor was rapped over the knuckles. He'd also been drinking quite a lot at lunch-time – no more than I did, but then he'd had drugs as well. As a matter of fact, we'd been celebrating Maria being pregnant. His wife thought it was an accident. She said he was always surprisingly punctilious about money – not about borrowing it, but about keeping tabs on it. If he'd really intended to kill himself, she said, he'd have made a will or at least left a note making sure everyone received what was due to them. She and the brother, she said, were going to try to arrange that as Andrew would have wanted it. They disagreed about whether it was suicide or not, but they were obviously both fond of him. The mother, on the other hand, I thought, probably disliked him. She spoke as if he'd always been a disappointment to her – not in front of the inquest, of course, but afterwards. She didn't actually say so, but she implied that she thought it was suicide.'

They had reached the pedestrian precinct of South Molton Street and sat down at a table in the open. The waiter brought them glasses of white wine and a sandwich for Simon, who'd had no lunch. James waited courteously until he'd eaten it and then got out his pipe.

'You used to smoke that thing in Balunda,' said Simon. 'I always thought it was a ploy, to make yourself look like a pukka colonial administrator.'

James smiled. He and Simon had never had a cross word together, but for some reason it seemed they'd always detected insincerity in the other.

'Maybe,' he said, 'but now I'm simply addicted to it.'

'It looks more natural now,' said Simon.

'I've grown round it, I expect. The way a rose stalk as it gets older grows round a piece of string you've used to secure it.'

Simon told him about Maria having a rose named after her.

'What colour is it?' asked James.

'I don't think he mentioned that.'

'You're not going to inspect it first?'

'I think he means to introduce it at next year's Chelsea Show. Maria will christen it then.'

'I do think you ought to see it first. Some new roses are hideous.'

There was a pause. They both sipped their wine. Simon seemed to be nervous. Perhaps not nervous so much as cautious, unsure of himself or of James. James unwisely introduced the topic of the Falklands, never far from his mind.

'Wonderful news about Goose Green,' he said.

'I hate it,' said Simon. 'It makes me very angry.'

'You're against the war?'

'Utterly against it.'

'What else could the Government have done, once the Argentinians had invaded?'

'Negotiated.'

'But that would be giving way to bullies, wouldn't it?'

'I don't think these simple analogies are helpful. Nations are not the same as individuals. They don't die or disappear. We have to go on living in the world with Argentina and they with us. It's totally and abysmally primitive – and useless – to go at each other with missiles and machine-guns instead of sitting round a table and sorting it out.'

James remained silent. He disagreed profoundly with Simon, so profoundly that he saw no point in arguing. They would just be making enemies of each other at this very moment when they had come so near being friends again.

'From a selfish point of view, I suppose I'm glad that this thing has happened,' said Simon. 'It's crystallized so many issues for me. That bloody task force! It's made it clear to me that there's only one real task in modern times – and that's to make the world habitable for as many of the people that live in it as possible. There's no room for these old macho attitudes, these ancestral preenings and posturings. Nationalism of the kind we're seeing at the moment is not just silly, it's evil. Evil because wasteful – of lives and resources – and backward – it impedes the spread of civilization and prosperity. National dignity is the direct enemy of human dignity. It's an excuse for oppression, aggression and armed robbery. It brings out the worst in everybody, winners as well as losers.'

James was moved by Simon's strong feelings. He even agreed with him in general. But not on this issue. The Argentinians were in the wrong on this issue. They were the aggressors. Simon's arguments should be addressed to them, not to the British who, if they had given way to Argentinian nationalism, would surely have made the world a more dangerous, not a better place.

'What does Maria think about it? The same as you?'

James didn't really care what Maria thought about it, but it was a way of getting the topic off their little café table, preparatory to losing it altogether. Simon, still leaning forward belligerently with his arms crossed on the tabletop, relaxed a little.

'More or less the same as me. Quite frankly we've hardly talked about it.'

Simon sat back on his white metal chair and looked contentedly around. There were three or four other tables outside the cafe, all occupied, and the street was full of passers-by, laughing and talking. It dawned on James that Maria had had her baby. He had seen a small paragraph about it in *The Times*. No doubt it would have been given much more coverage if it hadn't coincided with the news of the victory at Goose Green. Perhaps it had had more space in the tabloids. Simon caught the waiter's eye.

'The bill, please,' he said.

'No, bring us two more glasses of wine!' said James, smiling mysteriously. 'We have to celebrate, don't we?' he added, as the waiter went inside. 'You're a proud father.'

Simon looked confused. 'I don't know,' he said.

'Surely I saw something in the paper?'

'Yes, you're quite right. Yes, Maria had her baby yesterday.'

He stopped and eagerly took the fresh glass of wine brought by the waiter.

'Many congratulations!' said James, raising his.

'If I was with Maria,' said Simon, 'I couldn't do this. Sit at a table in the open. It has its advantages, being a person like her, being married to one, but it's a great loss of freedom. Sometimes one feels one's in the same position as a cat – kept and petted, very privileged – but not, ultimately, independent.'

'I wonder if that's because Maria is who she is,' James said in a calm, offhanded way, though inwardly he was overjoyed that Simon should confide in him, 'or because you've been living on your own for so long. Marriage is a trading-in of total independence for – what? – support, I suppose, mutual support.'

That sounded banal and pompous. He hadn't at all meant to come the old married man, only to keep the topic open.

'It's more complicated than that,' said Simon. 'Maria is who she is because of what she is.'

He paused and James suddenly thought he understood why Simon had buttonholed him in Bond Street, why he'd initiated this unexpected reunion, why he'd been hungry not for a sandwich but for a conversation. When William, his own first child, was born, James had also felt a sudden need to find a friend to talk to and discuss Judy in a way he'd never normally dream of doing. It was as if their close relationship had been temporarily suspended, so that, although she remained the one person he knew intimately, she was also now a separate person again – instead of an almost indivisible partner – and could be thought about and analysed in the way one thought about and analysed all other friends, relations and acquaintances. With this rare objectivity, of course, went also a sense of betrayal and that was probably what made the whole thing so nervous and exciting.

'A TV personality,' said Simon, 'is almost *per se* a face, an appearance. They don't have hidden depths. All their energy, all their charm, cleverness, knowledge, charisma is spread out on the surface. The rest of us go about saving it up, letting it out in dribs and drabs. It's like light bulbs. We may all be on the same voltage, but when *we* shine it's a 40-watt mushroom and when *they* shine it's a 100-watt flood. Do you see what I'm getting at?'

'Yes, but I'm wondering if a mushroom-bulb has hidden depths.'

'All right, the metaphor's poor. I'm trying to say that the person I've married is almost exactly what you see on the screen and read about in the papers. No less and no more. She's a kind of innocent. That's the wrong word too. No one could be less innocent than a TV Personality. She's without shadows. That's what I meant by the floodlight analogy.'

Simon paused again, marshalling his thoughts. James glanced surreptitiously at his watch, not because he wanted to go, but because he was always afraid he might have to. There was still plenty of time.

'What I suppose I'm trying to say is that when she's raped by or gives herself to another man – a completely odious man – the light hardly flickers. The child is hers and because it's hers, it's all part of that surface brilliance. It's subsumed into the public appearance.'

James was appalled and must have looked it.

'You find that shocking,' said Simon. 'So did I, of course. But you have to believe that really she didn't. A public person loses the ability to see anything in the round, with shadows. That's the conclusion I've come to and in many ways I find it admirable. I now think that my own attitude was shabby, irrational, desperately commonplace and purely selfish.'

'But how did it happen?'

Simon told him about the picnic by the river and its outcome.

'Well, you've seen the baby now,' said James, 'what do you think? Isn't it yours?'

Simon's introduction to fatherhood had been after all rather different from James's. When Judy entered hospital to give birth to William, she was caught up in an institutional world from which James was excluded. Nevertheless, she and James continued to have time alone together; she shared her new world with him so far as she could and he brought news of his outside world to her. But from the moment Maria entered hospital, she became altogether public property. The pressmen were only admitted to her private room for one brief and carefully supervised photo call, although their spies remained posted in the entrance hall downstairs. The room, however, was almost never free of somebody. Nurses, cleaners, tea ladies, doctors, the book lady, the chaplain, friends, colleagues, TV executives, other personalities passed in and out of it as if not only the hospital but much of the entertainment world revolved round it. Simon himself felt, he said, like Joseph in a Nativity scene, a vaguely appropriate figure in the background grouped with the ox and the ass, while the innumerable shepherds and wise men paying their respects and bearing gifts hogged the foreground. Maria, radiant and queenly, propped on her pillow and surrounded with flowers, held court and treated Simon less as her consort than her flunkey, daily deputed to fetch and remove books, clothes, cosmetics, etc., to open the heaps of mail that poured in from well-wishers all over the country and supervise the distribution of the countless boxes of chocolates and bunches of flowers among deserving people in the hospital and old people's homes throughout the borough. Yet he knew that if he stayed away, as he seriously considered doing, the press would be buzzing round him in a moment. Joseph might be a minor figure in the scene, but he was none the less absolutely necessary to it and would never be allowed to leave a hole where his head should be.

After two or three days of this and with still no sign of Maria actually giving birth, the consultants decided the baby must be induced. The pregnancy had been mainly straightforward, but the foetus was small and there could be no question either of sending Maria home again to wait a little longer or of allowing the royal levée in the hospital to continue indefinitely. At last Simon had Maria more or less to himself, but whereas before she had projected herself outward towards the troops of visitors, now she turned inwards. Although he sat by her side, comforting her while she groaned and moaned with pain and terror, he felt more like a nurse than an intimate and less use to her than a nurse, since he shared her ignorance and fear and winced at her pain.

It was the worst twelve hours of his life. The labour began at about lunch-time and continued intermittently through the afternoon and evening. At about 11 pm the elegant surgeon, dressed in an immaculate pale grey summer suit, who visited the cubicle regularly to monitor Maria's blood pressure and the dial showing the heartbeats of the foetus, decided, as he put it, 'to draw stumps'. He would operate on Maria and bring the baby out by Caesarean section. His manner was calm and abstracted, as though he were indeed choosing the best way to ensure the success of his cricket team, but Simon thought he would hardly take the trouble to change out of his suit into all the paraphernalia necessary for an operation if he'd not been alarmed by what he'd seen on the dial.

Simon was directed to a small waiting room on a lower floor and told that the baby would be brought down in the lift in half an hour or so and then he'd be able to see it. At first, as he sat exhausted in the waiting room, he was relieved that the thing was almost over and that he wouldn't have to witness the final stages of Maria's ordeal. But gradually, as the half hour elapsed and then another and then another, he was filled with cold misery and horror. He couldn't believe that this was really happening to him or that anyone could be expected to bear such concentrated psychological torture without going mad. He began to walk round and round the small room with jerky steps, sweating all over, talking to himself, anything to beat away his sense of time past and passing. It was Maria he thought he was going to lose. He hardly thought of the baby at all.

At the end of two hours – could it have been so long? – a middle-aged black woman came into the room and sat down on one of the chairs along the wall and began to chat to him. Who was she? Presumably the aunt or mother or sister of another woman in labour. What did she talk about? He had no idea, not the faintest recollection of anything she said. It was just neighbourly, friendly chatter and it drove him wild. It was the final torment. He was waiting to hear that Maria was dead and his life laid in ruins and this woman was engaging him in normal, everyday conversation as if the circumstances were ordinary, as if he were not being racked and thumb-screwed in front of her eyes.

Then he heard slow, soft footsteps coming from the far end of the corridor. He left the woman in mid-sentence and went out of the open door. The surgeon, still in his grey suit, was coming towards him. This was it. This was the horrible news. Horrible task for the surgeon too, he had time to think – to have to say that something had gone wrong, to offer excuses and condolences to the bereaved. After that he would have to justify himself to the waiting press and nation. No wonder he was walking so slowly. Simon tried to rush towards him to get the deadly business over, but his legs were almost out of control. He was staggering, fending off the wall of the corridor like a drunk. They stopped, facing each other, and there was silence. Simon looked at the surgeon and looked away. He couldn't speak. He wanted to know, he didn't want to know.

'Your wife's fine,' the surgeon said in a low, throwaway voice through half-closed lips, as if the fact was almost too boring to mention.

Simon was still unable to speak. A condemned man needs time to understand that he is going to live after all. He managed a kind of gurgle. And then it occurred to him that there had been two lives at stake, one of which he'd hardly considered until now.

'And the baby?'

'Haven't you seen it?'

'Seen it?'

'She came down an hour ago. Didn't they tell you? Quite small, but all there. I'm sure she'll be as beautiful as her mother.'

'A girl?'

'Quite definitely a girl. Go and ask the sister. She'll show her to you. And you'll be able to see your wife in half an hour or so when she comes round from the anaesthetic.'

The surgeon turned and began walking slowly away.

'I think we were wise to declare when we did,' he said over his shoulder.

Simon's eyes were brimming with tears. He wanted to run after the man and crumple his suit with a passionate embrace, but instead he made his way to the ward office, where he found the night sister.

'Oh, there you are, Mr Carter!' she said, as if she thought he'd been callously neglecting his duties, out drinking or whoring while his wife bore the brunt of the day. 'Yes, that's your daughter. We haven't quite finished washing her.'

She went out to attend to something else, leaving him alone with a transparent plastic cradle in which lay a naked, almost hairless creature, smaller than a cat, the colour of a boiled shrimp, speckled here and there with blood.

'My daughter?' thought Simon. Of course it was his daughter, he'd have known her anywhere. At the same time, strangely enough, she wasn't his at all, but already a person quite separate and independent, a new person he'd have to get to know. He stood there with tears of love pouring into his moustache and off his chin, until the sister returned, wheeled his daughter off to be washed and sent him to his wife's bedside.

'What are you going to call her?' asked James.

Simon blinked. He was on the verge of crying again at the mere thought of his daughter.

'I don't know,' he said. 'I suppose if she'd been a boy I might have called her Percy.'

'That's an unfashionable name.'

'Maria wants something quite ordinary. Caroline or Jane.'

'What's that character in *The Winter's Tale?*'

'Hermione?'

'Her daughter. The baby dumped on the beach in a storm because her father thinks she's illegitimate.'

'Perdita.'

'Perdita. Lost and found.'

'I like it,' said Simon.

'I'm not sure it goes with Carter.'

'She can be Perdita Dobson. I'm not fussy about conserving the Carters. They're an extinct species.'

They began to part, promising to meet again soon. James and Judy were to come to supper in Hammersmith as soon as Maria and the baby were home and fit. As they were about to turn away, Simon to the Bond Street tube station, James towards Oxford Circus, James suddenly found himself saying:

'By the way, I'm still trying to write something about the Butlers.'

He felt foolish as soon as he'd said it. Why was he exposing himself in this way, unnecessarily, wilfully, when their conversation was over? Perhaps it was a need to seal their restored friendship with a potentially damaging secret of his own in return for Simon's.

'Both of them?' said Simon. 'That's splendid. What view do you take of their relationship?'

James was already anxious to leave the subject as soon as possible.

'I don't know. It seems to have been a very happy marriage. Almost exemplary for two people with such powerful personalities and separate careers.'

'Was it? That was my view at first. But the more I looked into it, the more I had doubts. I think he probably wrecked her career. For all his liberalism in public, he was a classic autocrat at home. And let's face it, her career was infinitely more valuable than his. He was a remarkable man, a distinguished soldier, but only one of many. She was unique. Yet after she married him her work hardly developed at all. Something wrong there.'

Strolling round by the raspberry canes but finding them nowhere near ripe, James encountered Judy on hands and knees weeding the rockery.

'I thought you were working,' she said.

'Taking a breather,' he said.

'If you're not doing anything else,' she said, 'the front hedge needs clipping.'

'Your word is my command,' he said.

He went to the shed and fetched the shears, pleased to have something positive to do which would carry him through to supper and so to the news bulletin and the latest on Port Stanley. At the time he hadn't taken much more account of what Simon had said about the Butlers than of his opinion on the Falklands, but now as he worked steadily along the inside of the hedge, a new idea struck him which must have been maturing secretly over the last two weeks. If William Butler had really been a tyrant to Elizabeth and she had knuckled under but almost unconsciously resented it, then perhaps in her old age when he was long dead and she was reviewing the whole stretch of her life, she might begin to recognize the damage he'd done to her painting. Or not so much to recognize as to reveal the truth without meaning to. Her narrative, in that case, would be shot through with irony and even bitterness. The subject would take on another dimension. It would have a distinct flavour of Browning.

James had moved round to the pavement side of the hedge. He was clipping fast and accurately, but his mind was mainly occupied with the delightful prospect of rereading Browning. Yes, he would even make another stab at *The Ring and the Book*, which he'd never managed to finish. He became aware that three large youths had stopped to watch him. They were a bit older than William, no longer schoolboys, but not quite men – about the same age as Tim Rutland.

'That's a nice hedge,' one of them said, mockingly.

'Thank you,' said James, pretending to take it as a straight compliment.

'You're a hard worker,' said the second.

'Not really,' said James and resumed his clipping.

'You've missed a bit here,' said the first, pulling a branch so that it stuck out.

James became alarmed. They were probably a bit drunk and looking for a quarrel. He went back through the gate and inside the hedge, as if he wanted to finish off something there.

'Woo-hoo!' said one of the youths, sticking his head over the gate and round the hedge.

James ignored him. There was a brief pause and some whispering and then suddenly all three of them flung themselves at the hedge from outside and pushed it inwards. James stood quite still. The youths roared with derisive laughter and went on down the street. James emerged cautiously to make sure they'd really gone. The hedge was in a frightful state, dented and sad like a car after a collision. Raging at himself for his pusillanimity, but also relieved that the hooligans hadn't attacked him personally, James began to pull the broken and tangled branches back into place and to try to restore the overall shape. Then he finished the clipping and swept up the bits. Judy came out to call him in for supper. She noticed the dent.

'What's happened there?'

James was too ashamed to tell her. 'Looks as if some children have been vandalizing it,' he said.

'I suppose it will grow back,' she said.

After supper they watched the news. The battle for Mount Longdon, Wireless Ridge and Tumbledown Mountain – the hills overlooking Port Stanley – was still going on, though there seemed little doubt of the issue. The Argentinians were fighting stoutly, but the British had most of the advantages in equipment, training and morale. James found that he had lost much of his relish for the affair and when, next day, the Argentinians were finally driven off the hills and surrendered Port Stanley, it seemed more of an anti-climax than a glorious victory.